"A GRACEFULLY RENDERED STORY . . . RICH WITH HISTORY, MYTHOLOGY, FOLKLORE, LANGUAGE, AND EMOTION. . . . A NOVEL THAT WILL SURELY BE READ AND VALUED BY FUTURE GENERATIONS."
—Hemingway Foundation/PEN Award for Fiction Finalist Citation

"HUMANITY . . . SHINES THROUGH IN HER STORYTELLING."
—*The Wall Street Journal*

"ONE OF THOSE BRAVE NOVELS OF RESILIENCE AND THE POWER OF LOVE THAT SURFACE ONCE OR TWICE IN A GENERATION, LIKE KHALED HOSSEINI'S *THE KITE RUNNER*." —*The Buffalo News*

"WHAT A LIFE. AND NOW, WHAT A BOOK." —*USA Today*

"LYRICAL . . . IT'S RAAMI'S MOTHER WHO WILL STAY IN YOUR HEART . . . SOMEHOW SHE RETAINS THE WILL TO SURVIVE AND THE STRENGTH TO HELP OTHERS, FIERCELY TELLING HER DAUGHTER, 'REMEMBER WHO YOU ARE.'"
—*People*, ★★★★

"VADDEY RATNER'S DEBUT NOVEL BEARS WITNESS TO THE ATROCITIES OF CAMBODIA'S KHMER ROUGE, AND . . . IT CAPTURES THE BEAUTY AND RESILIENCE OF THE HUMAN SPIRIT." —*Yahoo! Shine*

"EVOCATIVE, LYRICAL. . . . ACCESSIBLE AND PROFOUNDLY MOVING, *IN THE SHADOW OF THE BANYAN* IS DESTINED TO BECOME A CLASSIC."
—*School Library Journal*

Praise for *In the Shadow of the Banyan*

"Incredible."—San Francisco Chronicle

The New York Times Book Review Editor's Choice
The Christian Science Monitor 10 Best Novels of the Year
The Columbus Dispatch Top Books of 2012
Kirkus Reviews Best Fiction of the Year and
Best Debut Fiction of the Year
About.com Best Books of the Year
TimeOut New York Best Books of 2012
BookBrowse.com 2012 Favorites

"One of the most extraordinary acts of storytelling I have ever encountered . . . utterly heartbreaking and impossibly beautiful. There are moments in this story that are among the most powerful in literature. This is a masterpiece that takes us to the highs and lows of what human beings can do in this life, and it leaves us, correspondingly, both humbled and ennobled."
—Chris Cleave, author of *Little Bee*

"The powerful story of how even the most brutal regime lacked the power of a father's love for his daughter."
—*The Daily Beast*

"A truly important literary event."
—Robert Olen Butler, author of
A Good Scent from a Strange Mountain

"Moving . . . luminous."
—*The Columbus Dispatch*

"With lyrical and breathtaking prose, Ratner plunges us into the midst of the nightmare that was thrust upon her, and yet, even amidst the darkness of starvation and violence, she never abandons us to despair. She always offers us the glimmering thread of hope and of love. She offers us wings."
—Naomi Benaron, author of *Running the Rift*

"The resilience of the human spirit and body, the ability to hope even in the face of extreme hopelessness: this is what carries the reader through this touching masterpiece of a novel."

—Historical Novel Society, Editor's Choice

"Knowing that the story was culled from Ratner's experiences as a child brings . . . immediacy to this heartrending novel."

—*Library Journal*

"An astonishing book, unlike anything else that has emerged from Cambodia and its tragedies. In contrast to other books dealing with the Khmer Rouge period, this is not a memoir—it is literature, and literature of a high order."

—Philip Short, author of *Pol Pot* and *Mao: A Life*

"By countering the stark and abject reality of her experience with lyrical descriptions of the natural beauty of Cambodia and its people, Ratner has crafted an elegiac tribute to the Cambodia she knew and loved."

—*Booklist*

"A child's eyewitness account of Cambodia's genocide, overlaid by the soul of a poet."

—*The Christian Science Monitor*

"Often lyrical, a painful, personal record of Cambodia's holocaust."

—*Kirkus*, starred review

"Touching and beautifully written . . . celebrates the human spirit, the power of story and imagination and the triumph of good over evil."

—Shelf Awareness

"A remarkable achievement . . . one of those novels that lead writers like me to believe that real truth is best found in fiction."

—*The Washington Independent Review of Books*

"Poetry in prose . . . a fascinating, moving work that offers a powerful leitmotif of optimism."

—*The Independent on Sunday*

"As the great human drama unfurls in this sensitive and impassioned telling, it is impossible not to be moved. . . . Ratner is a fearless writer."

—*The Guardian* (Manchester)

"A landmark book. . . . The vividness of Ratner's writing and the richness of her story . . . mark this novel as an extraordinary literary achievement."

—*The Financial Times*

In the

Shadow of the

Banyan

Vaddey Ratner

SIMON & SCHUSTER PAPERBACKS
NEW YORK   LONDON   TORONTO   SYDNEY   NEW DELHI

Simon & Schuster Paperbacks
A Division of Simon & Schuster, Inc.
1230 Avenue of the Americas
New York, NY 10020

First Simon & Schuster trade paperback edition June 2013

SIMON & SCHUSTER PAPERBACKS and colophon are registered trademarks
of Simon & Schuster, Inc.

For information about special discounts for bulk purchases, please
contact Simon & Schuster Special Sales at 1-866-506-1949 or
business@simonandschuster.com.

The Simon & Schuster Speakers Bureau can bring authors to your live event.
For more information or to book an event, contact the Simon & Schuster Speakers
Bureau at 1-866-248-3049 or visit our website at www.simonspeakers.com.

Designed by Nancy Singer

Manufactured in the United States of America

10   9   8   7   6   5   4   3   2   1

The Library of Congress has cataloged the hardcover edition as follows:
Ratner, Vaddey.
 In the shadow of the banyan / Vaddey Ratner.
    p. cm.
1. Cambodia—History—1975–1979—Fiction. 2. Refugees—Cambodia—Fiction.
I. Title.
 PS3618.A876I52 2012
 813'.6—dc23   2011033320

ISBN 978-1-4516-5770-8
ISBN 978-1-4516-5771-5 (pbk)
ISBN 978-1-4516-5772-2 (ebook)

For my mother

In the memory of my father,

Neak Ang Mechas Sisowath Ayuravann

In the
Shadow of the
Banyan

one

War entered my childhood world not with the blasts of rockets and bombs but with my father's footsteps as he walked through the hallway, passing my bedroom toward his. I heard the door open and shut with a soft click. I slid off my bed, careful not to wake Radana in her crib, and snuck out of my room. I pressed my ear to the door and listened.

"Are you all right?" Mama sounded concerned.

Each day before dawn, Papa would go out for a solitary stroll, and returning an hour or so later, he would bring back with him the sights and sounds of the city, from which would emerge the poems he read aloud to me. This morning, though, it seemed he came back as soon as he'd stepped out, for dawn had just arrived and the feel of night had yet to dissipate. Silence trailed his every step like the remnant of a dream long after waking. I imagined him lying next to Mama now, his eyes closed as he listened to her voice, the comfort it gave him amidst the clamor of his own thoughts.

"What happened?"

"Nothing, darling," Papa said.

"What is it?" she persisted.

A deep, long sigh, then finally he said, "The streets are filled with people, Aana. Homeless, hungry, desperate . . ." He paused, the bed creaked, and I imagined him turning to face her, their cheeks on the same long pillow, as I'd often seen. "The miseries—"

"No matter what awfulness is out there," Mama cut in gently, "I know you will take care of us."

A breathless silence. I imagined her lips pressed against his. I blushed.

"There!" she exclaimed, the insouciant ring and chime of her voice returning. Then came the sound of slatted shutters being opened, like wooden birds released, suddenly taking flight. "The sun is brilliant!" she enthused, and with these easy words chased away the morning's gravity, threw "Nothing" back out the gates like a stray cat that had clawed its way onto Papa's shoulder.

A shaft of light fell on the front of the house and spilled into the open hallway from the balcony. I imagined it a celestial carpet thrown from the heavens by a careless *tevoda*—an angel. I ran toward it, my steps unencumbered by the metal brace and shoes I normally wore to correct the limp in my right leg.

Outside, the sun rose through the luxuriant green foliage of the courtyard. It yawned and stretched, like an infant deity poking its long multiple arms through the leaves and branches. It was April, the tail end of the dry season, and it was only a matter of time before the monsoon arrived, bringing with it rains and relief from the heat and humidity. Meanwhile the whole house was hot and stuffy, like the inside of a balloon. I was slick with sweat. Still, New Year was coming, and after all the waiting and wondering, we'd finally have a celebration!

"Up, up, up!" came a cry from the cooking pavilion. It was Om Bao, her voice as voluminous as her ample figure, which resembled an overstuffed burlap rice sack.

"Pick up your lazy heads!" she clucked urgently. "Hurry, hurry, hurry!"

I ran around the balcony to the side of the house and saw her roll back and forth between the women's lower house and the cooking pavilion, her sandals smacking the dirt with impatience. "Wash your faces, brush your teeth!" she ordered, clapping as she chased a row of sleepy servant girls to the clay vats lining the wall outside the cooking pavilion. "*Oey, oey, oey,* the sun has risen and so should your behinds!" She whacked one of the girls on the bottom. "You'll miss the Tiger's last roar and the Rabbit's first hop!"

The Tiger and the Rabbit were lunar years, one ending and the other beginning. Khmer New Year is always celebrated in April, and this year—1975—it was to fall on the seventeenth, just a few days away. In our house, preparations would customarily begin long in advance for all the Buddhist ceremonies and garden parties thrown during the celebration. This year, because of the fighting, Papa didn't want us to celebrate. New Year was a time of cleansing, he reminded us, a time of renewal. And as long as there was fighting in the countryside, driving refugees into our city streets, it would be wrong for us to be celebrating anything. Fortunately, Mama disagreed. If there was a time to celebrate, she argued, it was now. A New Year's party would chase away all that was bad and usher in all that was good.

I turned and caught a glimpse of Mama standing in the corner of the balcony just outside her bedroom, lifting her hair to cool the nape of her neck. Slowly she let the strands fall in gossamer layers down the length of her back. *A butterfly preening herself.* A line from one of Papa's poems. I blinked. She vanished.

I rushed to the broom closet at the back of the house, where I'd hidden my brace and shoes the day before, pretending I'd lost track of them so I wouldn't have to suffer them in this heat. Mama must've suspected, for she said, *Tomorrow then. First thing in the morning you must put them on. I'm sure you'll find them by then.* I pulled them out of the closet, strapped on the brace as quickly as possible, and slipped on the shoes, the right one slightly higher than the left to make my legs equal in length.

"Raami, you crazy child!" a voice called out to me as I clomped past the half-open balcony door of my bedroom. It was Milk Mother, my nanny. "Come back inside this minute!"

I froze, expecting her to come out and yank me back into the room, but she didn't. I resumed my journey, circling the balcony that wrapped itself around the house. *Where is she? Where's Mama?* I ran past my parents' room. The slatted balcony doors were wide open, and I saw Papa now sitting in his rattan chair by one of the windows, notebook and pen in hand, eyes lowered in concentration, impervious to his surroundings. *A god waxing lyrical out of the silence . . .* Another line from another of his poems, which I always thought described him perfectly. When Papa wrote, not even an earthquake could disturb him. At present, he certainly took no notice of me.

There was no sign of Mama. I looked up and down the stairway, over the balcony railings, through the open doorway of the citrus garden. She was nowhere to be seen. It was as I'd suspected all along—Mama was a ghost! A spirit that floated in and out of the house. A firefly that glowed and glimmered, here one second, gone the next. And now she'd vanished into thin air! *Zrup!* Just like that.

"Do you hear me, Raami?"

Sometimes I wished Milk Mother would just disappear. But, unlike Mama, she was always around, constantly watching over me, like one of those geckos that scaled the walls, chiming, *Tikkaer, tikkaer!* I felt her, heard her from every corner of the house. "I said come back!" she bellowed, rattling the morning peace.

I made a sharp right, ran down the long hallway through the middle of the house, and finally ended up back at the spot on the balcony in the front where I had started. Still no Mama. Hide-and-seek, I thought, huffing and puffing in the heat. Hide-and-seek with a spirit was no easy game.

Pchkhooo! An explosion sounded in the distance. My heart thumped a bit faster.

"Where are you, you crazy child?" again came Milk Mother's voice.

I pretended not to hear her, resting my chin on the carved railing of the balcony. A tiny pale pink butterfly, with wings as delicate as bougainvillea petals, flew up from the gardens below and landed on the railing, near my face. I stilled myself. It heaved as if exhausted from its long flight, its wings opening and closing, like a pair of fans waving away the morning heat. *Mama?* In one of her guises? No, it was what it appeared to be—a baby butterfly. So delicate it seemed to have just emerged from a chrysalis. Maybe it was looking for its mother, I thought, just as I was for mine. "Don't worry," I whispered. "She's here somewhere." I moved my hand to pet it, to reassure it, but it flew away at my touch.

In the courtyard something stirred. I peered down and saw Old Boy

come out to water the gardens. He walked like a shadow; his steps made no sound. He picked up the hose and filled the lotus pond until the water flowed over the rim. He sprayed the gardenias and orchids. He sprinkled the jasmines. He trimmed the torch gingers and gathered their red flame-like blossoms into a bouquet, which he tied with a piece of vine and then set aside, as he continued working. Butterflies of all colors hovered around him, as if he were a tree stalk and his straw hat a giant yellow blossom. Om Bao suddenly appeared among them, coquettish and coy, acting not at all like our middle-aged cook but a young girl in the full bloom of youth. Old Boy broke a stem of red frangipani blossoms, brushed it against her cheek, and handed it to her.

"Answer me!" Milk Mother thundered.

Om Bao scurried away. Old Boy looked up, saw me, and blushed. But finding his bearings right away, he took off his hat and, bowing at the waist, offered me a *sampeah*, palms together like a lotus in front of his face, a traditional Cambodian greeting. He bowed because he was the servant and I his master, even though he was ancient and I was, as Milk Mother put it, "just a spit past seven." I returned Old Boy's *sampeah*, and, unable to help myself, bowed also. He flashed me his gappy grin, perhaps sensing his secret would be safe.

Someone was coming. Old Boy turned in the direction of the footsteps. *Mama!*

She made her way toward him, her steps serene, unhurried. *A rainbow gliding through a field of flowers . . .* Again a line fluttered through my mind. Though I was no poet, I was the daughter of one and often saw the world through my father's words.

"Good morning, my lady," Old Boy said, gaze lowered, hat held against his chest.

She returned his greeting and, looking at the lotuses, said, "It is so hot and now they've closed again." She sighed. Lotuses were her favorite blossoms, and even though they were flowers for the gods, Mama always asked for an offering to herself every morning. "I was hoping to have at least one open bloom."

"And you shall, my lady," Old Boy reassured. "I cut some before dawn and placed them in iced water so that the petals stay open. I shall bring up the vase to your room when His Highness finishes composing."

"I can always count on you." She beamed at him. "Also, would you make a bouquet of the closed buds for me to take to the temple?"

"As you wish, my lady."

"Thank you."

Again, Old Boy bowed, keeping his gaze lowered until she'd floated past him. She ascended the stairs, her right hand pressed on the flap of her silk *sampot* to keep her steps small and modest. At the top, she stopped and smiled at me. "Oh good, you found your brace and shoes!"

"I've practiced walking slowly in them!"

She laughed. "Have you?"

"One day I want to walk like you!"

Mama's face went still. She glided over to me and, bending down to my level, said, "I don't care how you walk, darling."

"You *don't?*"

It wasn't the pinch of the brace or the squeeze of the shoes, or even what I saw when I looked in the mirror that pained me the most. It was the sadness in Mama's eyes when I mentioned my leg. For this reason, I rarely brought it up.

"No, I don't . . . I'm grateful you can walk at all."

She smiled, her radiance returning.

I stood still and held my breath, thinking if I so much as breathed, she'd disappear. She bent down again and kissed the top of my head, her hair spilling over me like monsoon rain. I took my chance and breathed in her fragrance—this mystery she wore like perfume. "It's good to see that someone is enjoying this stifling air," she said, laughing, as if my oddness was as much an enigma to her as her loveliness was to me. I blinked. She glided away, her entire being porous as sunlight.

Poetry is like that, Papa said. It can come to you in an intake of breath, vanish again in the blink of an eye, and first all you'll have is

A line weaving through your mind
Like the tail of a child's kite
Unfettered by reason or rhyme.

Then, he said, comes the rest—the kite, the story itself. A complete entity.

"*Oey, oey, oey,* there's not a minute to waste!" Om Bao rattled on from below. "The floor must be mopped and waxed, the carpets dusted and sunned, the china arranged, the silver polished, the silk smoothed and perfumed. *Oey, oey, oey,* so much to do, so much to do!"

The branches of the banyan tree in the middle of the courtyard stirred and the leaves danced. Some of the branches were so long they reached all the way to the balcony, the shadows of their leaves covering my body like patches of silk. I twirled, arms stretched out, mumbling an incantation to myself, calling forth the *tevodas,* "Skinny One, Plump One . . ."

"And just what are you doing?"

I swung around. There was Milk Mother in the doorway with Radana on her hip. Radana squirmed down to the floor and immediately started stomping on the shadows with her chubby feet, the tiny, diamond-studded bells on her anklets jingling chaotically. It was normal for Cambodian children to be covered with expensive jewelry, and my much-adored toddling sister was bedecked in the most extravagant way, with a platinum necklace and a tiny pair of hoop earrings to match her anklets. This was not a child, I thought. She was a night bazaar!

As she toddled around, I pretended she had polio and a limp like me. I knew I shouldn't wish it on her, but sometimes I couldn't help it. Despite her bumbling and babyness, you could already tell Radana would grow up to look just like Mama.

"Eeei!" she squealed, catching a glimpse of Mama floating through one of the doorways and, before Milk Mother could stop her, she ran jingling through the hallway, calling out, "*Mhum mhum mhum . . .*"

Milk Mother turned back to me and asked again, with obvious annoyance, "Just *what* are you doing?"

"Summoning the *tevodas*," I told her, grinning from ear to ear.

"*Summoning* them?"

"Yes, I'd like to meet them this year."

No one ever met the *tevodas*, of course. They were spirits and, as with all things spectral, they lived in our imaginations. Milk Mother's *tevodas*—at least as she'd described them to me—sounded suspiciously familiar. With names like Skinny One, Plump One, and Dark One, I'd say she was describing herself, Om Bao, and Old Boy. By contrast, my *tevodas* looked nothing like me, but were as lovely as court dancers, wearing their finest silk and diadems with spires reaching all the way to the sky.

Milk Mother wasn't listening to me, her ear tuned to a different kind of noise. *Pchkooo!* Again, the tremor of an explosion. She strained to hear, her head tilted in the direction of the din.

The explosions worsened. *Pchkooo pchkooo pchkooo!* A series of them now, just as I'd heard in the night.

Turning to me, Milk Mother said, "Darling, I don't think you should put too much hope on the *tevodas* coming this year."

"Why not?"

She took a deep breath, seemed about to explain, but then said, "Did you wash yet?"

"No—but I was about to!"

She shot me a disapproving look and, nodding in the direction of the bath pavilion, said impatiently, "Go on then."

"But—"

"No arguing. Grandmother Queen will join the family for breakfast, and you, my bug, cannot be late."

"Oh no, Grandmother Queen! Why didn't you tell me sooner?"

"I was trying to, but you kept running away."

"But I didn't know! You should've told me!"

"Well, that's why I called and called—to *tell* you." She heaved, exasperated. "Enough lingering. Go. Get ready. Try to look and behave like the princess that you are."

I took a step, then turned back. "Milk Mother?"

"What?"

"Do *you* believe in *tevodas*?"

She didn't answer right away, just stood there and looked at me. Then finally she said, "What can you believe in if not the *tevodas*?"

I went down the front steps. That was all I needed to hear. The rest was easy to figure out. They were things I could see and touch—lotuses opening their petals, spiders weaving tiny silvery hammocks on wispy branches, slugs slipping through watered green grass . . .

"Raami." Looking up, I saw Milk Mother leaning over the balcony railing. "Why are you still dawdling?"

I placed one foot in front of the other, swaying my hips slightly. "I'm *practicing* my walk."

"For what—an earthworm contest?"

"To be a *lady*—like Mama!"

I broke a sprig of jasmine blossoms from a nearby bush and tucked it behind my ear, imagining myself as pretty as Mama. Radana appeared out of nowhere and stood in front of me. She cooed, transfixed for a second or two, and then, as if deciding I didn't look anything like Mama, bounced off. *Where are you?* I heard Mama sing. *I'm going to get you . . .* Radana shrieked. They were playing hide-and-seek. I had polio when I was one and couldn't walk until I was three. I was certain Mama and I didn't play hide-and-seek when I was a baby.

From above, Milk Mother let out an exasperated sigh: "For heaven's sake, enough lingering!"

Later that morning, in an array of brightly colored silks that almost outshone the surrounding birds and butterflies, we gathered in the dining pavilion, an open teak house with a hardwood floor and pagoda-like roof, which stood in the middle of the courtyard among the fruit and flower trees. Again, Mama had transformed herself, this time from a butterfly to a garden. Her entire being budded with blossoms. She had changed into a white lace blouse and a sapphire *phamuong* skirt, dotted with tiny white flowers. Her tresses, no longer loose, were now pulled back in a chignon tied with a ring of jasmine. A champak blossom, slender as a child's pinkie, dangled on a single silk thread down the nape of her neck; when she moved to adjust herself or to reach for this or that, the blossom slid and rolled, smooth as ivory on her skin.

Beside her, in my metal brace and clunky shoes and a ruffled blue dress, I felt ungainly and stilted, like a sewing dummy on a steel post, hastily swathed in fabric. As if this wasn't humiliating enough already, my stomach wouldn't stop rumbling. How much longer would we have to wait?

At last, Grandmother Queen—"Sdechya," as we called her in Khmer—appeared on the balcony, leaning heavily on Papa's arm. She slowly descended the stairs, and we all rushed to greet her, queuing on bended knees in order of importance, heads bowed, palms joined in front of our chests, fingertips grazing our chins. She paused near the bottom and, one by one, we each scooted forward and touched our forehead to her feet. Then we trailed her to the dining pavilion and claimed our appropriate seats.

Before us was an array of food—lotus seed porridge sweetened with palm sugar, sticky rice with roasted sesame and shredded coconut, beef noodle soup topped with coriander leaves and anise stars, mushroom omelets, and slices of baguette—a dish to suit everyone's morning taste. At the center of the table sat a silver platter of mangoes and papayas, which Old Boy had picked from the trees behind our house, and rambutans and mangosteens, which Om Bao had brought from her early morning trip to the market. Breakfast was always an extravagant affair when Grandmother Queen decided to join us. She was a high princess, as everyone constantly reminded me so that I would remember how to behave around my own grandmother.

I waited for Grandmother Queen to take her first bite before I lifted the cover off my soup bowl; when I did, steam rose like a hundred fingers tickling my nose. Tentatively, I brought a spoonful of hot broth to my lips.

"Be careful," Mama said from across the table as she unfolded her napkin and laid it across her lap. "You don't want to burn your tongue." She smiled.

I stared at her, mesmerized. Maybe I had seen a New Year's *tevoda* after all.

"I thought I'd visit the temple in Toul Tumpong after breakfast," she said. "My sister will send her chauffeur. I'll go with her, so our car is free if you'd like to venture out." She was speaking to Papa.

But he was reading the newspaper, his head slightly cocked to one side. In his usual muted attire of brown wraparound pants and beige *achar* shirt, Papa was as solemn as Mama was radiant. He reached for the cup in front of him and began to sip the hot coffee mixed with condensed milk. Already he'd forgotten the rest of his breakfast as he immersed himself in the news. He hadn't heard Mama at all.

She sighed, letting it go, determined to be in a good mood.

At one end of the table, Tata offered, "It'll be nice for you to get out a bit." Tata was Papa's elder sister—half sister actually, from Grandmother Queen's first marriage to a Norodom prince. "Tata" was not her real name, but apparently when I was a baby, I came to identify her as my "tata." The name stuck and now everyone called her this, even Grandmother Queen, who, at the moment, reigned at the other end of the table, blissfully ensconced in old age and dementia. I'd come to believe that because she was a high princess—Preah Ang Mechas Ksatrey—Grandmother Queen was more difficult to grasp than the *tevodas*. As a "queen" who ruled this family, she was certainly unreachable most of the time.

"I shouldn't be long," Mama said. "Just a prayer and I'll be back. It doesn't seem right to start the New Year without offering a prayer first."

Tata nodded. "The party is a very good idea, Aana." She looked around, seeming pleased with the start of the day, noting the preparations being made for the celebration to take place on New Year's Day.

In the cooking pavilion, Om Bao had started steaming the first batch of the traditional New Year's *num ansom*, sticky rice cakes wrapped in banana leaves. These we would give out to friends and neighbors during the coming days as each batch was made. On the balcony of the master house, the servant girls worked on their hands and knees waxing the floor and railings. They dripped beeswax from burning candles and rubbed it into the teakwood. Below them Old Boy was sweeping the ground. He had dusted and wiped the spirit house so that now it stood sparkling on its golden pedestal under the banyan tree like a miniature Buddhist temple. Several long strands of jasmine adorned its tiny pillars and the spire on its roof, and in front of its entrance, a clay pot filled with raw rice grains held three sticks of incense, an offering to the three pillars of protection—the ancestors, the *tevodas*, and the guardian spirits. They were all there, watching over us, keeping us out of harm's way. We had nothing to fear, Milk Mother always said. As long as we remained within these walls, the war could not touch us.

"I couldn't sleep a wink." Again Tata spoke, spooning brown sugar from a small bowl and sprinkling it on her sticky rice. "The heat was awful last night and the shelling was the worst it's ever been."

Mama put down her fork gently, trying not to show her exasperation. I knew, though, what she was thinking—*Couldn't we talk about something else?* But being the sister-in-law, and a commoner among royals, she couldn't speak out of turn, tell Tata what to say or not to say, choose the topic of a conversation. No, that would be graceless. *Our family, Raami, is like a bouquet, each stem and blossom perfectly arranged,* she'd tell me, as if to convey that how we carried ourselves was not simply a game or ritual but a form of art.

Tata turned to Grandmother Queen sitting at the other end of the table. "Don't you think so, Mechas Mae?" she asked, speaking the royal language.

Grandmother Queen, half deaf and half daydreaming, said, "Eh?"

"The shelling!" Tata repeated, almost shouting. "Didn't you think it was awful?"

"What shelling?"

I suppressed a giggle. Talking with Grandmother Queen was like talking through a tunnel. No matter what you said, all you could hear were your own words echoing back.

Papa looked up from his newspaper and was about to say something when Om Bao stepped into the dining pavilion, bearing a silver tray with glasses of the chilled basil-seed drink she made for us every morning. She placed a glass before each of us. Resting the tip of my nose on the glass, I inhaled the sweet ambrosia. Om Bao called her drink—a mixture of soaked basil seeds and cane sugar in ice-cold water, scented with jasmine flowers—"little girls hunting for eggs." When Old Boy picked the blossoms earlier they had been tightly closed, but now they opened up like the skirts of little girls with their heads dipped in water—hunting for eggs! It hadn't occurred to me before, but the basil seeds did look like transparent fish eggs. I beamed into the glass, delighted by my discovery.

"Sit up straight," Mama ordered, no longer offering me a smile.

I sat up straight, pulling my nose back. Papa glanced at me, mouthing his sympathy. He took a small sip from his glass and, looking up in surprise, exclaimed, "Om Bao! Have you lost your sweet touch?"

"I'm terribly sorry, Your Highness . . ." She looked nervously from Papa to Mama. "I've been trying to cut down on the cane sugar. We don't have much left, and it is so hard to find at the market these days." She shook her head in distress. "Your servant humbly regrets it's not so sweet, Your Highness." When nervous, Om Bao tended to be overly formal and loquacious. "Your servant humbly regrets" sounded even more stilted, when across the table from His Highness, I was lapping up my soup like a puppy. "Would Your Highness—"

"No, this is just right." Papa drank it up. "Delicious!"

Om Bao smiled, her cheeks expanding like the rice cakes steaming away in the kitchen. She bowed, and bowed again, her bulbous behind bobbing, as she walked backward until she reached a respectful distance before turning around. At the steps of the cooking pavilion, Old Boy relieved her of the emptied tray, quick as always to help her with any task. At the moment he seemed unusually agitated. Perhaps he was worried that I'd revealed his and Om Bao's morning canoodling to Grandmother Queen, who forbade such displays of affection. Om Bao patted his arm reassuringly. *No, no, don't worry,* she seemed to say. He turned toward me, obviously relieved. I winked. And for the second time this morning, he offered me his gappy grin.

Papa had resumed reading. He flipped the newspaper back and forth, making soft snapping noises with the pages. I tilted my head to read the headline on the front page: "Khmer Krahom Encircle City."

Khmer Krahom? Red Khmers? Who had ever heard of that? We were *all* Cambodians—or "Khmers," as we called ourselves. I imagined people, with their bodies painted bright red, invading the city, scurrying about the streets like throngs of stinging red ants. I laughed out loud, almost choking on my basil-seed drink.

Mama gave me another warning look, her annoyance now easily piqued. It seemed the morning hadn't gone in the direction she wanted. All anyone wanted to talk about was the war. Even Om Bao had alluded to it when she mentioned how hard it was to find cane sugar at the market.

I hid my face behind the glass, hiding my thoughts behind the little floating jasmine skirts. *Red Khmers, Red Khmers,* the words sang in my head. I wondered what color Khmer I was. I glanced at Papa and decided whatever he was, I was too.

"Papa, are you a Red Khmer?" It came out of me like an unexpected burp.

Tata set her glass down with a bang. The whole courtyard fell silent. Even the air seemed to have stopped moving. Mama glared at me, and when a *tevoda* glared at you like that, you'd better hide or risk burning.

I wished I could dip my head in the basil-seed drink and look for fish eggs.

The afternoon arrived, and it was too hot to do anything. All preparations for New Year came to a halt. The servant girls had stopped cleaning and were now combing and braiding one another's hair on the steps of the cooking pavilion. Seated on the long, expansive teak settee under the banyan tree, Grandmother Queen leaned against the giant trunk, her eyes partly closed as she waved a round palm fan in front of her face. At her feet, Milk Mother sat swinging Radana in a hammock lowered from the branches of the tree. She pushed the hammock with one hand and scratched my back with the other as I rested my head on her lap. Alone in the dining pavilion, Papa sat on the floor writing in the leather pocket notebook he always carried with him, his back against one of the carved pillars. Beside him the radio was playing the classical *pinpeat* music. Milk Mother began to doze off as she listened to the chiming melodies. But I wasn't sleepy, and neither was Radana. She kept sticking her face out of the hammock, wanting me to play with her. "Fly!" she squealed, reaching out for my hand. "I fly!" When I tried to grab her wrist, she pulled it back, giggling and clapping. Milk Mother opened her eyes, slapped my hand away, and gave Radana her pacifier. Radana lay back down in the hammock, sucking the pacifier like a piece of candy. Grandmother Queen clucked her tongue in encouragement, perhaps wishing she too had something to suck on.

Soon all three were asleep. Grandmother Queen's fan stopped waving, Milk Mother's hand rested on my back, and Radana's right leg hung out of the hammock, fat and still, like a bamboo shoot, the bells on her anklet soundless.

Mama appeared in the courtyard, having returned from her trip to the temple, which took longer than she'd planned. Quietly, so as not to wake us, she climbed the few short steps to the dining pavilion and sat down next to Papa, resting her arm on his thigh. Papa put down his notebook and turned to her. "She didn't mean it, you know. It was an innocent question."

He was talking about me. I lowered my eyelids, just enough to make them believe I was asleep.

Papa continued, "*Les Khmers Rouges,* Communists, Marxists . . . Whatever we adults call them, they're just words, funny sounds to a child, that's all. She doesn't know who they are or what these words mean."

I tried repeating the names in my head—*Les Khmers Rouges . . . Communists . . .* They sounded so fancy and elliptical, like the names of mythical characters in the tales of the *Reamker* I never tired of reading, the *devarajas,* who were descendants of the gods, or the demon *rakshasas,* who fought them and fed on fat children.

"Once you shared their aspirations," Mama said, head resting on Papa's shoulder. "Once you believed in them."

I wondered what kind of race they were.

"No, not them. Not the men, but the ideals. Decency, justice, integrity . . . I believed in these and always will. Not only for myself but for our children. All this"—he looked around the courtyard—"will come and go, Aana. Privileges, wealth, our titles and names are transient. But these ideals are timeless, the core of our humanity. I want our girls to grow up in a world that allows them, if nothing else, *these*. A world without such ideals is madness."

"What about *this* madness?"

"I hoped so much it wouldn't come to this." He sighed and went on. "Others abandoned us long ago at the first sign of trouble. And now so have the Americans. Alas, democracy is defeated. And our friends will not stay for its execution. They left while it was still possible, and who could blame them?"

"What about us?" Mama asked. "What will happen to our family?"

Papa was silent. Then, after what seemed like a long time, he said, "It's extremely difficult at this juncture, but I can still arrange to send you and the family to France."

"*Me and the family?* What about *you?*"

"I will stay. As bad as it looks, there's still hope."

"I will not leave without you."

He looked at her, then, leaning over, kissed the nape of her neck, his lips lingering for a moment, drinking her skin. One by one he began to remove the flowers from her hair, loosening it and letting it spread across her shoulders. I held my breath, trying to make myself invisible. Without saying more, they stood up, walked toward the front stairway, climbed the newly polished steps, and disappeared into the house.

I looked around the teak settee. Everyone was still asleep. I heard droning in the distance. The drone grew louder, until it became deafening. My heart pounded, and my ears throbbed. I looked up, squinting past the red tile roof of the master house, past the top of the banyan tree, past a row of tall skinny palms lining the front gate. Then I saw it! Way up in the sky, like a large black dragonfly, its blade slicing the air, *tuktuktuktuktuk* . . .

The helicopter started to descend, drowning out all other sounds. I stood up on the teak settee to better see it. All of a sudden it swooped back up and went the other way. I stretched my neck, trying to see past the gate. But it was gone. *Zrup!* Vanished completely, as if it had only been a thought, an imagined dot in the sky.

Then—

PCHKOOO!!! PCHKOOO!!! PCHKOOO!!!

The ground shook under me.

two

That same afternoon Om Bao went missing. A servant girl told us she'd gone out to the market near the airport. The girls knew it was dangerous but they couldn't stop her. She told them she needed to buy supplies for the New Year's party and was adamant she would find more there than in the shops of Phnom Penh. She'd been gone since just after breakfast, and although now it was evening, there was still no sign of her.

"It's been long enough," Papa finally declared. "I'm going out." His tone meant he'd made up his mind and no one could stop him, not even Mama.

He went to the carport, where his motorcycle was parked. Old Boy got up from the floor where he'd sat listening to the news on the radio and rushed to open the front gate. Papa, hunched over his machine, roared into the street, not a glance back.

Mama and Tata rose from their seats, walked toward the master house, and climbed the front stairs, their steps heavy.

"Can I stop now?" I asked, looking down at Grandmother Queen, my arms strained from massaging her all this time.

She groaned and, nodding, rolled onto her back. "You're a good girl," she mumbled, trying to sit up. I helped by pushing her back with mine. "All this is merit for your next life."

"Where do you think Om Bao is?" I whispered.

Grandmother Queen gave me a blank look, seeming only interested in the next life. Anything to do with this one was a huge void to her. I wondered if she even knew there was a war.

"People are fighting . . ."

"Yes, I know," she murmured. "There will remain only so many of us as rest in the shadow of a banyan tree . . ."

"*What?*" I stared at her, thinking not only did she look like some kind of spirit but sometimes she sounded like one too, speaking in obscurity. "*The explosions,*" I persisted. "Don't you hear them? A rocket must've dropped on Om Bao's head—"

I stopped, remembering what Milk Mother often said—*Turn your tongue seven times before you speak. This way you'll have time to think if you ought to say the things you want to say.* I turned my tongue seven times, but I wasn't sure if it counted when I'd already said it.

"There will remain only so many of us as rest in the shadow of a banyan tree," again Grandmother Queen murmured, and I didn't understand why crazy people always feel the need to say the same thing twice. "The fighting will continue. The only safe place is here . . . under the banyan."

The front gate creaked. I turned to look, but it was only Old Boy opening the toolshed behind the carport. He took out a large garden clipper and, for the first time, left his vigilant post under the hanging bougainvillea bush where he had waited since Papa left.

He walked about the gardens, trimming the trees and bushes. He cut off the leaves of the torch ginger so its flame-like blossoms would have more room to grow. He clipped the stems of the roses and rearranged the hanging orchid pots so that those with flowers went in the shade and those without would be ready to receive sunlight when morning came.

Night fell and still there was no Papa, or Om Bao. Old Boy put away his gardening tools. He picked up a broom and began to sweep the ground of thorns and broken branches. He gathered the fallen frangipani petals into a basket—white, yellow, red. A gift for Om Bao on her return. Every morning he would clip a stem of the red frangipani, whose fragrance was like vanilla—her favorite spice—and put it on her windowsill, a token of his appreciation for the sweetness she had shown him over the years, the desserts she had snuck into his room night after night when all the cooking chores were done, when she thought no one was looking or listening. He had lost most of his teeth because of her sugary concoctions. Theirs was a secret affair, one I'd witnessed—*spied* through the cracks in the walls and doors—in the furtive glances they'd give each other all day long, in the early morning blossoms he'd exchange for her late night desserts. But now, while waiting for her return, he'd gathered the fallen petals from the ground. He believed she was dead, and so did I. As soon as I told myself this I turned my tongue seven times . . .

. . . and seven times more.

Absence is worse than death. If you suddenly disappear without a trace, it's like you have never lived. To say Om Bao was missing, that she was suddenly absent from our life, was to deny she had ever existed. So everyone treated her "being gone" as a kind of death, a moving on into the next life. A couple of days later, a Buddhist ceremony similar to a funeral was held at a temple near the airport, the site where Om Bao might have last been alive, and because it was outside the city, where artillery shelling was most intense, only Papa and Old Boy attended. When they returned home, they brought back an urn with a lid shaped like the spired dome of a stupa.

"The cinder remains of her most cherished belongings," Papa said, nodding at the silver vessel Old Boy cradled in his arms.

How disconcerting to think that this was all that was left of Om Bao, just her things, reduced to ashes. Old Boy had carried a bag with him when he left at dawn for the ceremony. I hadn't thought then to ask what was inside the bag. I imagined spice boxes, wooden ladles and spatulas, frangipani blossoms . . .

"The *achar* tossed them into a fire," Papa explained, looking exhausted, his clothes crumpled and smeared with dirt, smelling faintly of soot. "In lieu of a corpse . . ." Then, noticing me for the first time, he said, "I should go change."

"Yes," Mama was quick to agree. To Old Boy, she said, "You should change too and get some rest," and, handing the urn to Milk Mother, "Would you put it away before you leave?"

"Of course, my lady," Milk Mother said, all dressed and ready to go. She was taking one day's leave to be with her family. "I'll find a proper place for it."

"Oh," Mama told her, "enjoy your time with your family. Our regards to them."

"Thank you, my lady."

Everyone got up to leave. I followed Papa and Mama. As they climbed the stairs, he said, "She is fated to be an absent ghost."

I stopped in my tracks. *Absent ghost?* How much more absent could you be if you were already a ghost? Invisible to the world?

"She's here with us," Mama said, squeezing Papa's hand, "in spirit."

I was tempted to ask if the New Year's celebration was back on. It had been canceled because Om Bao was gone. If she had returned, even if only in spirit, should we still celebrate?

I felt a hand on my shoulder. It was Milk Mother. She pulled me aside and said, "You must promise me you'll behave while I'm gone."

"You promise you'll be back tomorrow?"

Mama had insisted Milk Mother go and be with her family. It was good to have a break, even if we couldn't celebrate.

"It's New Year tomorrow," I reminded her.

She examined me. "The *tevodas* will come, darling. But it's not to celebrate New Year. It's not possible now. They will come to mourn her as we do."

"But you'll be back then, right?"

"Yes, most likely in the evening. Until then, promise me you'll keep yourself out of trouble?"

I nodded but did not say what I truly felt—that I didn't want her to go, that I feared she too would be "gone."

A little while later, when everyone had retreated into the cool silence of the house, an apparition in white appeared in the courtyard. It was Old

Boy. He had changed into clean clothes and now stood before the spirit house, making an offering of red frangipani blossoms. He gave me a handful of the blossoms so I could place them on the spirit house's tiny steps.

"Why are you dressed like that?" I asked, wondering why he was wearing funerary white when there was no funeral.

"I'm in mourning, Princess," he replied, his voice faltering.

I wanted to reach up and caress his face, as Om Bao had done in those moments when they thought themselves alone. But he looked so fragile, I was afraid if I touched him he might crumble to pieces. How was it that in a matter of a couple days, his age seemed to have caught up with him? I couldn't stop staring.

"When you love a flower," he said, as if wishing to explain his altered appearance, "and suddenly she is gone, everything vanishes with her. I lived because she lived. Now she is gone. Without her, I am nothing, Princess. Nothing."

"Oh." To mourn then, I thought, is to feel your own nothingness.

Tears rimmed Old Boy's eyes, and he turned his face away from me.

I let him be. I knew what I must do. I headed straight for the citrus garden in the back. Papa said that when he wanted to escape from something unpleasant or sad all he needed was to find a crack in the wall and pretend it was an entryway into another world, a world where all that was lost—yourself included—would again be found. Inside the bath pavilion, I found a portal much more generous than a crack—a row of tall, slender windows with the shutters swung open for air and light. I chose the middle window, as this gave me a full view of the whole grounds at the back of the estate. First, I saw the usual—ankle-high grass rippling like an emerald pond, tall bamboo vibrating with the whispers of a million tiny creatures, red and yellow birds-of-paradise frozen in flight, swooping bracts of lobster's claw hanging like Mama's jewel necklaces, and towering coconut trees like giant sentinels guarding an entrance. I looked harder, more carefully. Then I saw it!—this other world of which Papa spoke, where the lost was found, where a part of you always resided. It was quiet and lush, at once earthy and ethereal. There were no rockets or bombs exploding, no people crying or dying, no sadness, no tears, no mourning. There were only butterflies, fluttering their gossamer wings, each as brilliant as a dream, and there, near the trunk of a coconut tree, was Om Bao. She was in the form of a rainbow-colored moth, bulbous and bright, as she'd been when she was our cook. All along she'd been here waiting for Old Boy, while he waited for her. *Should I go tell him?*

No. Not yet. He was still mourning her. He wouldn't see what I saw. He wouldn't believe me. When he was ready, I would show him this secret world, where all he thought he had lost was in fact only hidden—transformed. And only then would he discern the invisible, the magical, only then would he find among these flowers he cared for a butterfly he had once loved.

three

Papa came running through the gate, calling out, "The war is over, the war is over!" He jumped up and down, like a schoolboy. I'd never seen this boisterous side of him. "No more fighting! No more war! The Revolutionary Army is here!"

"What? Who?" Tata demanded. "You mean the Khmer Rouge?"

"Yes, and everyone is cheering for them!"

"Are you mad?"

"The streets are full of well-wishers," Papa explained, unable to curb his excitement. "Even our soldiers are welcoming them. They're waving white handkerchiefs and throwing flowers!"

"Impossible." Tata shook her head. "This can't be true."

"You have to go out there." Papa remained exuberant. "The smiles, the cheers, the shouts of greeting!" He picked up Radana from the teak settee and started spinning with her, singing, "It's over, it's over, the fighting is over!" He grabbed Mama and kissed her full on the lips in front of us, in front of Grandmother Queen. Mama pulled away, mortified. She took Radana from him.

I tugged at Papa's shirtsleeve and asked, "Will Milk Mother come back for sure then?" It was New Year's Day, and she was due back from her visit to her family on the other side of the city. I had been worried about her being outside the safe enclosure of our walls, but now that the war was over, there wasn't the risk of her not returning.

"Yes!" He lifted me up and kissed my forehead. He looked around the courtyard, beaming. "All is well again."

In expectation of Milk Mother's return, the servant girls were granted an immediate leave for the holiday, and given that there would be no celebration, with Om Bao gone, they could have longer than usual. Once they departed, I took my copy of the *Reamker*, a Cambodian adaptation of the *Ramayana*, and went to wait for Milk Mother by the gate, even though it was still morning and she would most likely return in the evening. But just in case she returned sooner, she would see how glad I was to have her back. I chose a spot under the hanging bougainvillea where it was shady and cool and began to read once more from the beginning:

In time immemorial there existed a kingdom called Ayuthiya. It was as perfect a place as one could find in the Middle Realm. But such a paradise was not without envy. In the Underworld, there existed a parallel kingdom called Langka, a flip-mirror image of Ayuthiya. There, darkness prevailed. Its inhabitants, known as the *rakshasas*, fed on violence and destruction, grew ever more powerful by the evil and suffering they inflicted. Lord of the *rakshasas* was Krung Reap, with fangs like elephant tusks and four arms bearing the four weapons of war—the club, the bow, the arrow, and the trident. He, among all the beings of the three realms, most coveted Ayuthiya. Banned from it, he sought to destroy this paradise, creating all sorts of havoc and disturbance, shaking the mountain on which Ayuthiya rested, sending reverberations that could be felt all the way to the Heavens above. The gods, weary of Krung Reap's vices and villainy, beseeched Vishnu to fight the king of the *rakshasas* and restore balance to the cosmos. Vishnu agreed, and, assuming an earthly incarnation, descended as Preah Ream, the *devaraja* who would inherit Ayuthiya and bring it everlasting peace. But before this happened, the cries of battle resounded, blood was spilled, bodies of men and monkeys and deities alike littered the ground.

I had pored over the words countless times now, and this last bit—
bodies of men and monkeys and deities alike—still unsettled me. I imagined
a scene of such carnage that you couldn't tell who was who among the
dead. I knew enough of the tales to know that the rest of the *Reamker* was like this, that ogres could often turn themselves into beautiful
creatures, and that Preah Ream could transform himself into a being as
scary-looking as Krung Reap, with multiple arms and fangs and weapons. One entity could manifest as another, and if you didn't know who
was who to begin with, then how were you to recognize the *devas* from
the demons?

I continued reading: *At the time our tales begin, Ayuthiya was ruled by
King Tusarot. Of the four princes born to the king, Preah Ream was noblest*—
Suddenly I heard voices shouting in the distance: *Open the gate, open
the gate!* I put the book down and stilled my thoughts to listen. *Victory!
Victory to our soldiers! Welcome, brothers, welcome!* The voices were getting louder, as if they were just around the corner, *Open the gate! Leave!*
But I couldn't be sure. There were other noises—horns, bells, sirens, and
countless engines—all competing. Then the ground rumbled. Something
enormous heaved and rolled toward us. The air turned unnaturally hot,
laden with the odors of burnt rubber tires, heated tarmac. The reverberation became deafening, and around me the leaves and flowers trembled. A monster, I thought. A monster with rolling metal feet! Children
screamed, "Look, look! More of them!"

As they rumbled past, these monsters with diesel breath, grinding
the tarmac with their feet, cheers and applause broke out high in the
air—*Welcome Revolutionary soldiers! Welcome to Phnom Penh! Welcome!* A
few carnations landed on the walls of our gate, like birds falling from
the sky, followed by a chorus of voices singing, muffled and crackling
through some sort of loudspeaker:

> *A new day has arrived, Comrade Brothers and Sisters.*
> *Carry your Revolutionary flag with pride,*
> *Lift your face to the glorious light of the Revolution!*

The procession of monsters and voices moved farther up the street, until the loudspeaker's harsh bellowing softened to an unintelligible din. I heard the sounds of doors and windows being closed as people went back into their homes. Motorcycles and cars, which had stopped for the procession, seemed to be starting again, and bicycles and cyclos resumed their journeys, bells ringing incessantly. Then, after a while, all the noises faded, until our street was as completely quiet as before.

I waited to see if there was more to come, my ear pressed to the stucco wall. But there was nothing. No one. Where was Milk Mother? Maybe she got lost in all the commotion. Maybe she was trying to get back but couldn't make it through the dense traffic.

Then all of a sudden I heard loud banging a few houses away. My heart skipped. The banging continued, followed by the urgent squeaks and rattles of gates being opened, along with voices talking, shouting and arguing: *Who the hell are you? Get out! No, you get out! This is our house! BOOM!* Something exploded. A gunshot or maybe just a car tire, I couldn't tell. More banging, louder and nearer now, and before I had time to figure out what to do, someone was pounding on our gate, *BAM BAM BAM!* I jumped back a step or two, and one of the carnations that had been teetering on the wall fell to the ground near my feet. Just as I was about to pick it up, a voice commanded, "OPEN THE GATE!"

I looked around the courtyard, but not a soul was in sight, not even Old Boy. I knew the rule—no grown-up, no open gate. At least when there had been war. But now there was no war. My heart pounded, my breath quickened.

"OPEN!" again came the voice. "OR I'LL SHOOT IT DOWN!"

"Wait!" I croaked. "Just wait a minute!" I looked around and spotted a footstool partially hidden under a gardenia bush a few feet away. I brought it over and, standing on top of it, pulled back the latch—

A column of smoke burst in. He was all black—black cap, black shirt, black pants, black sandals. He stared down at me.

"Good morning!" I greeted. "You must be Dark One!" Of course I knew he wasn't a *tevoda*, but I was determined not to be afraid.

"*What?*" he asked, seeming more confused than I.

"Dark One!" I rolled my eyes, drawing him into my game. For a *tevoda*, fake or real, he wasn't very polite.

"*What?*"

He wasn't very smart either.

"I've been expecting you."

"Look," he growled, half exasperated, half threatening. "I don't have time for your stupid game." He brought his face close to mine. "Where are your parents?"

"Where's Milk Mother?" To curb my fear and stall his intrusion, I pretended to look past the gate to see if she was hiding in a corner somewhere.

"Go!" He pushed me. "Tell your parents to come out. Now!" He pushed me again and I nearly tumbled headlong into a flower bush. "Go!"

"All right, all right." I ran and skipped, calling out to everyone, "A *tevoda* is here!"

"He's a Revolutionary soldier," Papa said.

What? He didn't look like a soldier. Soldiers, I thought, were men who wore fancy uniforms decorated with stripes and medals and stars. This boy was wearing the plain black pajama-style shirt and pants that peasants wore for planting rice or working in the fields, and a pair of black sandals made from—of all things—a car tire! The only color in his entire ensemble was the red-and-white checkered *kroma*—the Cambodian traditional scarf—that belted his pistol to his waist.

Tata came out and gasped, "*Le Khmer Rouge.*"

I was even more shocked. *This is a Khmer Rouge?* Where was the many-named larger-than-life deity I'd expected?

"Stay here," Papa said to all of us. "Let me talk." He went over to greet the boy, his manner unusually respectful.

"Pack your things and get out," the soldier ordered.

Papa was taken aback, stammering, "I-I d-don't understand."

"What's not to understand? Get out of the house—get out of the city."

"*What?*" Tata demanded, forgetting Papa's warning as she marched toward them. "Look here, young man, you can't just burst in—"

Before she could finish her sentence, the soldier pointed his pistol at her. Tata stopped in her tracks, her lips parted, but no sound came out.

"Comrade," Papa said, touching the soldier's arm. "*Please.* There are just women and children here."

The boy looked around, his gaze moving from Papa to Mama, to Tata, then to me. I smiled. I wasn't sure why, but I held the smile. He put down his gun.

The air moved again, and I felt my heart beating once more. Still, for a moment there was only silence. Finally, Papa spoke. "Comrade, where are we supposed to go?"

"Anywhere—just get out."

"For how long?"

"Two, three days. Take only what you need."

"We'll need a little time to pack—"

"There's no time. You must leave now. The Americans will bomb."

Papa appeared flustered now. "You must be mistaken. They're gone. They won't—"

"If you stay, you'll be shot! All of you! Understand?"

Without further explanation, he turned and marched out the gate, the pistol now held high above his head as if to shoot the sky. "Long live the Revolution!"

We had to move fast. If the Revolutionary soldier came back, he would shoot us. We didn't know when that would be, if he would come back in an hour or a day, or if it was all a bluff. But Papa said we couldn't take any chances. We had to leave now. Tata argued, "I refuse to be chased out of my own house like a rat!" Papa gave us no choice. Mama broke into a sob. Radana, on the bed, hugging her beloved bolster pillow to her chest, began to howl at the sight of Mama's tears. Mama rushed over to comfort her. "I don't know what to take," she whimpered, looking at the large armoire with all her clothes still on their hangers. "We take money and gold," Papa said matter-of-factly. "Anything else we can buy on the street." He unlocked Mama's old vanity dresser and scooped out her jewelry from their boxes—necklaces, earrings, rings, and a jumble of other valuable items. He grabbed Radana's bolster pillow, which made her howl all over again, and sliced the seam open with a pocketknife. He stuffed all the jewelry into it among the cotton batting and hurried out of the room. He rushed through the house grabbing books, pictures, boxes of matches, anything he could think of, anything he came across. Outside, he tossed everything into the trunk of our blue BMW.

I caught him by the sleeve. "Where's Milk Mother?"

He stopped, looked at me, and sighed. "I don't know."

"Aren't we going to wait for her?"

"We can't, darling. I'm sorry."

"What's revolution?"

"A kind of war."

"But you said the war was over."

"That's what I thought, what I hoped." He looked as if he was about to say something else but then changed his mind. He was utterly distracted.

I let him go. He rushed back into the house.

I sat in the backseat of the BMW, sandwiched between Grandmother Queen and Tata. In the front Mama held Radana on her lap, pressing her lips to my sister's head, rocking back and forth. In Mama's arms, Radana had calmed down, lulled into sleep by the rocking, exhausted from her earlier crying. Papa slipped into the driver's seat and started the car. His hands shook as he gripped the steering wheel.

Old Boy walked to the gate, his back bent as if he were carrying a sack of rice. He was not coming with us. He would stay behind to take care of the gardens. He would rather face the soldier alone than let his flowers die in the heat. No one could convince him otherwise.

When you love a flower, and suddenly she is gone, everything vanishes with her.

As he held the gate open, Papa inched the BMW forward. I stretched my neck and looked into the rearview mirror. I saw the balcony, vacant and still. Had it always been like this, like no one had ever lived here? Suddenly I realized what it was that had followed Papa into the house, trailed his footsteps like a shadow several mornings ago when he returned from his walk. It was this moment. Our leaving. Our "being gone." We hadn't yet left, but already I saw and felt what it would be like without us here. How was it possible? I didn't understand. But there it was. Our prescient absence.

Everything began to recede. The cooking pavilion where Om Bao reigned with her spatulas and spices. The women's lower house on whose wooden steps the servant girls gossiped, relaxed, enjoyed their freedom from household chores. The master house where every morning I greeted the day, where stories spread their wings like the birds and butterflies in the surrounding trees. The dining pavilion that held all the conversations and meals and visits. The banyan tree under whose shadow lay sacred ground. The gardens with their clusters of bumblebees and blossoms.

Then, at last, the whole of the courtyard.

Only Old Boy remained, standing by the hanging bougainvillea bush near the gate where he had always stood. He waved. I turned and waved back.

He shut the gate.

four

The streets were packed. People, cars, trucks, motorcycles, mopeds, bicycles, cyclos, oxcarts, pushcarts, wheelbarrows, and things that didn't—*shouldn't*—belong on the streets of a city: ducks, chickens, pigs, bulls, cows, mats, and mattresses. I couldn't have imagined a water buffalo caked with mud, or an elephant carrying the mahout and his family. But there they were, part of the throngs that pushed and pulsated in every direction.

Beside us, a farmer pulled his pig by a leash. Panicking, the sow squealed as if being slaughtered. A bit farther away, a yellow Volkswagen Beetle barely escaped a horse rearing in fright when a truck suddenly blasted its horn. Papa kept a firm grip on the steering wheel as he maneuvered the car inches at a time through the dense traffic. When we left home, he had briefed us on the route we would take—we'd go to Kbal Thnol and meet up with my uncle and his family. This was the meeting spot they'd agreed on in case of an emergency. From there, we'd drive together to our weekend house in Kien Svay. He'd made it sound so easy. Now it seemed hugely complicated to cross a small intersection or even move in a straight line.

Next to me, Grandmother Queen began to moan. She wanted Papa to turn the car around, take us back home, but of course we couldn't go back. Revolutionary soldiers were everywhere, dressed in black from head to toe like the one who'd burst through our gate, waving their guns, ordering everyone to leave. Families poured into the streets, dragging suitcases cramped with belongings, cradling baskets stuffed with dishes and cooking pans, wooden stools and chamber pots. A woman balanced two baskets on a bamboo pole over her shoulders, a child in one basket and a stove in the other, with a rice pot perched precariously on top. An old blind beggar shuffled barefoot along the street, a walking stick in one hand and a begging bowl in the other. He groped his way through the swarm of bodies. No one stopped to give him change. No one seemed to pity him. No one even noticed. "GET OUT OF THE CITY!" bellowed voices through bullhorns. "THE AMERICANS WILL DROP THEIR BOMBS!"

Soldiers pushed and shoved anyone in their way, not caring who was old and who was young, who could walk and who couldn't. A man on crutches fell down and tried several times to pick himself up. A Khmer Rouge soldier saw him, yanked him up, and pushed him on. At the entrance to a hospital, a sick old woman clung to the arm of a young man who looked as if he might be her son. A young nurse in uniform wheeled a patient out on a hospital bed, adjusting the intravenous bag above the patient's head as she went. Nearby, a doctor ripped off his surgical mask, gesturing emphatically, as if trying to reason with the soldiers. One of them put a gun to his forehead, and the doctor stood suddenly still as a statue, arms raised in the air, his latex gloves smeared with blood.

A young father passed by, carrying one son on his back and another in front, the rest of him loaded with bundles and necessities—food, kitchenware, sleeping mats, pillows, blankets. His wife, with a child on her hip and another one on the way, hung tight to his arm as they twisted their way through the crowded street. A teenage boy pushed past them, holding his bleeding stomach in his hands as he tried to look for help. No help came his way. I was seeing a million faces at once, and everyone looked like everyone else. Scared. Lost.

We crawled by a half-destroyed building, with pieces of rebar protruding from the blocks of broken cement. In nearby alleys and corners, half hidden behind mounds of rubble, government soldiers frantically shed their forest-green uniforms and threw them into bonfires. In the back of a noodle stand a man was about to take off his camouflage shirt when a couple of Khmer Rouge soldiers spotted him. They dragged him out and pushed him into a truck full of other government soldiers.

In front of a school bookshop a group of students huddled close together, hugging their books to their chests. A Khmer Rouge approached a middle-aged woman, who looked like she might be a teacher, and tore the glasses from her face. He threw them to the ground and smashed them with the butt of his rifle.

Smoke was everywhere, as black as the soldiers' clothes. On sidewalks, books and papers burned in piles. Ashes flew up into the air, like burnt butterflies. I wondered why they were called Khmer Rouge—"Red Khmer." There was nothing *red* about them. Why did they have so many names? *Revolutionary soldiers, Communists, Marxists,* was how Papa would invariably refer to them, and Tata never failed to retort, *Khmer Rouge, rebels! Thieves! Jungle rats! They won't last.* She predicted their victory would be short-lived and called for their punishment. *They should be hanged like the common criminals they are. Revolutionaries,* Papa would insist, his tone tentative, as if he himself had yet to discern their true name, their intentions. *You must be careful how you speak of them.* I wondered what they were really. Soldiers or peasants? Children or adults? They looked neither like *devarajas* nor *rakshasas,* the mythical gods and demons I'd imagined them to be; in those plain black clothes they looked more like a race of shadows, each one a repetition of the others.

We came to a huge crowd gathered in front of a tall wrought-iron gate, behind which I could see part of the façade of a white-pillared villa. People pushed and shoved one another, fighting to get to the entrance. Those up front banged on the iron bars, pleading to be let in. Some tried to climb over the high wall, cutting themselves on the sharp metal prongs lining the top edge. A few made it over, but most were pulled back down by the competing horde below. Two men punched each other, then two more, three. A fight broke out. Women screamed, children whimpered and howled like puppies.

A shot resounded.

The crowd became suddenly still. A soldier stepped through the half-open gate, pistol held high above his head. He issued an order, waving left and right, and quickly the crowd divided to allow for a narrow path in the middle. The other soldiers standing guard began plucking out the foreigners and letting them through, while pushing the Cambodians back out onto the street.

Beside me, Tata murmured in disbelief, "Good god, they're doing what they said they would—they're expelling all foreigners."

"Is it a diplomatic sanctuary then?" Mama asked, turning to Papa.

"A temporary one, it looks like," Papa replied, staring straight ahead at something.

"They're not letting anyone in without a foreign passport."

I followed his gaze to where a young couple stood a little apart from the crowd. The man was a *barang*, one of those white giants with hairy arms and a protruding nose; the woman Cambodian and heavily pregnant. He was telling her something, an earnest expression hovering over her frightened one. She nodded, tears streaming down her cheeks. He took her face in his hands and pressed his lips to hers. A Khmer Rouge soldier marched over and shouted at them, his face contorted with disgust. The *barang* tried to explain—*My wife, my wife,* his lips seemed to be saying in Khmer—but the soldier paid no attention. Two more strode over and pulled the couple apart. The man cried out, the woman sobbed. A mob quickly came between them.

Papa pushed forward with the car. I looked back, searching for the *barang,* but he'd disappeared. I looked for his wife. She too was gone. I blinked, once, then again. Still, I couldn't bring them back. They were lost, as if erased from the human landscape.

We headed away from the villa, turning left onto Norodom Boulevard, which cut through the middle of the city. Papa had thought traffic would move more quickly here since it was a main thoroughfare. But it turned out to be even more congested, its lanes no longer visible as tanks and army trucks crawled alongside smaller vehicles, its once cleanly swept sidewalks now littered with indiscretions: an old man spitting into his chamber pot, a little boy relieving himself, a woman going into labor.

Papa wanted to get off the road and head toward Sisowath Quay along
the river instead. But every turn we came to was crammed, impossible
to penetrate.

We had no choice but to push on, weaving our path now around
the Independence Monument, whose giant mauve flame steeple seemed
dwarfed by the unbroken mass surrounding it. Voices echoed from every
direction through bullhorns: "DON'T STOP! KEEP MOVING! THE
ORGANIZATION WILL PROVIDE FOR YOU! THE ORGANI-
ZATION WILL LOOK FOR YOUR LOST RELATIVES! KEEP
MOVING! GET OUT OF THE CITY! THE ORGANIZATION
WILL TAKE CARE OF YOU."

Who was this Organization? The Khmer name—"Angkar"—
sounded to me like "Angkor," the ancient stone temples whose steeples
bear the carvings of giant faces looking down at you. I imagined the
Organization to be a living version of one of those carvings, a deity of
some sort, or a very powerful king. I propped myself up on one knee,
chin resting on the headrest, and looked out the back window. My eyes
followed the movement of a Khmer Rouge soldier as she headed toward
our car. She stopped just a few feet away to talk to a skinny old man who
reminded me of Old Boy. The old man put his palms together, pleading
with her, his hands like a bobbing lotus in front of her face. It seemed
he wanted to go up the steps of the Independence Monument, maybe to
rest, to find someone, to get his belongings, I could only guess. The girl
shook her head and pointed in the direction she wanted him to go. He
persisted, pushing against the flow. The girl slipped her hand under her
shirt, pulled out a pistol, aimed. A shot rang in the air. It echoed, like
three separate shots, one after another. People screamed, pushed against
one another, tried to run but couldn't.

"What was that?" Mama asked, jerking to full alert.

The old man dropped to the ground. A dark pool bloomed around
his head. A halo of blood. Crimson like the betel nut juice dripping out
the side of Grandmother Queen's mouth.

"What *was* it?" Mama asked again.

Still, no one said anything.

"KEEP MOVING!" The Khmer Rouge soldier marched past our car now, her arm raised high, gun in hand. "KEEP MOVING!"

I turned and faced front, sliding into the seat, closing my eyes. The noises outside beat on my eyelids, and I felt my lashes fluttering like a pair of wings severed from the burnt body of a butterfly.

"GET OUT OF THE CITY! THE AMERICANS WILL BOMB! THE AMERICANS WILL BOMB!"

"Pray to the *tevodas,* child," Grandmother Queen said, patting my head. "Pray to the *tevodas.*"

"DON'T WORRY ABOUT YOUR HOMES AND BELONGINGS! JUST GO! GO! THE ORGANIZATION WILL TAKE CARE OF YOU!"

I prayed to the Organization.

By midafternoon, we arrived at the edge of the city and found a place to wait on the side of the road under a cassia tree. Just ahead lay Kbal Thnol, the traffic circle where Papa had told his younger brother to meet us. To the left stretched Monivong Bridge, which would take us out of the city toward Mango Corner, our weekend house. We would wait and cross the bridge together with my uncle and his family. This way we wouldn't run the risk of being separated and sent in opposite directions.

We searched among the hundreds and thousands of faces that went by, but there was no one we recognized, no one who resembled my uncle or aunt or their twin sons. Once or twice when a Khmer Rouge soldier glanced our way, Papa restarted the engine and inched the BMW forward, pretending to move along with the crowd. I took in the faces drifting past us.

Among the scared and confused, a few seemed unafraid of the soldiers, indifferent to the threat of the Americans' bombing. Near us a woman walked up and down the street selling fried bananas, waving a dishrag to keep the flies away. A little girl came along dangling an assortment of jasmine garlands around her arms. She traded a small garland for a fried banana. "New Year's jasmines!" she called out. "New Year's jasmines!" She had a voice, I imagined, a New Year's *tevoda* would have—crisp, clear, like a bell ringing at a temple in the early dawn.

The little girl crossed the street, nibbling on the banana. She must have felt Mama staring at her, for she swung around, smiling, and ran to our car. Mama chose a garland with a long bright red ribbon spiraling down like the tail of a macaw and handed some money to the girl, who flashed us a big smile when she saw the amount. She went skipping away toward the fried-banana seller.

Mama detached the ribbon from the garland and gave it to Radana to play with. Then she hung the jasmine on the rearview mirror, letting the fragrance fill our car. When I looked again, the little girl had disappeared among the crowds, but I could still hear her voice singing, "New Year's jasmines, New Year's jasmines, get them while they're fresh . . ."

A large fire suddenly shot up in front of a row of shop houses a block away. Cries and gasps rippled through the streets as small crowds gathered to watch. Through the flames and smoke, I saw soldiers hurl armfuls of paper into the roaring blaze. Several pieces fluttered about like stringless kites, only to fall back into the fire. I caught sight of a little boy lunging forward to grab a sheet the size of a banknote. A soldier seized him by the neck and threw him aside, which had the effect of keeping others away from the burning pile, now smoldering with heat waves as palpable as membrane.

All of a sudden Papa restarted the car and aimed for the bridge. A Khmer Rouge soldier was marching straight toward us, a pistol in hand. Again, I prayed to the Organization.

The soldier—a boy with freckles a shade darker than his cane-sugar skin—walked alongside our BMW, finding ways for us to move along the crammed, narrow lane around the traffic circle. I'd thought he was coming to shoot us. When he slapped the hood, Papa steered to the right, and when he slapped the side, Papa steered to the left. As we got on the bridge, Papa poked his head out the window and said, "Thank you, Comrade!" The boy broke into a smile and saluted Papa. Then just as quickly, he turned back and started directing other vehicles onto the bridge.

We inched forward, bumping into baskets, carts, cars, people, and animals. Beside us a woman pulled her injured husband in a wheelbarrow, her shoulders entwined in a cotton scarf tied to its handles, like an ox harnessed to a cart. Her husband lay on top of their belongings, his bandaged legs stretched out stiffly in front of him. Papa steered the BMW to the left, inadvertently blocking her way. The woman glowered, muttering under her breath, cursing us, I was certain. Finally, she let us pass, pausing to wipe the sweat from her forehead.

Up and down the bridge people kept honking their horns as if this would make everything move faster. Two men got off their Vespas and started pushing each other back and forth, arguing over who had the right of way. A Khmer Rouge soldier strode toward them and the two men quickly separated, scrambling onto their mopeds, pushing forward with their feet against the ground, like criminals hurrying to escape.

Suddenly there was no more room to move. In front of us the crowd became confused. People screamed and pushed one another. Some tried to go back, but there wasn't even room to turn their bodies around. The crowd behind us kept pushing forward. Our car rocked back and forth as if we were on a swinging wooden bridge instead of a concrete one. Papa stuck his head out the window and asked a man standing next to our car, "What's going on?"

"They're bringing prisoners through," the man replied.

"*Prisoners?* Who?"

"Government officials and military people, those who tried to run— Here they come!"

"Don't look," Tata ordered. "Keep your head down."

I lowered my head and then lifted it back up as a group of Khmer Rouge soldiers passed, escorting not several but *one* prisoner. He stumbled forward, blindfolded with a *kroma,* the traditional cotton scarf, hands tied behind his back. Blood dripped from the corner of his mouth, his face was bruised and swollen, his skin broken everywhere. He was a big man, but his injuries made him seem small and vulnerable. Khmer Rouge soldiers, two in front and three in back, hit and kicked him. The crowds pulled back and made a path for them. Everyone was silent.

As he neared, I saw that both his ankles were tied with an arm-length rope, which had the effect of making him waddle instead of walk. With his injuries, it seemed, he couldn't run even if he wanted to. He brushed past our car. The soldiers took turns whacking him with the butts of their guns to hurry him on. He didn't retaliate or react but plodded on, dragging his despair with him. I kept my gaze on him until he disappeared from sight.

The crowds converged and the noises returned. Everything and everyone pushed forward, trying to get ahead, get as far away from the possibility of capture as they could. Loudspeakers from either end of the bridge bellowed, "THE ORGANIZATION AWAITS YOU! THE ORGANIZATION WILL WATCH OVER YOU!"

I looked everywhere for the Organization, but all I saw was confusion. Desperation. A man climbed the side barrier of the bridge and was about to jump when a soldier caught his shirt and yanked him back down. The soldier moved on. The man stood there shaking as the crowds moved about him, his life saved and ignored all in the same moment.

When it seemed we would never get through, we came to the end of the bridge, and the road split in two. Papa turned left off the main road onto a smaller road along the river. Something caught his attention. A black Mercedes-Benz parked along the shoulder of the road. I recognized the car. Papa headed toward it. I stretched my neck, trying to see past the windows. Only when Big Uncle rose like a *yiak,* a mythical giant, out of the Mercedes, unscathed and stately, did my heart finally stop hammering.

He strode toward us, followed by Auntie India and the twins. The boys bounced excitedly when they saw Radana waving the red ribbon.

Papa turned to us and said, "Let's get out of this mess."

five

At sunset we arrived in Kien Svay, a small town just outside Phnom Penh. It had taken us the entire afternoon to traverse the short distance. Even so, it seemed we were among the luckier ones to have escaped the city at all.

Our country house, Mango Corner, was the only French-colonial-style bungalow in a row of Khmer-style teak houses along the Mekong. Situated on a two-acre plot shaded by mango trees, it faced a small dirt road that rarely saw cars or motorized vehicles. Most of the town's residents were fruit growers, rice farmers, or fishermen, and except for ox-carts or boats, they owned nothing more than a bicycle. Now it seemed the whole city had descended on the town and overflowed into our once quiet enclave as people from the city, seeking refuge for the night, parked their vehicles in any open space.

To keep others out of Mango Corner, our neighbor, the caretaker of our property, had parked his oxcart in the entrance between the two rows of mango trees that gated our front yard from the road. When he caught sight of our cars, he rushed to remove the oxcart and let us through. "It's a relief to see Mechas and the whole family," he said, addressing Papa, his knees bent, head bowed, speaking the royal language. He quickly greeted all of us in the same way, and then again turning to Papa, said, "I didn't know how much longer I could keep them off the property." He motioned to the crowds in front of his own house. "I couldn't turn them away, Highness."

Papa nodded, thanking the man. The caretaker waved to his teenage sons to come help with the luggage. We went inside.

I headed straight for the double French doors that opened onto the colonnaded balcony. Beyond the row of coconut trees that marked the border of our property, the Mekong heaved like a waking serpent. Boats crowded the surface of the water as they would during the Water Festival, except I knew it wasn't a festival of any kind. There were no colorful buntings or streamers decorating the boats and oars, no crowds cheering from the shore, no singing and dancing, no light, no music. There was only the sound of loudspeakers ordering people to keep moving, to cross to the other side before nightfall. "GO! YOUR COMRADE BROTHERS AND SISTERS WILL HELP YOU! THE ORGANIZATION WILL FIND YOU SHELTER! GO!" Hundreds, maybe thousands of people skirted the sandy shore. Khmer Rouge soldiers kept guard everywhere. When a boat appeared, a family would rush to board it, dragging with them what they could of their belongings—pots and pans, pallets and pillows. Bigger items—stuffed mattresses, tables, chairs, paintings—lay abandoned on the bank. I watched as boats returned emptied of passengers and as many more, loaded with people and belongings, headed across the river. Ants floating on leaves, I thought. As they moved farther away, they merged with the blue-black backdrop of the forest at dusk. I wondered what was on the other side of the forest. A new world? Maybe the edge of this one? I didn't know.

Papa came out and stood next to me on the balcony. I turned to him and asked, "Where are they going?" I feared that we too would have to leave, that the soldiers would come storming in and order us back on the road.

Papa didn't answer, staring instead at the river in silence, his eyes following the flow of people. He stood like this for a minute or two. Then a shadow crossed his face, and he finally turned to me with a look that mirrored my own confusion. "The Mekong is a powerful river," he said solemnly. "So powerful that every rainy season it changes the course of another river"—he pointed in the direction of the city—"the Tonle Sap."

I knew the Tonle Sap River well, as did every child who lived in

Phnom Penh. It stretched along the eastern edge of the city in front of the Royal Palace. The riverfront was a wonderful place for bike rides, kite flying, or an evening stroll. During the Water Festival in November, people would come from all over the country to watch the boat race and above all, to pay respect to the spirits of the water.

"In the next several months," Papa continued, "when the monsoon arrives, the Mekong will rise so high that the water will flow upstream through the Tonle Sap River into the Tonle Sap Lake in the northwest. Over there." Again he pointed, this time in the direction far beyond the city.

I paid close attention, expecting him to weave me a tale of the Underwater Kingdom where the mythical *naga* serpents lived.

"Then near the end of the rainy season, the level of the Mekong begins to fall and the built-up water of the Tonle Sap Lake drains back into the Tonle Sap River, reversing its course."

I knew the Tonle Sap River reversed course. That was part of its magic. But I'd always thought it had to do with the direction in which the *naga* serpents were swimming. At least, that's what Milk Mother had told me.

"Life is like that." Papa turned once again to the Mekong. "Everything is connected, and sometimes we, like little fishes, are swept up in these big and powerful currents. Carried far from home . . ."

"If the river brought us here," I ventured tentatively, "then when it reverses course, it'll carry us back."

Papa gazed at me. Finally he smiled and said, "You are right. Of course it will."

I nodded, relieved.

He lifted me up, and even though I didn't like to be carried as if still a small and helpless child, I let him do it this time, too tired to resist. I closed my eyes and rested my head on his shoulder, the sound of that gunshot echoing through my mind, like a thought beating against my skull. A question no one could answer. *Why?* Again and again, I saw the old man drop to the ground.

• • •

Inside we found respite from the heat and turmoil. It was cool and clean, thanks to the caretaker's wife, who swept and dusted and aired out the house every day, always keeping it ready for us. She had brought out the silk cushions from the tall Chinese camphor chest by the living room entrance and placed them on the chairs and settees. I felt safe and protected among these brilliant colors. They reminded me of home and our courtyard with its profusion of flowers. I grabbed a cushion and settled into a low armchair by the doors. Nearby the twins were playing. They had dug out a broom from somewhere and were now riding it around the living room, pretending it was a horse. They zigzagged between pieces of furniture and luggage, making galloping sounds. Radana, waking from her car-ride stupor, slid down the teak recliner where Mama had put her and started to chase after them, demanding her turn. When they wouldn't give it to her, she stomped her foot, crying out, "Mine, Mama, mine!" Just then Big Uncle walked in, a suitcase in each hand, and, seeing the distressed look on Mama's face, boomed, "Attention!" The twins stopped, dropped the broom, and stood at attention, midget soldiers fearful of their towering commander.

Papa chuckled. Big Uncle burst out laughing, then just as abruptly stopped, adopting seriousness again when he caught one of the twins fidgeting. He growled, and the twins straightened, their little chests puffed out even more. They seemed rooted to their spot now. Auntie India—nicknamed so for her dark-skinned beauty and melodious, lilting voice—placed a hand over her mouth to keep from giggling. On the antique settee Grandmother Queen and Tata exchanged amused glances. Big Uncle, certain of the boys' obedience, went to one of the bedrooms to put away the suitcases, smiling to himself.

Mama went about the house opening doors and windows. A sigh traveled her body and escaped her lips every time she pushed a shutter open. I got up and followed her, helping with the hooks and latches, mimicking her every movement and breath. She looked down and gave me a smile. As long as Mama smiled, everything would be all right. Papa winked, as if reading my thoughts. Then, reaching over the coffee table, he pulled on the long chain attached to the ceiling fan.

We waited, holding our breaths in hopeful anticipation. But the wooden blades wouldn't turn. As we suspected, there was no electricity. Even in the city, electricity was erratic.

"The power line must be damaged," Papa said, coming over to where Mama stood. He gave her hand a quick squeeze. "I'll look for some lanterns in the storage shed." He went down the side stairway, whistling, his steps light.

I went over to where Grandmother Queen was sitting. Tata had left to prepare their room, and Grandmother Queen patted the cushion for me to sit down next to her, but as the tiles were cool against my feet I sat down on the floor instead, my head resting on her knees. "This is home, too," Grandmother Queen said, caressing my hair. I nodded.

The twins had resumed their game, riding their own invisible horses, chasing after Radana, who now had possession of the broom. The boys, four years old, were named Sotanavong and Satiyavong, but because next to their giant father they looked more like little bubbles hovering no higher than his knees, their long names were ignored, and we called them simply "the twins" or "the boys." If you asked which of them was older, one would declare, "I am!" and the other would quickly add, "Only by fourteen minutes eleven seconds!" Then the two would elbow and punch each other, competing for supremacy, until someone like me came along and smacked some sense into them and told them how it really was: that two of them combined didn't equal one of me. Needless to say, for this reason, they preferred to play with Radana, as they were doing now, pursuing her like warriors on their make-believe horses while she shrieked, a princess in peril. For the first time, though, I wasn't annoyed with the ruckus they were making. The three of them playing—even as they wrangled over a stupid old broom—made everything seem normal, like all the other times we'd come here for a holiday.

I stretched out on the floor, closed my eyes, and let the hard coolness of the tiles lull me to sleep.

I woke and found Radana next to me on a bed with a mosquito net over us. I looked around the room, letting my eyes adjust to the dark. Quietly, so as not to wake Radana, I got up and went out to the living room. The house was mostly dark except for a muted glow from the kitchen. Hungry, I went toward the light and found Mama and my two aunts sitting on footstools. They were busy arranging foods, their faces illuminated by the kerosene lantern burning on the tile counter just above their heads. Auntie India was telling Mama and Tata something when she saw me standing in the doorway. "There you are!" she chimed, her voice melodious even when she said the most mundane things. "You must be starving!"

I went over to Mama, needing to be reassured by her closeness. I had dreamt of Milk Mother, of her absence. She was a void as black as the night, and even though I felt her presence, I couldn't touch her, couldn't find her face in the darkness.

"Everyone has had their dinner already," Mama said, parting the wisp of bangs from my eyes. She pulled out a wooden footstool for me. I sat down and pressed close, my head against her shoulder. "Are you all right?" she asked, lifting my face to hers.

I nodded, wanting her to keep talking. Her voice calmed me, chased away the fears that lingered at the edge of my waking. She smiled and handed me the plate of fried rice she'd saved from dinner. I looked at it, hesitating, not sure if I wanted to eat now. "You'll feel better," she said, "once you've had some food."

"We didn't think you'd wake up," Tata said, squinting at me from where she sat. "The way you just lay there on the floor."

"Still as a squashed bug!" Auntie India chimed in, laughing.

As soon as I took a bite of the food, my stomach grumbled with hunger. Surely we must have had lunch, but I couldn't remember. Everything was a blur. How long had I slept? Had it only been one day from the moment the soldier banged on the gate? As I ate, the women resumed their tasks, sorting perishable foods from the dried and canned goods.

Mama seemed to have gotten control of herself and was again the woman who could run a household by herself or host an extravagant New Year's party without a drop of sweat on her silk. She was in charge now, telling my two aunts what was essential and practical to keep and what we could do without, like the bottle of brandy Auntie India had brought along for the men, or the unopened can of butter Tata had somehow managed to grab from the refrigerator before we left. Auntie India, nodding vigorously, deferred to all of Mama's suggestions and instructions. Tata, even as she continued to hold herself regal and erect, conceded authority to my much younger mother and admitted openly, "What would we do without you, Aana? And yes, what was I thinking? Butter in this heat! I guess I panicked and grabbed what I thought would be impossible to find."

"Don't worry about it." Mama laughed. "We can use it for tomorrow's dishes—maybe make mango crepes for the children. Or we could trade it for real meat—some fresh beef from a local butcher, perhaps. Same with the brandy." She gave Auntie India a teasing nod. "That is, if you haven't told the men yet."

All three laughed. Then it turned serious again when Auntie India inquired tentatively, "Do you think it's wise to leave the property, to trade or for any reason?"

There was silence. Mama turned to me, as if not wanting me to hear the conversation. But before she could say anything, Tata said, "I know what you mean. It's just too horrible." She shook her head. "They're everywhere, shooting people left and right. Barbarians, that's what they are."

"They say anyone with glasses reads too much," Auntie India offered. "The sign of an intellectual."

I looked at Tata and noticed her glasses were not where she'd always had them, hanging from the gold chain around her neck. Then I remembered she'd taken them off in the car sometime during our journey. Suddenly the whole day's events came back to me—leaving the house, the crowded streets, the rash shootings and separations, the chaos everywhere.

I stopped eating. Mama noticed. "Don't you want to have some more food?" she asked, worried by my abrupt change of appetite.

I shook my head. I felt sick to my stomach.

• • •

I found Papa and Big Uncle settled like two shadows in the low wicker armchairs on the balcony, a bottle of red wine on the coffee table between them. Except for a tiny glow from the cigarette between Big Uncle's fingers, they were sitting in the dark, deep in conversation. Before them the Mekong coursed like a dark glittering snake as boats lit with torches glided across its surface. Campfires had sprung up along the shore. Here and there stood the dark silhouette of a Khmer Rouge soldier hugging his gun, keeping constant watch. From somewhere high in one of the coconut trees radio music crackled through a loudspeaker:

We are the Revolutionary youth!
We must rise, rise! Take up arms!
Follow the glorious path of the Revolution!

I went over to Papa, and he lifted me up onto his lap, saying to Big Uncle, "I just don't understand . . . It doesn't make any sense, Arun." The wine in his glass seemed untouched, while Big Uncle's glass was empty, except for a darkish ring at the bottom.

We must bring down the enemies!
Smash them with all our might!

"What's clear to me," Big Uncle said, extending his arm to keep the smoke as far from me as possible, "is that reprisals will be taken against those with links to the Republic and the monarchy." He got up with ashtray in hand, took a drag, and exhaled. Then, stubbing out the cigarette, he returned to his seat. Auntie India said Big Uncle smoked when he worried.

Papa nodded. "People like us, I suppose."

I looked up at the night sky, searching for signs among the stars. At night, Milk Mother said, even the sky told a story. A blinking star means a child is about to be born, and a shooting star means someone has died and the spirit is passing into the next world. But at the moment I saw nothing, heard nothing, nothing that revealed to the world what I alone knew—I'd be shot because I too was an intellectual, an avid reader, a lover of books.

"They're starting with a clean slate," Big Uncle noted, brow furrowed. "It might be weeks or even months before we can go back. In the meantime a new rule, a new regime will be established in our absence."

"But why empty the city?" Papa wondered.

"Chaos. It's the foundation of all revolutions. This one is just beginning, and I'm not sure what it is. It has yet to be named."

How strange, I thought. Everything had a name. Even the *preats*, spirits condemned to wander homeless and hungry, had names. The soldiers themselves had names, indeed many names: Red Khmers, Communists, the Khmer Rouge, Revolutionary soldiers.

"You mustn't have any illusion about these soldiers, Klah," Big Uncle said, calling Papa by his nickname, Tiger. "These children."

Once again I saw the face of the Khmer Rouge soldier who'd aimed her gun at the old man's head. It occurred to me that the look on her face, as she shot the old man, as she watched him fall to the ground, had no name. It was neither anger nor hate nor fear. It was absent of rage or anything recognizable, and I remembered thinking that she had looked neither like a child nor an adult, but a kind of creature all to herself, not altogether unreal, in the same way a nightmare monster is not unreal.

"You see that they are children, don't you?" Big Uncle waited for a reply.

For a long time, the two men remained quiet, each lost in his thoughts. From the river a chorus of voices sang through the loudspeaker:

Wonderful, glorious Revolution!
Your light shines on our people!

Papa broke the silence. "What do we do now? Do we stay here?"

"We can't," Big Uncle said. "Sooner or later, they'll tell us to leave again."

"But where do we go?"

"I don't know."

The singing stopped, and a voice bellowed, "Today is the day we liberated the Cambodian people! April seventeenth will be remembered, etched forever in the memories of every Cambodian! Long live the Kampuchean Socialist Revolution! Long live the Organization! Long live Democratic Kampuchea!"

"I expected them to be more our age," Papa murmured, "or even older, and not so coarse with their manner and speech."

"Ayuravann"—Big Uncle adopted a tone that sounded like he was reprimanding his elder brother—"they're not the same men you studied philosophy and history and literature with in France." He looked at Papa until Papa returned his gaze. "Nor are they people whose daily struggles and aspirations you've tried to capture and convey in your poetry. They are children who've been given guns—power beyond their years."

"Can one not be sympathetic to their cause?" Papa said, his voice tentative. "To the ideals they're fighting for?"

"And what's their cause? We don't know, do we? And I'm quite certain neither do these children. As for *ideals,* I don't think they even know what the word means."

Papa made no response.

The next morning I woke with a start, my heart hammering in my chest. Old Boy was dead. I had dreamt it. He was shot in the head and his blood was the color of the early dawn sky.

six

Several days passed in relative calm at Mango Corner. Then one morning I heard the loud thud of feet running up the steps. "They're coming, they're coming!" the caretaker shouted, breathless with fear. "The Khmer Rouge soldiers are coming!" Before Papa could ask anything else, the caretaker raced away to warn others in the neighborhood.

We rushed about packing—grabbing whatever we could. It was the same madness all over again. There was no time to think, no time to argue. Suddenly shots rang through the air, and before we could take cover, three Khmer Rouge soldiers burst into the house, waving their guns and shouting, "GET OUT! GET OUT!" Radana bawled, the twins grabbed hold of Auntie India's legs, Grandmother Queen started chanting Buddhist prayers for the dead, and Tata couldn't stop whimpering, "Oh no, oh no, oh no . . ." Big Uncle yelled out something, and one of the soldiers turned to him. "YOU!" He pushed his gun hard into Big Uncle's rib cage. "MOVE!" Big Uncle took short, tentative steps, his arms in the air, his chest rising and falling. The soldier kept shouting, "OUT! OUT!" Papa took my hand in his and squeezed it tight. We followed Big Uncle out the door, the other soldiers pushing us from behind.

Outside, the ground in front of our property had been cleared of the refugees we'd allowed to camp there. Two of the soldiers tromped off, heading for the neighbors' houses. Only the youngest remained. He looked at us, then at Big Uncle. He ordered Big Uncle to kneel. Big Uncle lowered himself to the ground, slowly, cautiously.

The boy, his gun now aimed at Big Uncle's head, shifted left and right on his feet, eyes darting from face to face. Then his eyes caught the glint of Big Uncle's watch flashing in the sunlight. An Omega Constellation, I remembered. Identical to Papa's. Both gifts from Grandmother Queen to her sons. My eyes went to Papa's left wrist. No watch there. He must have taken it off and put it somewhere.

"OFF!" the boy shouted. Big Uncle made no move. "TAKE IT OFF!" the boy thundered. Finally Big Uncle lowered his arms, took the watch off his wrist, and handed it to him. Nervous, the boy dropped the Omega on the ground, and when he bent down to pick it up, a Mercedes emblem—round and shiny—slipped through his open shirt collar, dangling in the air from a string around his neck. It gleamed—a secret treasure. He quickly shoved it back inside his shirt, pocketed the Omega, and looked up to see us staring at him.

Big Uncle's eyes darted to the hood of his car and then back to the boy, nodding as if to say, *You could have that too.* Was he mocking the soldier? A smile, a sneer, I couldn't tell what Big Uncle was feeling or trying to communicate. The boy looked tempted. Then all of a sudden something rose in him and, straightening his stance, he spat on Big Uncle's face. There was a nervous pause as he waited to see what this titan would do. Big Uncle remained as he was, the spit sliding down his face.

The boy laughed, first forcefully, then more shrilly, thrilled that he could command the obedience of a giant. "IMPERIALIST PIG!" He lifted his foot and kicked Big Uncle in the stomach. Big Uncle fell on his haunches. The boy took a step or two back, still pointing the gun at us, and once at a safe distance, proclaimed, "DOWN WITH IMPERIALIST PIGS!"

He turned and dashed out of the property. Again, shots rang through the air. Papa cupped his hands over my ears. Mama pressed Radana to her chest.

Stillness returned. No one moved or said anything. No one knew what to do. Big Uncle got up, caught the twins and Auntie India looking at him, their eyes shiny with tears, and suddenly his face quivered with shame. "Curse the woman who gave him birth!" he thundered, his face contorted, nostrils flaring, looking as fearsome as the *yiak* I'd always thought he was. He picked up a rock and hurled it in the direction where the soldier had disappeared.

Auntie India, shaking from head to toe, begged, "Please, Arun. The gods—they are listening." Her voice, robbed of its birdsong melody, rang with dread. "Please, they will hear you."

"Damn them all!" Big Uncle roared, his anger as magnificent as his bulk and height. "Their revolution and their gods!" He kicked a small sapling and broke it in half and hurled that too at the road. Then, looking even more ashamed for losing control, he got in the car, slammed the door behind him, and started the engine.

We followed, our car behind his, roaring out the entrance.

But we didn't get very far. Again the road lining the Mekong was crammed, and before we could decide whether to veer left or right, a group of soldiers appeared holding up hand grenades, ordering everyone out of the cars and down to the river, threatening any who remained in their vehicles.

We found a spot under the shade of a rain tree, hurriedly sorted through the items we'd brought with us—food, kitchenware, sleeping mats, mosquito nets, blankets, clothes, medicines—and retied them into more portable bundles, while discarding the heavy and bulky suitcases. Radana's little pillow, resewn and heavy with jewels, was saved. But Big Uncle's small shortwave radio, Papa's thick volume of classic Khmer verses, and Mama's mother-of-pearl music box containing photos and letters had to be left behind, scattered on the car seats like offerings to a rapacious god who hid, invisible, salivating amidst the spoil.

From my copy of the *Reamker*, which I'd grabbed at the last minute when we were leaving the house, I tore out the page with the ornate gold-colored illustration of Ayuthiya and stuffed it in my pocket, reciting quietly to myself the words I remembered by heart: *In time immemorial there existed a kingdom . . . It was as perfect a place as one could find . . .* I would miss reading it, but it didn't seem right to tear out a page with words. If another child found it, I thought, I wanted her to have the complete story, from the beginning.

All around us others were doing the same, figuring what to take and what to leave behind. Families wondered if their vehicles should be locked, if the soldiers would guard their belongings during their absence, and when they could be expected to come back. The soldiers had no answers.

Papa, with rolled-up straw mats strapped to his back and two heavy sacks slung over his shoulders, picked me up and pressed me close to him. Mama, with her own bundles and sacks, carried Radana. Auntie India and Tata, in addition to what they carried, each took a twin, while Big Uncle, the biggest and strongest, carried Grandmother Queen on his back and a load on his chest. Together we descended the silty incline toward the Mekong's mangrove-covered shore, grabbing on to branches and vines and one another to keep from sliding.

At the bottom a line of boats waited along the shallow edge, swaying like hammocks rocked by all the coming and going, while many more littered the deeper waters. The boats were setting out loaded with passengers and returning empty. There was no time to decide if a boat was safe or not, if there would be too many of us in one vessel. A young Khmer Rouge soldier gestured to us, then pointed to a fishing canoe that looked as weather-beaten as the old fisherman who stood in it. I swallowed and felt the whole river rushing down my throat.

As we approached the long stretch of shore on the other side of the river, the old fisherman maneuvered the canoe into a space between a rock and another boat. In front of us a crowd was gathering to look at something that had washed ashore. There were murmurs and gasps. Mama turned back to look at us, unsure whether to stay or get off, her face blanched with motion sickness. I got up, wanting to have a look, but Papa quickly pulled me back down. A soldier marched toward the gathering crowd. "What use is it to gawk?" he thundered. "She's dead! Move before someone else ends up like her! NOW!" He turned, waving his gun in our direction. "OUT! WHAT ARE YOU WAITING FOR—A CARRIAGE TO CARRY YOU? OUT!"

Mama clutched Radana in her arms and scooted off the boat. The rest of us followed close behind, rushing past the dark mound lying on the sand. Papa tried to keep me from looking, but I saw it anyway. The body. It lay there on the muddy sand, facedown, with strands of jasmine wrapped around the neck and entangled in the hair. I didn't see her face, so I couldn't be sure if it was the same girl we'd encountered that day leaving Phnom Penh. It was unlikely. There were countless other little girls selling jasmine garlands every day. Still, it was her voice I remembered, her voice I heard now calling out to customers: *New Year's jasmines! New Year's jasmines!*

A couple of Khmer Rouge soldiers picked up the body and threw it into the nearby bushes. They wiped their hands against the leaves as if they had just thrown away a dead fish. More soldiers came and hurried us along. A young female soldier pushed Mama forward, yelling, "MOVE! MOVE!" Frightened, Radana cried out and wrapped her arms around Mama's neck, the red ribbon still tied to her wrist like a good-luck string.

"MOVE!" echoed the other soldiers. "MOVE!"

Papa picked me up and we followed the surging throngs, scrambling up the sandy riverbank toward the dark expanse of the forest.

The soldiers led us across a jungle-like terrain, where vines bore thorns as steely as metal prongs and where trees looked like *yakshas,* giant sentinels who guarded the entrance to a hidden world. Mama screamed when what she'd thought was a branch suddenly slithered across her path. Papa paused in his walking to flick a scorpion as large as a lizard off his forearm. When a wild boar came charging at us out of nowhere, the soldiers fired rounds of bullets in its direction. None hit the animal, but the clatter managed to scare it away.

On we pushed, bathed in sweat, braving sun and heat, fighting hunger and thirst. Only at nightfall when we met with water again did it become clear we'd journeyed across an island. At first I thought this new stretch of water was an ocean because it was bigger than any river I'd seen and looked much deeper than the river we'd already crossed. But Papa said it was still the Mekong. Pointing across the water toward the lights that dotted the otherwise pitch-black landscape, he explained that the closer lights probably came from barges and fishing boats and those farther away from small towns and villages along the shore. In the dark, even the lights looked lonely and forlorn. I couldn't imagine there being anything out there except those lost-soul *preats,* and now it felt likely we were being sent to join them.

Before us loomed the silhouette of a wooden boat as big as a house. This type of craft, Papa said, was used for transporting livestock, which was why it looked as it did—cavernous and windowless. Now it would transport us. "Don't worry," he reassured us. "It'll be just a few minutes." Looking at the coffin-like monstrosity, I didn't think I could bear even a second inside.

On deck stood several Khmer Rouge soldiers holding torches crested with bright orange flames and coiling black smoke. The smells of burning tar and hay filled the night's air and, even though the river was right in front of us, I couldn't smell it. The odor of fire, of burning, overwhelmed all others. Shadows and lights skimmed the surface of the water, entangled in one another's folds and grasps, like water sprites fighting in anticipation of their nightly feed.

Once again we had to line up. The soldiers did not speak, just grunted and shoved. They seemed younger and more closemouthed than those we'd met coming out of the city. During our trek across the island, they had hardly spoken even to one another, let alone us. A door, riddled with moth-shaped holes where the wood had rotted out, swung down from the belly of the boat like a tongue sticking out of a gaping mouth. A couple of Khmer Rouge soldiers guarded the entrance, one wielding a long-barreled gun, the other a torch with its tar-smoked flame. One by one people trudged past the lit entryway and disappeared into the dark within.

When our turn came, Papa rolled up his pants legs and, with me in his arms, waded through the water to get to the wooden gangplank. Mama and Radana stuck close behind, followed by the rest of our family.

At the door, the soldier with the gun stopped us, the tip of his weapon brushing against Papa's arm, barring us from entering. "What's this?" he demanded, eyeing the metal brace on my right leg.

"My daughter needs it for support," Papa told him.

"Is she crippled?"

Indignant, I blurted out, "*No.*"

The soldier's eyes flashed at me. I lowered my face.

"She had polio," Papa explained.

The soldier looked at him. "Throw it in the water."

"Please, Comrade—"

"Take it off and throw it in the water! It's a piece of machinery!"

"But—"

"The Organization will cure her!"

It seemed to take forever, but finally Papa got the brace off and cast it into the water. It sank like a toy ship. Now, I thought, I'd never walk like Mama. I had always hated the brace, but knowing I'd lost it, I wanted it back. At least we got to keep my shoes. The soldier moved his gun away and let us through.

Inside the boat it was dark, except for a small kerosene lantern that hung from the middle beam high above our heads. I couldn't breathe. It smelled of rotten hay and manure, as if we'd just stepped into the belly of a cow instead of a boat. Cages, crates, buckets, and bales of hay lay scattered on a wooden floor stained with dark patches. We found a spot near a large wire cage, the kind used to transport chickens and ducks. Papa moved the cage to one side and Big Uncle covered the floor with clean hay for us to sit. There was no possibility of escape. Up high on either side, small round openings, like slatted moons, lined the otherwise windowless walls. They provided the only glimpse of the outside world. I kept my eyes on them.

The last person entered. The door slammed shut, a giant mouth closing on us. No one would hear us again, I thought, panicking. No one would know we existed. I opened my mouth and screamed at the top of my lungs.

• • •

"Feel better now?" Papa asked, once I'd quieted down.

I nodded.

"That's good," he said, ruffling my hair. "You scared me."

By the time the ship docked, it felt as if we had spent the entire night inside. We stumbled out onto a makeshift pier next to a small floating village. There were thatched huts on stilts rising from the water, boats with woven rattan canopies, and sampans with wing-like sails. Lights glimmered here and there, and in the half-lit dark I could see silhouettes of people moving about their nightly tasks—a fisherman cleaning his net, a woman bathing with her child on the inundated steps of their hut, a family sitting down on the floor for dinner under the bluish glow of a kerosene lantern. They watched us from afar, silently curious and aware, as if all along expecting our arrival. Yet no one waved, no one called out a greeting or welcome. Still, I was grateful to be outside again. There were stars in the sky, fresh air. People. Trees. Grass. It was as if we had been swallowed by a sea creature and were being spit back out, whole and alive, all our senses intact. I could smell the river now when I hadn't been able to before, and it carried with it a faint scent of the monsoon. Had it rained while we were inside the boat? I wished it would now. I wanted to wash the odor of manure off my body and clothes.

A pair of torches lit our way as we walked down the wooden gangplank. I proceeded slowly, cautiously, clinging to Papa's arm for support, as I stepped onto the uneven ground. Without my metal brace, my corrective shoes were practically useless, and the sandals I wore now did not help at all with the limping. Without support, my right leg tired easily. Even so I was ecstatic to be released from the cattle boat and be outside again.

On the shore, more Khmer Rouge soldiers waited for us, guns slung on their shoulders, swarthy as the night. We would have to spend the night here, they said. The soldiers led us away from the floating village to a clearing interspersed with coconut trees. Pointing to the darkness beyond, the commander of the group said, "No one leaves this area. Runaways will be shot on the spot. If someone tries to escape, then the whole family will be shot. You're not to fraternize with the locals. We will decide whom you can make contact with and where you will go. If you disobey, you die."

People quickly began to lay claim to the area closest to the river. There was no fighting, no arguing. "It isn't worth getting shot for," a man told his wife. "It makes no difference what spot we choose. Everybody's sleeping on the ground."

We found a place just a few yards away from the water, by a coconut tree that stretched horizontally toward the river. Papa and Big Uncle put down their heavy loads and immediately went to work pitching camp. They cut down thorny bushes and shrubs using a pair of kitchen cleavers we had brought along. They pulled out vines and cleared away what might be poisonous climbers, stomped on the grass, and checked for scorpions and tarantulas. Big Uncle recruited the twins to help him haul away the cut debris. While all this was going on, Grandmother Queen and Radana sat among our sacks and bundles clucking at each other like a pair of wild pheasants, curiously contented to be still. Papa unfurled one of the sleeping mats on a space he'd just cleared so that Grandmother Queen would have something to lie on. A few feet away Mama was busy starting a fire. She broke some dry branches, stacked them in a little mound, and lit the mound with a match. Flames leapt up, sparks flew, crackling with life, and as the bigger branches caught on, embers began to glow. She placed three stones in a triangle around the fire, filled the kettle with the water she'd brought from the river, and perched it on top of the stones. Again, she'd taken charge, figuring out what we could eat from our limited food supply and how much. She'd assigned my aunts specific tasks so as not to overwhelm them. Except for Mama, all of us had had servants our whole lives, and suddenly we were simultaneously without help and home.

Tata was now preparing the rice for cooking. She untied the rice bag, measured into a pot the number of cups Mama had suggested, and rinsed the rice with water. Beside her, Auntie India was occupied wiping excess salt off dried fish with pieces of a banana leaf. Mama showed her how to place a strip of the fish between the fork of a small branch, tie the ends with a piece of vine, and lean it against the kettle to grill. When Auntie India got the hang of it, Mama started another fire for the rice.

All around us everyone was doing the same. Before long the whole camp became alive with movements and sounds. People borrowed one another's pots and pans, dishes and cups, baskets and knives. They exchanged dried goods—a can of condensed milk for a cup of rice, a clove of garlic for a spoon of sugar, salt for pepper, dried fish for salted eggs. There was an atmosphere of gaiety, like at a market, and the glow of cooking fires only made it feel more festive.

Even the Khmer Rouge soldiers, who paced the periphery of the camp, guarding and watching, didn't seem as threatening as they had initially appeared. They divided into smaller groups and, from a distance, looked like us, like families gathered to prepare their meals. While I couldn't hear what they were saying, I could tell they were joking with one another. Every now and then laughter broke out, thunderous, like birds flapping their wings. I felt a mixture of fear and curiosity.

Papa came toward us, a coconut in his hand, grinning from ear to ear. "Look what I've got! Appetizer!" He sat down next to me and, with his cleaver, hacked the outer shell, pulling the hard, wiry brown husk off until he got to the hard inner shell. Then, with one clean whack, he cracked it in the middle, poured the juice into a bowl, took a sip, and gave the rest of the juice to me.

Just then a frog the size of my fist leapt out of the grass from under Mama's bottom and onto the leaning coconut tree. Papa and I looked at each other, eyes wide, and broke into a laugh. Mama frowned with embarrassment. She turned her back to us, pretending she didn't know what we were laughing at. Papa and I roared. "If it were under *my* bottom, that frog would've been dead meat!" he exclaimed, hooting like a gibbon. "To think we almost had stuffed frog for dinner! A fine delicacy!"

Mama snapped, "You're so crass!" But in spite of herself, she also started giggling uncontrollably.

Papa rolled over, delirious with glee, as if being here, in the wild, he was becoming wild himself. It was contagious. Pretty soon the others—Grandmother Queen, Auntie India, Tata—were chuckling too. Even

Radana, who I was sure didn't understand a word of this whole exchange, was chortling. She bounced up and down, as if she alone grasped the irony, the last innuendo Papa made, and this of course only sent another peal of laughter through him.

Finally, breathless, he pulled himself together and sat upright again, sniffling and wiping tears from his eyes. He picked up the coconut, which had rolled to the side during the course of his laugh attack. "Would you like some, darling?" he asked Mama, in a voice as serious as he could muster. "It's delicious—I don't mean to toot my own horn!" Again he hooted, but with a glare from Mama quickly got control of himself. He turned to me instead. "You want some?"

I nodded, the coconut juice whetting my hunger.

During the journey across the island, we'd been allowed only a quick meal: a packet of rice and broiled fish the soldiers had handed out to everyone. They'd said the food was from the Organization, and I'd imagined the Organization was a rotund cook like Om Bao sitting in some kitchen wrapping rice and fish in lotus leaves, tasting everything, surrounded by mounds of packets. Where was she now, this gluttonous deity? Was she gorging on food meant for us?

Papa peeled the hard white meat from the shell, broke it into chunks, skewered each chunk on a stick, and handed one to each of us. We held the skewered coconut pieces over the flames leaping from under the pot of rice now set to cook. The smell was exquisite. I inhaled until my lungs hurt. When it was done roasting, I pulled my coconut off the stick and bit into it, huffing and puffing with renewed hunger.

Big Uncle emerged with two more coconuts, followed by the twins, each cradling a fruit in his arms. We attacked those as well while we waited for our dinner to cook.

"Listen up!" the Khmer Rouge commander called out. He stood in the middle of the camp, backed by his whole troop, light from fires and shadow flickering across his face like alternating masks. People moved closer in to better hear him. "Tomorrow you will be taken to your next destination—"

"Next destination?" someone from the crowd interrupted. "What about home?" The man stood up, shaking with suppressed anger. "When will we go back to Phnom Penh?"

"There's no going back," the commander growled. "You'll start a new life—"

"What do you mean a *new* life?" someone else asked, and then others started speaking as well, barking with fury. "What about our home? What will we do here, in the middle of nowhere? We want to go back to the city! We want to go home!"

"The city is empty!" the Khmer Rouge commander thundered. "There's nothing to go back to! Your home is where we tell you!"

"But we were told we could go back!" challenged the man who had started it all. "Three days, you told us. Three days! Well, it's been more than three days! We want to go home!"

"Forget your home!" the commander thundered. "You'll build a new life out here—in the countryside!"

"This is nowhere! Why should we leave our home for a life here?"

"It is the order of the Organization!"

"The Organization, the Organization!" another voice shouted from the throng. "*What* or *who* is this Organization?"

"Yes, tell us who they are! Give us a face! We want to know!"

"Tell us something we can believe!"

"Yes, stop telling us your Khmer Rouge lies!"

BANG! A bullet resounded in the night sky.

The voices stopped. No one stirred. The commander put down his pistol. "You will stay and go as you are told, understand?" He waited.

No one responded. A defiant hush all around.

"UNDERSTAND?" he roared, his gun sweeping across the wall of people in front of him.

The crowd murmured and nodded submissively.

"GOOD!" The commander lowered his weapon. He made as if to go but then turned and faced his challengers once more. "We are *Revolutionary soldiers,* and if you say 'Khmer Rouge' again, you will be shot." He marched off.

The whole camp fell silent. A long time passed before anyone fell asleep.

An army camion trundled into view, looking like a giant metal scrap heap, smelling of gasoline and burnt rubber. Once again the commander emerged from his post, a bullhorn held to his lips, announcing, "In a short while, you will be divided into two groups. Those of you with relatives in the surrounding areas must declare yourselves. You will be taken to your respective town or village. If your town or village is far, then you'll go by oxcarts. If it's close, you will walk. Those of you without any connection whatsoever will be taken by truck. You will continue your journey until further orders come from the Organization."

We quickly ate our morning meal, packed, and readied ourselves. The other Revolutionary soldiers came around again with their guns and started dividing people into two groups, as the commander had instructed. As our family had no connection or ties to the area, we were in the group bound for the camion, which, up close, was even scarier than its silhouette had suggested. It had a mud-covered floor, dented metal benches, burnt canvas top, sides punctured by bullet holes, and missing front doors that might have been blown off by rockets or grenades. The thing looked as if it had gone through hell, and I imagined it would likely go there again, taking us with it this time.

"Don't worry," Papa said, lifting me up, holding me still to him. "I'm here."

As we climbed in I looked back at the row of oxcarts we'd passed, which seemed preferable to this machine with its battle wounds and scars. Others began to board. First one family, then two, then three, and then a countless horde simultaneously. Finally, with everyone squeezed in tight, the camion trumpeted, like an ancient war elephant coming to life, and charged forth.

seven

Flame trees in full bloom blazed our trail, like offerings of fire to the gods. The trees gave way to denser, greener growth, and eventually all we could see were forests and sky and patches of water. Sometimes we'd come upon a sapling growing in the middle of the road as if it had been months since any vehicle had driven through. Our driver and the four Revolutionary soldiers accompanying him—two in the front and two on the roof—would take turns getting out and clearing the young saplings with an ax. If a patch of growth was especially stubborn or unruly, then everyone would get out and help clear away the vines. When we passed rice fields, quite often we would have to wait for a whole herd of cows to cross the road, and always one of the animals would stop and stare stupidly, refusing to budge until the herder—usually a little boy who seemed to be the only person around, a sprite appearing out of nowhere—came along and pulled it out of the way. As we moved on, a village would appear and disappear in the blink of an eye.

In the land of rubber plantations, where the trees stood scarred and bleeding milk-white blood, we crossed small wooden bridges that looked as if they would collapse under the weight of our truck and avoided others the soldiers suspected were rigged with land mines. When one of them jokingly clapped his hands and made an explosive sound with his lips, his comrade elbowed him disapprovingly in the ribs, to which he responded in kind. They continued like this, playfully hitting each other, as we looked on. I thought how ordinary they seemed, horsing around like that. At some point they started talking with us and we learned they were village boys who'd joined the Revolution because—as one put it—"guns were a lot lighter to lug around than plows." They seemed in awe of the driver, who knew how to maneuver the camion. They said most of their comrades, until recently, had never seen any car or truck or motorcycle, let alone knew how to handle one. But some, like our driver, had had to learn quickly when they started capturing these vehicles from the enemies. When asked if they missed their families, they shrugged, feigning indifference, and for a long stretch after remained silent with melancholy. But then a bump in the road caused them to knock shoulders and once again they became animated, pushing each other back and forth, playing with every leap and lurch that came our way.

Mama, noticing me staring at them, gently pulled my head down to her lap. I didn't resist, but curled up on the tight space between her and Papa, my head on her lap and my feet on his. For a long time I lay there, closing and opening my eyes, dozing in and out, the landscape rippling past me like a windblown sheet.

When the sun shone high above our heads, we stopped at a village by a small stream to eat another meal of rice and fish, brought by a group of Revolutionary soldiers who, like the others before them, seemed to have appeared out of nowhere. There wasn't a lot of talking. We ate quickly and hurried to cool ourselves in the stream. We rolled up our pants and shirtsleeves, splashing water on our faces and bodies. Mama scooped water with her hand and wet her hair and Radana's. Papa soaked his *kroma* and gave it to me to put on my head. He took off his shirt, soaked it as well, wrung out the water, and put it back on. Big Uncle grabbed the twins and dunked them, clothes and all. The driver sounded the horn. Dripping wet but rejuvenated, we rushed to the camion.

Once more we resumed our journey. Again and again, forests, rivers, and rice fields came into view, then rolled away as soon as they'd appeared, swallowed by the horizon. My head throbbed; I tried to sleep but couldn't. Each time I nodded off I was jolted back to waking by my own breathlessness. It was suffocating, with all the arms and elbows around me, the smell of sweat, the thick layer of red dust that coated my lips and tongue, my nostrils, the whorls of my ears.

Finally, when it felt like we'd traveled to the edge of the world, one of the soldiers announced that we'd reached Prey Veng, a province whose name means "endless forest." An archway lettered with the name "Wat Rolork Meas" in fancy old-Khmer script appeared on the left side of the road. Our camion turned and trundled through the narrow passage, its sides scratching against the cacti hemming the road. Passing a series of sugarcane fields and cashew orchards, the road brought us to a small town, where a throng of wooden houses rose in the distance and a Buddhist temple gleamed nearby, like a dream in the late afternoon sun.

At the entrance to the temple, a statue of a Walking Buddha lay on its back as if Mara, the god of desires, tempter of man, had come along and knocked it off its stone pedestal. Two small figures rose, waking from their nap under a gigantic banyan near the entrance. They ambled sleepily in our direction, stretching and yawning, their long-barreled guns hanging from straps on their shoulders at a slight angle to keep the tips from brushing the ground. Our soldiers jumped out, slapping dust off their bodies. The two sides spoke, and confirming this was the place we ought to be, the driver nodded for us to come down.

Everyone kept a respectful distance from the fallen Walking Buddha statue, avoiding the ground above its head. Some of the elders, their palms in a *sampeah,* bowed and muttered a prayer. The boy soldiers leading us showed no such deference. Earlier one had spat on the trunk of the banyan tree and now the other was blowing his snot on the ground just as he passed the statue. We followed them toward the main open-air prayer hall that stood not facing the road as was common of temples but parallel to it, rising higher than all the surrounding structures. The prayer hall had a roof of painted gold and gables carved with upswept tips resembling wings or flames. A pair of glass-tiled *naga* serpents encircled the outer pillars of the hall, their heads guarding the entrance to the front steps and their tails intertwined in the back. In the middle of the stenciled tile floor sat a large Buddha statue painted in gold, legs crossed, eyes gazing past a lotus pond to the distant marsh and forest.

I followed the statue's gaze, noticing how green and wet the land was, the rain apparently having arrived early in this part of the country. The pond brimmed full of lotuses, the marsh rippled with water lilies and hyacinths, and the rice paddies burgeoned with knee-high stalks as supple as a baby's hair. I'd once read about premonsoon clouds that could gather randomly in one place and burst like punctured water balloons, drenching everything under their shadows, while only a short distance away it would remain sunny and dry. I imagined little *tevoda* children floating in the bulges of clouds above us, testing the clouds for ripeness with the tips of their gold javelins before freeing the rains to warn us of the impending monsoon.

A cool breeze blew, jostling the lotus pads, sending little transparent spheres of water gliding across the green surfaces. Somewhere a frog croaked, *Ooak oak oak!* and a toad answered, *Heeng hoong, heeng hong! Ooak oak ooak! Heeng hoong, heeng hong!* Back and forth they went as if announcing to the other animals, warning unseen spirits and beings of this sudden intrusion.

I kept walking, my eyes taking in everything. I loved the way temples made me feel. Papa also loved them, so much so that he'd named me Vattaaraami, which in Sanskrit means "small temple garden." I didn't know if others felt as I did, but always I sensed a certain lingering familiarity upon walking into a temple, even if it was a completely strange one, as if I were returning to a place I'd known from another time, another life. I wondered about this temple, though. Why it was so quiet, so empty . . .

It looked prosperous for a provincial temple, yet it appeared abandoned, as if the inhabitants had disappeared abruptly. Evaporated. There were no children laughing on the shaded grounds, no monks reciting their dharma lessons, no townspeople chatting on the steps of the prayer hall. Instead there were echoes everywhere.

I sensed a presence. I whispered, *Anyone there?* No reply. Just echoes of the hollowness here and there, ricocheting against the emptiness.

To the right of the pond stood a white stupa, a bell-shaped dome with a long golden spire that rose and tapered off until it blended with the sky. A stupa is built to house a relic of the Buddha, a piece of cloth, hair, tooth, or often, as Papa once told me, our wish for the eternal, for immortality. Looking at the hugeness of this stupa I thought perhaps it housed all the wishes imaginable, those of the living and the dead, whose ashes would be in the surrounding *cheddays,* smaller versions of the stupa.

To the left of the pond were four buildings, painted a mustard yellow, with wooden slatted shutters all around, just like my school in Phnom Penh. The buildings faced one another to form a square, and in the middle of the square stood a flagpole, tall and slender, with only the tattered remains of a flag at its base, and next to it, a patch of ground worn by children's playing. My eyes fell on the charcoal outline of a hopscotch board drawn in the dirt. A rock was left in the center of the board in one of the squares to mark the place of the last person who had played it. I wondered who—who had last been here? Again, I thought I heard an echo. A ghost whispering in my ear. Or maybe my own thoughts ripping through the silence. I picked up the rock and put it in my pocket, an amulet for good luck, for protection.

We were left to ourselves to get settled. The school buildings were empty, so there were more classrooms than families. They were all open to us. We would have space to spread out and could choose any room we wanted. But why did it feel we were intruding? Why did I sense we were being observed?

Our family chose a classroom with a row of windows that opened to the rice fields, the marsh, and the expanse of forests beyond. Inside, the desks and chairs were gone. Only their outlines were left on the tiled floor. The blackboard remained, and at the top someone—maybe a teacher, a monk who was a teacher—had written, *Knowing comes from . . .* , each word a different color. The rest was erased, a rainbow of chalk dust left behind.

We put our belongings in one corner and looked around. It wasn't much, just space, an empty room, but it was better than sleeping out in the open among the night creatures and insects. There was enough space for us to be comfortable while keeping close to one another. Big

Uncle opened a slatted wooden door and found that it led to another room, quite a bit smaller than ours. A supply room perhaps, but it had nothing in it. Tata suggested we claim it before another family did. But to be on the safe side we decided just to put our extra belongings there and sleep together in one room. The twins, having slept almost the entire afternoon in the camion, could not keep still. They ran back and forth through the open doorway, with Radana squealing after them. Big Uncle made use of their energy and put all three to work. He gave the boys a rolled-up straw mat—the one we used for eating—and told them to take it over to the smaller room. He gave Radana a pot and told her to follow the boys. She toddled after them, banging the lid against the pot.

Papa, who'd stepped outside momentarily, returned with a couple of straw brooms, some rags, and a bucket of water. Together we dusted, swept, wiped, and mopped. On the wall near our room's entrance there were several crimson stains—paint or perhaps dried blood—in the shape of hands and fingers stretched to shadowy lengths.

Papa caught me staring at the stains, came over with a wet rag, and scrubbed hard until they merged into one big pinkish blob on the wall. Then, turning his attention to the blackboard, he erased all the marks and scribbles. His gaze traveled up to the words at the top, *Knowing comes from* . . . He put the rag down and, with a piece of chalk from the pile of swept-up rubbish, finished the sentence, so that now it read, *Knowing comes from learning, finding from seeking.*

We unpacked our belongings and spread out the straw mats. The sun had set, and the sky darkened to the color of a water buffalo's skin. Mama said she would get started on dinner. The Revolutionary soldiers hadn't come back to offer us rice or food. Auntie India suggested maybe we should wait. They might still come. Big Uncle reminded her that those two boys didn't look like they knew where *their* dinner would come from, let alone ours. "We'll have better luck with the frogs in the pond," he added, winking at me, harking back to the previous night's incident with the frog. "*Oak oak oak,*" Papa croaked, imitating the distant muffled cry from outside. "Stop it, you two!" Mama chastised. The twins and Radana, hearing the word "frogs" and croaking, started jumping about on all fours across the room. Once again, we all burst out laughing, Tata the loudest. Then all of a sudden her laugh turned to a cry. "We won't ever go back home, will we?" she sobbed. "We'll die here." Her entire being shook, and my otherwise formidable aunt, always poised and erect with self-assurance, was now a dribbling mess. No one knew what to say or do.

Radana toddled over, and with one arm around Tata's shoulder, kissed her on the cheek, like she would a fragile doll. "Tata hurt?" she asked. Tata nodded. Radana kissed her again and, puffing her cheeks out, blew the hurt away. "All gone!" she declared, palms splayed, chubby and cheerful. Mama's eyes watered. She turned and walked out the door, taking the rice bag and pot with her.

Darkness fell all around us, save for the small flame from the half stick of candle Papa had taken from the prayer hall, and as we prepared to settle for the night, I felt the spirits among us, their shadows commiserating with our shadows, their whispers imitating our thoughts, *Knowing comes from learning, finding from seeking* . . .

Raami, they called out to me. *Raami, wake up, wake up* . . . I opened my eyes and in the dark saw Papa's face above mine. "Wake up, darling," he whispered. "I want to show you something. Come—before it dissipates." I sat up, rubbing my eyes, and scooted out of the mosquito net as Papa held the edge open for me. Gathering me in his arms, he carried me tiptoeing across the room.

Outside, it was bluish grey, dawn's dark gown laced with strips of fog. The ground was wet and the air held the memory of rain, which, I recalled now, had traipsed in during the night like some nocturnal sojourner, waking me with the patter of its steps, and, as I fell back into sleep, slipping seamlessly into my dream.

Papa put me down and we walked hand in hand through the sieve-like mist, the cool air filling my nostrils and lungs, coaxing me awake. I looked around. All was still. Through the open doors and windows of the school buildings I could see patches of mosquito nets and felt everyone breathing deeply, collectively, as if dreaming the same dream. The whole place seemed under a spell, wrapped in serenity as palpable as brume.

We came to the prayer hall, and it was like entering that mythical cloud-bound kingdom of the *Reamker*. Ribbons of fog, thick as vapor in some parts, surrounded the open-air prayer hall, weaving the spaces between the pillars and balustrades, winding their way up to the ceiling, then down again toward the pond, where they gathered in loose swirls, like smoke contours left behind by vanishing dragons.

"It looks like Ayuthiya," I murmured, afraid that if I spoke too loud it would all evaporate. I wasn't able to find the torn page from the *Reamker*. It must've fallen out of my pocket while traveling. But I didn't need the illustration. Here was the real thing. "It's so beautiful."

"It is, isn't it?" Papa squeezed my hand. "That's why I want you to see it." He let out a long, slow breath, adding to the vapor around us. "It's a gift to be able to imagine heaven, and a *rebirth* to actually glimpse it."

"Is this heaven then?" I asked, blinking away the last remnants of sleep, thinking perhaps I was still dreaming.

"At least its mirror image. If one glimpses heaven's reflection on earth, then somewhere must exist the real thing." Papa's eyes went to the pair of carved serpents along the balustrades. "The *naga*—from the Sanskrit *nagara* for 'city' or 'kingdom'—is a symbol of divine energy, our link to the heavens. This place—this land of *naga* pillars and steeples and spires—was born of divine inspiration, so goes one legend among many. My favorite story is one of Preah Khet Melea, the son of Indra and his earthly consort. One day, the twelve-year-old Melea receives an invitation from his father to visit him." Papa looked up and pointed at the carved image of a mythical creature, part human and part bird, adorning the top of every pillar of the prayer hall. "Perhaps on the wings of one of those—I like to imagine—Melea ascends the heavens."

"It's Kinnara," I said, reminding him of the creature's name. In the countless tales I'd read and heard, Kinnara could traverse back and forth between the world of the humans and that of the gods.

"Yes, that's right." Papa nodded, smiling. "Once there, Melea gazes in awe at his father's celestial kingdom—the many-tiered-steeple palaces covered with precious stones, moats and pools shimmering as if made of liquid diamonds, causeways and bridges stretching to eternity and back.

You will have your own earthly kingdom, Indra says to his son, in the image of this one. Whatever you so desire here, I shall send my celestial architect to replicate it. Melea, moved by his father's generosity, dares not request a replica of Indra's own palace. Instead he humbly asks to recreate only Indra's cattle stable."

"*That's it?* Just the cattle stable?" My mind was roused by the story.

Papa chuckled, "Ah, but even Indra's cattle stable gave rise to the great Angkor temple, which became the inspiration for all later temples that adorn this land of your birth. You see, Raami, as beautiful as this temple is, it's only a tiny, modest glimpse of what is divinely possible in all of us. We are capable of extraordinary beauty if we dare to dream."

I kept quiet now, imagining Papa as Indra and myself Melea.

"Do you know why I named you Vattaaraami?" He knelt on one knee and looked into my eyes. "Because you are my temple and my garden, my sacred ground, and in you I see all of my dreams." He smiled, as if allowing himself the indulgence of an early morning's pondering. "Perhaps it's natural for a father, for every parent, to see in his child all that's unspoiled and good. But if you can, Raami, I want *you* to see it in yourself. No matter what ugliness and destruction you may witness around you, I want you always to believe that the tiniest glimpse of beauty here and there is a reflection of the gods' abode. It is real, Raami. There exists such a place, such sacred space. You have only to envision it, to dare to dream it. It is within you, within all of us." He straightened up again, letting out another long breath. "I see it all the time."

He took my hand and we climbed the steps into the prayer hall. Turning, we faced front, looking out to the pond. Light was gathering quickly, breaking through the thinning mist, and with each breath I took, I could see more and more in front of us—the lotus pads and blossoms emerging like tentative brushstrokes in an artist's painting. *Whatever you so desire here, I shall send my celestial architect to replicate it.* Somewhere I felt, even as I couldn't express it, that a god was rendering my dream into reality, for all the loveliness around us seemed true and touchable. I believed we had walked into heaven, had been led through its gate. I felt certain our arrival wasn't accidental.

There came shuffling by the gate. A hunched figure was slowly making its way toward us. My heart leapt and I blurted out, "Old Boy?" But it was a temple sweeper, with a broom in his hand. Every temple had one, this half-invisible, half-forgotten being. Often it would be an old man, the poorest of the poor, who, nearing death, felt that keeping the temple clean was his final plea to the gods, that when he died his effort would earn him enough merit for a better rebirth, so that he wouldn't again suffer as he had in this life. The figure coming toward us now moved like a hermit crab in a human shell, his back bent as if he'd spent his whole life, not just old age, sweeping the grounds of this temple.

Papa left my side and hurried down the steps. "Here, let me help you," he said, offering the old sweeper his arm. "Thank you, Neak Ang Mechas," the sweeper said, using Papa's full title, which meant he knew who Papa was. *But how?* On a few occasions during our journey people had turned to stare upon hearing us speak in the royal language. Papa had suggested that we should speak in normal Khmer as much as possible so as not to draw attention to ourselves. He hadn't said anything just now to reveal who he was. How did the sweeper know? Maybe he was one of those mystic sages who could see into your soul and know exactly who you were.

The old sweeper put his palms together and lifted them up to his forehead in an effort to greet Papa, but because his back was so curved his head only came up to Papa's chest. "I am a great admirer of your poetry, Your Highness," he said and then began to recite:

Once, in a journey's dream,
I came upon a child bearing my soul.

"I read it many years ago," he explained, smiling, "when it was first published in *Civilization*." He tilted his head sideways to look at Papa, his expression one of awe and amazement. "It is truly incredible that Your Highness should stand here before me."

Papa smiled, slightly embarrassed. "Let me help you," he said again, one hand taking the broom and the other supporting the sweeper's elbow.

"Thank you," the sweeper replied. "I'll just sit here." He lowered himself onto the steps of the prayer hall.

I went over and offered him the traditional *sampeah*. He returned my greeting and, gazing at me in a rather peculiar way, added enigmatically, "You must be the child in the dream."

I looked to Papa for an explanation, but he only shrugged, seeming glad to have the old sweeper's attention shifted to me.

Then, to my astonishment, I realized he'd meant the poem! My confounder grinned, delighted that I'd caught on.

"A pleasure, my dear princess." Again, I thought how like Old Boy he was, addressing me as he did, the formality of his language and manner, the playfulness of his grin. What was it that Old Boy said? *When you love a flower, and suddenly she is gone . . .*

"The late abbot . . . ," the old sweeper started to explain, his voice wavering, choked with sorrow. He stopped, steadying himself, and tried again, "His Venerable Teacher, who was also an avid admirer of your poetry, Your Highness, would often bring various literary journals from Phnom Penh. Over the years I've familiarized myself with your words as well as photos of you, which sometimes accompanied them. When I saw you yesterday, of course there was no mistaking who you were. My eyesight is my only remaining youth. Everything else . . ." He gestured to the rest of his body. "Well, as you can see, Highness." He let out a sigh.

"You were here yesterday?" Papa seemed bemused. "I didn't see you."

"I was in the meditation pavilion. You'd just arrived, and the soldiers were with you. One does best not to be seen by them—to be invisible."

Papa nodded. "Yes, all my life I've sought invisibility, but I've yet to attain it." He smiled at our companion. "Even out here I am recognized."

The sweeper flushed with guilt. "I'm sorry," he said ruefully, and then, as if struck by a brilliant idea, asked, "Would you like to have a look at the meditation pavilion?"

I followed his gaze to a simple wooden structure on the edge of the pond, its silhouette partially obscured by the trunk of a banyan. I had seen it when we arrived, but, in awe of the more ornate prayer hall and stupa, I hadn't paid it much attention.

"It is an ideal place for reflection, for poetry writing. One could be invisible there," the old sweeper added amenably.

"Is . . . is that all right?" Papa waffled. "I mean, for us to have a look? I wouldn't dream of it if the monks—" He stopped, the smile on his face gone. He hadn't intended to bring up the monks.

The sweeper nodded, his solemnity returning. "Yes, at this hour, the monks would be in there meditating." He struggled to stand up, and Papa again offered him his arm. "But now their presence is no more than mist. If Your Highness comes, I will show you."

We took off our shoes and climbed the four short steps of the meditation pavilion. The old sweeper unlocked the wooden doors with a heavy skeleton key he wore on a band around his wrist. It was dark and humid inside and the smell of stale incense filled the small, tight space. Papa undid the hooks and pushed open a row of collapsible shutters, revealing the pond and marsh and forest beyond. It was a beautiful vista, so still and serene it made me think I was looking at a painting.

"Another story . . . ," Papa murmured, looking at the murals, painted in gold and black and red lacquer on the walls and vaulted ceiling.

"Yes, scenes from the Jataka tales, from the Buddha's birth to his Enlightenment," the old sweeper said. "Do you know, Princess?"

I nodded, and he seemed pleased. Turning to an unadorned wooden Buddha carving in one corner, he knelt down and bowed three times, letting his forehead touch the bare floor each time. Papa and I followed his example. "O Preah Pudh, Preah Sangh," he chanted, invoking the name of the Buddha, the spirits of dead monks, "forgive our intrusion. We've come with pure intentions. Bestow upon us calm and insight."

We remained on our knees, our palms on our laps, looking up at the Buddha statue. Again I felt the ghosts among us.

"What happened here?" Papa asked, his voice barely a whisper. "What happened to the monks?" It seemed that since he'd made the mistake of broaching the subject in the first place, he must have thought it best to ask right out.

"They came last harvest, these soldiers," the old sweeper began.

"They emerged from every direction of the forest. They said they'd come to liberate us, set the town free. From what? We weren't imprisoned. Why had they really come? we demanded to know. They couldn't explain. They were just boys, freshly out of the jungle, hardly knowing left from right, let alone right from wrong. But they were polite enough, I suppose, asking us gently to abandon our old 'feudal habits,' speaking a strange Revolutionary language they themselves didn't seem to fully comprehend. They didn't convince us, of course. On the contrary, they made us weary, and we made things difficult for them, so much so that they retreated. Then, their commanders came, like a band of *kakanasos.*"

In the *Reamker,* Kakanaso was Krung Reap's black bird, the harbinger of dark omens. While Kinnara was half human, Kakanaso was half demon.

"They headed straight for the temple," the old sweeper continued, "knowing, as we all do, that this was where important and trusted members of our community gathered. Perhaps they thought, rightly so, if they could make the temple submit, then the rest of the town would follow." He paused for breath, eyes squinting, remembering. "They ordered the monks to defrock and go back to their families, claiming that there was to be no more religious practice in the new liberated Democratic Kampuchea. You can well imagine, Highness, the shock and protest that followed. The monks refused to renounce their vows, the town stood by them, and the soldiers, abandoning their Revolutionary slogans and rhetoric, resorted to violence. They turned the whole place upside down and forced the monks out of their sleeping quarters. Most of the novices did indeed disrobe and return to their families, but the few senior monks remained, standing by the abbot, sticking to their faith . . ." Again, the sweeper paused, his voice faltering.

We waited quietly, giving him time to collect himself.

"For the next couple of days, they sought refuge in this pavilion—the abbot and the remaining monks." He looked around the room. "They meditated and fasted, taking only water. To our great surprise, the soldiers left them alone. Then on the third day, a group of soldiers returned and seized the abbot, forcing him down the steps. We pleaded to know why they were taking him. 'To be reeducated,' their commander shouted."

The old sweeper shook his head. "To be *reeducated*? I don't understand what this means, Highness. Monks are our country's first teachers. Without them, a boy like me would never have learned to read. What could these illiterate soldiers have to teach our *teachers*? They know not a word of the Buddha's dharma or a line of poetry. What could they know of learning when all they seek is blood?"

Papa made no reply. Then after a moment, he asked, "Where did it take place?"

"I will show you, Your Highness," the sweeper said, struggling to stand up. "You must see with your own eyes their evil."

As we exited the meditation pavilion, I glanced back at the mural. The old sweeper's recounting of what had happened was nowhere as real to me as the story of the Buddha's journey painted on the walls and ceiling. Here was a tale I could literally see and run my hand across, its message explained to me countless times: peace comes to one who understands. So to palliate my disquiet, I convinced myself I understood— that the disappearances of those whose presence I could still feel were a kind of *nippien,* a passing from this life into a place as desirable as the gods' celestial realm.

He brought us to the monks' sleeping quarters—a cluster of wooden houses on stilts. Torn leather-bound dharma books, children's lesson books, pencils, rulers, boxes of chalk were scattered on the ground among broken alms bowls. Sleeping mats, pillows, chests of drawers, bookcases, along with the children's desks and chairs, which must've come from the school buildings, were tossed into the surrounding shrubs and brush. Piles of saffron robes lay near an outhouse in the back, and flies as big as bumblebees buzzed about them in a steady drone.

"They made the abbot take off his robe there and put on civilian clothes," the sweeper said, pointing to the festering mounds. "I don't know why they bothered, if they were going to do what they did. Perhaps they feared the cloth more than the man. I don't know." He looked at me, then at Papa, seeming uncertain if he should continue. Papa gave a slight nod, and he went on, "The abbot offered his life, in hope that they would spare the others. They took him to the forest." He nodded toward the impenetrable green beyond the rice fields. "A shot was heard . . ." Tears brimmed the sweeper's eyes and he fought them back. "Then . . . then they came for the others. The rest of the senior monks. The old *achars* and nuns who had thrown themselves on the ground pleading on the abbot's behalf. The orphaned boys who had known no other home except here, in whose desecrated classrooms you now seek refuge . . ."

Again, the sweeper fought back tears. "No shot was heard this time, but if a sound could move the heavens, it would be the screams of those children. I shall never forget it. It will follow me into my next life."

Papa remained silent, his eyes taking in everything. I followed his gaze, from one mound to the next, and for a fleeting second, I thought I saw echoes of ourselves, our own ghosts among the evanescent, mist-like presence of the slain monks, nuns, and orphans. I blinked the image away. Papa was right, I thought, dream and reality were one and the same. What existed in one could well be replicated in the other. We were far away from home, but even out here, I thought, my dream and reality were shaped by the adults who loved and cared for me. On this temple ground, Papa had constructed for me, as Indra's celestial architect had for Melea, a world that *was* lovely and good. I had only to look past the stench and scattered heaps to see the glimpses of beauty. No sooner had I thought this than there it was—a jewel beetle resembling a giant blow-fly, its metallic body reflecting green and gold. It emerged from the dark folds and crevices of the monks' soiled robes, carrying with it the colors of these exquisite and broken things.

Papa and the sweeper saw it too. They watched it with the silence of those paying respects to the dead. The beetle, as if feeling our presence, spread its wings and flew off.

We walked back to the prayer hall, Papa escorting the sweeper as the old man spoke of the town, how since a new breed of leaders had replaced the traditional chiefs, Rolork Meas was not the same carefree place it had been. The townsfolk, once gregarious and generous with one another, became withdrawn and taciturn, fearing retribution if they fraternized and spoke freely. They kept to themselves, wanting nothing to do with anyone new, and so we shouldn't be surprised if no one came to visit us.

"You must be careful, Your Highness," the sweeper warned, pausing in his steps as if to lend weight to his warning. "These soldiers and their leaders are watching . . ."

We kept moving, the fog having completely evaporated. Morning arrived, and with it, the sounds of waking. Birds chirped and flapped their wings, a rooster crowed in the distance and another answered, and over by the pond, frogs croaked and a fish broke the surface of the water. The sky wore a pinkish veil, borrowing the hue of the lotuses unfolding below. The marsh shimmered, as if at any moment it would spit out the sun, which, I imagined, it had soaked all night and polished to a new shine. When a soft breeze blew, the water rippled in long gilt bands, and it was obvious why this town was called "Waves of Gold."

At the gate, the old sweeper pointed across the road to a small thatched hut. "My little corner of heaven," he said. "If you should ever need anything, you can always find me there. Though I have not much to offer"—he smiled—"except for winds and rains."

"Can we accompany you back?" Papa asked.

"Thank you, Your Highness, but I'll make it fine on my own." Then, nodding in the direction of the meditation pavilion, he added, "I'll leave it unlocked, so that Your Highness will have a quiet place to write."

Moved by the offer, Papa clasped the sweeper's hand. The latter returned his gesture, and then, letting go, began to shuffle toward his hut, his torso curved like a scythe.

Papa watched him. Then his eyes shot to the distant hut and he murmured, partly to himself, "Its walls are the winds and rains . . ."

Behind us, a group of men had come out to enjoy the morning air. Papa approached them and asked if they could help him raise the fallen Walking Buddha back to an upright position. "Of course, Your Highness!" they chorused from the steps of the prayer hall. Papa smiled, grateful for their enthusiasm.

While the men were busy with this, I snuck back to the meditation pavilion. Inside, I studied the murals, thinking of the many tales carved into the balcony and walls of the house we'd left behind, how I thought they were fixed to that place. But, looking at the murals, I had the feeling the tales had followed us here, moving along with us on our journey, manifesting themselves in all sorts of ways.

Knowing comes from learning, finding from seeking.

It was clear what the message meant. If I looked hard enough, if I sought, I would find what I was looking for. Here, on the banyan-shaded ground, the temple harbored minute reflections of the paradise we'd left behind.

eight

I left the meditation pavilion and returned to the temple. The whole place was abuzz with activities, with the happy sights and sounds of a new day's beginning. People had come out to chat and stretch their limbs, looking as if they had always belonged here, talking to one another like longtime neighbors.

In the prayer hall, a group of elders was paying homage to the large Buddha statue. An old man, assuming the role of the *achar*, began with the familiar refrain "We offer homage to Him, the Holy, the Pure, the Enlightened." The rest of the group followed, intoning, "In the Buddha, we seek refuge. In the Dharma, we seek refuge. In the Sangha"—the temple—"we seek refuge . . ." Children ran about, infusing the morning with laughter and playfulness. The smaller ones played hide-and-seek, weaving their paths between the pillars, bouncing up one stairway and skipping down another. If they became too loud or came too close to the Buddha statue, an elder would gently admonish, reminding them to keep a respectful distance. The bigger ones—a group of boys—volleyed a *kroma* wound tight into a ball, while the girls skipped rope barefoot on the soft, moist ground.

Papa, his back against the pedestal upon which the Walking Buddha statue once again rested, sat scribbling in his leather pocket notebook, which he must've saved among our belongings when we were forced to cross the river. I looked around to see if any Revolutionary soldiers were watching, but I could see none. We were safe. Seeing Papa with his note-book made me think of the *Reamker*. Surprisingly, though, I didn't miss it as I'd thought I would. It was clear to me now that while books could be torn and burned, the stories they held needn't be lost or forgotten.

In the pond, a bright red bird flew out from among the lotus pads, sending a spray of water into the air, to the delight of the observing chil-dren and parents. I recalled a fable Milk Mother had once told me about a male bird that got trapped in a lotus blossom when it closed at sunset. Only when the blossom opened again at dawn the next morning was the bird finally able to escape. He returned to his nest, beautifully fragrant.

Milk Mother said that stories are like footpaths of the gods. They lead us back and forth across time and space and connect us to the entire uni-verse, to people and beings we never see but who we feel exist. I felt that somewhere, somehow, Milk Mother was still alive, safe. I realized that with us she'd found temporary security in the enclosed space of our love and then, like that bird released from the lotus blossom, had flown back to her family.

As I approached him, Papa looked up from his scribbling and took a deep breath, tucking the notebook and his silver fountain pen in his breast pocket. "Shall we go back?" he said, standing up.

I grabbed his waist and pressed my whole face into his shirt, smell-ing him, sniffing for hints of the world in his notebook where he'd lost himself. Papa laughed. Then, just as I was thinking maybe we should go back to the pond, he reached back and pulled something from the waist of his pants. "For Mama," he said, handing me an open blossom bobbing on its stem. "I thought you might like to give it to her."

"How did you know?"

He shrugged, pleased that he could read my every thought.

"What were you writing?" I asked as we headed back to the school buildings.

"A poem."

"Of course it's a poem! But what's it *about*?"

Papa turned; his gaze shot across the rice fields to the sweeper's hut. "I'm not sure," he said. "I'll tell you when . . . when I figure it out."

"Promise you won't forget?"

His brows furrowed in uncertainty, but he acquiesced. "Promise."

I nodded, satisfied, and we continued on our way, hand in hand, arms swinging.

Back at the school buildings, people had begun preparing breakfast. They'd made a ring of cooking fires in the inner quadrangle, and patches of steam and smoke drifted about like the earlier haze. The smells of burnt wood, cooked rice, and grilled dried meats now permeated the air, masking the dewy scent of morning. Outside our doorway, a pot of rice porridge simmered over the fire Auntie India was stoking. "Well, good morning!" she greeted us with her musical voice, her dark complexion flushed by the warmth of the fire, her eyes radiant with the morning's glow. *Indra's earthly consort,* I thought. In her former life, Auntie India could've been that woman who wooed Indra to earth, who bore Melea and gave us the story that connected us to the divine, linked our world to the gods'. She chirped, "The whole family is looking for you!" She made everything sound like a declaration of joy. "You'd better go in!"

We went inside. "Oh, there you are!" Mama said, her voice taut with worries. She was sitting on the sleeping mat, folding the blankets and mosquito nets. I went over and handed her the lotus. She brightened and, glancing up at my father, gave him that tender look they often shared when thinking themselves completely alone. Mama inhaled the blossom's faint fragrance. Then, as there was no vase, she broke off the stem and, turning to the drinking bowl on top of our sleeping mat, let it float in the water. Tucking her long hair behind her ear, she leaned forward and kissed my cheek. Beside her, Radana mimicked her every movement and expression, brushing her wispy curls aside and planting kisses on her own chubby palm.

"Where have you been?" Mama said. "You were gone so long."

"I'm sorry," Papa told her. "I guess we lost track of time." Then, winking at me, he added, "We visited Indra's palace." His face betrayed no evidence of all we'd seen or heard.

To this, Big Uncle quipped, "Indra's palace! And you chose to return to earth? Be among us mere mortals?" He stood by the doorway leading to the adjacent room, legs apart and barechested, a twin hanging off each arm, alternately lifting them up and down like weights while the boys gurgled with glee. "How was it up there?" he said between intakes of breath. "Heavenly?"

"Just like here," I replied, and turned to Papa, expecting him to smile at my cleverness, my ready witticism. Instead, his eyes clouded over. I didn't understand.

Mama must've understood, for she gave him an empathetic look and, changing the subject, merrily suggested that he and Big Uncle take us children to wash before we all sat down for breakfast. At this, Tata murmured gravely from her corner of the room, "Could you bring me back some water to wash? I can't go out there. I just can't do this anymore . . ."

She seemed stupefied by all the change, and the night's sleep hadn't lessened her shock. Looking at her, it was hard to believe she was the same strong-willed aunt who in her youth had defied all societal expectations, not to mention Grandmother Queen, by refusing to marry, who was forever fond of reminding me that a girl didn't need a man, that she could do anything herself. Now she couldn't will herself to move even an inch from her spot.

Big Uncle put the twins down and said, "All right, boys, who would like to balance a bamboo yoke on his shoulders?" The twins jumped up and down excitedly, echoing each other, "Me me me!" Big Uncle clapped his hands and threatened, "Settle down or I won't use you."

The twins stood completely still. This drew a smile from everyone, because no matter how many times Big Uncle made this threat, it always worked with the boys, as if to have their father *use* them was life's greatest privilege. Even Tata couldn't help herself. "Thank you," she said to Big Uncle, a shadow of a smile crossing her lips, and to the rest of us, "I'll pull myself together soon enough."

"Let's go!" Big Uncle said, grabbing a checkered *kroma* and a shirt and throwing them over his muscular shoulders. "We have work to do— get ourselves clean and bring water back for Tata!" He strode through the doorway, the twins scrambling after him.

Leave it to Big Uncle to turn the smallest task into a game and simultaneously imbue it with a sense of purpose and importance. Papa and I grabbed a change of clothes and dashed to catch up with them. From the doorway Auntie India called out in her singsong voice for us to bring back some more lotus blossoms. "As an offering to the Buddha! And be careful with the boys, Arun; don't let them swim out too far!" Big Uncle turned and reassured his wife with an exaggerated bow of servitude, mouthing, "*Oui, ma princesse.*" But to me—as I skipped up to him—he chortled, "We'll *use* them as bait for the crocodiles!" The twins exclaimed in unison, "Oh Papa, you don't mean that!" Big Uncle snorted, a stallion provoking his colts to action, nuzzling them forward with his nose. They bounced toward the water.

If one looked from the temple, it appeared the pond spilled into the marsh, but a long stretch of dike separated the two, then wound its way about the verdant landscape and diverged into innumerable branches among the rice paddies. As was his habit when we arrived at someplace new, Papa oriented me to the four directions. The sun would rise and set in a slightly different place, he said as we walked, depending on the time of year. In the east, past the marsh, the sun had risen above the forests and was now arcing westward at an almost imperceptible speed. We made our way along the northern edge of the pond toward the dike, Big Uncle leading with long, carefree strides; followed by the twins, one behind the other, shouldering a bamboo yoke and a pair of buckets between them; then me, a plastic bowl in one hand and a stick I'd found along the way in the other; and Papa in the back, arms around another bucket, thumbing it gently like a drum. To the south, the town of Rolork Meas lay in a blaze of morning light, golden and serene—a lovely patchwork of traditional wooden houses and fruit orchards. Papa promised we would go exploring later, maybe take some city items like a lighter and a bar of soap to trade with the townsfolk for rice and eggs. The Revolutionary soldiers had said we could, provided that we not try to run away but return to the temple as expected. Now that we'd settled in I didn't see any reason to run away and seek shelter elsewhere. We were comfortable here. We couldn't have hoped, I was certain, for a safer haven.

We'd reached a part of the dike that separated the marsh and the pond. Big Uncle stopped and took the bamboo yoke and the two buckets from the twins. Families gathered along the grassy embankment to wash and chat, hemmed on one side by water hyacinth and on the other by lotuses. Nearby two women were washing their children. "How long do you think we'll be here?" one asked, scrubbing the back of her child's ear with the edge of her sarong, and another answered, "My husband went into town last night and the locals told him they'd been ordered to prepare their houses for the 'new people.'" The first woman seemed puzzled: "Who did they mean?" The second replied, "Us, no doubt. They're going to settle us here. For a while, it seems." The first admitted, "The town's nice, I suppose. We could end up someplace much worse."

Papa and Big Uncle looked at each other but said nothing. Big Uncle, the checkered *kroma* around his waist for modesty, slipped his pants off and placed them atop the buckets and bamboo yoke. He stepped into the water, pulling a naked twin on either side of him, like a tugboat with a pair of buoys. Also in a *kroma*, Papa followed them, taking the bucket he'd brought along, pushing away stringy plants as he went. When he got to a depth where the water was clear, he dipped the bucket in and carried it back for me.

"Sure you don't want to come in?" he asked, setting the bucket down on the dike. "I could carry you."

I shook my head, slipping off my shirt and leaving only my elastic-waist sarong on for washing. I didn't know how to swim, and the twins would laugh if they saw me being carried like a baby.

Papa went back in, submerging himself like a crocodile. Big Uncle swam over to him. The two men stood talking, splashing water on their torsos, while the twins doggy-paddled around them. All the while Big Uncle's expression grew more troubled, and once or twice his gaze shot in the direction of the monks' sleeping quarters. I couldn't hear them from this distance, but I guessed that Papa was recounting what the sweeper had told us, what we'd seen at the back of the temple. With the plastic bowl, I scooped water from the bucket and poured it over my head, pausing now and then to study the two men. The contrast between Papa's calm solemnity and Big Uncle's agitated reaction began to disturb me. They went on talking for a while in this manner. Then Papa patted Big Uncle on the shoulder, as if to comfort him. Big Uncle nodded, his gaze now turned to some figures in black pacing the distant rice fields. I couldn't tell whether they were Revolutionary soldiers or farmers, if what they had slung across their shoulders were bamboo yokes or guns.

"Look!" suddenly Sotanavong yelled out. "A turtle, a turtle!" Satiyavong screeched, "Where, where? Oh, I see it! There!" They pointed to the spot directly in front of them. Slick as an eel, Big Uncle dove for it, and at the very same moment Papa slapped the surface of the water with his hand. In the blink of an eye, he snatched the creature by its shell, held it up above his head like a prize he'd just won, and spun it around for all to see. People around us clapped and cheered, and one man piped from among the water lilies, "We can have turtle soup!" Papa laughed, sank heavily into the water, like a drowned man, and then reappeared a few seconds later, the turtle gone from his grasp. Everyone groaned with disappointment. Big Uncle roared, and the twins chorused, "Do it again, do it again!" as if it was some sort of magic trick my father could repeat on demand. I shook my head, smiling. Papa shrugged, palms open in innocence, as if to say the turtle had simply escaped on its own from his grip. But, of course, he'd let it go. There would be no turtle soup.

We finished bathing and changed into clean clothes. Big Uncle hooked the full buckets to the bamboo yoke, one at each end, and hoisted the yoke onto his shoulders. The twins protested, speaking in turns. "But Papa, you promised! You said you'd use us!" Big Uncle plopped a wet *kroma* on their heads. "Here, you little tadpoles, you can carry—"

Before he could finish, a loud rumble came from the road. We whipped around to look. Amidst a blooming cloud of dust emerged the silhouette of a camion similar to the one that had brought us here the day before. It roared past the stupa, then reversed clumsily back to where the entrance was. *Oh no,* I thought with dread, *we'll have to leave again.* Everyone rushed back to the temple.

• • •

As it turned out, the camion had brought another load of passengers. Two more followed in immediate succession. More than a hundred people, it seemed, tumbled out from under the blue tarpaulin covers into the morning light, looking more bedraggled and rattled than we had when we arrived. As they gathered on the temple grounds, it was clear from their conversations that they had come straight from Phnom Penh and, having been driven through the night, were sleep deprived and disoriented and had no idea how far they'd traveled. One elderly man fell prostrate, forehead touching the bare ground, weeping loudly to the Walking Buddha statue. I couldn't tell if he was overjoyed to have at last arrived somewhere or burdened by sorrow for having traveled such a long distance to nowhere. A young woman quickly helped him up, murmuring, "Come, Father, come," as if she were the parent trying to comfort a child. "We're here now." She looked numbed by fatigue and shock. She turned toward the group of Revolutionary soldiers accompanying them. One met her gaze and quickly looked the other way, pretending he hadn't witnessed her distress or her father's. The rest of the soldiers—about eight or nine of them—were busy collecting their guns and ammunition. They seemed to be more stern than the ones who had traveled with us. Two or three soldiers appeared to have just joined this new group, and it was clear they had come from the town because they seemed rested and their clothes were clean and neat. They gestured to the school buildings and ordered us to help the newcomers. "Show them the way," one shouted, hands cupped around his mouth in place of a bullhorn. He appeared to be the leader of the pack and spoke with confidence. "More will join you! You must make room! The sooner you settle in the better!"

More people are coming? I didn't know whether to feel excited or worried. Another camion snorted into view. It was smaller than its predecessors but was packed so full that some of the passengers were hanging off the sides. Seeing this, the lead soldier tried to disperse the throng lingering at the entrance. "GO!" His voice grew louder above the rising murmur of the crowds. "THIS IS ONLY TEMPORARY! THE ORGANIZATION WILL DECIDE LATER!"

A frightful feeling came over me. What if these trucks were also here to take us away—out with the old and in with the new?

I had to find Papa and alert him. I found him by the front steps of the prayer hall talking with a young couple. I hurried over, and he, noticing me beside him, said excitedly, "Raami, this is a former student of mine and his family." He gestured to the couple, the husband balancing a heavy valise on either side of him, the wife cradling a small baby in her arms, a *kroma* draped over her head and shoulders to protect the little one from the elements. Papa noticed my nervousness, took my hand and squeezed it, and in that instant I felt my anxiety begin to ebb. "Mr. Virak took several poetry classes with me when he was a university student," Papa explained happily—to me as much as to the young wife—as if this was just another serendipitous meeting. "He was the only engineering student interested in literature."

His unworried manner further quelled my apprehension, and I found myself staring at the baby. The wife smiled and parted the *kroma* to reveal more of the tiny infant. She nodded at me as if to say I could come closer and touch it, but I stayed where I was. It looked too small, too precious for hands as dirty as mine. My eyes went to the tiny earlobe. No earring there. I guessed it was a boy. He was deep in sleep, his hands wrapped in thin white cotton mittens that resembled tiny boxing gloves. When he felt the air brushing against his skin, his arms jerked in reflex, a boxer taking punches at the air.

"And now you're a civil engineer." Papa turned to Mr. Virak, beaming proudly. "Working for a foreign firm, you said."

"*Was*, Your Highness." Mr. Virak sighed. "I was working in Malaysia, but I came back at the beginning of the year. Now, I'm . . . well . . ."

Just then the new arrivals began heading in our direction. Among them was the old man who had thrown himself to the ground weeping, and as he shuffled past, moving along with the throng toward the school buildings, I noticed a bamboo flute tucked in the *kroma* around his waist. When he caught sight of the stupa and the surrounding *cheddays*, he let out another despairing sob.

"Poor man," Mr. Virak said, shaking his head. "His wife suffered an asthma attack and died on the journey. We had to leave her on the side of the road. Imagine you're a funerary musician and you've played your music at all these funerals, but when your own wife died, you couldn't bury her, couldn't even play a single note to mourn her death. It is a nightmare, Your Highness. A nightmare. I feel as though we are journeying through *thaanaruak*—an underworld."

Papa looked at me, and turning back to Mr. Virak, said, "Well, you are here now. This is a sanctuary."

Mr. Virak looked around. He seemed skeptical. I could see why. It wasn't the same place now with the soldiers everywhere shouting, the camions churning up dust and debris, people milling about in a confused mob, uncertain where to go except to follow those in front of them.

As another throng pushed past us, Papa suggested we ought to hurry. With so many families, the classrooms would fill up quickly. He told Mr. Virak and his wife about the room adjoining ours, which was a bit small, but they ought to take it, as they would have more privacy than they would sharing a bigger room with another family. He then took the two valises from Mr. Virak, who stammered in protest: "Your Highness, I cannot let you . . ." Papa told him, "You are among friends now. There is no need for formality or status. Here we are the same. Address me as you would a friend." Mr. Virak's eyes flashed with understanding. "Yes, of course, of course."

We headed toward the school buildings. I rushed ahead to alert the rest of our family, thrilled now to have the couple and their baby joining us, comforted by the sheer number of people, a larger presence around me. Soon it would be just like home, I thought happily. This place would be filled with people we knew, with friends and family. More would join us, the soldier had said. Hope flitted through my heart.

We moved our pots and pans and whatever else we'd scattered on the floor and gave our friends the small adjoining room. It took them no time at all to settle in as they had only the two valises, one full of clothes, and the other food. In the fright of being ordered to leave at gunpoint, Mr. Virak explained, they had neglected to pack any kitchenware. "Not even a spoon," his young wife admitted, shaking her head, blushing with embarrassment. Not to worry, everyone assured them. They could use ours. "Do join us for some porridge!" Auntie India sang. "It's ready!"

It was almost noon, but with all that was happening, we had yet to eat our morning meal. Radana and the twins were delirious with hunger. They banged their spoons and bowls, making a head-splitting ruckus as they waited to be fed. Auntie India, with characteristic cheerfulness, spooned some porridge into a large bowl and led the three to the doorway, where she sat down to feed them, giving each a turn from the same spoon and bowl. *A mother bird feeding her chicks,* I thought. The three chirped and clucked, swallowing the porridge with insatiable relish.

The rest of us gathered in a circle on the eating mat like one big family. Mr. Virak's wife had brought out a container of sweetened ground pork and a can of pickled turnip to add to our usual but dwindling portion of dried fish. Everyone joked at how the meager spread looked like a feast, how everything seemed to taste so good. Maybe it was because of the fresh country air, Papa pointed out. Yes, Big Uncle agreed, maybe it wasn't a bad thing after all to be brought here. "Maybe they're right, city life was corrupting our appetites—our taste buds!"

At the mention of "city," everyone turned serious, and soon we were all listening quietly to Mr. Virak's descriptions of Phnom Penh and the ordeal that had carried them here.

Like us, on New Year's Day, he and his wife were told to leave their home, but as it was already evening, they decided to wait. The next day when they opened their gate they found a flood of humanity as impassable as the Mekong during a thunderstorm. Again, they thought it wise to stay put and wait it out. They would wait and see what happened in the next few days, if the seething mass would let up, and maybe then they wouldn't have to leave at all. They locked the doors, pretending they weren't home, hiding most of the time in a small storage closet under the stairway of their house, holding their breath whenever a Revolutionary soldier banged on their gate, fearful the cry of their two-month-old infant would be heard through the layers of doors. Meanwhile, without their realizing it, the world outside their home plunged into darkness, and by the time they emerged—forced out at gunpoint by a soldier who had blasted open their padlock with a single shot from his pistol—it was not the same place they had known. Destruction was all around them— buildings reduced to rubble, vehicles abandoned and burnt, corpses of people and animals alike rotting in the heat, an overwhelming stench everywhere.

"Phnom Penh is no longer," Mr. Virak murmured quietly, stirring the porridge in his bowl. "We can never go back. Never. It's the end." He kept stirring, unable to take his first bite, the porridge starting to congeal. Then he looked up and added, hesitantly, "When . . . when they drove us through the city, one of the Revolutionary soldiers—their commander, I believe—pointed in the direction of the Cercle Sportif and said they'd executed the prime minister and other important leaders. *Traitors,* the commander called them. *We've no need for such men in the new regime.* Those were his exact words. You must be careful."

Papa and Big Uncle exchanged looks but said nothing. A deathly silence settled upon the room. Mama nodded at me, and I realized I'd been holding my spoon in my mouth, riveted by the whole account. I had listened to Mr. Virak's every word, hoping for glimpses of a familiar street or corner of the city—for home. Instead he'd painted a picture of an unrecognizable place, an "underworld" where gods and *tevodas* were not revered but captured and shot like caged animals.

Mr. Virak continued, "In a matter of a few weeks, they've done what they said they would—take us all the way back to nothing. It's clear that not just Phnom Penh, but the whole country is being rearranged. It seems those living in provincial cities and towns are now being evacuated also, under stricter and harsher rules. People can't choose which way to go—if they're directed to go south, they go south, even if their hometown is to the north. In countless instances, we've seen family members being separated, some pushed in one direction and some in another. It's an elaborate evacuation scheme, and it's only starting. I sense they'll keep moving us around—"

"But why?" Tata interrupted impatiently. "What good would that do?"

"It's how they will hold on to power," Mr. Virak said.

"Yes," Big Uncle echoed, nodding, as if seeing it all clearly, "they keep us fearful and helpless by destroying our most basic sense of security—separating us from family and preventing any connections from being formed. All the more reason to stick together."

We finished eating. The air felt heavy, bloated with foreboding. The grown-ups neither looked at one another nor said anything now, but moved about in their separate spheres of silence as they cleared away the dishes, rolled up the mat, and swept the floor. Mr. Virak and his wife excused themselves and went to their room. They shut the slatted door and walked about the tight space with hushed steps as they set up their home.

Through our doorway, I could see that some of the new arrivals had found themselves without a place and were heading, their belongings in tow, toward the monks' sleeping quarters. There, they would see what we'd seen, and they would turn around, unwilling yet to live among the ghosts.

Pulling himself up, Papa murmured something about a walk and asked if Big Uncle wanted to join him. Big Uncle responded with a solemn nod. They needed to talk. I knew better than to tag along. Outside they told Mama and Auntie India—who were busy washing the dishes—they'd be back shortly. "Just need to clear our minds a bit and work things out," Papa explained, and Big Uncle added, "Think of our next steps." The women murmured their consent, and once the two men were gone, Auntie India ventured cautiously, her voice lacking its usual singsong melody, "Do you think it's true . . . about the prime minister?"

"It doesn't help to imagine what we don't really know." Mama tried to maintain her calm, but I could tell she was getting tired of explaining, taking care of everyone's feelings. "We just have to do what we can *not* to stand out." She scoured the rice pot vigorously with a piece of coconut rind. Then, noticing Auntie India's lacquered nails, she looked up and said, "You should really remove the polish."

Auntie India seemed confused. "Pardon me?"

"The nail polish," Mama told her.

"Oh, yes, I know it looks awful—all chipped." She sounded distressed. "Makes my hands look like a market vendor's. But I forgot the remover, and the bottle I've found in my purse is the wrong color, and of course I can't—"

"Use a knife," Mama said. "Scrape it off."

Auntie India frowned but dared not contradict Mama. We had to rely on her judgment when it came to conducting ourselves as ordinary people, as commoners. Auntie India knew this. Still, Mama had to explain. "It makes you look like a city person."

"Oh, I see." Auntie India nodded. She let out a sigh. Then, changing the subject, she said, "We're almost out of rice. We may have to cut our meals. But the children and Mother—they're always hungry."

"They'll eat when they're hungry," Mama told her forcefully. "Even if the rest of us have nothing." She rinsed the rice pot, put it aside, and looking at Auntie India, added, more gently, "We'll take some things to trade this afternoon." She attempted a smile.

Auntie India looked somewhat reassured.

I felt a hand on my shoulder. "Come here," Tata beckoned, drawing me away from the door. "Help me set up a place for Grandmother Queen to rest." She handed me a straw mat to unroll. Then she started to mumble, "The problem with being seven—I remember myself at that age—is that you're aware of so much, and yet you understand so little. So you imagine the worst."

She was right. I didn't understand. There was so much to piece together. So I asked her what I sensed was most immediate: "Do you think we'll starve, Tata?"

She didn't answer right away. Finally she said, "No, Raami. No, we're not going to starve." She turned away, clearly upset.

I swallowed. I didn't know what troubled me more—the possibility that we might not have enough to eat, or the realization that Tata had just lied to me.

The problem with being seven . . .

I wondered at what age one understands everything.

nine

Several days later, at dusk, a group of solemn-looking men and women began to arrive at the temple. Like the Revolutionary soldiers, they were dressed in black from head to toe and walked with such furtive steps it seemed they appeared out of nowhere and were suddenly in our midst. They floated toward the school buildings, a black bat-like mass stirring the air with disquiet. Something about the way they moved, drifting like one giant shadow, made me think I'd seen them before. Then I realized indeed I had—days earlier when we were bathing at the pond, the black figures pacing the distant fields. They'd watched us surreptitiously from afar while pretending to survey the crop. The old sweeper had warned us of this. Now they'd come for a close-up, bearing baskets of rice and dangling chunks of cane sugar in bamboo nets as if to entice us like ants out of our holes.

"Strange-looking peasants," Tata murmured, watching from our doorway. "Wonder who they really are . . ."

They introduced themselves as the Kamaphibal, as if to distinguish themselves in our eyes from the Revolutionary soldiers. They spoke Khmer using village vernacular, sounding like rice farmers even though they looked like they could be teachers or doctors. One was even wearing glasses. *How are you, Comrade?* they inquired, moving from door to door, family to family, passing out the food they'd brought, startling everyone with their way of talking, the words they used, as if they didn't know adults from children, elders from infants. They invited everyone to meet outside. The man with the glasses stood over the charcoal outline of the hopscotch board. As he prepared to speak, the others stood back, opening the way for him with a resounding clap.

"You may wonder why you are here," he said, his voice even, monotonously soothing compared to the erratic booming we'd so often heard coming from the Revolutionary soldiers. "There is a reason, you see."

He had a slow-moving stare, like the lens of a camera taking in a large crowd, lingering now and then over a face.

"The war is over. We've won. Our enemies are destroyed. But the fighting does not end here. The struggle must go on. Anyone can be a soldier in the Revolution. It doesn't matter if you are a monk, a teacher, a doctor, a man, or a woman. If you give yourself to the Revolution, you are a Revolutionary soldier. If you know how to read and write, the Organization needs you. The Organization calls out to you to help rebuild the country."

His gaze rolled seamlessly from person to person, unperturbed by suckling infants or yawning elders, by coughing or sneezing.

"You're here because we believe there are many among you who could join us in our cause. While you may be new to the Revolutionary struggle, we need your proven expertise and skills, your practical knowledge and know-how."

I knew how to read and write well, but I doubted I could actually be a soldier. Perhaps he was exaggerating. As if reading my thoughts, he stopped and stared, his gaze steady on us. A smile or grimace, I couldn't tell. A knowing blink. Papa, on bended knees, one arm around my waist, faltered in his position, and I felt his grip tighten around me as he tried to regain balance. I turned to face him, wondering if something was the matter, but he'd lowered his face, hiding it from view. Meanwhile, the man's gaze didn't linger; he'd moved on to other faces. It was obvious he'd recognized Papa.

"Cambodian history is a history of injustice," he went on, his tone consciously calm. "Now we must write a new history. We must build a new society upon the wreckage of the old. Come. Do not be afraid. We shall build the new Democratic Kampuchea together. Come."

He waited. No one moved. He turned to the other members of

the Kamaphibal. They responded with a silent, collective nod. Then, as stealthily as they'd arrived, they began to leave, vanishing one by one in the gathering gloom, like shadows absorbed by the night.

Kamaphibal. "A Revolutionary word," Papa tried to explain. "Made up probably of older Pali or Sanskrit words broken up and strung back together." He went on, but I was no longer paying attention. My mind had caught on to the phrase "broken up," which I thought was strangely apropos of this group that had appeared out of nowhere, as if emerging from the bits and pieces of all they'd broken and destroyed.

For the next several weeks there was no sign of the Kamaphibal. Even so, their words, the language they spoke, continued to swirl like smoke following a magician's disappearing act. *If you know how to read and write, the Organization needs you. The Organization calls out to you to help rebuild the country.* A kind of desperate confusion spread across the temple ground as people argued over what it all meant.

Back in our room, Tata surprised everyone by wondering aloud if we oughtn't to put our trust in the Kamaphibal. "They're certainly a more educated bunch," she said, looking around for support. "Well, at least the one who spoke—he wore glasses, didn't he?" Big Uncle looked at her as if this last statement was as inane as the Revolutionary soldiers' justification to shoot someone for the very same reason. Tata tried to explain. "What I mean is that the man—whoever he is, the spokesman of the Kamaphibal—wasn't bred in the jungle like the rest of these barbarians." Big Uncle reminded her that stripped of their Revolutionary eloquence, and their peasantry pretense, the Kamaphibal were those same Khmer Rouge soldiers—those "vile Communists"—she so vehemently despised. To this, Tata pleaded, "But these people can reason! They made sense! It's true they will need people like us to put the country back together." Big Uncle looked skeptical but refrained from saying more.

Preoccupied with the Kamaphibal's words, no one was prepared when a group of Revolutionary soldiers appeared one evening armed with notebooks and pencils.

A boy—tall and lean with a smoker's dark lips and yellowish eyes—strode into our room, brandishing a notebook and a pencil stuck in its spiraled spine. His gaze shot through the open doorway toward the small adjoining room where Mr. Virak and his wife were tending their baby who, in the past couple of days, had developed a fever. Feeling the soldier's gaze on him, Mr. Virak straightened up, fist clenched as if ready for a fight. His wife placed her hand on his arm, holding him back. But the soldier ignored them, scanning our room now, his eyes on the twins, Radana, then finally me. "You!" He pointed with his notebook. "Come here!"

I got up and walked toward him, my steps heavy, slowed, as fear coiled itself like a snake in the pit of my stomach. Papa grabbed my shoulder and held me in place. He addressed the soldier, "Comrade—"

"SILENCE!" the boy roared, then again to me, "COME!"

I heard Radana bawling and Mama trying to comfort her, but I dared not turn to look. I stepped closer to the soldier.

"What's your name?" the soldier demanded, his stare bearing down on me, and I felt myself pushed into the ground, small and crushable as a bug. "Your name!" he thundered.

"R-Raami," I stammered.

"Who's the head of your household?"

I blinked, confused for a second or two—*we have no house, so how could there be a head?*—but before I could answer, Papa said, "I am."

"Klah . . ."—a breathless objection from Big Uncle. He started to come forward, but Papa told him firmly, "Arun, stay back." Big Uncle retreated into his place by the window. Again Papa told the soldier, "I'm the head of the household, Comrade."

"Is he your father?" the soldier demanded.

"Yes," I let out, gulping down a fistful of air in turn. Papa's hands grew cold and heavy on my shoulders. I heard heartbeats, fast and thumping, but I couldn't be sure if they belonged to me or to Papa, or even the soldier.

"What's his name?"

Again, Papa opened his mouth to speak and again the soldier yelled him down. "SILENCE!—I'm asking the girl!" He turned back to me. "Your father's name!"

"Ayuravann," I whispered, regretting it as soon as it came out of my mouth. Mechas Klah—the "Tiger Prince," as Papa was known among family members and close friends—would have sounded more impressive, intimidating.

"Full name," the soldier demanded. "Your father's full name."

"Sisowath Ayuravann," I rattled, saying the surname first, as Cambodians do. "And I'm Sisowath Ayuravann Vattaaraami." I thought if I just went ahead and also gave him my full name, then I would compensate for my earlier slowness.

But the soldier didn't care. Thrusting the notebook at Papa, he ordered, "Write it down. Name, occupation, family history. Write it all down."

Papa didn't see the pencil stuck to the notebook spine. Instead, as if by force of habit, he took the silver fountain pen from his breast pocket and began to scribble, first tentatively, then furiously, arms and shoulders trembling. I'd never seen him handle his pen this way, with such nervous haste. Writing for him, he often said, was synonymous with breathing, and his breathing was the most calming sound I'd ever heard. Now he was breathless with panic, and I could hear every scratch and stroke of the pen on paper.

While Papa kept writing, I stared at the pistol tucked in the *kroma* around the soldier's waist. A cobra rearing its head. I thought I heard it hiss. An echo of a shot resounded in my head, and again I saw the old man fall to the ground, a halo of blood spreading around him.

Papa finished and handed the notebook back to the soldier. He pulled me to him, arms like safety bars on my chest. The soldier looked at the writing, frowned, then as if deciding it was good enough for now, turned and left the room, taking long-legged strides across the playground toward the opposite building.

"You *shouldn't* have told them your father's name," Auntie India hissed when it was just us again, her voice accusing—harsh—its melodiousness gone. "*You shouldn't have.*" Each word like a finger jabbing my chest.

Big Uncle touched her arm, as if to placate her, but she turned at him, "Now they'll also know who *you* are!" and, angrily, venomously, back at me, "You should've kept quiet!"

I was scared. The harsh words, the screaming, Auntie India behaving as she did. None of it made sense.

"I'm glad she told them," Tata intervened, coming to my rescue. "Yes, they will realize soon enough who we are and give us some respect. If these idiots don't, the Kamaphibal will."

Papa ignored them both. He turned to Mama, but she was staring at her hands in her lap, refusing to meet his eyes, trying to calm her quaking shoulders. I looked from one face to the next—*What's going on?*—but no one would look at me.

Finally, Papa said, "You didn't know." His palm brushed my hair in that gesture he reserved for forgiveness when I'd done something wrong. "It isn't your fault."

Know what? What didn't I know? *What* wasn't my fault?

"I don't think the boy will remember," Big Uncle said, holding Papa's gaze to his. "He's too young to know what it means. He's just a child. Raami could've told him anything—said you were the king himself—and he wouldn't know." He turned to the others. "Really, there's nothing to worry about." He attempted a smile, but his face collapsed in uncertainty.

"I'm sorry to intrude." Mr. Virak spoke from where he stood by the door. "Did you write down everything he'd asked for?"

Papa nodded and, to me, said by way of explanation, "I wanted him away from you. Whatever it took, I wanted him to leave the room."

"You gave them your *real* name then?" Mr. Virak pursued, looking like he was puzzling over a gnarl in his mind. "You wrote 'Sisowath'?"

"Yes," Papa replied. "But I don't think the boy can read."

"His leaders—the Kamaphibal—they can read," Tata reasserted. "He'll know soon enough who we are, and when he does, he won't dare treat us as he did. None of them will."

Everyone looked at Tata like she'd become crazier than Grandmother Queen. "Well, he'll think twice," she said, trying to recover herself, and looking at Papa, "You are a Sisowath prince, for god's sake!"

"I don't think he cares," Papa replied, appearing more uncertain each minute. "I'm nobody to him."

Again, Auntie India turned to me and hissed through her sobs, "*You shouldn't—*"

"Leave her out of this!" Papa thundered. "Leave her out!" He punched the wall, then left the room, the earth trembling under his footsteps.

I shook from the reverberation. He was my god, peaceful and self-contained. Not even an earthquake could disturb him. Why would he let an argument over his name upset him like this?

ten

Ayuravann. *Ayu,* from Sanskrit, meaning "life possessing," and *ra-vann,* the combined abbreviation of *ras vannak,* "to shine with letter or word; to be renowned with a scholar's reputation." Grandmother Queen had said she gave Papa this name because, while she was carrying him, she'd dreamt the god Airavata, Indra's sacred elephant, raised his foot and touched her belly as if to impart his spirit to the life growing in her womb, and when Papa was born with the top of his right ear flipped back, like an elephant's, she was convinced he was an earthly incarnation of Airavata. When Papa became known for his poetry, Grandmother Queen was ever more convinced of his divine origin. *He's a vehicle of the gods, just as Airavata is a vehicle of Indra.* But I was not to be immediately persuaded. What about the Tiger Prince? Why was Papa called a tiger if he was in fact an elephant? To this, Grandmother Queen had impatiently replied, "Ah, ignorant child, a god has many manifestations!"

I found him near the meditation pavilion, at the bottom of some wooden steps down the slight incline to the pond. Dusk was gathering, and in the greyness around us, he manifested himself in yet another way—fragile and fractured, a small snail hiding in his shell. I had the urge to take him in my hand and mold him whole again.

I cleared my throat to let him know I was there.

He didn't turn but continued to stare at his hand, caressing it as if nursing an injured fish he'd rescued from the water. I went down the steps and sat next to him. "Let me see," I said, taking his hand in mine, examining it—the skin of his knuckles torn and bleeding. I blew on it, imagining the hurt escaping silently with my breath. *Ephemeral.* A magical word, he told me. *Nothing lasts. Not sadness, not pain.* "It'll be fine," I said, even as I felt a solidity to his wound, something far more enduring and deeper than this slight, superficial injury.

He turned to face me. "Do you know who I am?"

Of course. What a funny question.

"I am a prince. A Sisowath prince."

I knew this already. We were all princes and princesses. A prince wasn't *all* my father was. Art, he'd told me in response to Grandmother Queen's story, is our divine expression, and as far as manifestation is concerned, it's we humans, not the gods, who must be worthy to reveal ourselves. More than a prince, I thought, Papa was the poetry he wrote.

"Sisowath Ayuravann," he said now, as if uttering the name of someone who'd died long ago. "Do you know what this name means? The story that comes with it?"

I waited as he stared at the water, searching perhaps for a fissure that would allow him entry into another world.

"When I was about ten years old," he began, "I had a friend. He was a bread seller. Every morning, he'd come around hawking those little French baguettes on the streets outside my school."

The sky let out a distant rumble. I looked up. A small, wispy cloud was moving across the waxing quarter moon, like a veil pulled over a lopsided smile, trying to hide its amusement from us.

"His name was Sambath. He was poor, but I didn't know it—I didn't care. All that mattered to me was that he was my friend—my *best* friend."

The cloud passed and the moon seemed bigger and brighter, more like a full-lipped pout now. *Tousana,* Papa had called it, I remembered now, from the Pali word *dassana,* meaning "insight." When something seemed both familiar and new all in the same moment. We'd been talking about storytelling, how there could be many versions of the same story, many ways of telling it, and how each version was a kind of manifestation, as if the story itself was a living, evolving entity, a god capable of many guises.

"Being who he was—a poor boy—Sambath of course couldn't come into the school. During break, though, when the students were allowed to step out to buy snacks on nearby street corners, I'd go out to meet him. We'd sit and talk, sharing a baguette I bought from him, dipping it in steamy condensed milk I got from another vendor. I'd stay out for the rest of the break to be with him, even as other children retreated to the school compound to play with their own kind. Once, on the sidewalk near the guard station, we played a game of marbles. Sambath won, I lost. I was upset. I wanted the marbles back. He said no. He won them fairly—justly."

Papa had told me this story before, but he'd never mentioned any games they played, let alone disagreements between them. This was all new, and it struck me that not only did the story sound different, but that Papa seemed not to realize he was *telling* it. Instead he was visibly upset and confused, as if caught still in the middle of this quarrel over some marbles.

"*Justly?* Why would he use such a word with me? Had I been *un-just* to him? Rage filled my lungs. We fought, at first calling each other names—*Liar! Cheat! Thief! Shameless dog, you think you're better than the rest of us just because you're a prince!* Then I threw the first punch, and just like that, we were exchanging blows and kicks." Papa's hand balled up in a fist at the memory of that punch. "It was our first real fight. Why did he have to ruin everything by reminding me who I was? Prince or not, I was just his friend. He should have understood this. I kneed him in the stomach. Sambath kneed me back, twice as hard."

I could well picture the tussle, thinking how boys kick and punch and wrestle even when they're *not* angry.

"A school guard returning from his lunch break saw us and, instead of inquiring, started to beat Sambath with his club. Pounding him with it. I begged him to stop. He wouldn't. He kept beating Sambath. *This should teach you to know your place,* he growled at the mound collapsing at his feet. *You worthless garbage! Don't you know who you're talking to?*" Papa's voice was so harsh that for a second I believed it was the raging guard speaking. "*A prince! You're talking to a prince, you dirty worm!* Again and again, he reminded Sambath of this."

Another rumble resounded. I scanned the sky for lightning, but there was none. Still, I wanted us to go. It might start raining any second.

Papa seemed not to have heard the thunder at all. He swallowed, moistening his throat, and continued, "He kept referring to my name, my title, reminding Sambath and all the children gathered to watch, and I'd never been so ashamed of who I was as in that moment."

Something jumped in front of us. A silver-tailed fish. It flashed like a knife in the air and then disappeared again beneath the surface. Papa's gaze followed the ripples shimmying in the water, and for a moment he looked as if he would jump into the pond and follow the fish. He often looked like this—like he wanted to escape but knew he couldn't. "The guard didn't know better, you see. He thought he was honoring me by beating a boy—a worthless street urchin, in his eyes—who dared to curse me, defile my noble name."

Grandmother Queen had said that "Ayuravann" was a Buddhist monk's reformulation of "Airavata." The monk had interpreted Grandmother Queen's dream to mean that Papa would die young, as the gods would strike down any human who dared to assume their guise. The monk thus consulted a sacred Buddhist text and came up with "Ayuravann." The name would shield Papa from those who intended him harm and anchor him to this world. He would enjoy a long and prosperous life. We had nothing to fear.

"Sisowath Ayuravann. My wrong and redemption, Raami. Both strung into the story of this name. As a boy, I knew there existed different worlds, but I also believed that these worlds were traversable by friendship. Yet, when my friend was beaten, made to understand that certain boundaries could not and should not be crossed, I realized that not only did we live in different worlds, but *mine* was fiercely guarded." He turned to face me now. "I might as well have beaten Sambath with my own hands. The landscape of his face, bloody and broken, Raami. I could never put it back. It stays with me to this day. My culpability. I let it happen, you see."

I saw the lopsidedness of his revelation and couldn't keep quiet any longer. "But you didn't do anything."

"That's just it—I *didn't* do anything when I *could* have. I could have called for help. Could have kicked and scratched the guard. Could have taken the blows of his club myself. But I did none of those things. Instead, a man beat a boy because of my name. And, sooner or later, I'll have to answer for the injustice of it all. I'll have to pay for my crime."

"But it wasn't *your* fault," I reasoned. "Remember the turtle you caught? Well, we could have had it for soup. But you let it go. You couldn't even hurt an animal. How could you hurt a person?"

He didn't hear me, lost to despair. When he finally spoke, it was more to himself. "Yes, I am a prince, a minor prince, but still a prince . . . Sisowath. This name matters. It matters to the Revolutionary soldiers and the Kamaphibal. It has always mattered. I should've been able to do more with it."

It was just a name, I thought, no more meaningful than the nonsensical appellation the Kamaphibal had concocted for themselves, and, as far as Papa was concerned, I didn't care what name or title he answered to. Sisowath, Ayuravann, the Tiger Prince, His Highness . . . Even if he were to bear a hundred more names, he would still be my father, and there was no one, neither prince nor god, gentler than he.

"You'd still be the same person to me," I told him, my hand brushing his hair, "even if you didn't have a name. Even if you were nobody."

He pulled me to him and, resting his chin on my head, murmured, "Once, in a journey's dream, I came upon a child bearing my soul . . ."

"Once, in a journey's dream," I replied, knowing well the routine, the game we'd often play with the verses he'd written, tossing them back and forth, testing them aloud, "I came upon a reflection of myself."

A frog jumped into the pond, and the water rippled again, undulating under a sky that had darkened now to the color of despair. A father's bruised conscience.

"Words, you see," he said, looking at me again, "allow us to make permanent what is essentially transient. Turn a world filled with injustice and hurt into a place that is beautiful and lyrical. Even if only on paper. I wrote the poem for you the day you lay sick with polio. I stood over your crib and you looked at me with such mournful eyes I thought you understood my grief."

Maybe I did, I wanted to tell him. *I do now.* I certainly understood what it felt like to want to do more than you could.

A gust of wind blew from the east, sending water lapping at our feet. I felt Papa's sadness surge through me.

Night arrived, a giant wing closing on us, carrying in its folds the silhouette of another giant, a *yiak* with a gas lantern illuminated in his raised hand: Big Uncle stood next to the meditation pavilion, his shadow contending with its shadow, like a scene from a shadow-puppet play of the *Reamker*. "There you are!" he exclaimed. "I've been looking all over for you."

Papa turned. "What are you doing here?"

"I could ask the same of you," Big Uncle said, descending the wooden stairs toward us, his steps heavy and grave, like the rumbles of the sky, shaking the earth with their might. "It'll rain any moment, you know." He offered his hand. I grabbed it and he hoisted me to a standing position. We followed him up the steps. At the top he faced us and said, "The whole family is mad with worries."

Papa lowered his gaze, hands in his pockets, and murmured, "I'm sorry, I can't erase what was said—what I wrote."

Big Uncle shook his head. "I'm not talking about that. They're worried about *you.*"

We started walking. It was just the three of us outside. It appeared everyone else had sought shelter from the impending storm. A constant stream of cool wind was blowing now, stirring the trees and bushes around us, sending their shadows collapsing into ours. We passed the open prayer hall, and I looked up, to the tops of the pillars, expecting to see the statues of Kinnara coming alive and taking flight. But I could barely make them out in the dark, their silhouettes inanimate. Several yards away, the Walking Buddha statue guarded the entrance, reassuring in its solidity.

"How are you feeling?" Big Uncle asked after a moment's silence.

"I shouldn't have behaved as I did," Papa told him. "How's India?"

"It's understandable. Remember me at Mango Corner? We each have our moment, I suppose."

"I don't know, Arun." Papa shook his head, unconvinced. "I should've been able to behave in a saner way."

"You were scared, and so was India. But she's fine now. We move on. We take our next steps. Remember what we talked about? The plan to settle here with the townsfolk? Take up royal residence in Rolork Meas," he added jokingly. "Hey, that has a rather nice ring to it! What do you think, Raami?"

I didn't answer. It wasn't a time for jokes. Had they been planning this whole time to settle in Rolork Meas?

"Well, I think we should just do it," Big Uncle continued. "Make this place our home for now. Even if it means we'll be put in different households."

Different households? Live separately? I felt panic rising in my throat. Big Uncle kept walking, his steps light, nonchalant.

"But how?" Papa said. "We have no connection here."

"We could *declare* a connection."

"With what? With whom?"

"The old sweeper. He came looking for you," Big Uncle explained. "He brought some eggs from his hen. We could say he's Aana's rela-tive—a distant uncle, perhaps. It's plausible. Don't you see it? He could be our *peasant* connection. Our safety net."

Papa stopped abruptly and, letting go of my hand, turned to Big Uncle in the dark. "Have you spoken of this with him?" he asked, visibly upset.

"Of course not!" Big Uncle rumbled with indignation. "I haven't said a word to anyone. I wanted to talk with you first. See if it was even a possibility." He softened. "Besides, your friend was in no mood to talk; I couldn't discuss it with him even if I'd wanted to. He was all shaken up about something."

We continued walking, with me in the middle now. Papa kept silent, thinking. Then, after a moment, he said, "No, it's too much to ask of him. I'd be risking his life for mine. I'm in this alone."

It was Big Uncle's turn to be upset. "What do you mean you're in this *alone*? We're all in it together."

"No, it could be just me, Arun. Just me. Don't you understand?"

"What are you talking about?"

"I wrote my name and occupation," Papa began to explain, quietly, matter-of-factly. "Our family history is brief: I'm the only Sisowath; the rest of you are my in-laws. Commoners. You, Tata, and Aana are siblings, and your parents were formerly fruit growers—mangoes and bananas mostly—from Kien Svay. Your mother's alive. But your father died, drowned in the Mekong when his boat sank while transporting fruits to the city."

"But why? Why would you say all this? None of it makes any sense."

"Listen, Arun," Papa said, hands in his pockets, his manner strangely calm and casual. "I think that young cadre, the Kamaphibal's spokesman, I think he recognized me. I don't know how, but I think he knows who I am. If he doesn't, he'll find out. Tata's right—he's one of us. He could see right through me. When I'm called, I'll go. *Alone.* Please understand. I need you to understand, Arun."

I heard the lantern break against the hard earth as it dropped from Big Uncle's hand. "Oh, my brother," he heaved, breathless with horror, "what have you done, what have you done? You've clipped your wings. You have clipped your own wings."

Lightning struck, the sky roared, and the night cried a giant's tears, thunderous and inconsolable.

eleven

In the stillness, I woke to find Papa gone. Mama was also gone, her blanket gathered in a pile at the foot of the straw mat. I sat up, letting my eyes adjust to the dark that felt as thick as ink, becoming aware of the sound of a bamboo flute playing outside. A familiar melody. It weaved through my mind and I recalled the words that went with it:

Since I was a little girl, I've never been so scared,
As when Your Highness took hold of my hand.

A passage from a *lakhon* drama. But a *lakhon* out here? At this hour? There was a faint orange glow coming through the front doorway. In the room, no one but me was awake. I could easily make out who was who from the silhouette each person formed on the floor: in one mosquito net, Big Uncle a mountainous bulk, the twins a pair of nautilus-shaped knolls, Auntie India a slender hill of dips and curves, and in another net, Tata long and straight like a pestle, Grandmother Queen globular and malleable like a clay mortar in the process of being molded. No sign of Mama or Papa anywhere. Where could they be? I wasn't alarmed. On the contrary, I felt strangely subdued, calmed by sleep that hadn't quite left my body and by the music of the bamboo flute, which sounded more like the trill a bird would produce than anything a human being could conjure up with his lips.

Beside me Radana snored gently, hugging her small bolster pillow, her face squashed in doughy bliss, completely ignorant of Mama's absence. I pulled the blanket from the foot of the straw mat and covered her with it, gathering the edges in around her so she would be secure and safe within its soft enclosure. Then I let myself out of the mosquito net and went to the doorway. There I saw them.

They were sitting outside by a small fire, their faces turned so that I could see only the slight curves of their chins glowing like two quarter moons. She was in the middle of dressing the wound on his hand, with a strip torn from the *kroma* on her shoulders. She felt the bandage and, seeing that it could use one more layer, ripped another strip from the checkered scarf, Papa contemplating her every gesture and movement. Neither one noticed my presence, absorbed as they were in each other, their minds wooed to stillness by the bamboo flute. I wanted to say something to let them know I was there, but as my voice hadn't yet come to me, I swallowed my wordlessness and lowered myself to the floor, my senses slowly awakened by the cold air, which had set in after a night of pouring rain.

Please, Your Highness, I beg you let me go . . .
I belong to another, he who is humble as I.

I glanced in the direction the music seemed to be coming from and saw in the surrounding dark another shadow crouching in the doorway of the building across the school ground from ours. It was the old musician, the elongated silhouette of the bamboo flute extending from his lips. His fingers moved over the instrument's air holes, weaving a refrain:

Please, I beg you let me go . . .
Your Highness, please let me go.

He paused, played a couple of notes, and slowly moved into a tighter, more controlled piece. Again, I heard in my head the words that went with the music, the insults thrown back and forth between two adversaries, the thievish prince and the impoverished perfume seller:

O, you minuscule animal of the savage world,
Seeing a fire flaming hot, you imagine it a game!

O, mountain, you tower over all . . .
Your name places you in the family of gods—
Yet, you stand lower than grass!

It was from *Mak Thoeung,* a beloved Khmer classic told in verse. I knew the story well. I'd seen several *lakhon* performances of it and heard it read on the radio. It tells the story of a perfume seller and his beautiful young wife. One day while they are at a market selling fragrances and oils, a young prince spots the wife and takes her for his concubine. The perfume seller goes to the king and informs him what the young prince has done. The prince denies it. The king, on the advice of his most trusted senior court minister, orders the two men to carry a large, heavy drum to faraway fields and back, as punishment for their insolence. Unbeknownst to them, inside the drum crouches a little boy who is to note the conversation between the two offenders and report it back to the king. Thinking themselves alone, the perfume seller and the young prince begin throwing insults as sharp as blades:

Your race is heavenly,
So priceless and beautiful, as no word can describe.
Yet, you show not even human understanding,
But ignorance of the creatures below!

How dare you speak of me in such a manner!

Your Highness, I am speaking
Only of the one who has stolen my wife—

You ignorant fool—I am the one who stole your wife!

Papa said he loved *Mak Thoeung* for its poetry. But the real reason, I suspected, he cherished the story above all others was that its performance at a theater many years before had brought him and Mama together. They'd come separately to the theater to see the *lakhon,* but by some chance, they were seated next to each other and, during the performance, found themselves whispering back and forth the lines the various characters spoke or sang, behaving as if they'd known each other all their lives. While Mama was there with an aunt, her chaperone didn't discourage her from what would normally be considered highly inappropriate behavior for a young, unmarried woman. Instead the aunt pretended she didn't see or hear what was going on, knowing that the man sitting on the other side of Mama was none other than the Tiger Prince himself. If anything, she seemed to encourage the liaison, and when a year later Mama and Papa were married, the aunt claimed she'd brought the two together. Once when I asked Papa to clarify *which*—the story or the aunt—brought him and Mama together, he had responded, laughing, "Ah, Raami, the whole evening conspired to bring us together!"

Now I wondered if this night wasn't conspiring also in some way. I felt—even as I couldn't articulate it—this music, emerging through a husband's grief for his dead wife, seemed intended for my parents. As if by magic, the poetry they loved had found its way to them even in this dark hour.

I looked again across the school grounds toward the old musician. The next piece he played was so sorrowful I wanted to weep: the perfume seller and his wife are given the same punishment with the drum and, while carrying it to the faraway fields and back, they bare their souls to each other. I closed my eyes, hearing the lyrics in my head:

A flower of fallen petals cannot bloom again
Life once sprung forth is fated to pass away.

My life has ended for me already . . .

The music stopped. I opened my eyes and saw another shadow emerge in the doorway and hover over the old musician. It was his daughter. She bent down and tenderly touched her father's shoulder, her long hair spilling over him like silk. She said something, and I imagined her urging him to rest. He nodded and allowed himself to be led back into the room. My gaze came back to Papa and Mama.

They seemed unaware the music had stopped. They continued to sit there, holding each other's hands, ensconced in a sphere of light cast from the fire like an aura of protection. If I were Indra, I thought, I'd build them a world and keep them swathed in their solitary love.

Suddenly I remembered the dream I'd had before waking. Papa was a being much like that mythical Kinnara, at once human and divine, helpless and brave, who, unable to bear the pull of competing existences, impaled himself against lightning and fell to the ground. His wings severed and bleeding, he cowered in the rains, alone and unprotected. Having chosen a mortal life, he traded his immortality for a flash of hope in the darkness of night. The images circled my mind like strands of musical notes, and I knew then I hadn't woken all on my own. The bamboo flute had called out to me, drawn me to the door. There was no doubt in my mind now that the music was intended for *me*. It was trying to tell me something. A story I already knew.

A familiar refrain.

Just then the kettle gurgled and spewed steam through its spout. Surprised, Mama pulled her hands away and lifted it from the fire. She poured some water into the lid of the thermos beside her, handed the lid to Papa like a cup, and poured the rest of the water into the thermos to keep warm for later. Papa cupped the lid with his bandaged hand, breathing in the steam, as he waited for the water to cool.

Mama watched him and, after a moment, said, "It isn't too late. I can't let you believe that it is. The soldier's notebook could've gotten lost. We don't know with these soldiers—they may have not shown it to their superiors. It's all an act. You could invent another story. Give yourself a new name, a different identity." She tried to joke, "A perfume seller or *something*."

Papa remained silent, blowing on the water. He took a tentative sip and, looking at her, said, "You know, I am both the perfume seller and the prince." His hand holding the water shook. He stilled it with his other hand.

"No," she said, her voice taut with grief. "No, to me you are more. Always, you *strive* to be more. They must know this." A muffled sob. "They can't take you from me."

He put the thermos lid on the ground and, taking her hands in his, pressed them to his cheek. His body quaked and sobs escaped his throat. I suddenly recalled a photo on their bedside table back home in which they'd struck a similar pose: her hands in his, their foreheads touching. A wedding picture. For the longest time I had been jealous of it—the captured intimacy that, inside the glass frame, had seemed impenetrable—until one day Papa explained it was taken before I came along. *When it was just the two of us,* he'd said. That unsettled me even more, as I hadn't been able to imagine a time when it was just the two of them. But now I saw it. How it must have been when they were Ayuravann and Aana, not Papa and Mama, these two people whose togetherness had brought me.

"When they come," Papa said, looking into her eyes, "I ask that you let me go."

I should have recognized it right away, the bamboo flute's ghostly voice warning me in the dark, reminding me of the story's ending: back at the palace, the drum is opened and the little boy inside is revealed for all to see. He recounts every word he overheard, and the entire royal audience now knows the truth. The prince, angry, demands all must be killed and rushes toward the most frightened of them all, the young wife. But before he reaches her, she plunges her long hairpin deep into her chest, taking her own life. In the mayhem, the king, fearing a popular revolt, sees that everything must end here, once and for all. He orders the immediate execution of the perfume seller, the senior minister, and the little boy. Justice, as Papa had explained the tale's senseless conclusion to me, could be found inside that drum, but when we murder a child, we murder our own innocence.

"I ask that you give me your blessing," Papa sobbed.

My parents' love, it slowly dawned on me, this tenderness I now witnessed in the shadows, faced the threat of being stolen, and, despite my very grown-up desire to protect them, there was nothing I could do to prevent it, for outside their small sphere of light existed a greater incomprehensible darkness conspiring to tear them apart, and, like the little boy inside the drum, I would suffer their demise.

"If not that," Papa said, swallowing tears and sorrow, "then your forgiveness. I ask for your forgiveness."

Mama turned away from him, her face a full moon now, aglow and streaming tears. She saw me but did not attempt to hide her grief.

I went back inside and waited for the sun to rise.

The wind gave a long, drawn-out sigh, and from the giant banyan by the temple's entrance, a flock of birds flapped their wings, echoing the exhalation. A new day's radiance greeted us from every direction as we made our way across the temple grounds. Water lilies and lotuses threw splashes of color—yellow, pink, purple, indigo—across the verdant landscape. Gold and silver flashed off the roof of the prayer hall and the giant dome of the stupa, turning the temple into a miniature bejeweled kingdom. Above us the sky stretched high, blooming with thick white clouds, like a wide blue sea cradling floating gardenias. I marveled at how the sky imitated the earth and the earth imitated the sky. Pockets of rain dotted the ground, and each held in its reflection the possibility of another world much like the one welcoming us now.

We received greetings from those we passed: "Good morning, Highness! How are you? A day worth writing about, isn't it?" Papa nodded and smiled, acknowledging everyone, and by now everyone seemed to know who he was—a prince, a poet. *How could he change his name, his story?* The thought flitted through my mind, a night moth confused by the light and gaiety. I shooed it away. From the steps of the prayer hall an elderly woman remarked, "You make a handsome peasant, my young prince!" A gaggle of her toothless friends giggled coyly. Papa paused, bemused, then catching his reflection in one of the rain puddles—the rolled-up pants, the *kroma* around his waist, the buckets swinging on the bamboo yoke from his shoulder—threw his head back and laughed out loud. I recalled his quiet words—*I am both the perfume seller and the prince*—the desolation with which he'd uttered them hours earlier. Now he laughed, his happiness imitating the morning's brightness, renewing itself, as the day always seemed to renew itself.

We crossed the dirt road, on our way to collect drinking water from the town's well. But first we would pay a visit to the old sweeper and thank him for the eggs he'd brought us the night before. Papa led the way, whistling as he went, the buckets swinging from the bamboo pole on his shoulder squeaking companionably as he meandered around the rain-filled ruts that the wheels of the camions had gouged into the road. I followed at a leisurely pace, circling gaping tracts of water, jumping over smaller ones, leaping onto patches of grass, pausing now and then to observe the invisible gradually becoming visible.

On a bed of thorny weed, a spider peered from beneath her dew-glistened web, as if trying to decide whether to come out and search for food or stay in and cast her net from afar. Nearby, an unsuspecting praying mantis rocked on its hind legs on a long blade of grass, serene as a diver contemplating an early morning plunge into the cool sea. To my left, a dung beetle buzzed with the aplomb of a seaplane as it shook specks of clay and pollen off its wings. And directly beneath it, a pair of backswimmers scurried across a wide pool like circus acrobats daring each other to a magician's feat.

The ground was animated with these infinitesimal beings, and I remembered what Papa always said whenever we went out for a similar walk—"If you pay close enough attention, Raami, you'll realize that a single leaf can contain myriad lives imitating our own, and you'll know that there are always others traveling this world with you."

There was one now faithfully accompanying me—a dragonfly with yellow-and-black wings, the kind that came out after the rain. It flitted this way and that, sometimes leading me, sometimes trailing behind. Then as we neared the old sweeper's hut, it flew off, having seen me safely through my journey. *If you pay close enough attention,* I thought, *you know you're never alone. There's always someone or something guiding you. Tevodas,* it was clear to me now, were not celestial beings at all but earthly things, *beautiful* things I saw every day, and what made them beautiful was precisely that they were momentary, just a glimpse here and there before vanishing again.

I looked for the dragonfly but saw instead a butterfly with similar coloring—with black-and-yellow wings—flitting over Papa's head. Another god, another guise. Even the tiniest creature was capable of transformation.

At the old sweeper's hut only his hen greeted us, clucking in distress, scratching the dirt in a panicked search. Papa and I caught sight of the empty nest by the doorway. We looked at each other and shrugged, attempting to rid ourselves of guilt. The hen came near us, a gurgle of discontent escaping her throat, as if saying, *Your Highness, I'm speaking only of the one who's stolen my eggs!* I suppressed the urge to giggle. Papa tilted his head questioningly, not quite sure what was amusing me. I thought of telling him but didn't, afraid it would remind him of the sadness of the earlier hours. Instead I wondered aloud where our old friend had gone, and silently, apprehensively to myself, why everything was in such disarray, why the door of the sweeper's hut was left ajar and hanging askew on one unraveled rattan knot, as if something enormous had burst through. "Maybe it was a dragon tail," I offered, imagining that a *naga* serpent had risen out of the marsh during the night's storm and scoured the land, its tail whipping the air into a funnel that earned the monsoon whirlwind its funny nickname.

Papa made no reply. Instead he scanned the hut. The new coconut fronds he'd helped haul from the temple grounds one afternoon and put over the deteriorating thatched walls—in spite of the sweeper's insistence he was adequately sheltered—had not kept out the night's howling rain. Everything was drenched, a soggy mess, and there was this feeling of abrupt abandonment, as if the old sweeper had been sucked right out of bed by some force hurling through the front door.

"Maybe he's gone to find shelter in town," again I offered, more to calm my own worries than Papa's. Circling us, the hen gurgled indignantly, pulling her neck in and out, strutting with the air of one who'd been left high and dry: *You don't say, that old scoundrel ran off with my children! Still in their shells, I'll have you know.* She dipped her beak in a puddle and drank from it, throwing her head back every so often and gargling as if her throat was hoarse from having to explain her losses to a couple of two-legged carnivores.

Papa was oblivious to the hen's distress. His eyes lingered on the gaping doorway, then traveled slowly to the clay vat pressed against the front wall, under the lip of a bamboo trough. The vat was the only durable, solid form, while the old sweeper's few possessions—the soaked straw mat on the bamboo bed, a pair of frayed twig brooms nestling by the door, a threadbare shirt hanging on one wall, a discolored *kroma* on another— seemed on the verge of evaporating as their owner apparently had.

"He never spent the night here," Papa finally said as he walked over to the vat and, using his bandaged hand to lift the wooden cover, looked inside, his expression pensive as if working out some great mystery. "It's not full. You'd think he would've left it open to collect the rainwater." He turned to me. "I think our friend left before the storm came last night. Strange, though, that he went without saying good-bye to us first."

"Maybe when he brought the eggs, he came to say good-bye."

Papa attempted a smile, and as if to assuage his own worries, said, "He's probably out and about somewhere nearby."

"We can come back this afternoon."

"Yes, that's a good idea."

As we made our way along a dike toward the well, I scanned the area, hoping to catch a glimpse of the sweeper's curved silhouette gathering twigs under a tree or collecting wild herbs along a grassy patch among the rice paddies. But there was only the tattered frame of what looked like a scarecrow from last season in the cornfield to the right of us. I blinked, willing the scarecrow to straighten up and wave. If it did, it would confirm my suspicion that the old sweeper was a spirit of some sort, a *tevoda* in disguise. But it didn't move, not even when a flock of sparrows settled upon its stick arms, from which dangled strings of rusted cans. A breeze blew and the cans clattered, sending the sparrows fluttering like snippets of a lost lyric: *It's true mine is a life of poverty . . . my home a half-built thatched hut . . .* Papa said that some mornings he would wake up with his head full of words and images and the only way to still them was to write them down. It'd been like this for me since waking, my head full of half-remembered lines. *Its walls the winds and rains . . .*

"Well, did you ever finish it?" I asked, looking into the opaque water below, my chin resting on the edge of the well.

Papa didn't hear me. His head followed the flight of a hawk circling above us, its wings straight as metal.

"Did you finish that poem you were working on?" I asked again.

"Hmm . . . ," he replied, still watching the hawk.

"Is that yes or no?"

"Do you know why I write?" he murmured, smiling to himself.

"You can't answer a question with a question!"

He looked down into the well, and his blurred reflection said to mine, "I write because words give me wings."

"Wings?" I felt the palpitation of my heart but did not tell him about my dream.

"Yes, wings! So I can fly!" Laughing, he spread his arms and circled the well. "Be as free as that hawk!"

"You can't be a bird!" I shouted, my fear resurfacing. "You can't! Stop it!"

Papa stood still, surprised by the volume and harshness of my voice. He looked at me and then, as if coming to the same conclusion, said despondently, "Yes, you're right, of course. I can't be a bird." His gaze went back to the hawk, which was now circling the golden spire of the stupa. "'*Upadana dukkha,*' the Buddha told his disciples. 'Desire is suffering.'"

"What's desire?"

"To want something so bad your heart hurts."

"What's suffering?"

"When your heart hurts."

"Well, my heart hurts because I desire to go home."

Papa laughed, pulling me to him. He wrapped his arms around me, and they felt, I thought, as safe as a pair of wings. In the sky, the hawk circled the stupa a few more times before slipping into the white expanse.

Papa picked up a pail made from a carved-out palm trunk and

dropped it into the well, holding firmly on to the long bamboo pole fastened to its handle. He flicked the pole around until the pail began to submerge, filling up with water, like the funnel of a sinking ship. Then he pulled it back up and poured the water into one of our buckets, repeating the steps until both buckets were full.

We were ready to return to the temple. But instead of going back in the direction of the old sweeper's hut, we took a shortcut across a series of rice paddies that bordered the dirt road. Papa balanced himself on the narrow dikes, the bamboo yoke on his shoulder now bent like a large bow from the weight of the water, his body swaying left and right, his arms stretched out to steady the buckets so the water wouldn't spill. He looked more like a chicken trying to fly than a bird that could soar. I followed close behind, running, skipping, hopping, imagining the rice paddies a giant hopscotch board. Papa pointed out the different families of rice, reciting the names like a line from one of his poems. "Long grain short grain, fat grain sticky grain, grain that smells like the monsoon rains," I mimicked, singing it out loud.

"Sometimes when you look at the sky, you'll see *tevodas* bathing. The water falls to the earth and makes everything grow." He paused for breath, adjusting the bamboo yoke on his shoulder, and then moving again, said, "Yes, I did."

"Yes, you did *what?*"

"I finished the poem."

"I thought you never would!"

He laughed. "You have so little faith in me!"

"Hmm . . ."

He laughed again. "Do you want to hear it?"

"Of course!"

I kept pace with him, my steps following the rise and fall of his voice:

They say mine is a ravaged land,
Scarred and broken by hate—
On a path to self-extermination.

Yet no other place
So resembles my dream of heaven.
The lotus fields that cradle my home
Each flower a reincarnated spirit—
Or perhaps, like me,
A child who wishes to be reborn
Should dreams become possible again.

It's true mine is a life of poverty
My home a half-built thatched hut
Its walls the winds and rains.

"Yes," Papa admitted when I pressed him, "the poem is about the old sweeper. But, you see, it's also about Sambath. Myself. You, darling."

As he spoke, I turned and looked back at the abandoned, rain-soaked hut across the road. I realized with a start how the sparseness of one existence mirrored another, how an old man's poverty gave a glimpse of the hardship he must have endured when he was a boy, must have suffered his whole life, and that small, forgotten patch of ground, with its dilapidated hut and drenched belongings, held in its reflection the deprivation of Papa's childhood friend. It was clear the old sweeper was a version of Sambath, and just as I saw a manifestation of my father in everything that was noble and good, *he* saw a manifestation of his friend everywhere, in every poverty-stricken person he met, and tried to do for each what he hadn't been able to do for his friend.

"We are all echoes of one another, Raami."

twelve

It happened in half a breath. One moment he was alive and the next still, his silhouette faint on the straw mat, more like an incomplete thought, a tracery, than an actual person. It seemed no one expected him to die. It was just a fever, everyone said. He should've gotten over it. But I'd known since that day Mr. Virak arrived at the temple and I first laid eyes on the delicate form beneath the folds of his wife's *kroma*, like a partially unwrapped parcel, their baby was more spirit than flesh. And like all spirits, he belonged not entirely to our world. "The gods have reclaimed him, Raami," Grandmother Queen said of his departure. She was adjusting well to the change, never complaining about the diminishing food or the hard floor we had to sleep on. Once in a while she would ask for Om Bao or Old Boy, but when we explained that they were not with us, she would nod, as if suddenly remembering. Then her expression would become vague again and, as usual, her mind would wander to the otherworld. "In the blink of an eye," she whispered in my ear now, "in half a breath, he went, surprising even himself."

I wasn't sure if this was possible, but it did look that way—his tiny mouth still agape, his eyes refusing to close even after the adults' repeated attempts to shut them. Looking at him now, I couldn't help but think that maybe he wasn't ready, that, although infantile and knowing nothing of the world or himself, he was shocked by the swiftness of his own death.

I tried to imagine how that would feel, to die swallowing air, instead of letting it go. "He looks like he's yawning," I whispered, leaning into Grandmother Queen. "It must be horrible to choke forever."

"He'll be spared from a lifetime of sorrow and regrets." She nodded and kept nodding. "Yes, a lifetime of sorrow and regrets . . ."

She was the only person among the grown-ups not shocked by this sudden loss. Instead she observed it with the impartial gaze of one preparing for her own departure.

From her corner, Tata watched the whole scene with wide-eyed dismay, as if death, like a stranger uprooted and misplaced, had appeared out of nowhere and taken up residence with us, competing for its shared space in this refuge already haunted by so many ghosts. "This can't be real," she murmured to herself. "I can't be here."

A crowd had gathered. Mr. Virak crouched in the back corner of his room, his head in his arms, his body curled into a ball. Papa and Big Uncle had tried to take him outside, get him away from the screams of his wife, the stillness of his dead child, but he rejected them, with a silence so resolute that it now hardened him in his corner like an immovable boulder. He wanted to speak to no one. No one could possibly understand his grief. I wanted to tell him I understood. Not his grief, but the cruelty of the gods. How could they give a gift they themselves couldn't bear to part with?

There was a stir from the crowd near the doorway. The musician, dressed in black pants and the white shirt of an *achar,* came into the room holding not his bamboo flute but three sticks of incense and a large bronze bowl filled with water and lotus petals.

"It's time, my dear," he said, kneeling down on the mat beside Mr. Virak's wife. "It's time to let him go."

As one familiar with all the rituals of death, he would be the funerary *achar.* He would give the baby the ceremony he hadn't been able to hold for his own wife when she died on the road. "We must free our ghosts," he murmured softly, more to himself, to the ghost of his wife sitting beside him, perhaps. "May you find peace in your journey." He then turned toward the doorway, nodding at Papa and Big Uncle.

They came in, carrying a coffin, so small it looked like a desk drawer.

The crowd moaned, letting escape what the baby had swallowed in half a breath.

His was my first funeral. The elderly women washed and dressed him, wrapped his tiny body in one of Mr. Virak's white dress shirts, which, in the absence of a proper cotton sheet, served as the baby's funerary shroud. The women combed his hair, wetting it with water from the bronze bowl the musician had brought in, rewetting it several times more so the downy tufts would stay in place. But at the crest where two topknots whorled like a pair of snails, the strands kept springing up like young rice shoots. How strange, I thought, that his hair seemed the only part of him still alive, still fighting to live. Stranger still that a person's breath, indiscernible and weightless, should wield such influence over the body, that it had made the baby shake his legs and his arms in delight at the sight of his mother's face, and that without it, he should lie unaffected by her immense grief, rigid in his breathlessness, eyes staring past this world to another.

When the women finished preparing him, they gave the tiny white bundle to Mr. Virak. He cradled the corpse and, sprinkling it with water from the bronze bowl in a symbolic ablution, murmured, "I, your father, who have loved you in this life, cleanse you of your karma, release you from your suffering, so that you may be free to choose your own path." He handed the baby to his wife and she repeated his gesture and words.

Tears welled up in my eyes, and I remembered Om Bao, how I'd wondered what it was like to mourn her absence, what mourning was. A lifetime of sorrow and regrets, expressed in this single moment, in a mother's hiccupping sob that echoed her child's dying breath.

The musician took the baby from Mr. Virak's wife and placed him in the makeshift coffin, fashioned out of the wood from a desk found among the piles at the back of the temple. He closed the lid. I saw the words scratched on top in a child's handwriting: *Knowing comes from learning, finding from seeking.*

What was left to find? Everything was lost in that coffin. I began to feel anger at the gods for grabbing the smallest person they could find and claiming him as theirs. Who said they alone had the right to love a child? Who said they alone could love? Even a person as small as Radana could love another. She blew kisses at the coffin as it was being carried from the room, wondering, "Baby? Mama, baby?" Mama, nodding, replied, "Yes, darling. Baby's sleeping. Say goodnight to baby." She held Radana tighter in her arms, as if to say no gods or ghosts, however powerful, could ever match a mother's fierce attachment to her young.

Outside, a mound of twigs and palm fronds was set up in the middle of the school grounds. It was an unusual spot for a funeral pyre but, earlier, from his depth of silence, Mr. Virak had emerged and voiced this one request—that the corpse of his baby be immolated here—as if by witnessing it burn in front of him, in the very place where his child had lived, he would finally be convinced of the baby's death.

A monk who could no longer be a monk presided over the funeral. I remembered he'd arrived that same day with Mr. Virak, and how the others had moved around him with deference, how the elders had called him "Wise Teacher," even though he looked to be no more than thirty. He wore now what he'd worn the day of his arrival—a shirt and a pair of trousers, layman's attire—and his once smoothly shaven head bristled with new growth. Without his saffron robe he seemed naked, vulnerable, stripped of the invincibility I'd always thought monks possessed.

"Even as a lotus, endowed with beauty, fragrance, and color must fade," he intoned, his left arm cradling the bronze bowl the musician had given him, his right hand stirring the water with a sprig of jasmine blossoms, "so must our body wither away, become nothing." He sprinkled the water on the small coffin. "*Anicca vatta sankhara;* impermanence is the condition of all sentient existences. Nothing stays, nothing lasts, and we who cling and desire, we are caught in an endless cycle of births and rebirths, in the wheel of samsara." He circled the funeral pyre, sprinkling water on the closed coffin, the ground around it, the bowed heads of mourners gathered in small clusters around him. "*Cattari ariya saccani . . .*" His voice took on the resonance of a hundred monks chanting.

When he came to the grieving parents, he hesitated, the corner of his lips quivering, as if unsure what to say. Then he did something unusual, forbidden of a monk—he reached out and touched his worshipper. "Your grief will fade," he said, his hand on Mr. Virak's shoulder, speaking to him not as a monk but as a sharer of this sorrow. "It's hard to believe this now, my friend"—his steady gaze held Mr. Virak's glistened one—"but it will wither and, like a flower, leave behind always a seed of possibility."

He gave a slight nod to the musician, who with a lighter from his pocket knelt down and lit the funeral pyre. The desk-coffin, with the baby inside, burst into flame. Mr. Virak and his wife fell to the ground, weeping over the hopscotch board, one silently, the other loudly. A chorus of mourners joined them. An endless lullaby of tears.

The funeral fire was still burning when a group of Revolutionary soldiers came and called an evening meeting. Some of the children asked me to play hopscotch with them, but there was no room to play. The funeral mound had covered up the hopscotch board. Embers glowed and sparks flew about in the air, like fireflies gathered to mourn as we did. Only the Revolutionary soldiers seemed enthusiastic, fervent. "The Organization knows who you are! Who did what, who was rich and who was poor, who lived in a villa and who lived on the street, who is Cambodian and who is a foreign spy! The Organization has eyes and ears like a pineapple! There's no reason to lie, to hide! You must come out! Reveal yourself!"

The Organization was blind, I thought. Deaf even. He threatened and commanded, sent his shadows to enthuse and proclaim when he ought to tell them to weep and mourn, or, at the very least, be silent. Did he not know this was a funeral?

"Give yourself to the Revolution! Army officers, engineers, doctors, and diplomats! Those who held positions of any kind in the old regime! Come forward!"

Only the voices of ghosts were more ubiquitous, insistent. I heard them commiserating all around me. They must have come out of the *cheddays*. I looked up at the stupa, its long golden spire that in the porous light of dusk resembled a fishing rod dropped from the sky. *We got an-*

other one! Is it a fish? A tadpole? No, a seed. A seed of possibility . . . They sang and chanted, welcoming the baby back to their world. *We, who mistakenly gave you away, now reclaim you as one of our own.*

"You must come forward! You must give yourselves to the country! To the glorious cause of the Revolution! Come forward!"

No one went. A baby had died. It was enough leaving for one day.

"Look, Raami," Papa said, pointing at the moon high above us. "It's the second moon of the Lunar New Year." He counted the dates on his fingers. "And a full one, no less. No wonder it's so bright. Indeed, the Tiger must retreat and make way for the Rabbit."

We'd come out to sit on the exposed roots of the banyan in front of our room, and even though it was late, the night was luminous, as if in mourning it had abandoned its habitual black and swathed itself in funerary white.

"It wasn't full last night," I mumbled, feeling listless and hollowed, like I'd been on a long walk to nowhere. Inside, everyone had collapsed in exhaustion and numbness. "Is it even the same moon?"

Of course it was. I knew this, but it didn't seem right to say what I really thought—that the night was awash with light not from the moon alone but also from the funeral pyre, which had settled now into an ashen glow, as if a star had fallen and landed in the middle of the school grounds, incinerating everything in its path. The air, tinged with an acrid odor, reminded me of one time in Phnom Penh when a *chieeng chock* lizard had fallen from the wall of the cooking pavilion into Om Bao's earthen brazier, scorching in flames, and for a whole day I hadn't been able to eat because everything had smelled of charred flesh.

"Doesn't seem like it, does it?" Papa murmured, his eyes still on the moon. "Things are moving so fast, Raami, it hardly seems like the same day, the same world we woke up to."

Yes, it was hard to believe that only a single day had passed since we last looked at the moon, when it played hide-and-seek with us as Papa told me the story of his friend Sambath, and in that short span a child had lived and died, his death more felt than his life. I marveled at how so little a person could leave a void so huge as to make it seem like whole weeks had been sucked away, burned to cinder inside that coffin.

"But yes, it is the same moon," Papa continued, his voice as distant as that bright white countenance staring down at us. "Always, from wherever we look, it's the same moon." He paused, swallowing. "You know, I was born in the Year of the Tiger, 1938. Now I'm thirty-seven—an old man to you, I'm sure!" He let out a soft chuckle. Then, turning to face me, he said, "In one of his countless reincarnations, the Buddha was Tunsai Bodhisat—a bodhisattva, an enlightened being, in the guise of a little rabbit."

A rabbit Buddha?

"One night during the full moon"—Papa's voice wove a wispy trail around my head, the contour of another tale—"Indra decided to transform himself into an old Brahmin and test Tunsai Bodhisat for his kindness to determine whether the rabbit would merit a better rebirth. I'm so hungry, little one, he said to the rabbit. Would you not offer yourself as food to me? Tunsai Bodhisat, filled with compassion for this emaciated ascetic, agreed. He built a fire, shook his body free of all the tiny fleas and insects that clung to his fur, and jumped into the roaring flames. But just as he did so, Indra rushed to save him, seizing his spirit, and flew him off to the moon, where he carved a figure of Tunsai Bodhisat on its luminous surface. Henceforth, Indra told the rabbit, the world shall know of your kind deed."

Papa smiled and lifted his gaze to the sky again. "That's why, Raami, when we look at the full moon, we see a rabbit!"

I searched now for the filmy rabbit-shaped etching Milk Mother had taught me to decipher in that orb of light. She had her own story, though, for why the rabbit was there, why it always looked like he was bending over a fire, tending it. He's the keeper of the Eternal Flame, she told me. Now I wondered if the rabbit wasn't tending his own funeral fire.

"When the sky is dark, when all around us is black and hopeless, the moon is our only light," said Papa, cutting into my thoughts. "I should like to go to the moon. Raami . . ." He lowered his gaze to me, his lips parted as if he was about to say more.

I waited. He blinked and turned away. I kept quiet, sensing what he couldn't explain—that death is a passing, a journey from here to there, and sometimes it can lead us to a better place. The baby's body may have been eaten away by flames but his spirit had gone to the moon, and there, high in the sky, he would be out of harm's reach. Papa needed not explain everything to me. Some things are obvious, like wanting to escape, to be free of pain and sorrow. I wished him to know this, to know that I understood.

"Me too," I said. "I should also like to go to the moon."

But my unease remained. Something was not right. When I looked up at the sky again, I realized I couldn't see what Papa wanted me to see. I was no poet. I didn't have his vision to divine in the illuminated sphere of the full moon a metaphor for hope. I saw instead a huge, gaping hole in the sky into which he might disappear.

The moon came and went, but we remained where we were, bound to this enclave of the disappeared. I began to cling to Papa, terrified that somewhere glowered an untrusting Indra, who would indiscriminately pick him from a crowd and put him through some vague trial, which would inevitably result in me losing him. I'd trail his every step and watch his every move, wary of those who might be sent to whisk him away. When he got up to go anywhere, I'd rush to accompany him, often clutching his hand so tight he winced, perhaps regretting he'd told me too much too soon, or perhaps too little too late. One day when I accompanied him to town, we learned that the old sweeper, along with a truckload of Rolork Meas's more affluent residents—landowners, former town officials and bureaucrats, petty merchants—had been relocated to another place. Where exactly our friend was relocated to, or why—since he obviously did not belong in any of these categories—no one knew for certain, and none of the townsfolk were willing to say out loud what they felt or knew. Perhaps they were afraid the same fate would befall them. We could only speculate. When Papa tried to find out more from the Revolutionary soldiers doing rounds at the temple, one of them told him matter-of-factly, "If you're too rooted, you must be yanked out and planted elsewhere."

Rooted, yanked, planted. My head was filled with such words. Spoken as they were, they rang with concealed rancor and venom. Even as a seven-year-old child, I recognized a tenor of the absolute: you're either for or against the Revolution. There was to be no ambiguity, no middle ground. The old sweeper had too many "bad" connections—the town, the temple, the monks, and now us—therefore he couldn't be trusted. "Weeds must be uprooted before they multiply!" said the soldiers, and as if to reinforce their militant counterparts, the Kamaphibal would further intone, in the same calm manners and voices with which they'd greeted us at the beginning, "Brothers and sisters, comrades, together we must forge a new political consciousness. We must let go of our old habits and desires, make personal sacrifices for the greater good . . ."

Listening to them, seeing how they moved and carried themselves, you'd have to wonder if they had been young Buddhist novices in their earlier incarnations. If, like the old sweeper, they'd spent part of their adolescence sweeping the grounds of temples, while learning to read and write through the recitation of Buddhist principles: *Life is filled with suffering, the cause of suffering is desire, but we can end suffering, and we do so by choosing the right path . . .*

"The glorious path of the Revolution is not without obstacles," the bespectacled cadre asserted, standing once again in the middle of the school grounds outside the classrooms, flanked on either side by an older-looking member of the Kamaphibal. There were just the three of them this time, and it occurred to me that the young owlish cadre wasn't the leader of the clique, or even its spokesman, as we'd all assumed, but an apprentice. His elders were testing him out by letting him lead, in the same way senior monks would try out a novice, test his readiness to carry on their work by putting his knowledge of the sacred text to use.

"We've traversed jungles," he sermonized, "crossed rivers and mountains, and braved one battlefield after another to arrive at your doorsteps."

Something about him reminded me of Papa. A poet's sincerity

perhaps, a respect for words, as if each one had weight and value beyond the sound it made. He spoke solemnly, carefully. "Now we need you to help construct a new world. A Cambodia that is democratic, prosperous, and *just*."

His audience was unmoved; their tired faces stared back with indifference. They reminded me of worshippers who grew weary when a Buddhist sermon had gone on far too long, become too repetitious. Still, no one dared walk away from the meeting, which was being called more regularly now, every other evening around the same time, when the heat of day subsided, when the women were busy preparing meals for their families and only the men were free to attend. Perhaps this was the Kamaphibal's intention all along—to get to the men first. I would always follow Papa to these meetings, holding tight to his hand, sitting on his lap, or sometimes falling asleep in his arms when the speech droned on.

This evening, though, Mama had ordered me to stay in our room and keep an eye on Radana and the twins while she prepared our dinner. I watched and listened from a safe distance, my chin resting on the window ledge. Outside Mama and Auntie India chopped vegetables and set the rice to cook, looking up occasionally at Papa and Big Uncle standing several yards away, among a small group of men gathered outside the bigger circle around the Kamaphibal. Papa, his head bowed, his arms crossed over his chest, seemed the only one listening to their speech. He appeared unusually attentive. Beside him, Big Uncle kept rolling his shoulders as if to release some tension, stealing glances at his older brother, looking more anxious about Papa's contemplative silence than about the Kamaphibal's presence, their oddly familiar but impenetrable rhetoric.

"Comrades, you've only to look at the suffering around you to know you are needed. You must rise, offer your education and skills."

This seemed to resonate and the crowd stirred. Vacant stares flashed with understanding, heads reluctantly nodded in agreement.

The two elder members of the Kamaphibal noticed and, taking advantage of the opportunity, one of them pulled something out of his shirt pocket—a page from a notebook folded into four, the perforated edge frayed like lace trimming. He unfolded the paper and began to call out names. A long list of names: *Vong Chantha, Kong Virak, Im Bunleng, Sok Sonath, Chan Kosal* . . . I thought I heard our name, but I couldn't be sure. Maybe it was Sinn Sowath, which would be another name, another family entirely. So many Khmer names sound alike, Seysarith, Sireyrath, Sim Sowath.

. . . *Pen Sokha, Keo Samon, Rath Raksmei.*

The list ended. The senior cadre folded the paper along its original creases and put it back in his shirt pocket. He narrowed his eyes, searching among the faces staring back at him, like a magician looking for volunteers from an unwilling audience. No one moved, no one breathed. Even the sky seemed frozen above our heads, a still, white tableau. The senior cadre stepped forward, his feet pounding the ground. If no one was willing, he seemed to be saying, then *he* would decide. He would make a proffering, choose a sacrifice. Looking at the list again, he called out, "His Highness Sisowath Ayuravann. A prince—a prince and a poet."

Something crashed. My eyes shot in the direction of the sound. It was Mama—she had dropped the rice pot; uncooked white grains littered the ground like ants' eggs. My gaze shot back to Papa. He did not look up, or even stir, but remained as he was, head bowed and arms crossed, his every muscle still. Beside him, Big Uncle turned toward us with a look of stunned terror.

"We're honored to count you among us, *Votre Altesse,*" the senior cadre enthused. "You'll be an example to others. Please, come forward, *Altesse.*" He waited.

Still, not a leaf moved.

"Comrade Ayuravann, we know you are here. Please identify yourself."

Back in our room panic ensued. "It's a trick," Big Uncle rattled. "They pretend they know you're here to draw you out; if they really knew, they would've handpicked you from the crowd, they only have a piece of paper to go by, they don't really know you're here. It's a trick, you must wait, listen to me, Ayuravann, don't go, don't reveal yourself. They don't

---

know what you look like. You can vanish—be invisible. It isn't too late. *Please*—" He ran out of breath.

Papa said nothing, his eyes fixed on me and only me, his hands clasped and pressed against his stomach as if to cushion the fragile calm he tried to pass on to me amidst the fear and frenzy around us.

"You can't go," Mama declared, putting herself in front of him, forcing him to look at her. "I won't let you. Arun is right—it's not too late. I won't let you think so." She shook.

Papa couldn't comfort her. He remained where he was, his gaze still fixed on me as if all he could do at the moment was to make sure I saw him, right there in front of me, and that I knew all would be fine, that nothing was going to happen.

"You ought to run," Tata offered, hysterical. "But where would you go? There's a trap everywhere. They've trapped us like animals."

Papa remained silent and his silence was like a hundred voices whispering a hundred stories. I didn't know which I ought to listen to—to believe.

"Do you know why I told you stories, Raami?" he asked. We'd left the others, their panic and fears, and hid ourselves in the solitude of the meditation pavilion.

I shook my head. I knew nothing, understood nothing.

"When I thought you couldn't walk, I wanted to make sure you could fly." His voice was calm, soothing, as if it were just another evening, another conversation. "I told you stories to give you wings, Raami, so that you would never be trapped by anything—your name, your title, the limits of your body, this world's suffering." He glanced up at the face of the wooden Buddha in its corner of the room and, as if conceding to some argument they'd had earlier, murmured, "Yes, it's true, everywhere you look there is suffering—an old man has disappeared, a baby died and his coffin is a desk, we live in the classrooms haunted by ghosts, this sacred ground is stained with the blood of murdered monks." He swallowed, then, cupping my face in his hands, continued, "My greatest desire, Raami, is to see you live. If I must suffer so that you can live, then

I will gladly give up my life for you, just as I once gave up everything to see you walk."

I shook my head. I could not accept it—this senseless and cruel barter of one life for another. My outlook was simple—he was my father, I, his daughter; we belonged together. I could not fathom my existence without his. I wanted to tell him, but I couldn't find the words, I didn't know how. Again, I shook my head. *No.*

His whole face trembled, a still pond disturbed, rippling with agony, anguish. "I'm telling you this now—this story, for it is a story—so that you will live. When I lie buried beneath this earth, you will fly. For me, Raami. For your papa, you will *soar.*"

I didn't respond. I wanted him to stop talking. Whatever it was he was trying to tell me, it sounded like a good-bye.

He pulled back, inhaling. "I know you don't understand, but one day you will."

A stream of tears slipped from the inner corner of his right eye and trickled down the curve of his nose, caressing it, lingering at the flare of his nostril.

"Forgive me when you do. Forgive me that I will not be here to see you grow up—"

He couldn't say more; instead broke down in a sob, his face buried in his hands. A hundred *tevodas* joined him, their cries sounding like a flock of birds taking to the air, their wings beating across the dusky sky.

thirteen

"You must sacrifice for the Revolution!" the senior cadre thundered, smashing his fist against his palm, the veins in his neck bulging, his every word and movement exaggerated beneath the orange flames from the torches held high by the Revolutionary soldiers pacing the grounds. It was clear now that this senior cadre—the same one who'd read the list of names—was the leader of the Kamaphibal. "All your comrades here, including myself, have given up our families and homes in order to build Democratic Kampuchea!"

I couldn't tell how big a group they were, but there seemed to be hundreds of them now in this flickering, wavering light, their silhouettes like a series of paper cutouts, one a duplicate of another, strung together apparently by some silent vow of solidarity, some predesigned uniformity. The young apprentice cadre, with his glasses and a poet's solemnity, was the only incongruity, standing now to the side as if demoted from his place in the center for having failed in his duty to persuade and garner a following.

"You're not the only ones who have lost those you loved," the Kamaphibal leader continued. "We too have lost and suffered much. But our losses and suffering have liberated you and this country from the injustices of the old regime. Now you must join us in the fight! Come forward before it's too late! Before another child dies in your arms!"

He meant Mr. Virak's baby. I didn't think it was right to mention the dead baby in front of his parents, to use his name to get people to join the Revolution. As if recruiting living people wasn't enough, they had to recruit a dead child as well, use his death to stir the sadness of his parents.

"Those of you whose names were called, you'll be given a chance to reveal yourselves of your own accord. If you choose still to hide, or to run, we cannot guarantee your safety, or your family's." He paused, letting the words sink in. "Come forward, comrades. Now it's *your* choice."

There was a long silence. Finally, a man raised his hand. I saw the rolled-up sleeve of his white mourning shirt. Mr. Virak. The Kamaphibal clapped. *Kong Virak*. His name had been second on the list. He must've given it to the soldiers. How else would they know? Since the baby died, he hadn't been himself, and now just as everyone feared, he unthinkingly raised his hand. Next to him another arm went up, or maybe not. Maybe it was only a shadow of Mr. Virak's arm. Again, the Kamaphibal clapped. There were shadows everywhere. I couldn't be sure who was who or how many people had raised their hands. Mr. Virak stood up and revealed himself like a target.

Back in their room, Mr. Virak's wife cried. She begged him to explain his decision. He said he couldn't stay here. He couldn't stay with her. They had nothing between them now except sadness and tears and memories. He pierced her body with words that ripped holes and wounded like bullets. His anguish drove her wild. She ran into our room, crying, "Please talk to him!" She pulled on Papa's sleeve. "Talk to him!" Mama walked up to her and slapped her across the face. "Be quiet!" she ordered. "I can't hear myself think." Mr. Virak's wife fell to the floor in stifled sobs. Turning to Papa, Mama demanded, "*Why?* Tell me why you're giving up. There's still another way—an exit."

I didn't understand. What had he done now? Then it dawned on me—Papa had sat beside Mr. Virak. He'd raised his hand.

"There's a way out of this, don't you see?" Mama cried.

Papa took her hands and clasped them in his. He looked at her as if they were alone in the room, as if this were a private moment just between them. Then he spoke. "I know I've not always been present when you need me." He held her still, pulling her to him now, her arms trapped between his chest and hers. "Often, I lose myself in the constellation of my own ideas, forever searching for points of illumination. But no matter where I look, I find you, shining and bright, offering me whatever it is I seek. You are my one single star. My sun, my moon, my guide and direction. I know as long as I have you, I'll never lose my way. Even if I cannot touch you, I know I will see you, feel you, from anywhere. If I need you, I know where to find you." He brought her hand to his heart. "Here—you are always here."

Mama pulled away and ran out of the room, her long hair soaked with tears. Papa stood there, trembling, looking at me.

When I lie buried beneath this earth, you will fly . . .

I should have understood. Even now, he didn't attempt to hide his sadness or fear from me. He stood there swaying slightly, hand clutching his chest, lips parted, as if wanting to explain all that he knew, only to hold his tongue in the realization that no words or story could ever prepare me for his departure, elucidate his broken heart.

I know you don't understand, but one day you will. Forgive me when you do. Forgive me that I will not be here to see you grow up.

I didn't know that day would come so soon. That it was now. I understood, but I could not do a single thing. I could comfort neither him nor myself.

Getting his bearings, Papa turned to the others and explained what he'd already revealed to Big Uncle the other night—that he'd disconnected himself from the family and rewritten our story. "Look after them," he said to Big Uncle. "My children are yours." Big Uncle opened his mouth to protest, but seeing the look in Papa's eyes, he lowered his head in helplessness.

I didn't know so much sadness could exist in so small a place.

Mama slept with her back to us, hugging Radana to her chest. Tears had drained her, hardened her body like a board. Beside her, Papa lay so still that for a moment I'd thought he too had fallen asleep. But now

I saw that his eyes were moving, following the leaps of a small *chieeng chock* lizard on the ceiling. I didn't know why, but the lizard made me think of the baby. Maybe because of its smallness, the way it made that *tsssk tsssk* sound with its tongue, as the baby had done when he got ready to sneeze. I wondered if the baby had come back, reincarnated as this tiny lizard, its limbs trembling with the desire to live as it scaled the ceiling and walls looking for food, playing with the sphere of light cast by the kerosene lantern. Round and round it went. A thought slowly took root in my head. It had the feel and shape of a bird's flight, weightless and elliptical. It circled my consciousness like the hawk we'd seen circling the stupa a few days earlier when we were at the well. Round and round it flew, carving a moon, full and bright. "Papa?" I whispered, cautious with my discovery. "Will—will your spirit go to the moon then?"

He seemed to still himself completely. Finally, he said, his voice quivering, "Yes . . ." He steadied and continued, "I will follow you, and you'll have only to look at the sky to find me, wherever you are."

"Papa?"

"Hmm?"

"I wish in your next life you'll be a bird so that you can fly away, so that you can escape when you need to, and come back when you want to."

Silence.

Then he pulled me closer, his lips on my forehead, his tears on my skin, warm and overflowing. I hugged him until I could no longer feel him, feel his heart breaking against mine.

That night I woke up in the middle of my dream. I saw Papa's lips on Mama's, their bodies wrapped around each other like two snakes. *I want to swallow you, to hold you . . . keep you forever to me.* They were feeding each other poison, I thought, but I couldn't stop them, I couldn't speak up. It was only a dream, I told myself. A dream. I closed my eyes and went back to sleep. Sometime later I heard the sound of paper being ripped, slowly, cautiously. I opened my eyes and saw Papa bent over his pocket notebook by the doorway, in the partial light cast by the stars in the night sky. He was writing, or perhaps folding the torn page, I couldn't tell. Sleep was stronger than curiosity, locking me in its embrace, and I fell back into oblivion.

When I woke again, it was morning. Papa wasn't beside me on the mat. I ran outside to look for him. At the gate of the temple, a group of Revolutionary soldiers stood guarding a row of men—Mr. Virak, the musician, the monk, and others whose faces I knew—as they climbed into an oxcart loaded with belongings. Papa stood beside it, getting ready to board as well. I pushed through the crowds and found my way to him. "I've changed my mind," I blurted out, my arms around his waist, pulling him away from the oxcart. "I don't want you to go to the moon."

"Raami," he said, kneeling on one knee. "Listen to me, darling. I never lied to you. I will not lie to you now. I know you are only a child, but I have no time for you to become an adult. It's too late for me." He paused, looking at the ground. "Even when my heart hurts, I must go. I . . . I wish I could make you understand."

"But you're my papa," I cried, unable to say what I felt, what I understood—that in a world where everything real could disappear without a trace, where one's home and garden and city could evaporate like mists in a single morning, he was my one constancy. That he was my father and I his child, that he had incarnated first, from whatever previous existence he had lived, to lead the way, to love and care for me, was proof enough of some logic in this universe. The rest, however senseless and confounding, was allowable, even pardonable. But now I was to be without him? My eyes flitted from one soldier to the next, searching for one who would understand, who would know how I felt, but none glanced our way. I turned back to Papa and demanded, "Tell them you're my papa!"

He did not respond, his face still lowered, his eyes hidden from me.

"Tell them! You're my papa—I want you here! *Tell them.*"

He looked up, his eyes brimming with monsoon rains, like the inundated rice paddies surrounding the temple. He dared not blink or say more. I had never seen him so sad, but I couldn't comfort him. I felt only my own sorrow. I thought only of myself. "Take me with you then," I pleaded.

"Raami, my temple——," he started to say, but stopped, his voice choked.

"If you leave me here," I reasoned, "I will suffer, my heart will hurt." Yet I couldn't imagine my heart hurting more than it did now. Still, I tried to hang on. "Don't go yet—I want to hear another story. Tell me a story!"

He flinched and turned away, his whole body shaking.

"Please—one last story. *Please, Papa.*"

I seized the fire of grief and flung it in every direction, at every person who came near me. I refused to speak to Big Uncle because it was he who had held me in place that morning when I tried to run after Papa as the caravan of oxcarts started to move away from the temple. Mr. Virak's wife had done just that—she ran and pleaded with a young soldier who, whether out of pity or impatience, stopped the oxcart her husband was in and allowed her to join him. But not Big Uncle. His powerful embrace had borne me back to the classroom, undeterred by my tears and pleas, my kicking and screaming. *I want to go with Papa! Let me go! I hate you! I hate you—you big* yiak! Even as I bit and scratched him, he would not let me go. He'd only held me tighter. Now I resented his enormous presence, which, I felt, was somehow supposed to make up for Papa's absence. When the others—Tata, Auntie India, and Grandmother Queen—tried to comfort me, I turned my back to them, shrinking from their caresses and tender words, ignoring their shock and pain, unable to admit they might be reaching out to comfort themselves as much as me. I kicked and elbowed the twins when, wrestling on the floor, they rolled too close to me. I whacked Radana's arms when she extended them out in an offer of a hug. Only Mama left me alone, as if sensing that something ductile and tender had broken inside of me.

Words gave him wings, he had said. Not solace. *Wings.* These, I realized, he'd severed and handed to me so I could continue my flight.

Without Papa, I was suspended in numbness, drifting to and fro, as if this sorrow, which was like no other I'd known, had weight and mass exceeding my body. It was a complete entity, a shadow-like presence that sat and walked beside me, assuming its place as my new and abiding companion.

I went on, anguishing against the inexplicable, the incomprehensible, while holding on to my father the only way I could—by believing that his spirit had soared to the sky, and there he resided, ethereal and elusive as the moonlight. Eternal, free. At last.

fourteen

The following weeks passed in a blur as the Kamaphibal fervently sought to destroy our old world in order to create a new one, as they sent soldiers to unmask people's backgrounds—their education, jobs, social milieu—and decided who was good and who was bad, who would merit induction and who elimination. I didn't understand the reason for all the coming and going, the endless summoning and separation. No one did. No one saw through the coded rhetoric of solidarity and brotherly love to a deeply indoctrinated belief that *anyone* could be an enemy. At first the enemy was the intellectuals, diplomats, doctors, pilots and engineers, policemen and military officers, those of rank and reputation. Then the enemy was the office clerks, technicians, palace servants, taxi drivers, people with *mok robar civilai*—"modern professions"—which would include almost everyone at the temple, as the majority of us were from the city. Those who didn't lie and assume a new identity were called and brought out into the open, like rabbits forced from their holes. Then their families were given the choice to either follow them or remain at the temple and wait for their return. But because it was never clear when that would be—this "return"—or what it meant in the first place to "join" the Revolution or to be "wanted" by the Organization, most families chose to go, believing that, whatever fate had in store for them, at least they would face it together.

As they left, others came, not just from Phnom Penh but from all over the country, sometimes in a convoy of trucks, sometimes in a caravan of oxcarts. Each time I'd rush from the room or wherever I happened to be hiding and elbow my way through the throngs, hoping I'd find Papa among the new arrivals. My heart would leap when I caught a glimpse of a shirt that looked like one of his, hair that greyed at the temples, shoulders that seemed capable of bearing the weight of a mountain. But it was never him. No one had news of him. No one cared. Everyone had their own losses to tend to.

As for the new arrivals, each group seemed more dispossessed and desperate than the last. Their ordeals seemed to have hardened them, clouded their vision, and numbed their sensibility so that sometimes they appeared not to know right from wrong. They pushed aside statues of gods and guardian spirits and laid claim to the prayer hall, the monks' sleeping quarters, the dharma pavilion, and even the heretofore unviolated sanctity of the meditation pavilion. No place was off-limits, no nook or niche sacred, left untouched by needs. Two families fought over the ground directly beneath the Walking Buddha near the entrance, each pushing for a share of the space, while the statue remained upright, staring peacefully ahead, indifferent to the squabble. Once a haven, the temple now looked like a dumping ground, littered with trash and tragedies. People exchanged personal stories of loss and death as they would food items and articles of clothing. *Our home was torched. My parents were old—the journey was too much for them* . . . One ordeal gave companionship to another, and in this way everyone accepted the fact that they were not alone, that this awfulness was universal, inescapable.

As for our family, we kept to ourselves. We never spoke of our loss to anyone. We had a sense—a need to believe—that Papa hadn't entirely disappeared. His presence, amorphous like water from a tipped glass, seeped into everything, into all we said and did, into our stillness and silence, our split and splintered selves. Big Uncle became almost like two people, one smiling and lighthearted when he was with the family, and another grave and introspective when thinking himself alone, unobserved. He would play with Radana and the twins, rousing them from sleep with tickles, letting them bounce on him among the pillows and blankets. He'd give them rides on his back until the sound of their laughter filled the room so that for a brief second or two I forgot where we were, thinking ourselves safely back home. He would joke during mealtimes about giving up coffee, abstaining from this or that food he knew we didn't have. Or he'd contemplate fasting a whole day at a time, like a monk would when taking on certain precepts. Once, feeling the overgrown thickness of his hair, he pondered out loud, "Do you know why monks and nuns shave their heads?" When no one responded, he went on obliquely, talking to himself, "If one begs the gods for a miracle, I was told, one should do so with naked humility. Stripped of any human pride. Vanity." He ran his hand through the disheveled mane. "Maybe I should shave my head. Offer my humility for his return."

Mama got up and left the room.

I glared at him. *What are you waiting for then? Do it!* I raged in silence. *Shave your head. Bring back Papa!* I didn't know if I was angry at him for his useless pondering or astounded by the absurdity of a god who could be so easily coaxed into returning my father with a simple offering of his brother's hair. Papa was worth more than that. Big Uncle, blinded by his sadness, could not see my anger.

"I should at least learn to pray," he concluded gravely, absentmindedly.

Auntie India, unconvinced of her husband's sudden piety, gazed at him with quiet alarm, as if she thought him crazy, behaving one moment like his usual self, the jocular jester, then another like Papa, the silent, solemn thinker.

Tata, at once severely pragmatic and childishly naïve, intervened. "It's not the gods you need to appeal to, Arun. Talk to the Kamaphibal. Explain who we really are. Maybe we could still join him."

In her corner, Grandmother Queen, who had been observing this whole exchange, let out a rueful sigh and murmured, "The worst irony of motherhood is when you outlive your children." Then, just as suddenly, her expression dulled once more, without a clue as to why. A funerary silence fell in the room.

Tears welled up in Big Uncle's eyes and he fought them down with a smile. Later, behind the school building, thinking himself alone, he cried into his hands, unaware that I was watching.

Gradually things seemed to get better, or at least settle down. A new group of Kamaphibal, drawn mostly from the local peasantry, emerged when the former went on to other areas to sniff out more educated people like themselves to "recruit" to the Revolution. A sense of order took shape as the local Kamaphibal began assigning families more permanent shelters: those who wished could now go live in town, either by sharing houses with the townsfolk or by occupying the ones emptied by recently deported local families. Priority was given to those camping on bare ground, or to those—it wasn't openly discussed but everyone knew—who had bribed well-connected residents. A hut was given to a family in exchange for a watch, or a wooden house for a traditional women's belt made of pure gold. The yellower the gold, the more coveted it was by the town's peasants and the bigger the house it would fetch. A rumor went around that one of the wives of the Kamaphibal was willing to give up the villa she had "inherited" from an exiled Chinese merchant in exchange for such a belt. When Tata heard this, she reminded Big Uncle that we had gold—plenty of it. Maybe we could barter a belt or two for more suitable shelter.

Big Uncle said we couldn't trust anything or anyone—a rumor or a local resident. We had only to look at the Kamaphibal, he pointed out, whose members were always changing. Nothing remained long enough for us to rely on. We might be given a house one moment, he reasoned, but deported the next. So, after much discussion, we agreed the best thing to do was to stay put and, above all, not draw attention to ourselves.

As for our claim to be mango growers, the soldiers never returned to pursue further interrogation. Whatever the reason, for now at least, the disguise worked, kept us safely stationed in our classroom, which, as Big Uncle explained, would cloister us better than a house in town, where we'd be under the constant watch of the Revolutionary soldiers and the Kamaphibal and their conspiring relatives.

But the real reason we stayed, I sensed, was simply that we couldn't bear to leave the place where Papa had last been, where the ground echoed with his footsteps, the trees heaved his sighs, and the pond mirrored his tranquility. Here, we could still be with him, and, as much as we wished to free his spirit, to let it travel the invisible universe and look for a new home, we were not ready to let go. We clung to it—the possibility that he existed among us, even as a ghost, even as an echo or shadow—because to let go was to relinquish our hope, to admit and submit to utter, irreversible despair.

So, even as more people were leaving to set up a new life in town, we continued to stay at the temple, and, instead of bartering for an unfamiliar, ghost-free shelter, we traded our gold for food. A necklace fetched us a pillowcase of rice to supplement the sporadic rations we received from the Organization via the Revolutionary soldiers or the Kamaphibal. A pair of earrings would get us a block of palm sugar that we'd use sparingly, as a special treat now and then for Grandmother Queen and the little ones. A bracelet bought a slab of beef that Mama and Auntie India salted and sun dried and portioned out to last us a whole week.

Everyone—no matter where he lived, at the temple or in town—was now expected to work. Big Uncle would leave every morning with a group of men to dig irrigation ditches and canals to channel water from the rain-flooded marsh to distant fields. Mama and Auntie India were assigned to gather rice shoots from nursery beds along riverbanks or on hills and bring them to the plowed paddies for the rice farmers to transplant. Tata, because Mama had convinced the Kamaphibal of her chronic poor health, and I, because of my polio, stayed behind to take care of Grandmother Queen, the twins, and Radana. I would've liked to get away from the temple, but this was our assigned work—to care for the aged and young—so others could do theirs. We each must contribute our worth to the Revolution, so said the Kamaphibal.

Work, the rhythm and routine of the day's labor, the physical exhaustion at night, kept us from disappearing completely into our private grief, and when the Revolutionary soldiers started to bring rice and food at more regular intervals, when the Kamaphibal began to relax their control and stopped asking who was who, when no truck or oxcart appeared to haul anyone away, hope began to emerge that perhaps the worst was over.

"Get your belongings! Out!" There were ten, twenty soldiers—maybe more. They stormed onto the temple grounds and ordered everyone outside. "You, you, and you over there!" They pointed with their guns as if selecting animals for shipment, separating large families into smaller ones. "Only immediate family members together! The rest divide up!" Big Uncle, shielded by a crowd, quickly gathered us around him. "We're *one* family—a single unit. All children of *Grandmother*." He fixed his gaze on me as if I alone held the key to our unity. "'Grandmother,' no more 'Queen,' understand?"

Yes, I understood. We were no longer who we were. How could we be?

A couple of soldiers broke through the crowd and headed straight for us. Mama grabbed Radana and held her tight. One of the soldiers pushed her aside and, in a single long stride, cut across to Grandmother Queen. He demanded her to identify only her *koan bongkaut*—children she'd given birth to. Grandmother Queen pointed to Tata and Big Uncle. Auntie India, seizing the twins, rushed to Big Uncle's side. "I'm his wife—the boys, our children." The three of them clung to Big Uncle like buckets to a bamboo yoke. Alone, Mama stood frozen in place, Radana pressed to her chest, a bundle of clothes on each shoulder.

The soldier pushed her and Radana to the left, Grandmother Queen and the others to the right. Panic and confusion ensued. Big Uncle tried to say we belonged in one family. The soldier swung his rifle like a bat and struck Big Uncle across the face. Big Uncle faltered, blood gushing down his nostrils, his nose broken perhaps. The crowd divided and all of a sudden I found myself in the middle of an aisle between two throbbing masses: on one side, Mama and Radana, just the two of them, desolation; on the other, Big Uncle and the rest of my family, safety in numbers at least. I could choose. *But which?* Tears stung my eyes, clouded my vision.

"Raami, come," Big Uncle whispered, one furtive hand out to me. I stared at it, wanting to be held now in his strong embrace. "*Come.*"

I turned the other way and saw Mama, her lips parted but unable to speak, to say my name, to make any claim whatsoever. I blinked.

She needed me, and I needed her. I flew to Mama.

Big Uncle closed his eyes at the same moment that Tata and Auntie India broke into sobs, while the twins looked on helplessly. Only when the Revolutionary soldiers pushed us toward the entrance did Grandmother Queen blink in realization of what she had done—by forgetting to claim us, she had, in essence, thrown us away.

A row of dust-covered army trucks lined the road, a convoy of metal carcasses. I spun around, suddenly regretting my choice, searching for an escape route, but before I could even take a step a throng came at us, pushing forward at the command of a soldier. I heard Big Uncle's voice above the crowds, "Raami, Raami!" I looked around, but I couldn't see him through the sea of arms and hips around me. There was only his voice, desperate, despairing. "Aana! Aana!"

Mama did not stop or turn back to look. She held my hand firmly and, with Radana on her hip, pulled me along.

"Oh, Aana, where are you?" again came Big Uncle's breathless voice.

Madness surrounded us on all sides. The only direction we could move was toward the exit. Our exile.

On the truck, I stood on tiptoes and searched the crowds, gripped by the feeling that I was leaving behind some essential, irrecoverable part of myself. I had believed we were led to sacred ground and thus would be protected, never suspecting heaven and hell could coexist in the same space. I lost my innocence, and with it the illusion that I was safe. Now there was no Big Uncle, no Grandmother Queen, no Tata, no Auntie India or the twins. There was no Papa. Whichever way I turned, I was faced with the same stark reality—my family was gone. Without my spirit, my *pralung*, my untainted hopefulness, I felt like a kite with its string severed, drifting, drifting.

As the truck began to move, I closed my eyes and let the world vanish in a single flutter. I couldn't bear its slow disappearance, so I obliterated it before it obliterated me. I shut out the noise and chaos, the presence of others around me. I became aware only of myself, the movements of my body—how it seemed to be operated by the same mechanism or wiring that propelled this metal clunker forward, as if we were both skeletons of our former selves, stripped of the padding and niceties that had cushioned us until now against unexpected leaps and shocks. When the truck stopped, I felt myself smacked against a rock. When it gunned forward, I hurled through the air, moving as fast as the wind.

It went on like this, my mind jerking to and fro, my body cresting the waves of nausea and numbness. Once in a long while I would open my eyes and search for Papa, for Big Uncle and the others, for their shadows and silhouettes among the human-shaped trees and hills, for the possibility of their existence somewhere in this world beside ours. Mama, cradling Radana on her lap, freed one arm and drew me to her, pressing my face into the softness between her arm and chest. She held me tight. I closed my eyes and sank deeper into the shadow that was all my own.

fifteen

The old couple smiled, exposing their dark-stained teeth. Their open, cheerful grins made their shaved heads—an expression of Buddhist piety common among Cambodian elders—appear disproportionately larger than their bodies, and their somber peasant clothes seemed incongruous with their lively moods and manners. They were inexplicably happy to see us, as if we were long-lost relatives and our much-anticipated arrival had somehow burst open a bubble of excitement. "You're here, you're here!" the wife exclaimed as she hurried toward us. Mama and I offered our *sampeah*. The wife turned to her husband and enthused, "Oh, they're lovely!"

She welcomed us to their home, their village. Stung Khae, she called it—"Moon River." My heart skipped a beat. Did Papa send us here? Did his spirit guide us to this place that bore the namesake of his reincarnation? To these people whose wrinkled, earthy appearance and sheltering happiness made me think they must have sprouted from the same seeds and soil as the trees around them? The husband did not speak but stood comfortable in his silence, one hand holding a whittling knife, the other fingering a piece of wood, as if trying to decipher through its grains and texture its predestined form. The wife couldn't stop talking. "You're the answer to my prayer! Oh, how I've dreamt and wished for you!"

She chewed and spat, red betel nut juice staining the corners of her mouth and the ground near her feet. "I've waited for you since my bosoms were round!"

The husband smiled, not at all embarrassed by his wife's candor, a small tobacco quid moving inside his left cheek, rolling languidly like a word, a sentiment waiting to be spoken aloud. His face, creased and parched, resembled a dried-up riverbed, yet he smelled like damp earth, fresh mud. He tucked his whittling knife and piece of wood in the folds of the *kroma* that belted his loose *achar* shirt and took the two bundles from the back of the oxcart that had brought us. The wife, noticing how dirty our bodies and belongings were, ventured, "Oh, Lord Buddha, the wind must've blown you here!" She dusted the dirt from my hair with a familiarity that made me long for Milk Mother. "You need a good wash!" Radana, waking up to the noise around her, rubbed her eyes and, after one look at the old couple, buried her face back in Mama's chest, whimpering, frightened by their appearance.

But I did not think them ugly. To me, they looked like old trees that walked and talked, their rustling, noisy presence a refuge, a kind of sheltering from the aloneness that had trailed and shadowed us all day.

At the sound of wheels turning, our eyes went to the soldier still perched on the cart. The husband finally spoke, at last coming out of his silence: "The rain will come." He looked up at the sky, and then at our driver. "Maybe you should wait until it passes."

"Yes, stay—you can eat with us!" the wife offered, as if finishing his thought.

The soldier took off his cap, acknowledging the invitation, but his hands lifting the reins told us he would not stay. He turned to me and, noticing the bamboo branch in my hand, gave me a hint of a smile. Then, with his cap back on and pulled down low over his forehead, he turned the cart around and headed back toward the dirt path, retracing the steps that had brought us here.

The first part of the trip had been a blank—a silent depth. I'd slept through it, pulled under by the tide of grief. When I woke again it was to the sound of people talking around me. It seemed our truck had left Prey

Veng and was now entering Kompong Cham. They looked the same, one province and the next. Forests surrounded us on all sides, impenetrable and infinite. It looked as if it would rain but didn't. The sky hung low and grey, heavy with heat and humidity, a silent, unrequited mourning. But far off in the distance, past a mountaintop, it was blue and brilliant. I couldn't tell if a sanctuary was waiting beneath the light, where we'd reunite with the others, or the edge of the world, an abyss.

Mama squeezed my hand, as if reminding me she was still right beside me. On her lap, Radana continued to sleep. We both kept our gazes on my sister, unable yet to face each other after that moment when she'd stood still and I was forced to choose.

Gradually, the forests thinned out. The trees along the road became less wild looking, recognizable again—eucalyptus, cassia, acacia—their leaves and barks Papa had taught me to distinguish during our various visits to the countryside. Here and there, under the shade of these roadside trees, stood open-air huts built for travelers to rest. Rice paddies came into view again, and with them, silhouettes of towns and villages, dotting the muted landscape like murmurs and sighs.

We arrived in a country of sky-tall sugar palms. A group of village men, along with some children, waited for us on the steps of an open-air pavilion. I quickly scanned the group for Papa even as I knew he couldn't possibly be among them. As we descended from the truck, the men greeted us with reserved curiosity. One of the children, a girl with a rag-like elastic sarong and no shirt at all, came over to offer me water in a coconut shell. I stared at it, swallowing, imagining the water against my parched throat, but the girl's grubby appearance made me hesitate. She pushed the coconut shell into my hand and scuttled off toward the parked truck, where her older sister—it seemed, from the facial resemblance—had perched herself on the driver's seat, playing with the steering wheel. The other children, half naked and dirty like the two girls, circled the vehicle, equally spellbound, sniffing its gas-fume breath, banging on its hood and front doors, marveling at the headlights and rubber tires. They prodded it, kicked it, and tried pushing it forward and back, as if it were a mythical iron water buffalo that could be provoked to stir, teased into snorting at least.

A caravan of oxcarts appeared, each driven by a Revolutionary soldier. Again we were divided and sorted—a family in this cart to a village
in the north, another in that cart to a village in the south, and so on and
so forth.

Mama gathered our two bundles and lifted Radana and me into
our designated cart. The driver, his black cap pulled down low to shield
his eyes, didn't turn around to look at us, but feeling our settled weight,
flicked the reins and clicked his tongue at the oxen.

The cart jerked into motion and once again we trundled toward the
unknown, the path before us weaving through the green paddies, like a
snake lost among the grass. Thatched huts speckled the still, monotonous
landscape, and except for the swirls of smoke rising past the rooftops, it
felt as if we were moving through a painted canvas. The tall, slender sugar
palms, their dark silhouettes like charred torches, shot from the dikes of
the paddies, aspiring to an even loftier existence. Above us the sky hung
low and greyer than ever before, a giant belly about to erupt. Two bolts
of lightning crisscrossed silently like a pair of fencing swords clashing,
sending a shiver down my spine. I wondered how much farther we'd have
to go. If we didn't get there soon, we'd be caught in the full force of the
monsoon.

I stole a glance at our driver. The long-barreled gun that earlier had
hung on his shoulder now lay across his lap. He hadn't spoken a word.
The only sound I heard from him was the click of his tongue every now
and then as he tapped the yoked oxen gently with his bamboo goad.
He appeared unfazed by the gloomy sky, the lightning with its brilliant
flashes of muteness. Instead, he seemed part of it, part of the stillness,
the silence that was everywhere, that magnified the distance and spaces
around us.

My thoughts turned to the others. I closed my eyes, picturing their
faces: Grandmother Queen, Tata, Big Uncle, Auntie India, the twins,
first Sotanavong, then Satiyavong—separately, individually, as I rarely
thought of them. I counted each person on my fingers—one, two, three,
four, five, six—taking comfort in their numberness, if not their actual
presence. Where were they now? On an oxcart too, heading toward their

new home, their new life? Were they thinking of me as I was thinking of them? And Papa? Where was he? How often I would let myself
dream he would suddenly appear. That he could materialize even out
here, among the rice fields, a figure walking toward me.

I looked at Mama cradling Radana in her lap, a blue-and-white
checkered *kroma* across her shoulders, shielding my sleeping sister from
the elements. It was a good thing Radana was sleeping so much, that she
was easily lulled by the rhythm of a cart or truck on the move, allowing
Mama to rest most of the time. We'd hardly spoken to each other, Mama
and I, certainly not a word about the others. What was there to say?—*I
know you wanted to go with them. Yes, I did.*

I no longer regretted I'd chosen her over the rest, over my own sense
of safety in numbers. But I regretted what I saw, which all along I hadn't
wanted to see: her incompleteness, she without him, Mama without
Papa. Since he was gone, I'd avoided being alone with her, avoided looking into her eyes. I didn't want to witness her devastation—I could hardly
bear my own. Now here she was in front of me—her face gaunt, lips dry
and cracked, her entire being stretched to a breaking point. Where was
that beautiful butterfly with flowers in her hair? Sadness enveloped her
and she seemed to have changed from this weightless creature capable of
flight to someone who walked and moved with limbs of clay.

Those days and nights following Papa's departure, I'd often told myself that at least there was Mama: she would hold my hand, shelter me
from any storm. But when that moment came she'd stood frozen amidst
the surging throngs, unable to draw me to her, neither by gesture nor
word, and it was painfully clear that she'd needed me as much as I'd
needed her, that without Papa, she and I would always need each other
when calamity hit.

Now, as I gazed at her, as I felt her yearning for him, missing the
others, I thought maybe we mourned not only the dead but also the living. We felt their absence before we knew for sure they were gone.

Mama looked up and, perhaps ashamed of the way she appeared
to me, lifted the *kroma* over her head to hide her face. She let herself
be rocked by the movement of the cart, her body swaying, as though

she'd stopped fighting the exhaustion. In no time at all, she was asleep again, dreaming a joint dream with Radana, bound together at least by their unawareness of the dips and bumps along the way. I didn't blame her, nor did I envy this connection she and Radana shared. As much as I longed for the bond I'd had with my father, I knew I could not repeat it with anyone. Others would appear and disappear like fireflies; I could never know when. The best I could hope was to draw from each the light I needed to guide myself on this dark and uncertain path. The rest I'd have to do on my own. And my aloneness, this solitude, would be my strength.

Again lightning flashed, followed by what sounded like a mountain ripping in half. I jumped up and squeezed myself in beside the Revolutionary soldier, almost knocking the long-barreled gun off his lap. He didn't move or chase me back to my seat, or even laugh at my fear. Instead, he removed the gun and laid it parallel to the side of the cart to his right. Then he tapped the oxen again with his goad to hurry them on, murmuring tenderly some unintelligible terms of endearment I was certain they understood. The oxen hastened their steps, ears twitching, tails swishing, their hides rippling as if absorbing their master's sense of urgency.

I turned back to look at Mama and Radana. They were still asleep, not the least disturbed by the thunder and lightning or even aware that I had moved from my place beside them. I decided to stay in the front, feeling less alone next to the soldier, taking comfort in his vigilance and wakefulness. If I got struck by lightning, I thought, at least he would witness it. I wasn't completely alone.

Another clap of thunder resounded. I pressed closer. He didn't object. I didn't know if I was more scared of his silence or the roar of the sky.

We'd come to a part of the path made narrower by bamboo bushes growing on either side. The soldier pulled hard on the reins and the oxen came to a full stop. I thought he would wake Mama and Radana and tell all three of us to get off, that this was as far as he'd been instructed to take us, the rest we would have to brave alone. Instead he reached over the side of the cart, broke a long slender bamboo branch, and, without a word of explanation, handed it to me, nodding at the oxen, indicating

I should goad them. I tapped the one on the left, as gently as I'd seen him do it, then the one on the right. The soldier clicked his tongue and loosened the reins. Once again we were moving.

"So there were these two deity children, right?" he suddenly said, as if picking up a conversation we'd begun earlier. "A *tevoda* and a *yiak*." He didn't turn to meet my shocked gaze but kept his eyes on the path straight ahead. "They'd been studying magic with this hermit, a sorcerer." His voice was as composed as his profile, and I wondered if he himself wasn't magic, a trick manifestation of some sort. "One day the sorcerer gave them a challenge. He told them whoever collected a jar full of dew first would get the *keo monoria*."

I swallowed and asked, "What's that?"

"A crystal ball that contained light—power." He nodded toward the oxen, and again, I tapped them with my bamboo branch. "That night the two students went out, each with a jar. At dawn the next day, the *tevoda* came back with a jar full of dew. The *yiak* . . . well, his jar was only half full. The sorcerer gave the crystal ball to the *tevoda*. The *yiak* was upset. He deserved something too. So the sorcerer gave him an ax, also a weapon of great power. But the *yiak,* unsatisfied, took the ax and started chasing after the *tevoda,* and each time he swung his weapon at her, there came this awful, thunderous roar. The *tevoda* jumped out of the way to avoid being hit, tossing the magic ball into the air, sending out these brilliant flashes of light."

We bounced up and down on the oxcart, the path marked with holes and humps. I waited for the soldier to go on, but we'd come to a canal brimming with muddy water, and across its width lay a partly inundated crossing made from felled palm trunks. Leaning left and right, checking the positions of the oversized wheels, he guided beasts and cart across the precarious bridge.

"You shouldn't be scared of lightning and thunder," he said, once we were on dry ground again. "They're just two children playing with magic."

Silently, secretly, I wondered if this moment could be captured somehow, in a crystal vessel of my own, to be invoked again and again should I find myself forever alone. "I like magic," I ventured. "Do you?"

He didn't respond. And, just as unexpectedly as he'd spoken, he became part of the silence again.

At last, we came to a split in the path. The soldier turned the ox-cart, bearing to the right, and we trundled onto an even narrower track, hemmed most immediately on either side by an irrigation ditch, then by an expanse of green paddies spreading boundlessly into the greater distance. Up ahead the track opened onto a piece of slightly elevated land, surrounded by fruit trees. In the middle of the land, rising toward the open sky, a pair of sugar palms crisscrossed at the trunks, then curved like arms lifted to implore the gods. To the right of the palms, at a distance that seemed far enough to avoid falling fruits or fronds, stood a small thatched hut on stilts. From its bamboo steps, two shadows rose. My heart quickened. *Could one of them be Papa?* Always I hoped, seeing him everywhere, in every silhouette and form, in every gesture that might intimate he was still part of my world. One of the shadows waved tentatively, the other vigorously, ecstatically.

"Come," the wife urged, pulling my attention from the receding figure on the cart.

The sky rumbled and shook, enigmatic as its emissary, who was disappearing with the noiselessness of a mirage.

The wife grabbed Mama by the elbow and led her and Radana to the stairs. The husband and I followed, he carrying our two bundles, and I dragging my bamboo branch against the ground. "You came just in time," he murmured, looking up at the clouds moving overhead, as if the sky was his point of reference to everything, to every conversation he wanted to start. "It'll be a big storm when it comes."

His eyes went to the wooden weathervane spinning on the roof of the hut. It was in the shape of a rooster, and even though it wasn't a detailed carving, there was something about it that made it seem alive, like it was on the verge of flapping its wings and crowing. It spun left and right, then turned in the direction the clouds were moving, as if envying their flight, longing for its own release.

"I know you deserve more . . . ," the husband murmured, eyes still on the rooster, speaking to it. "You deserve better than our thatched roof."

I kept quiet.

At the stairs, the wife chimed, hands clasped in ecstasy, "Oh, I never thought at my age I'd be blessed with children!"

"Mae . . . ," the husband started, and again she finished, "Yes, I know, I know! I shouldn't get so carried away with myself!"

The husband nodded; his thoughts exactly.

On closer observation, it was clear that they were not so much two different people as they were complements of each other: he felt, she acted; he thought, she spoke. Two sides of the same revelation.

"They're not ours to keep," he cautioned. "They belong to the Organization."

She made as if to smack him on the shoulder. "You! Stop spoiling my happiness!" And to Mama, "Pok doesn't believe in miracles."

He smiled but did not refute his wife's accusation. Adjusting the weight of the bundles on his shoulders, he observed Mama, noting, as I noted, the wave of sorrow rising to her face as her eyes took in the surroundings: the small thatched hut with its ladder-like steps, each rung a section of roughly-cut bamboo; the bare-bones platform beneath the hut where, like our teak settee back home, I imagined, all the events of their lives took place; the dirt floor around it, scattered with baskets of dented kitchenware and household tools. "It's . . . it's not much," he said, cutting into her thoughts, his tone apologetic.

Mama flushed with shame. "No, it's not that . . ." She seemed about to explain but said instead, "It's lovely. It really is."

I focused my gaze on him. *You deserve better than our thatched roof.* He hadn't meant the rooster at all when he spoke these words.

Again, the wife seemed thunderstruck. "Maybe there's something to this new god after all. The Organization, the Organization! Everyone shouts his name. Oh, how I prayed and prayed to him! Now he's granted my wish! I couldn't have asked for nicer children!"

• • •

They called each other "Pok" and "Mae"—"Pa" and "Ma"—as if these simple terms of endearment they tossed back and forth bespoke not only their love for each other but also their shared longing—the children they would've liked to have had but didn't. "You're our children now," Mae kept saying. "Our home is your home." She fluttered about the room like a mother swallow building her nest, picking up the straws that had fallen onto the slatted bamboo floor and tucking them back into the thatched walls. "Don't be shy, make yourselves comfortable, anything you need, anything at all, you let me know, you help yourselves, all right?" She spoke merrily, continuously, switching without pause from house to history, telling us how since she was thirteen, married to Pok, who was fifteen, she had wanted children of her own, how over the years she had prayed and prayed, made offerings to every god and every spirit of every world, but none heard her pleading, until eventually she grew old and wrinkly and came to accept her childless fate. Not that she was complaining, in case the gods were listening now. Yes, she admitted, she and Pok were blessed in other ways. They had their land, planting was hard, but harvest brought enough, if not always plenty, and, aside from her barrenness, they experienced no grave sickness or catastrophe, which was nothing short of a miracle, considering all their years, the wars they'd lived through.

Then came the Revolution, and its Maker, whose presence was everywhere, whose power the soldiers endlessly touted—*No rain? The Organization will make sure water gets channeled to your fields. Not enough rice? The Organization will show you how to double, triple your yield the next harvest.* Who was this Organization? she wanted to know. Was he a demigod, like the king, or an enlightened sage, like the Buddha? He must be a divine being. If so, surely then she should heed his call to worship, to make the necessary offerings and sacrifices. The Organization needed volunteers, the soldiers told her. Neak Moulathaan—"Base People"—*true* peasants to house some evacuees from the cities. She didn't understand what was required of her but agreed to put herself and her home in the service of the Revolution, believing that this was the Organization's way of granting her and Pok their long-buried wish for children, for companionship other than their own, and when she saw us—*Oh, looking forlorn and forsaken!*—she knew she'd been called upon by some great power to mother, or at the very least to offer a shelter.

Mae looked around and, sighing, concluded, "But this could hardly be called a house. You need more," echoing Pok's earlier sentiment. "I feel so ashamed to offer you this."

Their hut had only one room, half the size of my bedroom back in Phnom Penh, and since we couldn't all fit—Mae, beaming again, laid out plans right then and there—we girls would sleep inside, and Pok would sleep outside, on the raised bamboo platform under the hut. Mama, putting Radana down on the floor so she could rest her arms, turned nervously toward Pok, eyes trailing him as he brought in our belongings. Mae immediately quelled Mama's worries. "He's grown up with the winds and rains," she asserted. "His leathery old skin's tougher than time!" Pok walked to the back and put the bundles near a pile of straw mats. He seemed to possess an easy calm about him, an unconcern for all things said in his presence, whether true or not. But, at his wife's nudging, he corroborated, "Yes, I like the fresh air." He faced us and smiled. Then as if to dispel our skepticism and give proof to his words, he happily slung a rolled-up straw mat over his shoulder and went back down the stairs, leaving us in his wife's charge.

"Oh, where are my manners!" Mae gasped, horrified to see us still standing. "I just talked and talked this whole time. You poor things. Sit down, sit down. Rest your tired souls."

sixteen

Mae pulled out three rolled-up straw mats from the pile against the back wall and spread them out over the slatted bamboo floor. These woven palm-leaf mats were our sleeping mats, she explained, not to be mixed with the eating mats woven from rice stalks, which we would never bring into the house because the smell of rice and fish would attract ants and all sorts of insects. We had to be careful out here in the countryside where bugs with teeth as sharp as saws could chew to dust in a week what people had taken months to weave.

Dusk had descended and, after a thorough wash and a dinner of hot steamed rice and broiled fish, I felt ready to rest—to plunge into a deep, long sleep. Mae's voice—its folksy rhythm and twang—relaxed my body, soothing every ache and strain.

From one of the covered rattan baskets, she pulled out a couple of faded, patch-filled blankets and shook them vigorously. "Hmm . . ." She frowned, vexed by their appearance. "They didn't seem this bad when it was just the two of us." She sniffed the blankets, and then, back to her enthusiastic self, joyfully declared, "Oh well, at least they're clean!"

She handed one of the blankets to Mama. "I put some dried kaffir leaves in to keep away, you know . . . *vor.*"

"Snakes" was what she meant. I remembered Old Boy would do the same—calling venomous snakes "vines"—as he went about watering our gardens, believing that to say their real name was to call forth their presence. It was a common country superstition.

"Thank you," Mama said, eyes glassy with exhaustion.

Radana echoed toothily, "Thank you, thank you." She was no longer scared of Mae's crinkly face and gash-like mouth. Instead, lips puckered in imitation, she seemed fascinated with how it always moved, how words and sounds constantly bubbled from it like water from a brook. She struggled out of Mama's lap and toddled about the hut, babbling nonsense, mimicking Mae's incessant speech and movements.

Mama began to sort through our belongings. She folded clothes, smoothed out the creases, and stacked them in three separate piles—hers, Radana's, mine. As reduced as our possessions had become, the bright colors seemed extravagant, ostentatious against the thatched walls and ceiling. There was Radana's satin dress, so white and shiny it glowed. Where would she wear that? It was all trees and rice fields here.

Mama put the satin dress at the bottom of Radana's stack and, emptying the bundle, took out the small bolster pillow, once hardened with jewels but now softened with loss. Papa had drawn a face on it one afternoon at the temple when Radana wouldn't stop pining for her beloved teddy we'd forgotten back in Phnom Penh. It was a silly cartoonish face—a bear with round eyes and ears and curly hair like a girl. "Princess Honey Bear"—Papa had anointed his creation with my pet name. Now I waited for Mama to laugh as she had that afternoon. But she could only stare at it, eyes brimming with tears.

Seeing the bolster, Radana rushed to take it out of Mama's hands. She squeezed it, hugged it, and kissed it several times over—her much-missed makeshift doll. Plunging her thumb inside her mouth, she plopped down in the middle of the room to cuddle it. "We sleep!" she announced, in case no one understood what she was doing.

"You do that," Mae chuckled. "Here, when the sky closes her eyes, we close ours, too."

"Sleep!" Radana said again, more forcefully this time.

"All right, all right, I'll shut up now."

Mae covered Radana with the blanket in her hand, sat down beside her, and, caressing the little one's back, hummed a familiar lullaby.

Radana fell fast asleep. Mae got up and, with hushed steps, set about putting up the mosquito net, the bamboo floor creaking softly beneath her feet as she moved from one corner to another.

Meanwhile, Mama had untied the other bundle, on top of which lay Papa's leather pocket notebook, his silver fountain pen, and the Omega Constellation watch—all loosely wrapped in one of the embroidered white handkerchiefs he used to carry in his pants pocket. He had prepared the bundle himself but must've decided at the last minute he wouldn't need it. Now, here it was—a funeral pyre of his personal effects. Suddenly, I recalled having seen him with the notebook the night before he left. I heard again the sound of paper ripping. Had it been a dream? Had he really gotten up to write and, perhaps not liking what he'd written, torn out the page? I felt the urge to snatch the notebook from the pile, but I couldn't bring myself to read his words without him being here. I couldn't bear his poetry without his presence.

A sound escaped Mama's throat, and she hunched over, cradling her stomach, her hair falling forward so that it curtained her face from me. One hand clamped over her mouth, she tried to muffle the sound, her body quaking from the effort. But I heard it anyway. Her grief flowed out of her, spreading like Mae's blanket, covering me with its tattered fringes and patched-up holes, and my heart broke again, not for my father this time, but for her, she who must bundle us up, the remnants of their once shared love, and continue without him.

Mae, sensing something wrong, paused in the middle of tying the mosquito net and asked, "Are you all right, child?"

Mama nodded and, pulling herself together, finished unpacking. Then she drew an eggplant-colored *sampot hol* from the pile and walked over to Mae. "This is for you," she said, holding it out to our hostess.

Mae looked at the handwoven silk sarong and, seeming overwhelmed by the gesture as much as by the loveliness of the gift, said breathlessly, "Oh no, I can't." She shook her head. "I can't—"

"Please. I don't know how to thank you . . ."

Again, Mae shook her head, then, recovering from her enthrallment, said sternly, "What would I do with it? This is cloth for *tevodas*, not an old crow like me."

"It'll be lovely on you," Mama told her, lowering her gaze to the silk and caressing it. "This color . . . it was my mother's favorite. Please take it. It would make me very happy."

Mae looked askance. Then, sighing, she said, "I'll keep it until you need it back."

Outside, dusk turned a shade darker and brought with it a mild, cool breeze, which now and then stirred the leaves and rice stalks, sending flocks of birds sweeping across the landscape. Still, the rain didn't come. I wished it would. I wanted the sky to cry, to lead the way for me.

I looked out the side window and saw the two crossed palms. "*Thnoat oan thnoat bong*," Pok and Mae called them. "Sweethearts." They swayed in locked embrace, serenading each other with a mournful creak. Lightning flashed in the distance, followed by a rumble. *They're playing with magic again*, I thought, seeing in my mind's eye the twins rolling, gnawing each other like puppies among the clouds, the ax and crystal ball changing hands. I stilled the image in my head.

Unable to stay erect any longer, I stretched out on my stomach beside Radana and looked through the narrow spaces between the bamboo slats. There, directly below us, was Pok, perfectly content on the raised platform, his feet dangling over a fire, which, from my perspective, appeared to be licking his toes. He was whittling the piece of wood I'd seen him with earlier, and when a stray chip flew into the flames, it smelled like boiled palm juice.

"That old man is always doing something," Mae said, reaching over to tuck in the edge of the mosquito net under the straw mat. "He can't keep still. He whittles and carves and chisels till he falls asleep and sometimes that never happens, and he'll end up staying awake till dawn. If you watch him, you'll never get any sleep."

"What's he making?" I asked, turning over on my back.

"A little calf for my cow," Mae said. "It died a couple of weeks ago. The calf, I mean. Poor thing. Now the mother pines and pines. Listen, you can hear her . . ."

I listened, and sure enough, from somewhere behind the hut, came the sound—*Maaw, maaw, maaw* . . . I'd met the cow earlier when it roamed over to the edge of the property while we were washing inside a nearby roofless thatched enclosure. It was the thinnest-looking cow I'd ever seen, and I'd thought it was going to eat the thatch. But it just stared at me, moaning, as it was doing now, *Maaw, maaw* . . .

"Pok thought he'd make her a little carving. To hang around her neck."

"You mean like a charm?" I felt certain that even an animal as dull witted as a cow would know the difference between her real calf and a miniature wooden replica. "Why? What for?"

"Oh, I don't know," Mae said, closing the front door. "I suppose he just wants to give shape to her sorrow."

"Oh."

Mama pulled Radana closer, sharing one blanket with her, while I shared the other with Mae. I lay sandwiched between Mae on my right near the door, and Radana on my left, next to Mama by the wall. Mae yawned, mumbled something or other, and then, after what seemed like a few short seconds, fell sound asleep, as though knocked out cold by the night.

Soon, she and Radana were snoring back and forth, like a pair of whistles answering each other's calls, while Mama and I searched the dark for the shapes of our sorrows.

Translucent drops of rain clung to the leaves and grass, like ladybugs whose vivid colors and patterns had washed away during the night's torrent. I lingered in the doorway, wrapped in Mae's blanket, my legs stretched out in front of me, yawning, waiting for sleep to leave my body, for dreaming to subside. Before me the quilted landscape of rice paddies and sugar palms unfurled as the sky peeled back its gauzy tier, revealing nearby tree-shaded huts standing much like ours on slightly elevated land and, at farther distances, the dark green silhouettes of neighboring villages rising like burls and whorls in an otherwise smooth fabric. Rainwater brimmed the paddies, and the slender green stalks appeared much taller than I remembered.

In one of the paddies closest to the hut, partly shielded by a screen of tender blades, a brown-speckled duck—female, I guessed, from her muted coloring—plunged into the chalky water, wiggling her tail in the air, then popped back up, shaking her head, burrowing her bill into her feathers. A private morning ablution.

On a strip of inundated land, a water buffalo stood swishing its tail, grazing the tufts of green flecked with lavender blossoms—water morning glory, judging by its elongated leaves. Nearby a man—the buffalo's owner, I assumed, from the ease with which the two kept company— with a *kroma* wound tight like a pair of boxers around his hips, plodded with careful steps, holding up a cone-shaped fish trap, which he suddenly plunged into the shallow water, his whole being riveted by the thrill of a catch. A *naga* serpent! I imagined something spectacular, my mind ever leaping toward a story, the possibility of escape, freedom.

How strange, I thought, that everything seemed so different. This place, which only the day before had felt like a chasm of stillness and silence we'd fallen into, now burgeoned with activities and sounds.

The water buffalo let out a loud snort, nostrils flaring, its huge head swinging in annoyance, its curved horns like a pair of sickles slicing the air. A flock of birds burst from a nearby bush, shocked into exhilaration. The man with the fish trap looked up, hand over his forehead, shielding his eyes from the hardening sun, as if contemplating the possibility of his own flight. Papa, I thought. He'd always wanted to fly. *Be as free as that hawk!*

A rooster crowed, followed by another, and another, setting off a chain of cock-a-doodle-doos that echoed from hut to hut, from one village to the next.

I went down the steps and walked barefoot across the wet ground. From somewhere high up, a man's raspy, reedy voice crooned, *Oh,* sarika-keo *bird, what are you eating? . . .* whistling when the lyrics eluded him.

I turned my gaze skyward and there was Pok coming down the trunk of one of the Sweethearts, a stringed bamboo flask swinging from a leather strap around his waist.

He looked down and, seeing me standing below, greeted, "You're up!" He hopped onto a patch of grass, agile and light. "Just in time!" He nodded at the bamboo flask. "Want some?"

"Palm juice?" I'd never had it for breakfast before.

"Ah, not just that, but the nectar of youth!" He smiled, his face all crinkly, his teeth so stained he looked toothless, a hundred years old. "Heaven's gift to us mortals! It keeps us young!"

"Does it?"

He laughed. "Well, maybe not."

I looked away, embarrassed by my slip, and tried to change the subject. "Where's everyone?"

Pok nodded toward the back of the house. "They've gone to the river to wash." He unhooked the flask from the handle of his sheath knife and hung the flask on the bottom-most notch of the bamboo pole snaking up the full length of the palm, like the vertebrae of a long-ossified dragon. "At this early hour, the juice is as cold as . . ." He seemed at a loss for just the right word.

"Ice," I offered, thinking maybe the day before I'd misperceived his reticence just as I'd misperceived everything else.

"*Clouds,* I was going to say." He grinned. "But yes, 'ice' is more fitting." Then, his brows furrowing, he added in an apparent tone of interest, "You know, I've never seen it. Ice, I mean. I've heard people talk about it, but I can't imagine this 'solid water.' Made by a machine no less, is that right?"

I nodded, thinking of the small refrigerator we had back home where we stored our supply of imported cheeses and pâtés, the little freezer up top with its metal trays for ice.

Pok shook his head in amazement. "No wonder these Revolutionary soldiers are so fearful of machines. What power indeed to turn water solid!"

I kept silent, letting him find his way.

He began to undo the leather strap that held the sheath knife and several pairs of bamboo clasps I recognized were the kind used for squeezing juice from palm flowers. "I can't say I understand what's happening," he went on, avoiding my stare. "What grace or misfortune has brought you here, to us—we who have nothing to give you."

It hit me what he was doing—he was trying to be a parent, to talk to a child as a father would. He must've guessed what we'd lost, for here we were, a young mother and two little girls and no father to speak of. He must've sensed how far we'd been flung, for there was a world that he, who'd lived through countless moons and seen just about everything, didn't know, couldn't possibly imagine, a world of "solid water." I wanted to describe to him this world, my whole life there. But tightness swelled in my chest, and when I opened my mouth to speak all I could muster was a muffled choke.

Pok stood still and observed me, as one would a bird, afraid of making a wrong move. After a moment, he said, "Let's have some palm juice."

I followed him to a stout young palm a few feet away. He cut a section of its frond with his knife, ripped the pliant part from the hard spine, and, with quick, deft movements of his hands, magically whisked it into a pair of cones. He poured some juice from the bamboo flask into the cones and handed one to me.

We strolled to the edge of the rice paddies, climbed onto the dike, and, as we stood there drinking our breakfast in companionable silence, more comfortable now without speaking, I thought maybe it wasn't necessary to explain anything at all. Maybe it was enough that I knew I was not alone, that, at the very least, standing here beside me was this one person, who, unbeknownst to me till now, had all along been journeying this same journey with me, only from the opposite direction.

I can't say I understand what's happening . . . Had I owned the words I would've told him what my heart intuited—that joy and sorrow often travel the same road and sometimes, whether by grace or misfortune, they meet and become each other's companion. But again I couldn't express what I felt. So I told him what I could—"Maybe we are *pok thor koan thor*."

Thor comes from the Sanskrit word "dharma," but to me it meant simply loving someone you did not expect to love, and thus *pok thor koan thor* was a bond between a parent and child who were not related by blood. *They're not ours to keep,* Pok had said, cautioning Mae against becoming too attached to us. Looking at him now, I knew we'd fallen into good hands. I knew also that like Papa, like any parent who understood the brevity of his role, the pithiness of parenthood, Pok was going to care for us as best as he could, teach us how to live like *neak srae,* how not only to plant the rice but to *imitate* it, to firmly anchor ourselves in ever-upturned ground and, at the same time, sway in the direction of the wind.

"Maybe we were supposed to meet," I said, sensing the possibility of my father everywhere. *We are all echoes of one another, Raami.*

Pok looked at me. Silence seemed to have overtaken him again. Then his face broke open like the morning sun.

seventeen

So began my education, with Pok as my guide and guardian, this gentle soul who called himself *neak prey*—a "man of the forest"—because he'd never seen a refrigerator or known the taste of ice, but who, with quiet patience and *thor*, would help us to withstand the rigors of our reincarnation from city people to peasants. To begin with, that morning, after we'd finished our second helpings of palm juice, Pok directed my gaze to the rooster weathervane turning at the top of the hut. Here, he explained, our lives were ruled by the seasonal change of the monsoon's breath, which when blowing from the southwest brought rains and rice, and from the northeast dryness and scarcity. He described in detail the layout of Stung Khae and its neighboring villages, dotting them on his palm with the tip of his finger in an S-shaped curve from north to south. Together there were twelve villages in the commune. Stung Khae, the fourth village from the north, was cradled right at the crook of a small river, the one Pok had just pointed out to me. The river, also called Stung Khae, threaded its way between ours and the third village, connecting up with Prek Chong, a large tributary of the Mekong, somewhere in the distant north.

At the mention of the Mekong, my heart went aflutter, my mind became distracted, and I asked Pok if he could take me there, to which he replied, "Oh, child, it's many forests and rivers away!" He admitted he'd never seen it.

"Papa said—" I stopped.

"Yes? Your papa said . . ."

I couldn't tell him. Couldn't bear to say more. Not yet. Pok understood. The newness of my loss was apparent to him.

"Come," he said and led me across the vast green expanse, to where a group of farmers were busy preparing the paddies for planting. The men, each in a field with his plow and water buffalo, churned the flooded ground, turning the turbid water and earth into thick, doughy mud. Nearby, on a patch of land where two dikes met, the women hoed dirt from a termite mound into rattan baskets for children to scatter in the paddies. The dirt full of termites—*dey dombok,* Pok called it, teaching me the proper names of things as he went—would get ground up by the plows and become potent fertilizer for the soil. Then, after another rain or two, when the upturned soil had settled and evened out but was still soft enough to push one's thumb through, tender rice seedlings would be brought from the village's *thnaal sanab* and transplanted into the paddies. The rains would continue, nourishing the rice as well as providing sanctuaries for minnows, tadpoles, snails, crabs, and countless other tiny creatures we could collect for food, for our own nourishment.

"What about leeches?" I wanted to know.

"Oh, they're everywhere!" He lowered himself on one knee, dipped his arm into a rain-flooded paddy, and pulled out a cylindrical bamboo trap—*troo,* he called it, which was different from *angrut,* the cone-shaped trap used for ensnaring larger catches, like catfish or eels. Inside the *troo,* a thick colony of gravel-sized snails clung to the bamboo strips, and, like a giant sentry keeping watch over these minuscule prisoners, a lone crawfish the size of my thumb scuttled from one end to the other, fearful of our presence. "It's your lucky day, little fellow!" Pok exclaimed and, sliding open the small woven cover at one end, let the panic-stricken animal go. "Come back when you have more meat!" He returned the *troo* to the water, his arm lingering near a thicket of grass.

"What are you looking for?"

"Don't let . . . the flat surface . . . fool you," he said, his voice straining from overreaching. "Underneath all this sameness . . . there's a thriving universe of these creatures." Suddenly he pulled his arm out of the water, and clinging to the underside of his wrist was a leech—black and quivering.

I pulled back, gasping.

Pok grinned and, grabbing a tuft of grass, scraped the leech off in one quick swipe. "If you try picking it off with your fingers, it'll reattach itself to your hand or another part of your skin. It's best to not touch these creatures." He wiped away a trace of blood on his wrist where the leech must have pierced him.

"Does . . . does it hurt?"

"You mustn't be afraid." He looked at me, his gaze suddenly penetrating. "You'll see them everywhere. Sometimes, a whole troop will surround you, blackening your sight. But it's the ones you can't see that you must guard yourself against." He scrutinized the water and, quickly pointing to a dark, wriggling cluster, said, "There! Needle leeches, they're called. They'll enter your body by whatever route possible and make you bleed from the inside."

I shuddered.

Realizing his misstep—that this might have added to my fear rather than lessened it—he tried to make light of it. "But there's one good use for these guys. Not the needle leeches, but the fat ones. Pickle them in rice wine and you'll have a drink with so much fire as to make a coward brave!"

I shivered with disgust. "You'd have to be brave in the first place to drink something like that!"

Pok laughed. "Can't say I've ever tried it myself!"

We made our way to one of the farmers, who stopped his plowing when he heard Pok call out to him. They greeted each other, exchanged pleasantries about the morning, and, nodding at me, Pok introduced, "My *koan thor*."

The man flashed me a smile, seeming to need no further explanation as to how or from where I'd materialized, but that I was with Pok was enough to warrant his welcome and acceptance. "The soil is as black as worm castings," he said and, scooping up a handful of the sludge, showed it to us. "See, plenty of *dey labap*, with just the right amount of silt and sand. We'll have a good crop this harvest."

There was something familiar about him. Maybe the way he moved in the paddy, barely stirring the water, or maybe the way he wore only a *kroma* around his waist. But, as I looked around, all the other men plowing the paddies were similarly clad, with the bare minimum, their bodies so lissome and brown and streaked with mud, and I understood now why they were called "people of the paddies." Their whole life seemed to take place in these muddy fields, and, like the rice stalks, they appeared at once youthful and ancient, tenuous and resilient, light-footed and permanently rooted. It wasn't difficult now to understand why the Revolution favored them, why there was this need to turn people like Mama and me—the entire urban population, as we'd come to learn—into *neak srae*. Who wouldn't want to be like them?

The man's water buffalo snorted, swinging its head in annoyance, impatient to get on with the work. I suddenly realized it was the same water buffalo that had grazed the morning glory earlier, and the owner was the same man who had combed the inundated strip of land with his trap! I swallowed my shyness and asked, "What did you catch?"

He seemed surprised by the question, but then realizing I must've seen him from Pok's hut, smiled broadly and tilted his head toward the trap a few feet away at a dike junction—"See for yourself."

I went to take a look. Inside the cone-shaped fortress wriggled a catfish as big as my forearm, in a puddle too small for its long body and whiskers. It thrashed about, perhaps sensing it was being observed, mouth open wide as if in a silent scream. Then it went still, its gills heaving, exhausted from the brief exertion.

"I think it's dying," I told Pok as he came and stood beside me.

He frowned, seeming more troubled by my concern for the catfish than by the fish itself. "Well, you know . . . ," he started to say but couldn't find the words to explain.

He didn't need to. I understood. Fish was food. I wasn't naïve. I knew what was going to happen. I'd seen live fish killed and gutted countless times, at the market, in our very own kitchen. Yet somehow that was different from seeing one so close to its natural habitat, trapped like this when freedom was all around it. I couldn't help thinking I was in a similar predicament—removed from all that I'd known, cordoned off in an unfamiliar place, yet probably not far from home.

One big jump and you'll be back in the water! Go on! Jump!

The fish made no response to my silent urgings. It focused what breath it had left on staying alive in this tiny puddle.

I stood up and looked around. If only I could see past the fortress of trees, catch a glimmer of the Mekong. *Sometimes we, like little fishes, are swept up in these big and powerful currents . . .* Papa's words flooded my mind, and I remembered his despair as he stood beside me on the balcony of Mango Corner overlooking the river, the tightness of his voice as he spoke. If only the currents would reverse, I thought, and carry me back to him. Or him to me.

Again, tears stung my eyes and I felt choked, this time with the realization that this was now my home, my life, that I couldn't keep pining for all I'd lost. What breath or energy I had left I must focus on making it here, becoming not only *koan thor* to Pok and Mae but *koan neak srae,* a child of these paddies.

When we got back to the hut, Mama wasn't upset or worried as I'd thought she would be. She smiled when she saw me, her arms raised to hang a sarong on the clothesline that stretched between two papaya trees near the thatched enclosure in the back. Her face was glowing, flushed with youth, with the freshness of the morning's wash, the night's cleansing. The rain healed everything, I thought. Or at least washed away the residues of a day's wreckage. She pulled a shirt—mine, the one I'd worn during our journey—from a basket of freshly laundered clothes and hung it next to her flowered sarong. Anxious to give a reason for my early morning grubbiness, I told her I was out exploring with Pok, who, at the moment when I most needed him to back me up, was quickly disappearing up the trunk of the other Sweetheart palm to finish collecting the sweet juice, which he said must be gotten in the morning, as opposed to the sour juice collected in the afternoon. Mama looked at my bare feet, the clumps of mud between my toes, the pieces of dead grass stuck to my skin. In the chaos of our departure from the temple, we'd lost my shoes and sandals. But I didn't miss them. I liked the feel of dirt against my skin, and it was easier to walk barefoot on the uneven ground.

Mama made a small frown, but then, smiling, said instead, "It must have been fun."

I stared at her, surprised not only that she didn't reproach me but that she seemed, as before, happy and playful.

She lowered herself on one knee and, with a wet *kroma* from the pile in the basket, began to wipe my face. Her touch, supple and damp, made me think of a mother horse I'd once seen grooming her foal, licking the baby until it was clean. She lifted my chin and wiped underneath it. I felt a rush to hug her—to confirm her realness and solidity against my chest, her heartbeats with mine. But I stayed still, afraid I'd unravel what the rain had mended, that my tenderness would break her all over again. So instead I told her, "There are these needle leeches, and Pok said the way to not let them enter your body is to wear black when you go into the rice paddy, so that you appear like them, like this dark mass floating in the water. This afternoon he will take me to catch eels."

Mama nodded, running her fingers through my hair, smoothing out the tangles. Then, cupping my face with both hands, she looked me in the eyes and said, "It's wonderful, all this exploring. But don't get lost. Remember who you are."

A warning or a plea, I wasn't sure.

Then, seeing my confusion, she added, "You know, you would've also adored my father. Do you remember I told you he passed away a year before you were born? At the monastery where he'd spent the latter part of his life. But . . . but he also loved the countryside—the rice fields, the mud, the leeches, everything about it."

It was clear what she was trying to say—Pok reminded her of her father, and it was all right for me to venture about with him.

She let go and, putting the used *kroma* aside, stood up to hang the rest of the laundered clothes, which, I noticed with a start, had become blackish blue, all the colors and patterns gone. Mae had said the

Kamaphibal required that we dye our garments in indigo juice. Everything must be silenced. Black was the color of the Revolution. Mama, with her jade-colored sarong and light pink shirt yet to be dyed, resembled a lotus shooting out of the mud. The colors, or maybe her—the brightness of her presence amidst this straw dwelling and dirt—made me want to hold on tight. I flung my arms around her slender frame, the tapered waist Papa had described as

> *the narrowing of a river,*
> *A strait into the unknown—*
> *That mystery of birth and origin.*

Mama was my source, my home.

"Doll!" came a squeal from behind me. I spun around and there was Radana on Mae's hip, waving a cassava stem with its oversized star-shaped leaf bunched up and tied with a string so it resembled a stick figure with a ponytail. "Doll!" Radana said again, whacking my head with it.

"I tried to convince her to play in the hut, but no, she'll have none of it." Mae handed Radana to Mama. "She wants you."

"Doll hungry." Radana thrust the cassava stem at Mama's chest, making a suckling sound. Mama gently pushed it away, looking somewhat embarrassed, but Radana babbled on, "*Mhum mhum mhum . . .*"

Mae tickled her, nodding toward the cow tethered to a pole among the haystacks. "You sound like her!"

I laughed. *Huh, you little bovine!* Radana, clueless, laughed with me.

Mae turned to Mama. "You go and feed the little ones." She nodded at the pot perched over a fire under the hut. "I'll finish putting up the clothes."

The smell of palm sugar renewed my hunger. Mae had stirred a small chunk into the rice porridge, now turning it a thick, golden brown. Mama spooned some into a bowl and handed it to me. I blew and stirred, blew and stirred, impatient for it to cool down, my stomach urging me on, moaning incessantly.

Mae came to join us. She put aside the empty basket, poured herself a cup of palm juice from the bamboo flask, and drank it down in one gulp. When Mama tried to offer her some of the porridge from the pot, she shook her head. "No, no, that's just for you and the little ones. All I need is a bit of this sweet nectar to carry me through the morning."

I didn't know if this was true or if she was just saying it because she didn't want us to feel guilty for eating their meager supply of rice. She poured another cup of palm juice and again drank it down in one go.

"Would you like to help me with my morning chores?" she cooed at Radana, who, looking at the ground still wet from the night's rain, curled her toes in fearful distaste. "I didn't think so." She laughed.

While we ate our porridge, Mae began sweeping the ground around the hut, a broom in each hand, looking all arms and legs, like a spider hard at work. She moved with the lightness of the coconut-spine broomstick, her arm no bigger than its handle, no less sinewy, and as I watched her leap briskly from one spot to the next, I wondered where she stored her energy, her ancient agelessness. She picked up the debris brought in by the wind and rain, working her way to the plot of vegetables at the edge of the land. I quickly finished my porridge and followed her. There she showed me how to pinch off the drooping blades of the lemongrass so that there was room for new growth, and while I did this she went about rescuing the half-buried stalks of turmeric and galangal, whose banana-like leaves gave off a faint scent that reminded me of Om Bao's curries. She lifted the bitter gourd vines back onto the bamboo trellis that stretched over a couple of rows of curly cabbage. It seemed childlessness had made her more maternal to everything that lived, everything that had fought to survive. "Soak up the sun!" she clucked at the green tomatoes, and at the kaffir limes, "Keep those *vors* away from my little ones!" She gave me a betel-stained grin and, shaking her head in incredulity, marveled again how at this juncture in her life, she should be blessed with children—"When it's almost too late!"

"Why?—Why is it almost too late?" I thought we'd arrived just in time.

She chuckled, blushing. "Pok and I are so old, you see, and soon we'll return to the spirit world."

"How old are you?"

"Older than I can count!" She laughed.

A rooster suddenly crowed: *Kakingongur!*

"Finally, he rises!" Mae declared, looking around. "Where's that scoundrel?"

I pointed to the clay vat near the thatched enclosure. The rooster, with its neck stretched out, bellowed again: *Kakingongur!*

Mae hollered back at him, "You're no use to me! I'm up half the day already, done all my chores, and you're just clearing your throat!"

The rooster flapped his wings as if to say, *I'll show you, old woman!* and for the third time asserted, *Kakingongur!*

We returned to the hut. Mae set aside the twig broom and, hitching up her sarong, squatted down in front of the cooking fire. She removed the porridge pot and placed it on the ground. Then, using a piece of firewood, she pushed the stones farther apart from one another to build a perch for a bigger pot.

"What are you going to cook?" I asked, swallowing, thinking perhaps she was going to steam some rice cakes.

"I'm going to boil some palm juice to make sugar." She coughed, hands waving away the clouds of smoke mushrooming from the fire when she added the piece of rain-dampened log. "I—I need your lungs, child." She gestured to the moribund embers, still coughing. "Give it a good puff."

I squatted beside her, huffing and puffing, until a flame burgeoned like a leaf and caught on. Mae poured what was left of the palm juice from the flask into a large soot-blackened wok, and just as I was beginning to think the wok was much too big for such a scant amount of liquid, Pok appeared, a cluster of stringed bamboo flasks jostling weightily on each shoulder. He removed the leaf coverings and emptied the flasks into the pot, filling it to the rim with sweet-smelling juice. Mae added more wood to the fire and set the liquid to boil.

Happy with the exhaustion of a morning climb, Pok lowered himself slowly onto the bamboo platform and, from a large box made of palm leaves Mae had set out for him with all their chewing ingredients, treated himself to a quid of tobacco. Then he began to tell Mae about our morning excursion, his hands busy all the while whittling his wooden calf into existence.

eighteen

We settled into Stung Khae during what Pok called the "lament of the monsoon," that period of the season when the rain came in a steady drizzle throughout the morning, then wailed inconsolably in the afternoon, before it softened to a sob that was to last through the evening and sometimes well into the night. While some creatures like scorpions drowned and died, others like frogs and toads multiplied, the rain driving them into a wild cacophony of rasps and croaks on the surfaces of ponds and puddles littered with gelatinous spawn. Out here in the natural world, it seemed to me, life and death were simultaneously celebrated and mourned, neither more noted than the other.

The rains did as much to transform the landscape as Revolutionary fervor did to alter the life of the countryside, so that at times it appeared the power wielding the monsoon was in cahoots with the power wielding the Revolution. Shortly after we arrived, part of Stung Khae and most of the outlying lowland became flooded, turning the once earth-solid geography into a moving lake of shifting compositions. Huge masses of water hyacinth appeared suddenly one morning as if by inspiration, like islands in an archipelago. For several days they glided lazily across the aqueous canvas, carrying silhouettes of birds that had come to rest on the thick spongy leaves or to drink from the pouch-like blossoms. Then a rainstorm, descending like the broom bristles of a god bored with the scene, swept the floating islands away and replaced them with fields of undulating lotuses. The lotuses bloomed, pink and white, and eventually gave way to sturdy green pods. Pok would take me out in his palm-tree dugout, and while he scoured the water for shrimp hatchlings and minnows with a bamboo *chniang*, I harvested the pods, breaking the stems at about an arm's length below the surface of the water so that they'd retain moisture and remain fresh until we returned home at lunchtime. Some days, though, we'd stay out all afternoon, lunching on the rice and pickled papaya shrimp Mae had packed for us, letting ourselves drift among petals and pods as if in a dream, and snacking on fresh lotus seeds whenever hunger struck us. We'd go on drifting like this, without a word exchanged, and if a need ever arose for amusement, or simply to confirm our presence amidst the stillness, I'd tear open a lotus pod, take a hollow shell that had yet to develop a seed, and smack it against my forehead. Pok, woken from his reverie by the loud pop, would slowly turn to me, and noticing the telltale red blotch on my skin, invariably respond with a pop against his own forehead. This much said, we'd fall back into our silence, drifting like two lost souls, needing neither to be found nor rescued.

Once when it drizzled gently, he and I forgot ourselves completely, caught as we were in our daydreaming. When finally we returned home at dusk, drenched and weather-beaten but bearing a boatload of pods and more minnows and shrimps than we could eat for the next several days, Mae was beside herself with excitement because of the bountiful catch and with worry because—as she put it—"Lord Buddha, I thought you were carried away by the ocean tides!" Pok and I exchanged amused glances, expecting her to be no less dramatic. But Mae wasn't entirely exaggerating, for from our perch of land, the surrounding waters did resemble linked inland pockets of the sea. As for Mama, she knew I was in good hands. In Pok's care, I'd learned to swim, not very well yet, but enough to propel myself to safety.

The flood brought both plenty and scarcity. Fishes, crabs, crawfish— not to mention throngs of unusual creatures and crickets the villagers considered long-awaited seasonal delicacies—swarmed the water, often right into our nets and traps, and what we didn't eat that day, Mae would pickle and preserve to carry us through the days and weeks ahead.

But rice—the lack of it—became a great fear for everyone. The flood had brought a whole host of problems, chief among which was the loss of already planted paddies to total submersion. According to Pok, these paddies, which lay smack in the middle of the flood zone, shouldn't have been planted in the first place, at least not until the monsoon began to abate. At such time a traditional method known as "rice-chasing-water" would be used, whereby farmers rushed to transplant rice seedlings where the floodwaters had just receded, following the path and curve of the moving ebb as if chasing the water. It was an effective, time-honored mode of planting, he explained, as the soil would be rich with nutrients and minerals brought by the flood from as far as the Tonle Sap Lake and the Mekong. But the Revolutionary leaders and soldiers knew nothing of rice-chasing-water and in their fervor to speed up and increase production had ordered the villagers to fill the paddies with precious rice seedlings, which had all drowned and died. Fragments of their blackened, rotted stems resembling those lethal needle leeches now floated everywhere, possibly carrying plant diseases that could affect other planted paddies.

Whether in response to the villagers' fear of a rice shortage or their own fear of the Organization—whose name punctuated every public utterance and exchange like an exclamation mark—the Kamaphibal rushed forward again with their plans, this time to communalize the villages' rice supplies into one big reserve. They sent Revolutionary soldiers to announce there would be a "broad political" meeting to establish a communal granary at the estate of a former landowner. Every villager was required to attend. Some, preferring solid ground, braved the winding muddy roads on their oxcarts, while many more took to the water. Strings of boats and canoes threaded the rolling current, like stitches in a silk cloth, as villagers from all over the commune headed toward the same destination. We got into our palm-tree dugout and eagerly joined the pilgrimage. Despite the serious purpose of the trip, there was an air of festivity to the whole scene. The day, bright and clear, boasted an after-rain glow—a brilliant blue sky with florets of still white clouds. A sun-scented zephyr brushed our faces and carried our greetings across the water to one another—"Afternoon, fellow seafarers! Afternoon, comrades! Let's race!"

But on arriving, the mood changed completely. Everyone stopped talking and the apprehension about the meeting enveloped us like gloom. Pok moored the dugout to a willow sapling clinging to the side of an embankment. We all got out and walked the short distance to the appointed place. On one side stood an expansive, tier-roofed house surrounded by aged fruit trees, and on the other, a granary under the shade of lofty, ancient-looking hardwoods. We followed the crowd to the granary where enormous farm tools—wooden threshers, winnowers, querns, mortars, and pestles—sprawled across the straw-and-husk-covered ground like the exoskeletons of giant insects. Children climbed the bulky equipment, ignoring their parents' warnings. But when the Kamaphibal appeared, all movements and sounds ceased. A man stepped forward and introduced himself as Bong Sok—"Big Brother Sok." He had the leanness of a giraffe and the hooded eyes of a nocturnal creature, one of those fabled *khliang srak,* whose cry was said to portend the death of a sick person. The others' deference to him told me he was the face of the local Kamaphibal, the leader of the pack. He wasted no time in pleasantries and started the meeting right away.

"This spot has great significance," he said, hardly moving his mouth, but with a voice so morose it had the effect of silencing even our breathing. "The estate, as we all know, once belonged to a rich landowner. But now, among these remnants of wealth amassed through greed, the spoils of feudalism, we shall build a cooperative of collective wealth." His brow arched, revealing a bit more of his hooded eyes, but his facial expression remained unaltered, impassive. "Reactionaries may question our effort to advance the Revolution . . ."

I'd come to recognize the eloquence of their threat. They all spoke like this, sugarcoating their malevolence with fanciful words. I had only to look at Bong Sok, hear his grim hooting, to be wary.

"But we know their voices when they speak, we know their faces even as they hide in our midst." He paused. "Go home. Prepare your rice. Your comrade soldiers"—he nodded in the direction of the soldiers gathered in a long open-air wooden structure—"will follow you shortly to collect your contributions."

With that, the meeting promptly ended, and the villagers scrambled to get back into their boats or oxcarts.

As we feared, by the time we arrived back in Stung Khae, the soldiers were there. They took away everyone's rice. In turn each family received a ration for the week, which amounted to about a small can of rice per person per day. So it was that the four of us—Pok, Mae, Mama, and I—together received only *four* tin cans a day, not *five* as it should have been. Radana was too small to count as a full person, the soldiers said. So she received none.

A week or so later came Pchum Ben, a sacred Buddhist festival in which the Cambodians commemorate the spirits of the dead. Under the Organization's rules, we were not allowed to celebrate any religious holiday, but Mae said we would honor it anyway. Knowing that my birthday preceded it, I realized I must have turned eight. Mama looked at me with remorse, but I did not feel sad or aggrieved that my birthday had come and gone without her remembering. It was better this way. We wouldn't have been able to celebrate it as we'd done back home, with family and friends, with abundant food. Besides, I thought, eight was wrong—inadequate somehow. I was almost certain I'd become much older and, in these past months, had come to regard the reflection of the little girl I sometimes caught in the surface of the water as a kind of sprite—a phantom of guilelessness passing under my gaze before she vanished again among the ripples. So when Mae made a surreptitious midnight offering of food and drink to the spirits of the dead, I offered a prayer for my own ghost, for I could bear to imagine my own death, but I could not—*would not*—allow myself to think of Papa's. When Mama did, praying along with Mae, whispering his name, invoking his spirit to partake in the measly offering of food, I resented her for luring him from the safety where I'd hidden him—the sky, the moon, that secret sphere of my hope and imagining—back to this awful, aching hole in my heart. I wanted to tell her I did not need this night, or any other, to commemorate Papa's spirit, to call forth his presence. He was always with me. The next morning Pchum Ben was no longer, and I welcomed the day for its ordinariness.

Aside from this invocation of sorrow, our memorial return to loss, we adapted well to Stung Khae—to our new life as peasants and Mae and Pok's "adopted" children, to the ever-changing rules of the Kamaphibal, the volatility of the Organization and his predilection for chaos, as if calm was suspect, itself an enemy. I quickly learned my way around not only the village but also the villagers, who were linked every which way, like the rice fields, their associations often overlapping and so circuitous that it seemed impossible at first to keep straight who was related to whom and in what way—by blood, marriage, *thor*, or all three. I learned also that peasants were no longer just *neak srae* but should be addressed as Neak Moulathaan, the "Base People," or more commonly, Neak Chas, the "Old People," meaning they were the "base" from which we'd all come, the "oldness" from which hereafter everything would begin anew. By contrast, city people like Mama and me were Neak Thmey—the "New People"—new to country life, or maybe "new" as with animals that had yet to be broken in, to be tested and tried. "Old" or "New," my two elders told me, people were people, and I must gauge for myself whom I could and could not trust. And so, as I navigated the human terrain, as I negotiated for my survival, I began to discern what Pok had wanted me to see that day when he walked us across the rice fields and showed me what lay beneath the paddy water—that hidden in the unbroken and seemingly imperturbable monotony of rural geography, existed those, like the needle leeches, who fed on blood and destruction. If I was to survive my uprooting and transplantation, I must grow and stretch myself as a young rice shoot would. I must rise above the mire and muck, the savagery of my environment, while appearing to thrive in it.

For her part, Mama did her best to assimilate. She tried to cover as much as possible that side of herself that would invite endless critique and criticism. Attuning her body to the habits and rhythms of country life, she would get up before dawn to help Mae and Pok tend to the various chores around the house, and by the time daylight broke she would have already washed our dirty clothes from the previous day and hung them up to dry on the line, cooked and packed our lunch, and readied herself for a day of planting. In the fields, she performed better than could be expected of a New Person, drawing on her girlhood experience of growing up in the countryside, while hiding the fact that she had been the daughter of a provincial landowner who owned vast tracts of land and throngs of servants and that what she knew of farming came from watching them rather than performing the labor herself. She dyed her clothes muted colors, hid her long hair under a *kroma,* and spoke the village vernacular, sometimes going as far as affecting the lilts and twangs of the rural accent. Her transformation was like the reverse metamorphosis of a butterfly back into a caterpillar. Her true nature, her core, lay quiescent like a pupa inside a chrysalis, and when alone, away from the watchful eyes of the Organization, she would hug and kiss us, pick wild jasmine and insert the faintly fragrant blossoms into the folds of her clothes, and comb her long hair with lazy, indulgent strokes. Once, while attempting to replace the broken handle of her toothbrush with a bamboo stick, she slipped, saying, "Grandmother Queen—" She was quick to correct herself: "*Grandmother,* I meant . . . Your grandmother said black teeth were a mark of beauty in ancient times. Now I know why. The stain seals your teeth, keeps them from rotting out when you don't have any toothpaste or a proper toothbrush." Then, without looking up at me, she added, "You mustn't think this is our life, Raami. This isn't who we are. We're more."

It was her usual refrain, and every time she said it, I couldn't help but believe ever more firmly that *who* we were resided in all we had lost, that the disappearance of home and family, this gaping hole left by Papa and the others, gave shape and weight to our persons, as air to balloons, so that we hovered and drifted, light-headed with grief, anchored to solid ground only by a flimsy thread of self-knowledge—this faint notion that once we had been more, that there had been more to ourselves besides loss.

"Remember, Raami," again and again she would tell me, amidst the clamorous directives of the Revolutionary soldiers and Kamaphibal: *Forget the old world! Rid yourselves of feudal habits and imperialist leaning! Forget the past!*

"Remember who you are."

Let go of the memories that make you weak! For memory is sickness!

"You are your father's daughter."

Whenever she said this, guilt gripped me. I wanted to tell her I was sorry I'd revealed Papa's name. I'd done so only because I was proud of him. I wanted to tell her I was sorry because even now I wasn't sure if I understood it—why my pride had taken him away. But "sorry" seemed too small a word, and whenever Mama reminded me that I was Papa's daughter, it felt more like a rebuke, as if I had failed to keep him close, to cherish him. She never said she blamed me, but once she came close—"However you loved your papa, Raami, you must learn to keep his memory to yourself."

One morning at the rice paddies, a group of women known to be the wives of the Kamaphibal came up to us. Standing on the dike so that they were a couple of feet higher than we were, Bong Sok's wife, Neak Thot—the "Fat One," as everyone referred to her behind her back instead of "Comrade Sister"—cleared her throat and croaked, "Comrade Aana, we're quite pleased you're doing so well. You've shown great Revolutionary material."

Mama straightened up from her planting and, with the back of her hand, wiped the beads of sweat from her forehead. She gave no reaction to the woman's praise.

The Fat One continued, "Most New People aren't as adaptable as yourself, you see. They've shown no progress at all since they arrived"—shaking her head in dismay—"despite our effort to reeducate them." She let out a prolonged sigh. "Ah, they're still the spoiled bananas they've always been! All mush on the inside!" Her cronies tittered. She silenced them with a look. "What was it that you did before Liberation?"

Mama separated a section of rice shoots from the bundle she was cradling and, with her back bent once more, pushed the shoots into the inundated soil. "I was a servant," she replied without looking up. "A nanny."

"I see. What exactly did you do?"

"I fed and took care of my mistress's children."

"Really!" one of the other women exclaimed, unable to hide her disbelief.

The Fat One crooned, "We never would've guessed looking at you." She squatted down on the dike and then reached over to caress Mama's arm. "Your skin is smooth as eggshell, Comrade Aana." Her eyes shot to Mama's hands, which were soiled with mud and plastered with plant bits. "You have the fingers of—how should I say?—a *princess*. Ah, so delicate and well preserved!" She let out a false laugh.

Mama stood frozen to her spot.

"Let's hope they don't get ruined in this muck," the Fat One simpered. Then, on her feet again, she sauntered away, as though she had only stopped for a brief friendly chitchat while on her way elsewhere. The others tootled along behind her. "You're right, Comrade Sister, they are like spoiled bananas!" one parroted, and another retorted, "Good for nothing except fertilizer!"

When they were out of hearing range, I turned to Mama and demanded, "Why did you say you were Milk Mother?" I felt inexplicably betrayed. "*You're not her.*"

Mama stared at nothing in particular. "I was wrong to insist you remember who we were. I was wrong. None of it matters now, Raami. All we had, what we were. None matters at all. We're here now, stuck to this place."

"You're *not* Milk Mother."

"From now on, you're the daughter of a servant," she murmured, staring at her murky reflection in the ankle-deep water, "and I'm that servant."

What about the story of us being fruit growers from Kien Svay? "Papa said—"

"Papa, Papa!" she snapped. "He would still be your father if—"

She stopped herself. But it was too late. I understood what she meant to say. Yes, he would still be with us, if I hadn't revealed him to the soldiers.

"There's no Papa!" Tears pooled in Mama's eyes but she bit them back. "If anyone asks, you have no father. You don't know him. You never knew him."

I said nothing. I felt a rift, like a fault line, that suddenly cracked open on the ground between us, widening as it lengthened. *You have the fingers of a princess.* As if afraid of the Fat One's words, all of a sudden Mama was choosing to forget, eradicating from her memory all that we had been, bunching up the facts and burying their roots in the quagmire of denials and unattended pain, as I became more determined to hang on to every detail.

She turned her back to me.

As much as I needed reassurance, I told myself I must not go to her. I must stay instead on my side of this divide and separate myself from her because this was the only way I would survive.

nineteen

Harvest was upon us and with it the endless work, the long days cutting and collecting rice in the fields, the late nights threshing. One evening, as the sky turned a dusky grey, we arrived at the communal granary and joined the excited throngs gathered to celebrate the first official festivity of any kind since our arrival in Stung Khae. Traditional music blared from a speaker nestled in the fork of a giant cashew tree, with an electrical wire connecting the speaker to a small black cassette player at the base of the trunk. Both the speaker and cassette player were rigged to—of all things—a car battery. I thought of the camion that had brought us to Stung Khae months earlier. *What ever happened to it? Was the battery pried from beneath its hood?* A group of seven or eight Revolutionary soldiers, all male, stood guard, keeping at bay a gaggle of children eager for a closer inspection of this strange music box with its mouthpiece high up in the tree, like a dismembered organ, a heart beating with the *thum-thum* resonance of a folk drum. A couple of the soldiers hooked arms and started dancing, playing off each other's steps as the sound of a bamboo flute and coconut lute mimicked each other's melodies. Others sang, chorusing in unison, *Oh, the glory and riches of Democratic Kampuchea, the strength and beauty of its peasants . . .* It was all very bizarre, like falling into a hole where familiar things—cassette player, car battery, and electrical wire—had been squirreled away and recycled into a patchwork of nostalgia. Still, I was wooed, my mind anesthetized by the traditional melodies

dubbed with Revolutionary-inspired lyrics and the atmosphere of cama-
raderie and merrymaking. It was harvest as we'd celebrated before the
war, before all this, when farmers would gather to give thanks to the earth
and sky, honor the sun and rain, make offerings of warm rice flakes to—

The moon, I thought, remembering that harvest celebration always
had a moon. I looked up and there it was, high above the giant cashew
tree, just a faint silhouette of it now, but surely there, round and porous,
like a giant bubble suspended in the sky, a hole into which I might slip
and find fragments of a story told to me on a night much like this one.

The music stopped, and my reverie was broken. The Kamaphibal had
arrived. People stopped whatever they were doing and gathered around to
listen. I searched among the faces for Bong Sok and the Fat One, but they
were not in the group. One of the other members began to speak: "The
work of the Revolution is far from done! We must forge on! We must
continue with our struggle! The Organization needs everyone, every single
able body, to help make Democratic Kampuchea prosperous and strong! A
glorious and shining example to the world, to the oppressed millions out
there, the suffering masses that have yet to experience our Socialist regime!"

"*Cheyoo, cheyoo!*" the Revolutionary soldiers shouted, and the crowds
echoed, "Hooray, hooray!"

The Kamaphibal continued, "There's no better time than now, the
first harvest since Liberation, since the emptying of the cities, to show
the world we have taken a huge stride forward!" He made a sweeping
gesture: "We have all this rice to prove it!"

Again, the crowds cheered, their shouts made more thunderous by
a long, resounding clap. Then, I saw her—the Fat One, standing some
distance away, surrounded by her entourage of portly peers. Dread swept
through me and again I broke out in goose bumps.

"At the end of the work night," the Kamaphibal droned on, "we will
celebrate, according to village traditions, with a feast of rice flakes! The
Celebration Committee has been set up"—he gestured in the direction
of the Fat One and her cronies—"and these extraordinary ladies will see
to it that each and every one of you has his fill!"

This time the cheers were deafening.

• • •

Night fell. Mounds of threshed rice surrounded us, their shadows link-
ing, wavering in the moonlight, creating an impression of sea and mountains, the karst topography I often imagined in mythical legends. We'd
been working long enough and it seemed we ought to have a break soon.
But the bell had not rung. I gathered several bundles of the cut rice,
offered one to Radana, and, pulling her along, kept to the path lit by
the fire pits dug deep into the ground to keep sparks from flying astray.
While we children were required to work, what and how much we did
were not strictly defined. Instead the expectation was that we help as
much as possible, and in between jobs we could run around and play,
provided that when called upon to aid we must immediately put aside
our games—"as good soldiers would when called to arms," said the Kamaphibal—and assume the task demanded of us. One of our duties was
to bring the bundles of cut rice for the grown-ups to thresh and in turn
take the remaining stalks to the collection saved for thatch and fodder.
In general the threshing and pounding, which required more physical
exertion than skill, were relegated to the New People, who, according
to the Kamaphibal, needed to be toughened up through as much labor
and strain as possible. The dehusking and winnowing, which required
special handling, were assumed by the Old People, who could easily ma-
nipulate the deceptively simple-looking winnow baskets without tipping
them over and spilling the rice, or spin the hand-operated wooden chaff
blower without grinding the grains into bits. Mama was among those
assigned to thresh. She'd taken up her usual place behind a propped-up
wooden plank, against which she beat a bundle until all the grains fell
out, before taking up another bundle from the pile next to her.

Seeing how utterly absorbed she was in her task, I marveled at her
transformation. It seemed her body, rawboned and strained, could no
longer support thoughts and feelings beyond food, work, and sleep. Since
that day at the rice fields, confronted by the wives of the Kamaphibal,
she'd stopped speaking of Papa completely, never once mentioned his
name again, not even to remind me not to talk about him to others. I

hadn't understood it then, but I did now, and I no longer resented her for it—this decision to bury him, to blot him out of our memories as if he'd never existed. It was clear that while food fed our bodies, gave us strength to work and breathe another day, silence kept us alive and would be the key to our survival. Anything else, any other emotion—grief, regret, longing—was extraneous, a private, hidden luxury we each pulled out in our separate solitudes and stroked until it shone with renewed luster, before we put it away again and attended to the mundane.

Mama noticed me staring, looked up, and attempted to smile. I went to her, bringing Radana along, and added our bundles to the pile. She paused, her body rigid, as if wanting to grab hold of us and smother us with kisses, but she dared not with the Kamaphibal around. Such wanton display of affection was against the teaching of the Revolution. She nodded for us to keep working. Picking up an armload of straw each, we continued on our way, heading toward the haystacks on the other side of the compound.

Finally the bell rang. We could stop working now and have our treat. Along with the rice flakes, everyone received a banana and a cone of sweet palm juice. "Come back later," one of the wives of the Kamaphibal told me when she thought I was trying to get a second helping. I explained I wanted a share for Radana, and on hearing me the Fat One exclaimed, "Oh, is she even old enough to receive her own share?" I froze. Laughing, she scooped out Radana's portion and offered it to me, along with a banana and another cone of palm juice. Hugging my hoard, I quickly left before the Fat One changed her mind.

I found Mama sitting on a spread of straw. Radana lay in her lap, yawning, looking as if she was about to doze off. At the sight of food, though, she suddenly sat straight up, bouncing with excitement, licking her lips, offering her arms to me in a gesture of a hug—sudden love. Mama seemed unable to bear the sight of Radana's hunger. She got up and, looking at the queues of people waiting to receive their shares of rice flakes, said, "It might take me a while . . ." She sounded especially tired. "Let your sister sleep when she's finished eating. Keep an eye on her. Don't let her out of your sight."

I nodded, cheeks stuffed with rice flakes and banana. Beside me Radana slurped the palm juice from the leaf-cone I held to her lips, making puppy sounds, reminding me of the twins, and without warning, tears sprung to my eyes, as I wondered if somewhere they too were hungry. I looked up at the full moon, allowing myself to believe the world was indeed small enough for this one orb of light to illuminate its entire surface, that somewhere under this same moon, this same sky, the twins and the rest of my family were safe and well fed, if only for this one single night.

We finished eating. Radana yawned, rubbing her eyes with her soiled hands, spreading the stickiness all over her face. I took the edge of my shirt hem, licked it, and wiped away the broken bits of food from her skin and hair, while she nodded and swayed, her body heavy with sleep. I steadied her and, with one arm supporting her neck, laid her down on the *kroma*. She fell asleep in an instant.

All around the compound, other children, especially the little ones like Radana, were seeking the comfort of their mothers' arms, and if their mothers were not available in that moment for one reason or another, then they sought the security of a soft nook at the base of a tree or a whorl amidst the straw. It was late, perhaps near midnight from the feel of it, but I couldn't be sure, it being so bright. Certainly it was time for sleep. Even the crickets and cicadas had quieted down. A hush now settled over the whole place as people moved sluggishly about putting away tools and baskets of threshed rice, gathering their belongings, readying themselves to return to their villages. We could all leave, but some people had yet to get their treat, many lingered hoping for seconds, and others simply wanted to rest and catch their breath, let food reenergize their bodies before starting the journey home.

Again, I looked up at the full moon, imagining Papa's face looking down at me. I felt his presence everywhere. I wanted to be alone, gripped with an urge to speak aloud with him in complete privacy. I looked down at Radana. There was no harm in leaving her here, I thought. She was fast asleep. Besides, Pok and Mae were just a few feet away, slouching against a tree trunk by one of the fire pits, eyes closed, leaning into each other, much as the Sweetheart palms on our land leaned into each other, their chests heaving in harmonious snoring.

I got up and weaved my way through the haystacks toward the woods beyond. There I took a familiar path, slipping seamlessly through the waist-high grass, my body light and inconspicuous as if I were a spirit, a shadow capable of moving through space without causing a ripple or break, until the grass reached all the way up to my shoulders. I walked round and round in the same spot, trampling the delicate, yielding blades to create a comfortable sitting place. It looked so inviting, the whorl I'd created, like a nest almost. It would be as good a place to sleep as any, I thought. The spot I'd chosen gave a clear, straight-shot view of the moon, with no tree or cloud in the way, and feeling safely nestled, I began to talk to myself, making no sense at all, testing my voice first before calling out to Papa, saying his name.

Suddenly I heard other voices. I stiffened and lowered myself to hide. The voices came from the direction of the footpath, accompanied by the sound of footsteps. Then came an abrupt swoosh, like someone slipping and falling. "Get up!" said a man, followed by the sound of a kick and a shove, then the footsteps moving forward again, and a second voice, "How dare you steal! Right under our noses!"

"It's harvest and we are starving," answered a third.

"Well, you won't have to starve anymore. We'll put an end to your misery. How do you like that?"

No response.

"So where will your final resting place be? The well over there, where the landowner and his family are, or the forest beyond, where we have taken all the others?"

Still no response.

"Let's take him to the forest."

They pushed and shoved. I dared not move from my spot.

I don't know what path I took, whether I walked or ran or crawled, how much time had passed. When I arrived at the communal granary, my arms and legs and face were all scratched up, grazed by sharp grass and whipping branches. Mama grabbed hold of my shoulders and, looking me up and down, demanded, "What happened to you? Where have you been?" She shook me so hard my head wobbled. "Where's your sister?"

A cry came from one of the haystacks: "Mama!"

There was a whole army of them. They were as big as flies. Radana screamed, her arms shielding her face from the mosquitoes as if she were on fire.

twenty

Back at the hut Mama whipped me. With the spine of a coconut leaf so thin it felt more like hot wire across my back. Pok and Mae pleaded with her. They tried to pull me from her grasp, but she reminded them, "I'm her mother!"—they had no business interfering—then back to me, "I told you to watch your sister. You were supposed to keep an eye on her. Instead you let this happen. Look at her!" She pointed to Radana lying on the straw mat, her body covered with swollen bites. Even so, I knew this wasn't about Radana, or me alone. This anger she unleashed was meant for something larger, for all that she'd lost. "You were careless. You deserve this. You've asked for this. Do you understand? You've asked for this!"

Yes, I understood. But I couldn't speak.

"Answer me! Where were you when you left your sister alone?"

"Papa!" I heard myself cry when the spine of the coconut leaf slashed the small of my back.

She whipped me harder. "He—can't—hear—you." A lash for every word. "It's—no—use—crying."

But I wasn't crying. I was only calling out to him. I saw him now through the open doorway. A luminous, fearless moon. He smiled, holding the world in his light. I wanted him to hold me, to caress my seared skin, to patch my broken love. I wanted him to hold Mama, make her gentle and lovely again, as he made the night seem gentle and lovely, despite the secret it shared with me.

"It's no use crying," she said again, tears rolling down her cheeks in long, lustrous strokes, like the lashes she lavished on my body. "He can't hear you, do you understand? He can't! He's gone!"

Yes, I understood. Everything and nothing at all.

"Gone!"

"I'm sorry!" I cried as the coconut spine lacerated my shoulder. "I'm sorry I let them take him away!"

She stopped, as if stunned by my words. She threw the whip away, fell to her knees, and broke. Like a beautiful and fragile dream she broke, and everything broke with her.

Later that night the sky wept. I opened my eyes and saw her sitting in the doorway. Outside, it was almost pitch-black, the moon now hidden behind a curtain of rain. Rain that came in the middle of the dry season, the last fall before the earth cracked open. *Pliang kok*. Borrowed rain, Mae called it. Borrowed from another night, another loss. Above us the roof was leaking again. Mae got up to place a pot under the leak. She went to Mama's trembling form in the doorway. "Come, child, come," she said, her arms around Mama's shoulders. Mama shook her head vigorously, like a child refusing comfort. Mae sighed and came back to lie down beside me on the mat. A minute or two passed, then I heard Mama's voice—"Countless times I ask myself, Raami, what I could've done to stop your papa from leaving. There was nothing. Nothing I could've done, or that *you* shouldn't have done. I know you think I blame you. Maybe a part of me wanted you to believe it *was* your fault, because, knowing why your papa did what he did—to save us—I couldn't be angry with him. But the truth is no one, none of us, could've stopped him. He was who he was—he did what he believed was right. He stuck to his convictions." She gave an ironic laugh. "Your papa's poetry took him to great heights, Raami. But he didn't see that up there he was fully exposed. They would eventually spot him, even if you hadn't said his name." She let out a breath, as if letting go all she'd kept hidden. "Words, they are our rise and our fall, Raami. Perhaps this is why I prefer not to say too much."

I closed my eyes, counting the raindrops as they hit the metal pot, *tdock, tdock, tdock . . .*

In the morning, I found Mama outside stirring a pot of boiled lotus seeds over the cooking fire. The pot of rainwater was nearby. I walked to it, scooped some out with my hands, and drank, my parched throat remedied. She handed me a bowl of the lotus seeds. At first she was silent, wouldn't even look at me. Then, as I sat down to eat, she said, "There was a mother . . ." Her voice was small, like the rustle of a leaf in an immense forest. "She loved her daughter so much that she'd give the child whatever the girl desired. One night while they were playing in the garden, the little daughter saw the full moon and wanted it. The mother tried to explain that the moon belongs up there. You can't just pluck it from the sky like you would a fruit from a tree. But like any small child, the girl didn't understand the moon isn't something you possess. She cried and cried. So what could the mother do but give her daughter the moon? She brought a bucket of water, and pointing to the reflection, said, 'Here's your moon, my love.' The little girl, delighted, plunged her arms into the bucket, and for hours she played with *her* moon, watching it dance and swirl."

It was the first time, I realized, Mama had ever told me a story. All the stories I knew came from Milk Mother or Papa. Why? I wanted to ask. Why had she never told me a story before? *Words, they are our rise and our fall . . .* Why now, when all that was broken could not be mended with words?

"I'd give you anything," she said. "Bring him back if only I could."

I searched her eyes, and in their watery depths thought I saw his face. She turned away, wiping the side of her cheek with the base of her palm. Then, taking the bottle of iodine, which she'd obtained in exchange for one of Papa's shirts, she colored the welts on my back, her touch as gentle and tentative, I imagined, as a brush on canvas.

I let her caress me, as she'd whipped me. One stroke at a time.

One afternoon, some days later, while we were cutting rice, Pok's silhouette appeared like a mirage in the midday sun. He hurried across the rice fields toward us. Mama abandoned her sickle on the ground and rushed to meet him. Malaria, he told her. Radana had malaria.

Back at the hut, Mama sat hugging Radana to her chest, a blanket around both their bodies, and I couldn't tell who was shaking, she or my sister. Mae came in, lugging a basket of heated stones she'd wrapped in some rags. Mama looked up, pleading, "I can't stop her from shaking! Please, tell me what to do." Mae took Radana from Mama and, swaddling the blanket tightly around my sister's tiny body, put her down on the straw mat. Then, one by one, she placed the heated stones around Radana, pressing them against the blanket. Still Radana shook, her teeth banging against one another—a horrible sound, like an animal chewing on its bones.

She'd been attacked with bouts of chills since the morning. The first one started soon after we'd left for work, Pok said, but since it was mild he and Mae thought it was a cold. Radana had had no fever, so they weren't too concerned. Still, they kept a careful eye on her. The chills became more severe, each attack lasting longer than the one before, until there was no doubt in their minds this was malaria, which they themselves had suffered, as had countless others in the village. They knew the course of attacks well—first the chills, then the high fever, finally the pouring sweat and pounding headache. The chills Radana was having at the moment seemed to reach a peak. The whole hut shook with her.

Mae used the last two stones, balancing one on Radana's chest and another on her stomach. Holding the stones in place, she draped her body over my sister's like a mother hen warming her hatchling. For a long time she stayed like this, until the violent shaking subsided and only a tremor rose from beneath her. She sat up, but seeing Mama paralyzed with fear said to me instead, "Your sister will want some water." She nodded toward the doorway. "Go out and see if it's ready."

Outside Pok was tending the kettle. The water had boiled. He lifted the lid from the kettle and fanned the water vigorously with a palm fan. I squatted down opposite him and, unable to look him in the eye, said, "I gave it to her, didn't I? I gave Radana malaria."

Pok stopped his fanning. After a moment he said, "A mosquito gave your sister the malaria. A mosquito. It isn't your fault."

As soon as he said it, I knew without a doubt it was. Why else would he try to convince me it wasn't? No, I didn't give Radana malaria, but all the same I failed to protect her from it.

We took the kettle of water up to the hut, and as Mae had said, Radana emerged from the bone-rattling chills wanting only water. She screamed for it, pulling her hair, scratching her throat, biting down on her lower lip until it bled. Then, as soon as she'd had enough, the chills returned, along with the bone-rattling shakes, followed by the high fever. On and on it went, as I watched helpless with dread and guilt, unable to escape the feeling that I was once again somehow to blame.

When I was as little as two or three I became aware that my right leg was shorter and smaller than my left, just as I was aware I had wavy hair instead of straight, a round birthmark on my right shoulder instead of my left. When I got older I noticed all the other children had two legs of equal size and length, and I realized what I had was not only *not* As-It-Should-Be but that it had a name. Polio. When I asked the grown-ups what it was and where it came from and, most curiously, why I got it and other children didn't, no one could really give me a satisfactory answer. "For everything taken away," Papa once tried to explain, "something even more special is given back." Love was that Something-Even-More-Special. It was the glittering package, the silk bow and satin paper wrappings that came with the gift I didn't want, the polio I hadn't asked for, and because it was so dazzlingly beautiful, I held on to it and cherished it more than I did the gift itself. Love was my consolation prize, and as a child I received it in abundance from those who cared for me, from all the adults who shaped my world. First, love cushioned me against the realization that I walked with a limp while other children didn't. Then, love cushioned me against all things big and small—the disappointment of discovering polio wasn't a gift at all but was in fact an illness that had left me handicapped, the hurt of seeing my moving reflection in a mirror or glass wall, the resentment of being told by complete strangers that I had a lovely face but too bad about my leg—and except for the sadness I sometimes glimpsed in Mama's eyes when she watched me walk, I'd learned not to care much whether or not I'd had polio. Love, in all its manifestations, in the care and affection and tenderness I received, in the safety and comfort and beauty of my physical surroundings, would cushion me, I believed, against all maladies.

Now there was malaria. I didn't know if it was a minor illness that would go away quickly or if, like polio, it would leave a lasting mark, impair my sister in some way.

For the next several days malaria attacked Radana, like a spirit that had entered her body and was doing its wild crazy dance. One moment she would shake and rattle, sounding like a train coming off the tracks. The next she would burn with a fever so high her skin felt like fire, her eyes dull with delirium, rolling into her skull. Then, after the fever had peaked, her body would drop in temperature, so much that she turned from flushed red to ghostly white right before our eyes, as sweat leaked through her skin, soaking her clothes and blanket and anything else that touched her, at which point she would shiver and shake so hard I thought her bones would break into pieces and her teeth would fall out like an old person's. Sometimes in between attacks she'd call out insanely, "Ice cream, Mama! Ice cream!" But, of course, there was no ice cream, or even ice. There was only boiled river water that we kept giving her as if it were some sort of magical cure. After the fever and chills came an array of pains and cramps, so severe that watching her suffer them drove us mad with grief.

Again, Radana had just had one of her attacks, and the effect of it made her cheeks look and feel like embers, and her eyes become glassy like a fish's. Mama cradled her, rocking her gently, chin pressed to her forehead. Beside her Mae sat crushing two tiny yellow pills in a teaspoon. Mama had found the pills wrapped in a piece of paper inside the breast pocket of one of Papa's shirts. At first I thought maybe they were aspirins, but the paper said "Tetracycline," in what was unmistakably Papa's handwriting, each sound and syllable spelled out in Khmer under what I assumed was its foreign name. Round yellow moonlets, I told myself. Little tokens of himself he'd left behind.

Mae mixed the crushed pills with some boiled water from the kettle.

She nodded, indicating she was ready. Mama clamped her fingers on Radana's nose as Mae quickly shoved the spoon into my sister's mouth. Radana struggled, gasped for breath, and swallowed the medicine. Mae took the spoon out, Mama released her fingers, and that instant Radana let out an angry wail. I didn't know what she hated more—having her nose squeezed shut or the taste of the medicine. Furious, she tried pushing Mama away. Mama held her tighter, rocking her until she settled down, until her scream became only a whimper. Then, looking down at Radana, Mama said, "She's always been a healthy baby. She was never sick. She was perfect when she was born."

I wasn't sure who she was telling this to, Mae or me, or what she meant by it. Was she comparing me to Radana, or was she trying to say that I'd ruined my little sister, made her imperfect like me? I turned to Mae, but she only sighed. She got up and left us to ourselves.

Mama put Radana down on the straw mat. She stared at my sister, who looked so pale I thought the ghosts might mistake her for one of their own. Radana breathed softly as she slept, eyeballs gliding back and forth under her lids, the corners of her lips curled into a grimace. I didn't understand a disease such as malaria, or any disease for that matter. Still, I thought, I had the antidote for it—I'd love my sister more than I had ever loved her. I would no longer allow myself to feel jealous that she was perfect while I was marred by polio. I would love her completely, selflessly.

Mama looked up and faced me. "When you were sick with polio, your papa was with me, and I could hardly bear it, the agony of having to watch my own child suffer. I don't know how to bear it now. I need you to be strong for both of us."

Tetracycline. I repeated Papa's one-word poem silently to myself, casting its moon-like aura around Radana's body against the tricks of malaria. *Tetracycline*. This, and my love, in all its selfless manifestations, would bring Radana back to health.

The next day back at the fields, we moved through the rice with the speed of a hurricane. When the evening bell rang, we gathered our hats and tools and ran back home to Radana. Drained and in sore need of rest, we passed out next to my sister. Only later in the night did we get up again and, realizing we hadn't washed, head for the river behind the hut.

There, I quickly bathed, dried myself with a *kroma,* and changed into clean clothes, then went to wait by the torch we'd placed in the ground near the bamboo grove. Above me something—perhaps a lizard—leapt across the branches. It felt as if all the night creatures had come out to watch us. Frogs croaked, crickets hummed, and, once in a while from somewhere in the middle of the woods, an owl let out a deep, long hoot, silencing all with its mournful cry. I wished Mama would hurry up. She stood there at the edge of the river, tilting a coconut bowl of water over her head. She seemed immobile, bound by an unfathomable weight. As I watched her, it struck me again how odd that she, evanescent as a butterfly, was still here, while Papa, solid as a stone statue, had become only a vision in my dreams.

She dropped the coconut bowl to the grass and squeezed water out of her hair. I walked over and handed her a dry *kroma.* She took it and wiped the water from her body, and wrapping the *kroma* around her, dropped the wet sarong to the ground as she slipped on a clean, dry one over her head. I decided to tell her the dream I'd had before we came to the river.

"Papa came back," I said, holding the torch out for her as she buttoned her shirt. "He brought me a pair of wings. But"—I proceeded cautiously—"but he took Radana with him."

Mama picked up the wet sarong from the ground and began rinsing it in the river.

"Soon we can also go home," I continued. "That's what he said. Soon you and I can also go home. Now he'll take only Radana because she's sick."

Mama stood up, wringing the sarong dry, gripping it forcefully.

"Radana's going to get better, isn't she?"

Mama paused, her body rigid. "Of course," she answered, her voice quivering like the surface of the water under the torch's wavering light. "Of course she will. Why wouldn't she?"

I shrugged, then said, "It's just that I dreamt—"

"You and your dreams," she said, cutting me off. "They're like your stories—they're not real."

I didn't understand. Why was she upset? I only wanted to tell her that the reason Papa took Radana was to make her better again. "But—"

She yanked the torch from my hand and, without saying another word, started walking as fast as she could, leaving me behind in the dark.

I ran to catch up with her. "What's your dream then?" I demanded, angry now at her sadness, her refusal to acknowledge my every attempt to make her happy. "What's your dream?" I wanted her to explain why Radana wasn't getting better, and if it was indeed my fault, I wanted her to tell me what I could do to make my sister better. If she couldn't tell me that, then at least she should tell me something I could understand, a story where everything would turn out right. "Tell me! Even if it's not true!"

She stopped, her back to me, her entire posture erect.

"A lotus opens at dawn, a bird is released and flies home to his family," she said, not turning around to face me. "This is why I love an open lotus. It speaks to me of freedom and a new day—a new beginning, the possibility of everyone being together. But do you know the rest of the story? No, of course not, because I taught Milk Mother to tell you only the happy parts. Well, as you know, the male bird, smelling of beautiful fragrance, comes home to the rage of his mate. While he was shielded in that flower, a forest fire ignited, burning their nest, killing their children. In her grief, she accuses him of betraying her in the arms of another. No, your papa never betrayed me in that sense. But, all the same, he's left me alone in the middle of a forest and I fear the fire will have no limit."

I wept, not understanding.

"Yes, your papa may have brought you wings, Raami," she said, whipping around to face me now. "But it is I who must teach you to fly. I want you to understand this. This is not a story."

Before dawn several days later, Mama got up, slipped Papa's silver fountain pen in her shirt pocket, and went off without a word of explanation. At sunrise she returned, with three ears of corn hidden in her shirt. "How's Radana?" she asked, going up the steps.

"The same," I answered.

"Did Mae give her the medicine?"

"Yes." I followed her up the steps.

"And the rice porridge, did she eat much?"

"All of it."

She stopped and looked down at me from the top of the stairs. "Did you say *all of it*?"

I nodded.

She hurried into the hut.

"The child is getting her appetite back," Mae said. "It's a good sign."

Mama smiled, and her smile was like the sun after the rain.

At the fields, she kept smiling all day while she worked.

"You are full of private thoughts, Comrade Aana," the Fat One said. "The Revolution does not recognize private thoughts."

Mama beamed. She radiated.

It appeared Radana was indeed getting better. She'd stopped vomiting. She had mild diarrhea, but at least she was eating again and most of what she ate stayed down. Color was returning to her cheeks. Still too weak to sit up, she now lay on the mat, playing with a spool of white thread. Mama sat close by, letting out the seams of the white satin dress we'd brought from Phnom Penh, so that when Radana recovered and gained back her weight she could wear it. I stared at the tiny pink silk roses along the collar and the butterfly-shaped bow in the back, wondering where my sister would prance around in such an un-Revolutionary dress.

Mae poked her head through the doorway, and smiling at Radana, gurgled, "Look what I caught for you!" She held out a string, at the end of which dangled a toy grasshopper woven from coconut leaves. Radana stared at her, then at the dangling grasshopper. She didn't react, her eyes listless. Mae turned to me and sighed, "It's really for you."

I took the grasshopper from her and dangled it in front of Radana's face. I bobbed it up and down, twirled it around and around, and made all sorts of noise. Still, Radana did not react. I kept trying, counting the tiny brown scabs on her face left over from the infected bites, which looked not unlike little eyes staring at me. *The Organization has eyes and ears like a pineapple,* I thought, giggling to myself, imagining Radana to be the Organization. Then all of a sudden Radana's lips curled into a smile and she let out a hiccup-like chortle. Mama abandoned her mending and moved closer to my sister. "Do it again," she said to me. "Make her laugh again."

For the rest of the evening, we tried to make Radana laugh, and she did, each time a bit longer and louder.

The next day we rushed home from work to see how Radana was doing. She lay on the straw mat where we'd left her, her head tilted to one side on her small bolster pillow, her eyes only slightly open. Mae sat massaging her tummy while Pok hummed some sort of folk tune, his voice raspy like the sound of a bamboo reed.

Mama knelt down beside them, her hand stroking Radana's cheek. "How's my baby?" she whispered, parting the wisp of bangs on Radana's forehead, now looking enlarged with her face so gaunt.

"She was calling for you today," Mae said, "*mhum mhum mhum,* and looking at me like I had full breasts!"

Radana licked her lips at the word "*mhum.*"

"She must be hungry again," Mama said, watching her with such enraptured love I thought that too must be un-Revolutionary.

"I fed her some porridge already," Mae told her. "She ate like a piglet!"

"What about the cassava?" I asked cautiously. On the way home, we'd stopped by a villager's house and traded Papa's watch—the Omega Constellation—for a cassava root. "Is that for Radana?"

I couldn't bring myself to ask right out for it. I felt horribly ashamed of my hunger, believing that this constant ache for food was a kind of greed, a weakness of character. The lumpy knot twisted inside my stomach.

"No," Mama said. "It's for you."

• • •

Mama handed me a plate with cut-up chunks of the boiled cassava, sprinkled with bits of palm sugar. One of the Sweetheart palms that was still giving juice had recently produced enough for us to boil down to make a small block. I breathed in the aroma, the heat from the cassava melting the sugar, making the smell even stronger. Lying on the mat, Radana put out her hand and murmured, "*Mhum . . . mhum . . . mhum . . .*" She sounded like Mae's cow, I thought.

Mama shook her head at me and said, "Your sister's stomach is not ready for it yet."

"*Mhum,*" Radana said, more forceful now. "*Mhum.*"

It was her word for milk. A baby's word, and as such it was also her word for Mama.

"I'm here," Mama told her. "I'm right here beside you." She clicked her tongue, trying to distract Radana's attention from my plate.

"*Mhum!*" Radana screamed, even though it wasn't much of a scream.

"I'll get you some porridge."

Radana pointed at my plate. I felt a sharp pang grip my stomach, then shoot to my chest and bloom, tentacular and radiant, like a jellyfish pulsating in the dark of the sea. I winced from the intensity of it. Mama looked at me, as if to ask, *What's the matter?* But I couldn't explain it, this sudden heart-searing love for my little sister, who, if anything, had been more or less the bane of my existence, not because of anything she'd done but precisely because she *was* my little sister; who now, though still immune to despair and lacking any real sense of herself, seemed driven by the same physical need as mine—to feed her hunger, to stay alive. She kept pointing at my plate.

"Yes, that's porridge," Mama lied. "I'll get you some."

"No!" Radana cried, shaking her head. "Want *that!*"

"I know you do." Mama lifted her up from the mat. "When you get better, you'll have some." Turning to me, she ordered, "Take it outside—hurry and finish it!"

I ate it so fast I burned my tongue.

. . .

Later that night Radana sobbed herself to sleep, murmuring, "*Mhum* . . .
mhum . . . *mhum* . . ." Outside, Mae's cow replied, *Maaaw* . . . *maaaw* . . .
maaaw!

I clamped my hands over my ears. They went on. It was unbearable.

twenty-one

adana died. Mama woke me up to tell me this. She wasn't crying. She just sat in a corner, hugging Radana's bolster pillow to her chest. "I wanted so much for her to get better," she murmured. "I wanted so much for her to get better . . ."

I don't understand. When did she die? How?

"But she died," Mama chanted, "she died . . ."

I rubbed the sleep from my eyes and saw Radana lying next to me. I shook her, first softly, then hard. She didn't move. I waited. There wasn't a sound. "Radana," I whispered, then louder, "Radana!"

"All she wanted was to eat." Mama rocked back and forth. "If I had known . . ." Her words spun around my head, like a noose twirling round and round, ready to strangle me. "But it's too late now. Too late for cassava. Too late for sugar. For everything." She laughed. "Her last meal."

I heard noises below us. I looked down and, through the slatted bamboo floor, saw a torch burning and Pok working beside it. He sawed and hammered. A coffin for Radana.

She died.

The stars had come out for her, gathering in the doorway, blinking in silence. Everything seemed familiar. I didn't know why. Had Radana died once before? I remembered Mr. Virak's baby, the quickness with which he'd slipped away. Radana couldn't be dead. She was getting better. This was a dream. It had to be. *Wake up!*

"Wake up, Radana. Please wake up . . ."

"Come, child," Mae said to me. "Help me prepare your sister." She lifted Radana into her arms. On the straw mat, I saw a wet shape. Radana's body print in sweat. Or maybe the shape of her spirit, a shell left behind. Mae undressed her and placed her in the big wok we used for boiling palm juice. There wasn't anything else to put her in.

I looked at her body, now that she was no longer in it. Her rib cage. Her arms. Her chest bones, like a pair of hands with fingers splayed, protecting her heart, each bone as slender as one of Mama's fingers. I poured water while Mae sponged her with a cloth. I wished I knew how to chant like a monk. I wondered what you'd say to bless someone who couldn't be blessed anymore—*I hope the forest where your spirit goes has no mosquitoes. I hope malaria doesn't follow you there. I hope your suffering ends here and now* . . .

When we finished, Radana smelled like burnt palm sugar. Mae dried her and brought her back to the straw mat. Mama moved from her corner, moaning, unable still to shed tears. I no longer had to imagine it— she *was* a ghost, her spirit leaving with Radana's. I wanted to ask Pok for a nail from the coffin. I wanted to nail Mama's spirit to her body. I wanted to nail her to me.

She chose the white satin dress she'd fixed for when Radana would get better, the un-Revolutionary dress with the shiny shantung bodice, the lacy tulle skirt, the row of pink roses at the collar, and the butterfly-shaped bow in the back that I imagined would flap like a real butterfly's wings when Radana ran. A white night moth chasing a girl-shaped dream. White. Yes, I remembered now. White, the color of mourning. Not black, like the color of the Revolution. Nor saffron, that of vanished monks.

Radana was gone.

She had died while I was asleep. Mama put the dress on Radana. "Go to sleep, go to sleep," she hummed, like a woman playing house with a lifeless doll. "It's not morning yet, go to sleep . . ." Was she speaking to me or Radana?

She had woken me to tell me Radana would not wake up again.

Ever. Temporary was forever and forever was now. Death was now and eternity. I'd always remember it.

Mama handed Radana back to Mae, who took the eggplant-colored *sampot hol* Mama had given her as a gift when we arrived and wrapped it around Radana, swaddling her like a newborn so that only her face was showing. Then she laid her next to me and covered both of us with a blanket. I put my arm around my little sister and held her tight, as if the warmth of my body could make her body warm again. "Still a baby," Mae wept. "A silkworm in her cocoon."

"A butterfly not yet born," Mama echoed, rocking back and forth. *But tomorrow is her funeral.*

In the morning while we gathered on the bamboo platform under the hut, the Fat One appeared wearing black and a smug look on her face. She'd brought the other wives of the Kamaphibal with her. Members of the Burial Committee, she said. "We're your comrades, Comrade," she reminded Mama. "We've come to offer you our support." Whatever it was—this support of theirs—it would not do. Mama wanted only Radana.

"You are adopting the correct attitude, Comrade Aana. Tears are signs of weakness."

The others murmured their agreement. They were as young as Mama, all with children of their own. But they didn't understand her sadness. They praised her for being strong—for not crying. "Regret is poison. Crying for the past is against the teaching of the Revolution. You're on your way to become a true Revolutionary."

Mama looked at them. She didn't answer. They surrounded her, like vultures surrounding a mother hen, their eyes on her dead chick, greedy and waiting.

Pok had finished building the coffin. He lifted Radana into it and as he did so a teardrop fell from his eye and rolled down her cheek so that it looked as if Radana were crying for herself, as if she grieved her own death. In the morning light her skin was as white as the dress she was wearing, and her eyeballs, I noticed, no longer glided back and forth under her closed lids as they would when she dreamed. *Dying is when you close your eyes,* Papa had once tried to explain. *Sleep without dreaming.* Radana died. She was no longer dreaming.

They would take the coffin to bury, the Burial Committee explained. Somewhere among the rice fields. A body shouldn't be wasted. Radana would fertilize the soil. She would be able to serve the Revolution better than she could when she had been alive. We should be proud. The men and women who had sacrificed their lives for the Revolution were buried this way. They had no coffin. Radana was lucky. She had a coffin. Hers was a bourgeois death.

"There will be no religious ceremony." The Fat One wanted to make sure we understood. "Ceremony is a feudal custom of the rich. And there will be no prayer. Prayer is false comfort. It won't bring the child—"

"Enough!" Pok cut her off. He closed the coffin and nailed the lid shut.

Mama handed the Fat One the rest of Radana's clothes, neatly folded and stacked in a bundle tied with the red ribbon, the same one she had bought from the little girl selling New Year's jasmine when we were leaving Phnom Penh, when red was her favorite color, when she was young and strong and beautiful. Did she want the ribbon and the clothes buried with Radana? "Please take this . . ."

"Your daughter won't need these things where she's going," the Fat One told her.

"But you can't send a child into the next world without her belongings!" Mae protested. "Have pity on her soul—"

"The dress she has on is enough!" the Fat One snapped. "The rest is bourgeois luxury!"

"Please," again Mama murmured, her whole body trembling as she held the bundle out. In her lap was Radana's bolster pillow, darkened with dried sweat stains from all those times Radana had lain on it burning with fever. It was too old and dirty to be taken into the next life or be of any use in this one. No one took notice of it. They all had their eyes on the bundle.

Finally, the Fat One took it. "We'll see what can be done," she said, tucking the bundle under her arm. "We can carry the coffin ourselves. None of you need to come."

Mama nodded, lifting Radana's bolster pillow to her chest.

I stared at her, panic rising in my throat. *Don't just sit there! Do something! Tell them to bring Radana back. She isn't dead! Why do you just sit there hugging that stupid pillow? Bring Radana back! She isn't dead! Bring her back!*

I jumped from my seat and followed the Burial Committee to the road, my heart hurling against my chest, like Radana's small fist banging on the coffin's lid as she screamed, *Out! Let me out!* Or was it my own rage? "Where are you taking her?"

"You don't need to know!" one of them hissed. "Don't follow us."

"Let her," the Fat One snickered. "Let her follow her sister if she wants."

When we were alone again, Mama let out a heartbreaking scream. I scooted closer, offering my heart—my love—for her to break so that hers wouldn't have to, but she only screamed louder, rearing her head like the mother cobra I'd once witnessed Pok and a group of men trying to catch for food. The men had dug a hole in the ground not far from its nest and placed a pot of boiling water in the hole. Hidden behind some bushes, they used a long bamboo pole to invade her nest and quickly rolled one of her eggs into the pot amidst the cobra's frantic hissing. The cobra reared her head at the pot with her egg in it, let out a hiss—so sorrowful and human that I wept for her—and plunged herself into the scalding water. Had there been a pot of boiling water in front of us now, Mama would've done the same.

"Give me back my baby!"

It was my fault, of course. Radana died because of me. The certainty of it overwhelmed me now, as I remembered all those times I had wished she too would have polio so that we would be the same. Now she was dead. I hadn't loved her as completely as I myself had been loved, and even though I'd vowed I would, it was too late. Death had already dug a hole in the ground and set its trap.

"My baby!" Mama screamed again. "Give me back my baby!"

Pok came in and pulled me away, his body shielding my body, blocking me from Mama's screaming—her shattering.

Later, I found refuge under the Sweetheart palms. I wanted to be alone, to hide from everyone, from the world. Pok came walking up the dirt road from the river, a fishing pole in one hand and two catfish strung on a leafy vine in the other. When he passed the cow by the haystacks he gave her a pat. She let out a plaintive "*Maaaw.*" She appeared like any other bovine, witless and uninterested, until she mooed, and only then you realized she was still grieving, capable of sustained sorrow, as if death, the awareness of it, is a universal consciousness, the *thor* that allows us to empathize with another that's not of our own kind. The wooden charm Pok had carved and fastened around her neck with a rope hadn't done one bit of good. It hung there, a constant reminder of the baby she'd lost, and, looking at her now, I wished for this grieving beast of burden a human disease—forgetfulness.

Pok nodded and moved on. I pulled back, pressing myself against one of the palms. I didn't want to talk to him. I just wanted to be with the palms. Their solitude spoke to mine, my sense of isolation. But Pok saw me. He came and sat down, his back against the other palm. For a minute or two we kept silent and avoided each other's eyes. Then he tilted his head back and, looking up, said, "Do you know which is *thnoat oan* and which is *thnoat bong*?"

I said nothing.

"One morning that one grew out of a seed," he went on, nodding at the palm I was leaning against. "Several mornings later this one peeped out." He turned and tapped the one he was leaning on. "Also from the same seed. We separated them and planted them in these two spots, with enough distance between them so that when they got big their fronds wouldn't overcrowd and they'd more likely bear fruits. But, the funny thing was, as they grew they kept leaning into each other, each year a little closer, until their trunks crisscrossed, as they are now. You see, we thought of them as our children. Or at least, the spirits of the children we could've had, wished we had, and that's why we called them *thnoat oan thnoat bong*."

All this time I thought they were "sweethearts," when I should've known *oan-bong* also means "younger-older siblings."

"Now, it seems, one has stopped giving juice, and from the look of those fronds, it isn't going to make it." He paused, swallowing. "But the other, we hope, will push on."

He let some minutes pass in silence, then, looking up again, said, "Those vultures! I've seen them for days now." He untied the *kroma* that belted his shirt and swung at the air above us, as if this was enough to chase the vultures away. "You and your sister will always be connected. You were her older sister. You watched over her, you protected her—you did— the best you could, and now she will watch over you and protect you."

"She's dead."

He got up and, with his trap and fish, went on his way. I felt worse. It wasn't his fault. He was only trying to help.

I lay down on the grass and watched the vultures circling above me. I closed my eyes and imagined what it would feel like to just slip away and float to the sky.

Where're you running to?

"Wake up, child! Wake up!"

I felt a hand shaking me. I opened my eyes and saw Mae's face looking down at mine. "You could've been bitten by an animal," she said, holding a torch. "You see how dark the night is? What are you still doing out here?"

I looked around, not knowing where I was. "Where is she?"

"What are you talking about? Where is *who*?"

"Radana."

"You must've been dreaming." She helped me up.

Where're you running to? That's what her name sounds like in Khmer when you say it really fast—*Rad'na. Where're you running to? Where are you hiding?* I'd dreamt we were playing hide-and-seek.

"Come, let's get you inside," Mae said, taking my hand and pulling me home.

I looked up at the night sky and saw a shooting star, and then a blinking one. Somewhere out there a child died and another was born.

Mae soaked a washcloth in a bowl of water and put it in Mama's hand. Mama looked at it, as if not knowing what it was. Then slowly she brought it up to her face and rubbed her cheek with it, in the same spot again and again. As I prepared for bed I tried not to make any noise changing my shirt and pants. The last thing I wanted was to remind her I was here instead of Radana. She dropped the washcloth to the floor and lay down beside it. Mae felt her forehead. "You're on fire," she said and handed her a tiny yellow pill. "I found it among your clothes."

Tetracycline, I remembered.

Mama stared at the pill, whispering, "It was my hope till the end . . ."

"Take it," Mae told her. "Maybe it'll help you."

Mama laughed. Mae lifted her head up, pried her mouth open, and placed the pill inside. Mama swallowed. She turned away from Mae and, seeing me, said, "You were my hope till the end, my hope till the end . . ."

"Let's finish washing you up," Mae said. "Here, lift your neck."

"Please, leave me alone."

"All right, child, I'll let you be."

"I want to die."

In the morning Mama looked better. Her fever was gone. Outside on the bamboo platform, she stared at the porridge in front of her, stirring it with the spoon. Mae tried to get her to eat. "If you're going to the fields, you need your strength."

Mama began to sing softly to herself, the words unintelligible, but the melody was a lullaby, the one she'd often hummed to Radana when putting my sister to sleep. At the other end of the bamboo platform, Pok looked as if he wanted to say something but couldn't. Mama's pain muted him. It cut off his tongue.

"It's a small village," Mae finally said. "Someone might have seen where . . . where she was buried."

"I don't want to know!" Mama cut her off. "If I do, I'll bury myself right beside her. I *don't* want to know!"Then she went back to her singing.

It was the most sense she'd made since Radana died. It shook me to the core.

At the fields, the Fat One came up to her. "What does this say?" she asked, holding something out.

Mama looked at it. "Omega Constellation," she said, her voice far away. "Once he left it in the rain and I worried it might've got ruined, but it's water resistant . . ."

"Water resistant? What does that mean?"

"Nothing can penetrate it . . . not water . . . not tears . . ." She walked away from the Fat One, drifting past me like a column of smoke.

twenty-two

It was planting season again and, like waves rolling across the landscape, the rice paddies turned from ocher to jade. An eternity had passed since Radana's death. While most people grouped themselves in teams of three or four as they planted, taking comfort in one another's company amidst the vast expanse, Mama worked alone, cutting herself off from others, from any attempt to comfort her, as if her grief was her memorial to Radana, the stupa she'd erected in defiance of this renewed greenness. No one could reach her. No one could break through her hardness. She'd float from one place to the next, inaccessible inside her harvest-colored sorrow, like a dragonfly beautifully preserved in amber.

One evening, hoping to break through to her, I decided to run away. I hid in the bamboo groves behind the hut. I wanted Mama to worry. I wanted her to think I had fallen into the river and drowned. She'd be sorry. She'd cry, as she never could for Radana, with tears that, if collected, would run deeper than the river in front of me. I comforted myself with the thought of her inconsolable sorrow over me, wrapping it like a blanket around my body.

The sky darkened and my heart grew weak with the knowledge that I missed Mama more than she probably missed me. Night came. I got too scared. I abandoned my resolve to make her stop grieving and returned to the hut.

Mama was waiting on the steps. But when I came near her, she didn't ask where I had gone. She wouldn't even look at me, and her refusal to do so, her unbreakable silence, her every movement and stillness, confirmed my worst fear—that I was the child who lived, not the one she wanted. She got up and went inside.

I followed her into the hut, and when she lay down on the straw mat, I lay down beside her. I put my arm around her, just beneath her breastbones, where I felt her heart beating like a small bird throwing itself against the bars of a cage. I wanted her to feel love, its weight and touch, even if it was only mine, not Papa's or Radana's. "Mama?" I whispered.

It was the word that opened the floodgate.

"Like you, Raami, I grew up listening to stories. Every night my father would tell me the story of the Buddha. The Buddha was just a man, he said. A prince who one day left his wife and children to seek the answer to why things are the way they are, why people get sick and die and so on. My father told me that great learning comes at great cost, and sometimes you have to give up the one thing that is closest to your heart. One day, when I was nine or ten years old, my father left our family to become a Buddhist monk. He left my mother with seven children to care for and a huge land of coconut orchards to look after and maintain. My mother was overwhelmed. She was miserable, to say the least. One afternoon she took a torch and burned the whole land and, afterward, set herself on fire.

"Her death confused and angered me. I didn't understand why she'd killed herself. I went to the temple where my father was a monk, to seek comfort in a father's embrace. But my father held himself back, as a Buddhist monk was forbidden to touch a devotee, even if she was his own child. I turned my anger at him. I wanted to know why he'd left. 'Remember the story of the Buddha,' he said. That was it. That was all he said. And I was sent back home.

"For years, I tried looking for the answer in my father's story—the answer to my mother's unhappiness. Her anguish and pain. I didn't understand. How could she have done this to herself, to us, to me? In the blink of an eye, it seemed, I lost everything—my home, my parents, and my brothers and sisters, who were divided and sent to live with various relatives. Everything and everyone gone.

"When you were born, I wanted something different for you. I wanted to give you a reality that was magical and lovely. A reality different from mine. So I created for you a world rich with things you can see, touch, feel, and smell—the trees, the flowers, the birds, the butterflies, the carvings on the walls and balcony railings of our home. These things are real, Raami. Real and concrete. Stories are not. They're made up—so I thought—to explain what is too painful to say in simple, plain language.

"I remember my parents fought all the time. They were not angry people but they were always angry around each other, with each other, and, as a child, I always thought it was because they were different from each other and they wanted different things. My mother wanted a life in the city among shops and restaurants. She wanted to be surrounded by countless neighbors and friends. My father was happiest when he was alone, away from everyone and everything. This was what I saw. What I didn't see, and what my father could have told me in simple, plain language, was that he and my mother didn't love each other. They never had, and this not only destroyed them but it destroyed us children, ripped our world asunder and tore us apart.

"So love, I decided, would surround my own children. I tried to build for you and your sister a world where everyone loved one another and where you both were loved in equal abundance. Love was your reality, and you should never have to make it up, search for it in obscure words, such as those uttered by my father—*Sometimes you have to give up the one thing that is closest to your heart*. No, these words didn't mean anything. They didn't tell me how much he loved my mother or how much he loved us children. Love should be plain and clear. It should exist in the everyday things you touch and see. At least this was what I thought . . .

"But love, I know now, hides in all sorts of places, exists in the most sorrowful corner of your heart, and you don't know how much you really love someone until that person is gone. I realize, to my regret, that all this time I've loved one child more than I did another. No, not love in the sense that I would exchange you for Radana or the other way around. But love in the sense of believing. You had polio and survived. You never got sick again, as if polio had given you immunity against all other diseases. Since then I've never wavered in my belief that you were born to live.

"But Radana was different. I secretly believed the gods lent her to me for my sorrow—the sorrow of seeing you walk and knowing that no one, no mother, will see you as beautiful as I see you, that your beauty was in your strength, in your ability to pick yourself up from a fall and walk again, as I've seen you do again and again, with the polio and with other things.

"So when Radana got sick, this was all I could think of—she did not have your strength, your resilience. She had never been sick, really sick. I didn't know if she would survive malaria, as you had survived polio. Watching her, seeing how she grew weaker and weaker, I believed she would die.

"In this sense I've loved you more than I loved your sister, because even though you are broken and imperfect I never wavered in my belief that you belong only to me. You are mine to love and hold even as my world breaks around me, even as everything is ripped from my heart.

"I have no stories to tell you, Raami. There is only this reality— when your sister died, I wanted to die with her. But I fought to live. I live because of you—for you. I've chosen you over Radana."

A lump formed in my throat. For so long I had envied her closeness to my sister, believing their bond stemmed from their physical resemblance, their shared loveliness. Now I saw her beauty for what it was—a forbearance against loss, her own stolen childhood. All these years she had drawn strength from silence, while I'd sought solace in words. I swallowed my remorse and held her tighter.

"There may be times when I cannot look at you, speak with you. But you ought to know that in you I see myself, in you I see my horrible grief. We're not so different, you and I."

How could that be? She'd lived a whole life already—at eighteen she married Papa, who was ten years older, then gave birth to me and Radana, mourned the death of my sister, and now faced the possibility of losing me. Had she really suspected all along my sister would die?

I remembered that shortly after Radana was born I'd accompanied Mama to see a fortune-teller who told her Radana wasn't meant to be. *What?* Mama was flabbergasted. The fortune-teller, unperturbed, went on to suggest that we give Radana away temporarily to relatives to fool the gods—to protect my sister. Mama, furious, stormed out of the parlor, forgetting to take me with her. She came back soon after, but in the brief time she was gone, the fortune-teller had turned to me and said, *You are the daughter closest to your mother's heart.* I was only five then, but with the indignation of a grown woman, I'd responded, *You are lying! We will not pay you!*

But now it seemed to me the fortune-teller had glimpsed something we couldn't have seen—the nearness of Mama's grief to mine.

One day out of the blue, we were called to Bong Sok's house for a meeting with the head of the Kamaphibal himself. As we entered the compound, I imagined the landowner's ghost walking beside me, taking in every detail of his erstwhile existence. Coconuts and freshly harvested sugarcane stalks and kapok pods sprawled across the ground beneath the house, resembling disembodied heads and limbs. Sacks of rice and corn and cassavas lined the stairway like squat headless sentries. Amidst the chronic scarcity and deprivation, this concentrated cluster of abundance seemed grotesque and filled me with nausea, and I had the distinct impression I was walking into an open grave where the ground was strewn with the belongings of the dead. From somewhere behind the house, among the trees and bushes, I heard the murmur of small voices—a boy and a girl laughing, whispering back and forth, watching us perhaps, discussing what would happen—but I dared not look for fear of seeing the ghosts of the landowner's children. I kept my gaze on the open doorway and followed Mama up the stairway, swallowing nervously, pushing down the urge to lean over the wooden railing and retch from fear. Mama's well-paced steps, her practiced calm, as if she knew what was coming, frightened me even more.

Inside, ruffle-fringed curtains, once perhaps a beautiful deep red but now dulled to an earthy brown, draped the latticed windows. Bong Sok and the Fat One stood barefoot on a straw mat in the middle of an otherwise empty room. Dressed in the usual Revolutionary black, they resembled a pair of statues that only came to life in the presence of another human being. Upon our entering the house, they stirred, moving their shoulders and limbs ever so slightly, but their postures remained erect, faces expressionless. They both acknowledged Mama with a solemn nod. Then Bong Sok bent down so that his head was at the same level as mine and, with his hand resting on my shoulder, examined me with his hooded eyes. "What is your name, little comrade?" he soughed.

"R-Raami," I stammered.

"What a pretty name. I'd like to remember it. Can you spell it for me?"

Before I could open my mouth, Mama cleared her throat and asked, "May I have some water?"

Bong Sok signaled to the Fat One. As she disappeared to the back of the house, he sat down on the straw mat, gesturing for us to do the same. "You know, often children make better Revolutionaries than we adults. They are honest. Isn't that right, Comrade Raami? Could you spell your name for me? It's very unusual. It doesn't sound Khmer. Perhaps it's French? Or maybe English."

I opened my mouth, but once again Mama cut in, "They are good storytellers."

"Excuse me?" Bong Sok raised an eyebrow.

"Children are good storytellers." Mama forced a smile. "Like this one. She has a story for everything."

"You must know a lot about stories then," the Fat One said, coming back into the room, bearing a coconut bowl of water, which she handed to Mama.

"Thank you," Mama said, and, instead of drinking it herself, gave it to me. I drank and handed the bowl back to her. After all the trouble of asking for it, she herself barely took a sip.

"Why don't you tell us a little about yourself, Comrade Aana?" said the Fat One.

"I'm a Revolutionary—"

"Don't play games with us, Comrade. Really, where were you educated, abroad or in our country?"

"I never had any schooling," Mama answered calmly. "I was a servant."

Bong Sok signaled his wife with a look for her to stop with the questioning. It was his job to interrogate and instill fear. "You don't know how to read or write then?" he asked.

"No."

"Not at all?"

"Yes—I mean no, not at all."

"Comrade Raami, is this woman your real mother?"

I looked at Mama. *Yes, she's my mother, and she's real.* I nodded.

"Was she a servant—a nanny?"

I nodded again. *Lie even when you're scared—especially when you're scared.*

"What did she do?"

"She fed us milk."

"She fed *who* milk?"

"Us—me and Radana."

"Don't you mean *them*—the children your mother looked after?"

I nodded. "Them too."

"I nursed my mistress's children as well as my own daughters," Mama explained.

Bong Sok took something out of his pocket. It was the Omega. He pushed it toward Mama. "Can you tell me what this all means?"

"If I knew how to read a foreign language," Mama said, without so much as a glance at the watch, "perhaps I could."

"And you *know* this is a foreign language?" he asked.

"No, I assumed it is since . . . since I can't recognize any of the letters."

"Let me tell you then what it says: *Omega, Automatic, Chronometer, Officially Certified, Constellation, Swiss Made,* and, as you told my wife—but for the life of me I can't find it written anywhere on the watch—*Nothing can penetrate it, not water, not tears* . . ." He paused, observing her from beneath his hooded lids. "I wouldn't know, but I suppose I'll have to take your word for it. After all, it's your watch, and you should know whether or not it's water resistant. You should also know that a servant couldn't possibly have owned such a valuable foreign instrument."

Again, he observed Mama, then after a moment, "Do you know how to read and write Khmer, Comrade Aana? You certainly know some English, may even be fluent in French, as often is the case with people of your class."

"No, I . . . ," Mama stumbled.

"Are you sure? Are you sure, Comrade, that you are telling us the truth?"

Mama did not respond. I didn't know what he was trying to get at, what he was trying to get Mama to admit that he didn't already know. No, she wasn't a servant, and yes, she knew how to read and write, yes, she was educated, but apparently so was he. He could read a foreign language even, or at least what was on the watch.

"Do you know the severity of your crime?" he asked. "This deliberate cover-up you've engaged in to fool us all?"

Mama didn't answer.

"In Democratic Kampuchea," the Fat One edged in, "we have no room for people like you."

Bong Sok silenced his wife with a look, and to us, concluded, "A punishment will be decided. You may go now."

Outside their two children were playing. I'd thought they were ghosts of the landowner's children, but in fact they were little copies of Bong Sok and the Fat One. The son pretended he was a Revolutionary soldier, and his sister the captured enemy, his soon-to-be executed prisoner. He aimed a branch at her while she stood blindfolded, ramrod straight against a tree, her wrists in front of her, loosely bound with a piece of frayed rope. When the boy saw us, he put down his mock weapon, and the prisoner, sensing something was up, untied herself and removed the blindfold from her eyes. The two of them walked over to us. "Comrade Brother," the girl asked, mimicking my movement, "why is she walking like that?"

Beside me, Mama began to moan, her hand reaching for mine. The dress the girl was wearing was too small for her plump body. The white satin had turned yellow from dirt and sweat, most of the silk roses along the collar missing, and the butterfly-shaped bow gone.

Mama let out a sob. I pulled her away—"It's just a dress, Mama. Just a dress."

That night a Revolutionary soldier burst into the hut. "Pack your things!" he ordered. "Not you!" He pushed Mae and Pok out of the way and pointed at Mama and me—"You two!" He forced us down the stairs. Mae let out a hysterical cry: "No, no, you can't take them!" Outside she threw herself at his feet. "Please don't take them!" Pok came running out with our belongings in tow. "Where are you taking our children?"

"They're not *yours*! They belong to the Organization! To us—to do with as we please!"

"Where are you taking them?" he repeated.

"You don't need to know!"

"Tell us why then? *Why?*"

"You've grown too close. The Organization is your only family. You should've remembered that."

"At least let us say good-bye then."

"No! There's no need!" He pushed us toward the oxcart parked at the entrance of the land. "Go! Get in!"

"I am a *peasant*, you stupid boy!" Mae shouted, no longer afraid, Pok's machete in her hand. "I've worked this land longer than you've been alive, and if that doesn't mean anything to you, I'll cut you up and throw you in the rice paddy, and you can rot, and the Organization will have to deal with me!"

Surprised by her bold anger, the soldier let go of our arms. He pushed us back toward her. "Hurry up," he said. "Say your good-byes."

She glared at him, and he backed away, giving us room.

Mae cooed and clucked, sobbing, feeling our faces in the dark. She turned to Pok. "I don't know what to say, I don't know what to say. Help me. Help me find the right words."

"We've always known you don't belong to us." Pok handed Mama Radana's little bolster pillow. "But still we love you—" He choked on his own words.

Mama was right. Love hides in all sorts of places, in the most sorrowful corner of your heart, in the darkest and most hopeless situation.

"That's enough!" ordered the soldier.

Pok and Mae let go of us. We climbed into the oxcart. A kerosene lantern hung high on the arched wooden prow separating the two oxen. Another soldier was perched at the front of the cart, and for a split second my heart leapt, thinking it was the same boy who had brought us to Pok and Mae. But it wasn't him. Our driver held the reins and bamboo goad aloft, ready to go.

Pok came around and put the rest of our belongings beside us. He reached over to ruffle my hair, opened his mouth to speak, his betel-stained black teeth looking even blacker in the night. But he couldn't say it, whatever it was he wanted to say.

Our driver clicked his tongue, shaking the reins, and the oxen began to move forward. He whipped them, and they cried out, *Maaaw! Maaaw!* In the dark, the silhouette of Mae's cow answered, perhaps thinking its calf had come back: *Maaaw! Maaaw!* It ambled over to where Pok and Mae stood watching us. "Yes, I understand," I heard Mae say as she patted the animal. "I share your loss."

As our oxcart rolled onto the narrow village road, I became aware for the first time how cold and damp it was. In the short time we had been out, the dew had settled on my hair and skin as if I'd been sprayed with a fine mist. I looked back in the direction of our hut. I knew Pok and Mae were still standing there even though I could no longer see them. We had chosen them as our family over the Organization. This was our crime, and for this, we were being sent away. Our offense was as vague as the punishment awaiting us.

We headed into a forest, the path in front of us dimly lit by the kerosene lantern. Mama handed me Radana's pillow. I hugged it for warmth and put my head down on her lap. *Sleep, baby, sleep,* I sang silently to myself. *It's not morning yet . . .*

The forest enclosed us.

twenty-three

We emerged from the dark into an open field awash with light. A bonfire was burning, and here and there were smaller fires, like offspring of the larger one, around which people huddled in clusters of four or five, their belongings on the ground beside them. Many more gathered around the bonfire, their heads bowed in silence, mouths moving in inaudible whispers, like mourners around a mass funeral pyre, paying respects to the dead. Our driver abruptly stopped the oxcart and grunted at us, "Stay." He jumped off his perch and went to talk with a couple of Revolutionary soldiers standing guard in the middle of a paved road large enough to be one of the national roads that ran from one province to the next. The other soldiers nodded and lifted their faces in our direction, their postures languid, indifferent. Our driver came back to us and said, "Wait with the rest." Then, without saying anything more, he climbed into the cart again, turned it around, and slipped back into the forest.

With our belongings, we weaved our way through the clusters of people. Some turned to look at us as we went past, but no one greeted us, no one said anything. The only sounds came from the bonfire as the branches hissed or crackled, and from the night insects humming incessantly, unseen in the surrounding brush.

We found a space under a tree with sparse, drooping foliage. A group of people, gaunt faced and emaciated, made room for us on a patch of the slightly damp grass. They stared at us, searchingly, perhaps thinking we might be lost family members whom they couldn't trust themselves to recognize right away. When they saw no resemblance, they lowered their faces to the ground, once again as if mourning the dead, mouths moving in a whisper, a collective chant.

I pulled my knees up, chin resting on top of Radana's pillow, my arms wrapped around my legs to keep warm. I missed her, the smell of her hair after she bathed, like rain-soaked grass, midnight dew on bamboo leaves. It was that time of the night when it was easy to fall back to sleep. I looked around, feeling drowsy, unsure of what I saw and what I imagined. At the far edge of the open field a deer, or maybe one of those rarely seen *koh preys*, was licking dew off the leaves of a bamboo. Just a few feet away, a man sat cross-legged, his upturned palms on his lap, as if reading a book. *Papa?* I thought. My heart quickened once more, even as my mind slowed with sleep. He looked up. No, it wasn't him. The man tilted his head back, his palms lifted, as if making an offering to the heavens, and I realized he was surreptitiously saying a prayer, perhaps imploring the gods to spare his life. Or chanting an incantation before his death.

I averted my eyes and instead focused my gaze on images closer to me, things I saw clearly. Near us a mother was breast-feeding her infant by one of the small fires, while the father sat with a blanket wrapped around him like a tent, holding their older child between his knees. Again, I saw Papa, missed him intensely, the feel of his arms around me, the similar pose in which he'd once held me. Perhaps, I thought, I shouldn't wish for him. I shouldn't want him here. I would see him soon enough, he and Radana. I felt them beside me—their spirits, their ghosts. Soon I'd be dead too. Why else would they have brought us here?

"Beyond this field lies our fate . . ."

"Yes, our shared grave."

Voices echoed in my head, and at first I could not separate them from my own thoughts. They swirled around me, like the night moths beating their wings about the field, playing with the bonfire, toying with my mind. Then it became clear people were talking. I'd thought they were whispering hushed prayers for the dead when in fact they were talking about themselves and what was going to happen to us all.

"These soldiers will kill us," one man said, and another answered, "There are only two of them and at least fifty of us. We could take them."

"They are armed."

"Yes, they could wipe us out with one sweep of their guns."

My eyes followed the Revolutionary soldiers' movements. They paced back and forth, their steps listless with boredom and sleep. Still, they held on to their guns, one balancing it on his shoulder, the other using his like a walking stick. They wouldn't put them down, not even for a second, as if awaiting an order that could come at any moment. Their gazes flitted along the paved road, which, at each end, disappeared into the dark. What were they waiting for? More carts, with more victims?

"Even if we could take them, then what? Where would we go?"

"There's no way out."

"We will not see sunrise. We will die here."

I blinked, desperate to stay awake. If we were going to die, I thought, I didn't want to die in my sleep. I didn't want to die like Radana. But how *did* she die? It occurred to me I'd never asked. Mama had woken me up when it was already too late, when Radana was already dead, and now I wondered if my sister had been conscious when she took her last breath. *Stop it!* I told myself. *It doesn't matter. She's dead!* What good would it do to bring it up again? It wouldn't change a thing. It wouldn't change what was going to happen to us.

I felt a pair of eyes looking at me from across the open field. I turned in that direction and saw, some yards away, a man slowly standing up. There was something familiar about him. But I told myself, no, it couldn't be. He rose, his shadow becoming one with the dark. He held himself still, appearing almost as tall and thin as the tree trunk behind him. In the leafy shadow, I couldn't see his face, I couldn't be certain if he was actually looking at me. I had felt he was, but now I wasn't sure. He started walking, limping slightly, his every step tentative, his whole body trembling. He stopped and stared, again steadying himself, stilling his mind, perhaps making sure we weren't ghosts, just as I was trying to convince myself he wasn't one. He resumed walking, first slowly, then as if his life depended on it, he broke into a run, his arms stretched out, and I knew who it was.

Raami, Raami! Oh, Aana, where are you? It seemed a lifetime had passed before I was able to answer him—*Big Uncle!*

When I finally did, time stopped, rewound itself, fear and space disappeared, and all we saw and heard was one another. "Is it really you? Is it, is it? Tell me it's you. Oh, merciful life, it is you!" Big Uncle shook with happiness and disbelief, grabbing my face, then Mama's, feeling us all over to make sure we were solid, real, not just shadows or air, and as if he still couldn't be convinced, couldn't trust his hands or his eyes, he pressed his lips to Mama's eyes, each one in turn, and drank her tears. "It's really you, it's really you," again and again he said, and again and again he pulled us both to him, pressing us so hard against his body I thought we might slip through his rib cage.

"A miracle," he finally declared, breathless with incredulity. Then he hugged and kissed us all over again, needing to be reassured a miracle wasn't just a trick of the light.

"That's enough!" one of the soldiers suddenly ordered, pulling us apart. "Enough!" His voice brought the night back and everything reappeared.

Solemn faces stared at us. No one spoke. Then, one by one, heads nodded, lips smiled, eyes brightened, glimmering like stars in a hopeless night. The soldier looked around, shook his head, and walked back to join his comrade at their post by the road. The other appeared impatient, pacing back and forth with vigorous steps now, as if expecting an imminent arrival, an order from up top. But I wasn't afraid any longer. Big Uncle was with us. He was here. He was still alive. We could still live. Anything was possible now.

I looked at him, and he looked right back at me. I felt his head, and he felt mine. He was bald, like a monk. "What happened to your hair?" I asked. He laughed, fighting back the tears brimming in his eyes, and I chastised myself, *What does it matter what happened to his hair? He's here, isn't he?* Mama glanced up at him and, noticing his baldness for the first time, buried her face in his chest, her whole body shaking. He pulled her closer to him, and despite being told that was enough, we continued to hold one another, so tight that not even air could come between us. If we died now it would be as a single entity.

Then, as if suddenly remembering, Big Uncle asked, "Radana—where is she?" He looked around for her. I felt Mama pulling away. He reached for her, but she would not let him touch her now. "Don't," she said, shaking. *"Don't."*

He blinked, and the tears brimming in his eyes began to flow down his face. He was a *yiak*. An invincible giant who could crush you with his bare hands. Now he cried like a little boy.

"Where's everybody?" I asked, looking around for the others, as he had searched for Radana.

"Come," he said, swallowing his tears.

Happiness surged through me. "You'll take me to them?"

He could only nod.

Them was only Grandmother Queen. Auntie India and the twins and Tata weren't there. "They didn't make it—," Big Uncle started to say, and his hands began to shake, violently, uncontrollably. He tucked them under his arms to keep them still, to hide them from us. I stared at him, confused. *They didn't make it.* But what did it mean? They didn't make it on the oxcart, the truck, whatever had brought him here? Was that what he meant? A look of shocked acceptance settled on Mama's face.

"Mother," Big Uncle whispered, touching Grandmother Queen on the shoulder. Grandmother Queen didn't stir, just sat with her back against the trunk of the tree, so still I thought she might've died. "Mother, Raami's here."

Still no movement. Maybe she would recognize my voice.

"Grandmother Queen?" I whispered, leaning close to her ear. "Grandmother Queen, it's me . . ."

She opened her eyes slowly, stared, and smiling cried, "Ayuravann!" She pulled me to her, her bony hands caressing my back. "You've come back, my son. You've come back."

"No, I'm Raami." I tried to free myself from her grasp. I didn't know what shocked me more, her confusing me with Papa or hearing his name spoken. "It's me, *Raami,*" I repeated.

She stared, the look of recognition gone from her face. Closing her eyes again, she leaned against the tree trunk and murmured herself back to sleep.

"She's closer to them than us," Big Uncle said. "To the spirits and ghosts. She no longer knows who we are. She doesn't know who she is. It's . . . it's the only reason she's still alive."

He didn't say more but instead looked at the ground in front of his feet, avoiding Mama's eyes now boring into him. His hands began to shake again of their own accord. He tried to hold them still, one fist in another. I remembered once, back in Phnom Penh, he had reached up to the wall of his house and grabbed a gecko with his bare hand. He'd gripped it too hard, killing the animal by mistake. Once, a long time ago, Big Uncle had seemed to me like a giant who rose as high as the sky, who didn't believe that killing a gecko was bad luck, who challenged luck by picking fights with the gods. Now, he cowered and crouched, his limbs trembling like those of the gecko. When he could not stop his hands from shaking, he quickly hid them in his pockets.

"Your head," Mama said, brushing his shorn temple with the tips of her fingers, feeling the large scar that rose like a ridged mountain above his right ear.

"Yes . . ." He moaned, as if lacerated by her touch.

Her hand hovered near his face, fluttering in tenderness, and I knew what she was thinking, that in this light, in this moonless night, he looked like his brother. *You are my one single star. My sun, my moon . . . Even if I cannot touch you, I know I will see you, feel you . . .* Papa's parting words.

"To mourn them," Big Uncle finally managed to say. "I could not give them the proper ceremony." He felt his shaved head. "It was all I could do."

Mama pulled her hand back and turned away, unable to look at him any longer.

Big Uncle reached for me. I hugged him, touching his head, caressing it. There were more scars, I noticed now, in a few different places on his head. A plowed field of tiny ridges and crests, unmarked graves.

"You shouldn't play with your uncle's head," Mama reprimanded.

"It's all right," Big Uncle said. "Once, a person's head was sacred. Now . . . well, now it can be cracked like a coconut." He looked at her, as if noticing her hair. "They let you keep it long?"

"It's not Revolutionary, I know."

"Neither is being bald."

They both tried to laugh.

"I'll cut it if . . ." She let the sentence hang. But I knew what she meant—she'd cut it if we lived through this night.

Big Uncle nodded, running his hand down the back of his head, feeling for his hair. His baldness made him look even thinner. It made his head appear huge and fragile, more fragile than a coconut, more like an egg that could fracture with a slight tap, crushed by the hand of sorrow, a wife's remembered caress. He was still a giant, his silhouette towering over everyone, but something had broken inside him. Something stronger than bones. Something that had pushed this mythical *yiak* out of a storybook and turned him into my uncle, as if his size and bulk alone had given him the right to walk into any world, claim his place among men. Papa had called it *mechas kluon*—"a mastery of oneself." Now this was broken and he shook and limped, frail as a shadow puppet, lacking the self-possession of a live being.

He examined Mama surreptitiously, watching her whenever she wasn't looking, and when she faced him, he turned away or looked down at his hands, nodding to himself, as if he understood something she had never even said.

He'd remain like this for a long time, and I knew he would not talk about the others, at least not here, not now. He didn't have to. Their ghosts invaded our every thought and silence, and whatever happened or would happen, I took comfort in us being together again.

twenty-four

I rubbed my eyes and found Mama and Big Uncle and Grandmother Queen still beside me. I didn't remember having fallen asleep, but my first thought upon waking was that I'd dreamt them up. Then I remembered that just as I was about to fall asleep, Big Uncle had told Mama the name of the district he was taken to and, as it turned out, it wasn't far from ours. Perhaps less than a day's ride on an oxcart, he'd said. To think that all this time we were living so close. Fear, not distance, separated us, kept us from seeking one another out. "It doesn't matter," he was saying now. His voice was as real as the sunlight falling on my face. I blinked and shook sleep away, glad he wasn't a figment of my imagination.

Around us people stirred in weary confusion. They felt their faces and the faces of loved ones, smiling when they were certain the sun had indeed risen and they were permitted to rise with it.

There was some commotion by the road. A truck had arrived, and the Revolutionary soldiers guarding us were trying to sort something out with the truck driver and the soldier accompanying him. A crowd started to gather around them as the two sides argued.

". . . a delivery to a town called Ksach, in Kratie Province," the driver was saying.

"No, no," said one of the soldiers guarding us, shaking his head, "they're bound for Battambang Province."

The driver, a cheerful-looking fellow with a boyish face, suggested brightly that since Kratie was closer and he was going that way anyway, it would be easier to take us there than to Battambang.

"The two provinces are in opposite directions!"

"True, but at least we're following orders."

"Even if it's the wrong ones?"

"Yes."

As if this made perfect sense, the four nodded happily, like little boys finally agreeing to the rules of a game. So Kratie it was.

The soldiers ordered us to gather our belongings. One of them came along and poked Grandmother Queen with his gun to hurry her on. Big Uncle and Mama, each taking her arm, quickly helped her up and escorted her toward the truck.

It was a strange sort of truck—a mishmash of different parts from different vehicles hammered and welded together to create what to me resembled a giant mangled dung beetle. I hadn't seen a truck or a car or any other kind of motorized transport since the one that'd brought us a long time ago to Pok and Mae's village. I'd thought anything with a motor—any machine—had been destroyed. The truck was rusted to the core; I didn't know how it had even gotten here, let alone how it would take us anywhere.

When our turn came to board, Mama and I got in first, climbing the metal bars roughly welded to the back panel that opened and dropped downward. Next, with the help of others, Big Uncle hoisted Grandmother Queen up. Then he himself climbed in. There were no seats or benches, just a bare metal floor with small holes where the metal had rusted out. We moved to the front, pressing close to one another so there was room for those still coming in. Grandmother Queen crouched in a corner among the elderly, while Mama and Big Uncle, with me sandwiched between them, stood against the side.

At last the truck was loaded, with the young and brave perched high in what was normally the luggage rack. There were at least fifty of us, I thought. Maybe sixty. The driver turned on the ignition, and the truck wheezed and coughed like a cat trying to regurgitate a hair ball. After several false starts, the engine finally groaned with a steady hum and then slowly began to roll. Grandmother Queen suddenly cried out, "Wait! Wait for my son!" Mama bent down to comfort her: "He will stay behind with the others." Grandmother Queen turned to the people near her and said, "Ayuravann, he's my son, you see." Toothless heads bounced up and down, nodding, "Yes, once we too had sons," they told her. "We too had a family."

Sometime in the afternoon we arrived in Kratie Province. The road became wider—smooth, no longer rough like a crocodile's back but tar black and glistening under the sun, like the back of a python. We entered a town, a linear town, it seemed, for everything in it huddled along the edge of the river. The road widened even more, hemmed now with fruit trees—mango, longan, sapodilla. A yellow-columned temple appeared, with its doors and windows boarded up. Then we reached what appeared to be an abandoned market center where smaller streets and footpaths crisscrossed one another like woven strips on a rattan mat. We kept to our path, passing by a school, two long mustard-colored buildings facing each other, its playground noisy with children. A red flag bearing a golden image of the famed Angkor Wat flapped in the wind high above their heads. When they heard the cough and sputter of our truck, the children jumped up and down, squealing, "Gas, gas! Mmmm, doesn't it smell good?" *Boonk boonk!* our truck sounded. *Boonk boonk!* The children clapped and cheered, delighted. Their teachers, also dressed in Revolutionary black from head to toe, seemed just as charmed. They waved, and our driver stuck his arm out and waved back.

I thought maybe we'd slipped through some invisible crack during our journey and entered another world. I resisted the urge to close my eyes, afraid that when I opened them again these signs of civilization would have disappeared and we'd find ourselves back in the forest.

We came upon a small wooden cart drawn by a pony-sized horse. The driver lifted his straw hat in greeting. Our truck slowed, groaning and shaking, and the soldier accompanying our driver stuck his head out to ask where the town center was, to which the other replied, "Straight ahead, the house with a large bronze bell." The soldier thanked him, and the cart driver nodded, stunned by all the gaunt faces staring at him from the back of the truck. How we must've looked to him, like a truckload of skeletons, beings not quite dead, not quite alive.

We picked up speed for several blocks before stopping in front of a spacious, tree-shaded courtyard. At the entrance, a large bronze bell hung from an intricately carved wooden beam held up by two round columns. In the middle of the estate stood a large teak house surrounded by smaller open-air pavilions of a similar style, with shingled roofs and spire gables.

Our driver jumped out and announced, "I guess this is it!" He banged on the truck, laughing. His companion went to greet a group of men meeting in one of the open-air pavilions. They stood up, looking confused as they shot a glance in our direction. The soldier handed one of them a paper. The man read it and shook his head, looking even more perplexed. He indicated for the soldier to wait as he hurried toward the teak house and disappeared up the flight of stairs. A moment later he reappeared and joined the others in the pavilion, speaking to them in earnest, presumably explaining something important, to which they all nodded in agreement. Our soldier marched back to the truck and climbed in, gesturing for the driver to do the same, and, with the engine coughing and sputtering once more, the vehicle began to chug forward, groaning with the weight of everyone's disappointment.

I closed my eyes, fighting back tears, ready to console myself with sleep for yet another long journey. Just then our ride abruptly came to an end. I opened my eyes and saw that we'd come to the part of the road where it curved and narrowed so that on one side was a row of houses, a mixture of traditional wooden structures and painted stucco villas, and on the other, a pair of giant flame trees leaning on a gradual incline toward the river, the ground beneath strewn with blood-red blossoms.

The soldier ordered us out of the truck. We descended quietly, orderly, taking turns, afraid that if we behaved otherwise we'd be ordered back inside. We gathered under the flame trees, the river before us, brimming with the season's rains, its strip of white-sand shore glistening under the afternoon sun, so bright my eyes hurt from looking at it.

By now a group of townsfolk, noisy with gaiety, had started to trail us, offering greetings and help. In no time at all we learned we'd arrived in Ksach, a former merchant town in Kratie Province on the edge of the Mekong. "It's a lovely place," assured a round-cheeked woman, giggling nervously, as if she thought there was a chance we wouldn't like it. "It's the best!" a girl standing beside her declared with greater confidence. Mother and daughter, I thought. They looked like paper cutouts of each other, only one was big and one small, both with round moon-cake cheeks and eyes that thinned into brushstroke lines when they smiled. "Father!" the girl called out as a group of men, the same ones who had gathered under the open pavilion, hurried toward us. Seeing them up close, I knew right away they were the town's Kamaphibal.

But something was oddly different about them. The girl's father grabbed Big Uncle's arm in that personable and familiar way men held each other. "I'm Comrade Keng," he said, full of enthusiasm and good cheer. "Welcome, welcome to our town!" They hadn't anticipated our arrival, he explained, his tone apologetic. They were expecting a delivery of tools. But obviously a mistake had occurred, and now that we were here, an arrangement had to be made on the spur of the moment to accommodate us. He pointed across the street toward a yellowish stucco villa under a row of milk-fruit trees. "You'll all be staying there, as a group, until everything is sorted out." Then, as if noting our terrified look, he reassured, "Don't worry, the district leader is aware of your arrival."

We entered the shady grounds of our temporary home. The long branches of the milk-fruit trees made a leafy canopy over the ground and balcony. Purple and green fruits, waxy and perfectly round, flecked the glossy foliage. Under each tree was a marble bench, the seat covered with dead leaves and branches. A thick layer of dirt coated the mosaic marble, and a long line of ants marched down one bench and up the next.

The villa stood several feet off the ground on rows of square columns. We climbed the front stairway to double doors that opened to a hallway extending all the way to what looked like the kitchen in the back. Inside, the floors and walls were covered with dust and cobwebs and dried bug carcasses. Except for discarded items lying oddly about, all the rooms were completely empty. "You can use anything you find in the storage rooms or closets," a member of the Kamaphibal said as they led us farther into the villa. "There may be some old pillows and blankets, as well as dishes, pots, pans, and other odds and ends."

While the others were quick to grab the bedrooms, we ended up in the kitchen. It was a rectangular room with a side door that opened to the back stairway. The walls were scratched and scarred and, on one corner of the floor where an earthen brazier might have sat, a quarter-moon shape was burnt onto the wood. Beside it, a bamboo basket of kitchenware gathered dust and cobwebs. There was nothing else. In its bareness the room looked immense, and it was all ours. It was perfect.

Dusk came, the evening mirroring our bruises from the long trip on rough roads. We gathered at the town center, which, as we learned, was also where the district leader lived. At the entrance, a young Revolutionary soldier rang the large bronze bell to let everyone know the meeting was about to begin. The townsfolk seemed as anxious as we were to know our fate. Many came with food, in dishes and pots, which they put on a trestle table under one of the pavilions and covered with large banana leaves to keep the flies away until the meeting was over. I stared at the spread and swallowed repeatedly, wondering when I'd last seen this much food, fighting off the urge to run along the table and gulp down everything.

The bell rang for the second time, and when it stopped, the Kamaphibal emerged from the teak house and descended the stairway. Leading them was a man, tall and broad shouldered, with a red-checkered *kroma* belted around his waist. He looked like an actor playing a village hero in a movie. As he strode into the courtyard, all eyes turned to him. "Where did he come from?" I asked, my voice breathless with awe.

Big Uncle gave me a strange look. "There." He nodded toward the teak house. "He lives in the house. You saw. He just came out."

"Oh." I thought the man had dropped from the sky. He had the gait of someone who could float through mists and clouds. "But who is he?"

Again, Big Uncle gave me a bemused look. "He's the district leader."

"What's that?"

"A leader who's in charge of one big area."

I thought he might be the Organization.

The district leader went around and offered his greetings, calling everyone by familial terms—*brother, sister, uncle, aunt, niece,* and *nephew.* He held his palms together in a *sampeah,* bowing slightly as he went from one person to the next. I was completely dumbstruck.

After he'd met everyone, the district leader went up to the stairway landing. "We didn't expect you," he said, addressing the crowd below. "But it doesn't matter. We're glad you're here. Welcome!"

The Kamaphibal, who had taken their places behind him, clapped. It was clear this was to be our new home. Everyone sighed with relief.

Nodding in the direction of the river, the district leader continued, "The monsoon season is upon us and soon the Mekong will overflow, turning land into sea. But together we will build embankments to control this mighty dragon. Together we will demonstrate that through our collective effort, we can build with our bare hands a mountain ridge from—"

Suddenly he stopped. A group of Revolutionary soldiers had appeared out of nowhere in an oxcart. They marched toward us. The lead soldier thundered up the steps and approached the district leader, whispering in his ear. The district leader shook his head; the Revolutionary soldier insisted, hissing into the district leader's ear. After a moment, the district leader faced us again and said, "You must excuse me." Without further explanation, he descended the stairway and, together with the Kamaphibal, left in a hurry, climbing into the oxcart waiting at the entrance.

The crowd was abuzz. The lead soldier spun around and faced us, and I noticed a long, sickle-shaped scar running the length of his right cheek. "Quiet!" he growled, the scar twitching violently. "Only the newcomers stay! The rest of you leave!"

No one moved.

"NOW!"

The townsfolk began to file past us, murmuring but not daring to meet our eyes, or his. They seemed to know exactly who the soldier was and their manners and attitude said this was not someone you argued with. Finally, when the last of the townsfolk were gone and it was just our group again, the soldier with the scar said, "Those of you with any family members missing, tell us your family history and background. Give us complete and accurate details—your real names, your relatives' real names. Tell us how you got separated from them, when, and why— the *real* story. We'll help you find them. But we can do that only if you tell us the truth." He looked around, his eyes darting, the scar on his cheek quivering as if it were a live thing. "Now, those of you with missing relatives, raise your hand."

Slowly, people began to raise their hands. Every single person, it seemed, except Big Uncle and Mama. The soldier narrowed his eyes at us. I broke out in a sweat.

twenty-five

Our arrival at Ksach seemed like a deliverance. The town had rules and rhythm, a kind of logic that didn't exist in Pok and Mae's village. First of all, the morning after our arrival, we were given rice, cloth, and other essential items to get us settled in. Then in the subsequent weeks, as the whole town gathered to receive the monthly ration, we were each allowed one can of rice per day. To keep it simple, we were told, no distinction was made between a child and an adult, each received the same amount, the rationale being a six-year-old boy who worked hard might eat more than an ailing old grandmother who couldn't eat much of anything. While market-style bartering was not allowed, a simple exchange of food or household items between neighbors and friends was acceptable. In our spare time we could grow vegetables or catch fish from the river to supplement our rations, but all livestock was the collective property of the town and reserved for communal feasting. Work began an hour after sunrise and ended an hour before sunset, at which time the large bronze bell at the town center would sound for all to hear. Children from ages five to eleven went to school, either in the morning or the afternoon, depending on our preference, and we could even switch back and forth. So off to school I went, sometimes in the morning, sometimes in the afternoon, depending on my mood, and in the month or two of my perfect attendance, all we learned were songs:

Red, red blood showers the ground,
Democratic Kampuchea our Motherland!
Shining blood of our farmers and workers,
Shining blood of our Revolutionary soldiers!
The Red Flag of the Revolution!

We didn't learn to read or write a single word, and even though I already knew how, I never let on. It was clear we must keep quiet, keep what we knew hidden. So we carried on, making ourselves fit in, and this time around it seemed easier, perhaps because Ksach was a close-knit community, yet open and welcoming in a way Stung Khae never was. People walked in and out of one another's homes as if they were one big family, exchanging dishes they'd cooked, borrowing one another's utensils and tools, sharing news and gossip alike.

It was in this spirit that Chae Bui, the round-cheeked woman, wife of Comrade Keng, came to visit us one night, bearing a basket of goods—"Gifts to fatten you up," she said, giggling, as she plopped herself down in front of the kerosene lantern on the floor, her round, bulbous shadow hovering behind her, filling half the room. To my disappointment, her daughter Mui was not with her, but then, I knew it was quite late and she must be asleep. Already in the mosquito net myself, and supposedly asleep, I watched silently as Chae Bui handed Mama a skewer of smoked fish, spiced dried beef, a bag of sticky rice, and a small block of cane sugar. Then she pulled out a packet of cigarettes and, handing it to Big Uncle, said, "American, one percent tobacco, ninety-nine percent imperialism." Again she giggled, her round tummy jiggling.

Everything about Chae Bui was round and jiggly, leaving the impression that she wasn't so much a person as a big bubble bouncing happily about. I'd never met a grown-up who bracketed almost everything she said with giggles.

Big Uncle thanked her, looking at the package. "I didn't know such things still exist . . ."

Chae Bui explained that Comrade Keng had just returned with the district leader from a trip to a town near the Vietnamese border. "Sometimes things leak through."

They were silent for a moment, and then Big Uncle asked, "Do you know why we're still here?"

"Remember that day you arrived, when the district leader had to leave abruptly in the middle of the meeting?"

Both Big Uncle and Mama nodded.

"Well, apparently, the leader of a neighboring district heard about your arrival and demanded that all of you be sent to your intended destination. The district leader refused, arguing why waste time and effort in transferring you to the other side of the country when you'd be just as useful here. The other leader accused him of being lenient and lacking a strong 'political standpoint' and threatened to expose him. It was not an outright threat, but this is what was hinted."

"But we are nobody," Big Uncle said, brows furrowing. "Why fight over us?"

"It's not about you. It's about them. My husband says there is a struggle between those who adhere to the Cause and those who are loyal to the Party. The district leader is probably among the few who still cling to the Cause, ideals that drew them to the Revolution in the first place."

"It's all so random." Big Uncle shook his head. "Like a bunch of boys playing rock-paper-scissors."

"If it's any consolation," Chae Bui offered, "you're very fortunate that you've ended up here. Battambang is a terrible place, where they like to send 'undesirable' people, and you were marked as—" She stopped.

"As that," Mama filled in. *"Undesirable."*

The room became completely quiet, except for Grandmother Queen's snoring.

After Chae Bui had left, Big Uncle lit a cigarette. He took his first drag, long and slow. Mama walked over, her lips quivering in the wavering blue light of the kerosene lantern. "May I?" she asked, shaking a cigarette out of the packet. He lifted the kerosene lantern to her, touching the blue flame to the tip of her cigarette, his eyes on her lips as she drew in breath. Then, with her arms crossed and the lit cigarette between her upheld fingers, Mama tilted her head back and blew out the smoke, with an ease that told me this wasn't the first time.

"It's funny what a man wants before he dies," Big Uncle murmured, bending down to put the kerosene lantern back on the floor. He ran his hand down the back of his head, playing with the new stubble. "In those hours I'd thought were my last, all I wanted was a cigarette." He gave a small ironic laugh.

Mama looked at him but didn't respond.

He turned from her gaze and kept talking. "The soldiers came one night to our hut. They said I needed to come with them. I asked them why. They got angry. They said I was a member of the CIA. They were young and illiterate, these boys. They didn't know east from west, let alone know what the CIA was, what those English letters stand for. But this was what they'd been instructed to say. If they want you, and you've committed no crime, this is what they'll accuse you of—working for the CIA. I suppose it's something you can't disprove, even if you try.

"I needed to be removed from the family, they told me. Why? I asked, again my anger getting the better of me. What the hell for? They threatened to kill the family right there in front of me. So I went with them, I let them drag me out."

He paused, taking another long drag. Mama waited quietly, the cigarette still in her hand, but she'd stopped smoking.

"They brought me to a forest, where there were huts and cages and dug-out trenches. A secret prison maybe. A military center of some sort. They were like boys playing war. There, they began my reeducation. They said I needed to purify my mind, purge it of imperialist thoughts. Memory is a sickness, they told me, and I was full of it. I needed to be cured. They took a coconut to my skull . . . There were many who died this way. But they couldn't crack me. I was too strong, they told one another. Too big to be broken so easily. I must have foreign blood. A pure Khmer couldn't possibly be this big, this tall. I must be the child of an American whore. They wanted me to confess. Who was my father, my grandfather?

What were their names? When I wouldn't say, they took bamboo stakes and slashed my scalp. They joked that they were looking for CIA codes, classified information. I told them I had no such things. I had no idea what they were talking about. They said they would find out from the women and children. They were convinced we'd been important people. They said they would go back to the village and bring the whole family, put them in the bamboo cage with me. They laughed, slapping one another on the back for coming up with the idea. So I told them I had foreign blood, I worked for the CIA, anything they wanted to hear, the most ridiculous improbable lies.

"When they thought they'd broken me, I was taken back to the village. The others, I found them. Hanged from the ceiling. Their bodies swollen. Blackened with flies. Tata had told them everything, they said. Our name. We were princes and princesses. One group interrogated me, the others murdered my family. There was never any communication between them. It was all a game.

"Only Mother was spared—too old for them to waste their effort. For days she'd lived with their bodies, and you wonder why she sees only ghosts, talks only to them . . .

"As I'd been reeducated, they let me live. It would've been better if they hadn't. I wanted to hang myself next to my wife and sons. After I buried them, I tied a noose around my own neck and closed my eyes.

"In the darkness of my mind, I saw everyone—the twins' smiling faces, yours, Raami's, and Radana's. Ayuravann's. Then I saw my own face, I heard my own voice, the promise I'd made to your husband that I would take care of you and the girls. Even as I readied myself to die, I hoped *you* were alive, somehow, somewhere. Then, hope—this thin filament of possibility that somewhere you were fighting to live—took hold of me. I grabbed it and knotted it around my neck. I let it lead me, pull me back to life.

"After that day, I began to ask about you and the girls, describing to people what you looked like, Raami with her polio, and pretty little Radana standing this high. Various descriptions. But no one had seen or heard of you. Then months later a truck was to take some people to

Battambang. I thought then since there was no news of you, perhaps you'd gone that far. I asked to be part of the group. The village folk looked at me as if I was mad. *Do you know where you're going?* some tried to warn me. I didn't care. I didn't have anything to lose. I had only the memories of India and the twins, our family and their horrible deaths.

"The night before the truck was due to leave, I shaved my head. To mourn them. To mourn myself also, my own death, for I'd died that day with them, strangled by the realization I couldn't—"

His hands shook and he dropped his cigarette to the floor. He bent down to pick it up, but he fell on his knees instead, crushing the cigarette beneath him. He crouched there, arms over his head, and when he spoke again, his voice cracked. "I couldn't save them. Even with all my lies, I couldn't save them." He wept openly.

Mama did not move. She stood watching him, this quaking heap at her feet. She pushed her cigarette hard into the windowsill, grinding it into bits against the wood, before throwing the butt out the window. Then, slowly, she lowered herself to the floor next to him.

Between themselves, I knew, they would never talk about the others again. It was understood that this was the least they could do for the dead—to bury their memories, if not them.

As for myself, I could not sleep. My night was broken up by jarring images of flies, ropes, and faces I could no longer recognize. At one point, I woke, tiptoed to the stairway, and threw up.

The days and weeks passed quickly as the whole town rushed to build barriers and embankments before the flood season set in. The mornings were mostly cool and sunny, but the afternoons were drenching wet, with the rains coming down in thunderous, prolonged streams. Then the evenings would be hot and humid, with the sun bursting through the clouds for one last glimpse, streaking the sky orange, before its rushed descent toward night.

This evening, the day seemed young still, not at all like dusk, the sky a brilliant blue after the usual deluge, brandishing a pair of rainbows, like Indra's crossbows, the god's declaration of war. The townspeople, resembling defeated soldiers, dragged their feet in exhaustion as they made their way home from a long day of hoeing and digging. Mama walked to the stairs and collapsed on the bottom step, her face and body smeared with mud. Big Uncle lowered himself on the dirt beside her. I went upstairs to our room, brought back some boiled water in a coconut bowl from our kettle, and offered it to them. Mama took a small, breathless sip and then handed the bowl to Big Uncle, who downed the rest in one noisy gulp.

"How many embankments did you build today?" I asked, imagining mountain ridges rising like giant centipedes across fields and floodplains.

"You wouldn't believe the amount of dirt we had to carry," Big Uncle said, breathing heavily. "You'd think we were building the Great Wall of China." He handed me the coconut bowl, and said to Mama, "Now to the river—need to get this mud off."

"I can't move another inch," Mama said.

"Stay," he told her, reaching for the yoked buckets nearby. "We'll bring the river to you."

The Mekong was in full spate. Men with *kromas* around their hips and women with sarongs pulled above their chests stood bathing as the water swirled around them. Naked children rolled about on the sandy shore, slick and glistening like rain-drunk carps, indifferent to their mothers' repeated calls to clean up. Every so often they shrieked when a frog hopped out of the grass or a crab scurried from its hole in the sand. Big Uncle put down the yoked buckets, took off his shirt, and dove into the water. He swam toward an islet with only its top now visible, his head bobbing in and out of the water, his arms beating across the currents.

My eyes traveled past the islet, to where the currents billowed like a sheet in the wind. A water-soaked log floated by, followed by a small sapling with all its leaves and roots intact. A youngster chasing after his elder, I thought. The Mekong traveled through many lands, Papa said, carrying to us the stories of places as far as China and Tibet. If the Mekong stretched all the way to China and Tibet, I thought, places I couldn't even see, carrying with it murmurs and echoes of those lands, then perhaps it would travel as far as the moon and carry my voice to Papa. What could I tell him? Nice things, of course. None of what Big Uncle had told Mama. Nothing about the others.

I looked around. In one spot a boy was washing his albino water buffalo so that it stood as transparently pink as a peeled pomelo, while ignoring the mud that caked his own body like tree bark. In another, Mui was busy plucking the tiny, slender leaves of a soap bush and rubbing them onto her hair until they dissolved into countless green specks oozing with bubbles. Nearby, Chae Bui, in a black bathing sarong that made her light skin look even lighter, was engrossed in scrubbing her shoulders and chest. Comrade Keng suddenly emerged from the water and surprised them. He snapped his jaws, pretending to be an alligator. Mui and Chae Bui splashed water at him, squealing and laughing. I closed my eyes and thought, *I must tell him all that I hear and see now.*

When I opened my eyes again, Big Uncle had reached the islet. He stopped and waved to me. As far as anyone knew, he was my father. *It's a story to disconnect us from the others,* Mama had said. *But in private, we are who we are, and he's your uncle still.* But, at a certain angle, from a distance, he looked exactly like Papa. In moments like this, when others had their fathers with them, I wished he were mine.

I took off my shirt and went into the water, the sarong blooming around me like a jellyfish I'd seen in the sea. Big Uncle began to swim back, faster than he'd gone out, perhaps afraid I might go in too far. But he didn't need to worry. I knew not to. Besides, I'd learned to swim from Pok.

Big Uncle paused, looking at me, and I waved to let him know I was all right. Reassured, he moved at a more relaxed pace, his right arm thrown forward, then his left, then right again, left, right, left, drawing a series of tiny rainbows in the air above his head. I knew he hadn't meant for me to hear what he'd told Mama, so I pretended not to know. I never mentioned the twins even when I missed them, even as I often wondered if they'd learned to plant rice, catch crabs and minnows, search the brush for bird eggs, all the things I'd learned. Once, I dreamt about them—just the twins—their faces swollen, the flesh partly eaten away by flies. Since then I resolved not to think of them before sleep, and if they slipped into my thoughts, I quickly chased the image away. I wondered now if they were where Radana was, if death was a place you could picture as you chose so that you wouldn't be afraid to go to it.

Big Uncle came out of the river. Gone were the mud and dirt that had caked his skin. He seemed clean. Cleansed. I followed him. He bent down to pick up his shirt from the ground and his head, spiky with new hair, brushed against my shoulder. I pressed my face to his cheek and hugged him. He stood hunched over, caught in midgesture, surprised by my sudden affection. Then, fingers folding gently over mine, he squeezed my hand, and I knew it was okay to love my uncle as I'd loved my father, in lieu of him.

With the two buckets of water we'd brought back from the river, Mama hid behind a bush in the back of the villa and bathed. As there was no soap or shampoo, she scrubbed her body and hair with a half-rotten lime we'd found on the ground. She'd finally cut her long black hair, and now the ends barely grazed her shoulders. Truly Revolutionary, I thought. It had weighed on her, as sadness would, I imagined, but she couldn't cut sadness in half. It wasn't like hair, it wasn't dead. Sadness was alive. Or maybe she'd cut it for the same reason Big Uncle had shaved his head. To mourn them. More than a year had passed since we were all at the temple together in Rolork Meas, Big Uncle said. Judging from the rains and the level of the river, we were at the peak of the wet season, maybe July or August, and, in two or three months when Pchum Ben came again, I would turn nine. I did not think we would ever stop mourning them.

"I can't reach," she said, handing me the lime. "Can you help me?"

I took it and ran it up and down the length of her back. The skin of her right shoulder was raw and broken, blistered from balancing baskets full of dirt all day long. I scrubbed harder, wanting to wipe away her sadness, all the hurts and wounds I could and couldn't see. She cringed from my roughness as much as from the sting of the lime.

I lightened my touch, and she poured water on her shoulders to soothe the burning, the water flowing down her spine, which rose in the middle of her back like a chain of mountains. I could count all her bones, the round notches and the long slender canes. The mountains, the Mekong, the Great Wall of China, I thought; Mama carried them all on her back. I felt it now, the full weight of her grief. I felt it in her breathing. In the words she couldn't and wouldn't say, in the tears that wouldn't come, the blood that wouldn't flow. She was no longer bleeding, she'd told Big Uncle one night when they stayed up to talk, thinking Grandmother Queen and I were asleep. *Because I couldn't keep a child alive, it seems the gods have taken away my ability to bear one. There are no gods,* Big Uncle had responded. *If they were the ones who gave life, created it, they'd know its value. There are no gods. Only senselessness.*

She stood up, emptying the last bit of water from the bucket onto her feet, and for a few seconds I saw her as she'd once been, light and effervescent, like a soap bubble swirling with iridescence, rising ever higher toward the sky, carrying the reflections of the trees, the mountains, the rivers, my sadness, hers, and Big Uncle's . . .

She was not one to explain things in detail, so she said, and yet it was she, I remembered, who'd shown me my first rainbow, pointing to the sky shimmering with raindrops and sunlight, saying, "Look, darling, a slide!" And since then, I'd learned to see things not as they were, but for what they meant—that even when it rained, the sun could still shine, and the sky might offer something infinitely more beautiful than white clouds and blue expanse, that colors could burst forth in the most unexpected moment.

. . . up and up she drifted, becoming more elusive and transparent, barely visible, and finally nothing. All the sadness seemed to disappear, melt away as if it had never existed.

twenty-six

Mui and I arrived at school to find a Revolutionary soldier sitting at our teacher's desk, his back pushed against the chair, his legs on top of the desk, and his gun balanced across his stomach. He wore no sandals, and the soles of his feet were almost as black as his clothes. He stared at us, chewing on a blade of grass like a bored ox. I recognized him by the sickle-shaped scar on his right cheek. Mouk, everyone called him. He was the town's top soldier and we rarely saw him, but when we did, he inspired only fear.

"Where's Comrade Teacher?" asked Mui, always the brave one.

"She's gone," Mouk mumbled, the blade of grass still in his mouth. The scar on his face chewed when he chewed, a creature devouring its own face.

"Where did she go?"

"Nowhere."

"Then why is she gone?"

He didn't answer. He pulled the blade of grass from his mouth and played with it, rolling it between his thumb and forefinger.

"But we have an assignment," another girl said.

We were supposed to have memorized the lyrics of "We, the Children, Love the Organization."

"Your assignment is this!" He suddenly bolted up, banging his gun against the desk. "Destroy this. This is all useless! Useless! Do you understand?"

We sank in our seats. No one breathed. The room was completely still.

Then Mui had to open her mouth again: "No."

"Stupid children!" Mouk said, kicking the chair back with a loud bang. "The Revolution can't be taught! It must be fought! Not with thinking and talking, but with action!" He picked up the chair and threw it against the wall. "Like this!" He kicked away one broken piece and stomped on another. "And this! It's useless! The chair is useless! Understand now?"

We all nodded.

"To keep it is no gain, to destroy it is no loss! Understand?"

We nodded again.

"Get out of here then!"

On our way home we encountered a throng of men erecting a huge bamboo stage in the middle of the street, right in front of the town center. No one would say what it was for. A group of sullen-faced soldiers kept a careful guard. The whole town held its breath as it gathered to watch. By the afternoon, the stage was finished, standing a foot or so off the ground and completed with an arch made of woven coconut branches and sprigs of areca blossoms. There was to be a wedding, we were finally told. A mass wedding. But the whole atmosphere was funereal. A while later when the brides and grooms appeared onstage, all dressed in black and solemn looking, we understood why. They stood in pairs under the arch, each bride with her groom, and there, close to the middle, was our teacher with her groom, a Revolutionary soldier on crutches, one of his legs gone except for a short stump that jerked back and forth as he moved. The crowd was stunned. At first no one knew what to say, then the whispers began: *Her eyes are all swollen and red. Looks like she's been crying. Wouldn't you if you had to marry that? I'm glad we've no daughter of marriageable age . . .*

Mouk appeared on the stage and, gesturing to the one-legged soldier, proclaimed, "Victory to our brave soldier who has sacrificed his body for the Revolution!" He clapped thunderously. The other soldiers, waiting in the wings, echoed in unison, "Victory to our brave comrade!" Mouk, barely acknowledging our teacher, addressed the one-legged soldier, still in that loud voice for all to hear: "The Organization has chosen a beautiful wife for you, Comrade! Let's hope she is worthy of you!" The other soldiers shouted their support: "Victory to our soldier!" Then, turning to the rest of the brides and grooms, Mouk pronounced, "The Organization unites you!" The soldiers shouted and clapped, and this time everyone felt compelled to do the same.

And just like that the wedding ceremony ended. The newlyweds walked off the stage and joined the crowd, but before anyone could ask questions or offer wishes, Mouk spoke again, silencing all with his voice: "Bring him out!" He nodded to a group of soldiers waiting in the back of the stage, and they, turning in the direction of the teak house, echoed to another group, "Bring him out!" A moment later, to everyone's shock, the district leader appeared, blindfolded and hands tied behind him. The soldiers pushed him up to the front of the stage. They hit his head and shoulders with heavy palm fronds until he fell on his knees. Mouk pushed the tip of his gun under the district leader's chin while another soldier removed the blindfold from his eyes.

"Look at the people!" Mouk ordered, excited by the sight and smell of blood, the scar on his face leaping wildly.

With effort, the district leader looked up, and we saw that his nose was broken and blood was running from one of the nostrils, his eyes were swollen and bruised, the skin torn over his eyebrows. He was unrecognizable.

Mouk turned to us and said, "This is the face of the enemy!"

"DOWN WITH THE ENEMY!" the other soldiers chorused. "HE MUST BE DESTROYED! DESTROYED! DESTROYED!"

The district leader said something, but we couldn't hear him. He tried again, hardly able to move his lips, his voice barely a whisper: "Why?"

"BECAUSE YOU'VE COMMITTED A CRIME!" Mouk screamed.

"What crime?"

"YOU'VE BETRAYED THE ORGANIZATION!"

"How?" Blood suddenly seeped from his other nostril, as if the effort of speaking was too much. "How . . . have . . . I . . . betrayed . . . the Organization?"

"It's not for us to tell you your crime! You must confess it!"

"I . . . have . . . committed . . . no . . . crime."

"THEN YOU'RE ALSO A LIAR!" Mouk spat on the district leader's face.

"TO KEEP YOU IS NO GAIN, TO DESTROY YOU IS NO LOSS!" the other soldiers roared.

They surrounded the district leader. There were at least twenty of them on the stage alone, not counting the others on the ground among us. They pushed the district leader with the butts of their guns, beating him until he fell over on one side. Mouk and another soldier picked him up by the arms and dragged him off the stage. The others roared, "DOWN WITH THE ENEMIES! DOWN WITH THE ENEMIES!"

They appeared out of nowhere, the new leaders. Suddenly they were here, as if they'd been here all along, waiting to come out. They were younger, quieter, and closer to the Organization. They wore the same mask-like expression. We couldn't tell who was the leader of the leaders. When they spoke, they had only one voice. In meetings, they would sit or stand in a row, watching and listening, surveying the faces before them with unblinking gazes. When they wanted to say something, they would whisper to Mouk, and he would speak for them. "You must dye everything black!" he told us at one meeting. "Not just your clothes but all your thoughts and feelings! You must blot out all un-Revolutionary elements! You must purge them out of your system!"

With the new leaders came new rules. We could no longer cook and eat at home. "If we work together, we must also eat together!" Mouk claimed, the scar on his cheek twitching, leaping constantly. "A father doesn't let his family eat in separate kitchens!" The Organization was our father, and we were his family. We must do everything together. We must share everything with one another—our spoons and forks, our pots and pans, our thoughts and feelings. If we had to, we would share the last grain of rice with our brothers and sisters. "We must say no to private property!" he thundered. "Private property is the evil of capitalism! Private property promotes greed and divides the commune! We will abolish all forms of private property!"

Back at the villa, people rushed to hide their belongings. They stuffed gold bangles inside dried-up gourds, pushed sapphires and rubies into wet clay balls and pressed them to the corners of the room. Some sewed necklaces and bracelets into the seams of their clothes. Others swallowed diamonds. Grandmother Queen wanted us to hide *her*. "Tell them I'm not ready yet," she whimpered. "Tell them I won't go without my children!"

"Tell who?" I asked. "No one's here. It's just us in the room."

"The spirits and ghosts—they are coming to get me. Tell them I'm not ready."

We heard loud footsteps coming up the back stairway leading to our room. Mama stood frozen in place, hugging Radana's pillow to her chest. Big Uncle yanked it from her and tossed it into a basket full of dry cornhusks saved for fuel.

The soldiers marched into our room, seven or eight of them all at once. At the sight of them, Grandmother Queen started to wail, "Go away! Go away!"

"Tell her to shut up," Mouk growled.

Big Uncle and Mama said nothing.

"She thinks you're ghosts," I told Mouk and his soldiers.

"Is she crazy?"

"Sometimes."

"Tell her to shut up then."

Mouk looked around the room, at everything, except the box of cornhusk near the doorway. He looked at Mama, eyes lingering, in a way that made Big Uncle clench his fists. Then, as if disgusted, Mouk turned and spat out the window. "Let's not waste our time," he told the others. "Keep a bowl, a spoon, and a kettle for the crazy old woman. The rest goes to the communal mess."

They left our room and moved on to search the rest of the villa.

For the next several days, Mouk and his "Secret Guards"—or Chlup, as they were called, spies who armed themselves with weapons and stealth, who watched and observed without you knowing—made the rounds to each household and categorized everyone. *You look like you could pull an oxcart. You're full strength! And you look like you haven't worked a day in the sun. You're medium strength then!* Both Mama and Big Uncle were full strength. Later that night Mama busied herself with packing. In the morning she and Big Uncle would leave with their assigned work unit to build embankments far from here. I begged to go with them, but Mama wouldn't hear of it. "You'll be safer here," she said. I was to stay with Grandmother Queen. How she would take care of me, I didn't know.

At dawn the next morning, Big Uncle lifted me from the mat and carried me toward the doorway. I looked around the room, bleary-eyed. We were heading down to the river to wash as we did every morning, except, I suddenly remembered, this would be our last time together. I caught Mama's moving silhouette ahead of us, like the end of a dream segueing toward daylight. I struggled to get out of Big Uncle's arms, but he was too strong. I felt my panic rising, but I bit it back and tried one last time: "I want to go build the embankment with you." I pressed my cheek to Big Uncle's chest. "*You* can take me."

"Stay with Grandmother Queen," he whispered, holding me tighter. "She needs you."

I glanced back at the room, to where Grandmother Queen lay on the mat, infirm and lost to the world.

"You'll be her child," Big Uncle said, descending the stairs. "You'll take my place. Answer her when she calls my name."

I stared at him. Maybe, I thought, it was just as terrible to leave your mother as it was to be left by her. Big Uncle gave me a wan smile, and for a moment I forgot my unhappiness, thinking how awful it was to be this giant with his enormous grief, with no one to comfort him, in the way that I, in my smallness, could be comforted.

At the river, Big Uncle dove into the water and swam out some distance so as to give Mama and me the privacy to say good-bye. I didn't understand why we would repeat this ritual of coming down together to bathe. Parting was parting no matter how disguised. Mama changed into her bathing sarong and put the clothes she would wear on her journey on a rock jutting out of the sand like the back of a large turtle. I purposely moved slowly with my clothes, hoping she would go in the water first. But she knelt down in front of me and began to unbutton my shirt.

"When I was four or five," she said, playing with a button, "very little—a baby still, according to my mother—I developed a love for Chinese opera."

I swallowed, bracing myself for one of her rare stories.

"Every time a troupe came through our district, putting on a story, performing an episode in each village, I'd follow it from one place to the next, attaching myself to a relative or neighbor I knew, negotiating a meal and a sleeping place with people I thought my parents knew or sensed I could trust, so that I wouldn't miss a single line of the story from beginning to end. My mother would forbid me to go, but I was a willful girl and always somehow managed to sneak out. I'd come back home days later, singing only Chinese opera. Once, so exasperated with worries, she called me Niang Bundaja, reprimanding me in front of everyone, saying what mothers never tire of telling their daughters—that one day when we have children of our own, we will know the agony of mothering. You know the story, of course."

I did. Niang Bundaja, a beautiful rich girl, falls in love with her servant, runs away with him, then becomes destitute and widowed, as her mother predicted. With two children to care for, she decides to return home, even if it means facing her mother's wrath. But halfway into her journey, she comes upon a river. She can carry only one child at a time across the strong currents, so she takes the older child first, then goes back for the baby. Meanwhile a vulture appears, circling overhead; she tries to shoo it away. The baby, thinking the mother is waving for her, walks into the river and drowns, and as this happens, the vulture swoops down and snatches the older child. It was a stupid story, I'd always thought.

"But what *I* want you to know is this, Raami—it's never a mother's choice to say which child will live and which will die. When I gave birth to you and then your sister and held each of you in my arms, I imagined a whole life ahead of you. Once I believed I would live forever. Death never entered my mind. Then one day, death surprised me. It caught my child's hand and yanked her from me, and I bled until I could bleed no more."

She let out a sob, the sound of it like silk being ripped, a page of poetry torn out in the night. If I had Papa's notebook and pen with me, I thought irrationally, I would draw a map of a village and it would have rivers of tears, oceans of sorrow as bottomless as Mama's eyes, and a bridge, as delicate and narrow as the bridge of her nose, which you could cross without the risk of drowning.

"I don't want to lose you, Raami. So, I ask you now to wait for me on this shore. Don't mistake my leaving for a good-bye."

When we returned to the villa, Big Uncle and Mama went inside to get their belongings. I waited on the stairway. A lizard scurried across the bottom step, pausing midway to look up at me. *Go away! Shoo!* The lizard puffed up its sack-like neck as if to ward off my despair. I stuck my tongue out at it. It dashed off.

There was a murmur from inside the room. I moved up closer to the doorway. "We must leave for a while." It was Mama speaking to Grandmother Queen. "But Raami is here with you. She will care for you."

I resisted the urge to go in.

There was a silence, then Big Uncle cleared his throat. "Mother," he said, stopped, then started again, "Mechas Mae," speaking now the royal language, as if not caring who might be listening, "I, your son, bow before you." I didn't have to look to know exactly what he was doing—pressing his forehead to her feet, paying his respects. "I ask for your blessing on this journey."

"Come back to me," Grandmother Queen murmured, and I couldn't be sure if she was responding to Big Uncle or if she was talking to the ghosts inside her head, repeating herself as always. "Come back to me."

"We'll meet again," Big Uncle reassured. "I will see you soon."

There were movements, the wooden floor creaking under their steps. I held myself still, as the lizard had done, my neck puffed up, my throat all choked. With fear or sadness, I didn't know. A sense of loss, of losing, surged through me.

Big Uncle emerged first. He descended the stairs and lowered himself next to me. Then Mama came out. Big Uncle got up and moved away to make room for her. But she remained standing, and I could feel her gaze on me, as if willing me to look up and meet her eyes.

"Wait for me—" A sob escaped her throat and she could say no more.

She rushed down the stairs, her whole body shaking as if a storm were passing through her. Big Uncle followed. I didn't try to stop them.

I settled into my role as caretaker, doing my best to look after Grandmother Queen, striving always to do more than I could but achieving only just enough to get by, to keep us going for another day. Still, I had my routine and tasks, which, ironically enough, gave me a sense of purpose, gave some measure of structure to an existence that was otherwise hanging by a thread. First thing in the morning after waking up, I would rush down to the river with a bucket, quickly splash some water on my face, rush back up the incline with as much water as I could carry, and dump it in the small vat near the back stairway. I'd dash back and forth a few more trips so there was enough to give Grandmother Queen a sponge bath and wash our clothes. Then, with a kettle set to boil over a fire, I'd scour the ground for longan pits, round like hazelnuts, and pulpy jackfruit pits, the size of a grown-up's thumb. These I'd toss into the fire for a bit of something to eat. Fruits found on the ground were supposed to be collected and pooled together with our neighbors' in a basket, then taken to the communal mess. If I was caught eating any fruit or siphoning off the collection, one or both of my day's meals would be held back. But hunger made me less afraid, less thoughtful about the consequences, and stealing became a habit. I might visit a vegetable plot in the back of a neighbor's house, yank a melon off its vine, tuck it inside my shirt, rush into the room, and feed it to Grandmother Queen, one bite at a time, softening it first with my own teeth, as I'd seen Mama do. Another morning I might slip into a cornfield, snap off an ear of corn, break it in half for easy hiding, and, back at the villa, discretely drop it in the kettle to cook. If there wasn't time, I'd pry off the tender kernels as quickly as I could and feed them raw to Grandmother Queen. The rest I'd eat myself, chewing even the core, sucking it dry, before spitting the remnants into the fire. Other mornings, when hunger made me woozy and completely overtook my fear of being caught, I would pluck a fruit off the lowest branch of a tree behind our house, eat it quickly on the spot, and toss the seed into the brush, not caring who might be watching.

This morning, along with some grasshoppers, I found an egg—a duck egg it looked like, white and large—in the sand along the river. Deliriously happy, I ran back to the villa, started a fire, and perched the kettle on top to boil. While waiting for the egg to cook, I skewered the grasshoppers on a bamboo stick and held it over the flames. Critters like these were plentiful in all seasons. They hopped around wildly everywhere and belonged to no one in particular. I could cook them in the open.

The water gurgled and, several minutes later, I decided the egg was cooked. I tipped the kettle, spilling some hot water onto the ground, and rolled the egg out with a stick. Then, once it'd cooled enough, I peeled off the shell and carried the steaming egg—hard and polished—in the hem of my shirt, climbing the stairs to Grandmother Queen. I sat her up and handed her the egg. But she seemed unable to discern what it was. She stared at it.

"It's food," I whispered. "Eat it."

She looked at me, wincing, from hunger or memory I couldn't be sure. Perhaps, I imagined, she was remembering a time when we had plenty, when every meal was a feast.

Again I told her, "You have to eat."

She blinked and her eyes clouded over, pain and memory dissolving into blankness. I sighed and began to feed her, starting with pieces of rubbery white. When I got to the beautiful, almost saffron yoke, I hesitated, imagining its rich velvety texture coating my tongue, melting in my throat.

I swallowed hard and, gathering my resolve, popped a roasted grasshopper into my mouth instead—wings, legs, and all.

Just as we finished eating, the bronze bell sounded, echoing through the town, announcing work time. "I have to go now," I said, laying her back down on the mat. "I'll be back in the afternoon. I'll bring you your meal then."

This time she seemed to understand and nodded. I dashed off.

At the town center, I met up with other children, the few who remained in town. They were all small, all under the age of six, assuming they or their parents hadn't lied. Anyone older would've been placed in mobile work brigades or sent to work alongside the grown-ups. I was the exception because of my polio, which, time and again, had proven a blessing in disguise. I could stay with the group or go off on my own. As long as I worked, it didn't matter.

The work itself varied throughout the day: collecting sticks and kindling in the morning, gathering plants and vines for weaving in the afternoon, beating palm fronds into pulp fibers for rope making in the evening. This morning the group would be picking wild morning glory, said the soldier in charge of us. The communal kitchen needed more of it to feed everyone. "To feed *all of you*," he emphasized, scowling at the tiny faces looking up at him. "So you should gather as much as you can. The more you pick the more you'll have to eat. Understand?" Little heads nodded in response. The soldiers then led us down the incline behind the town center and told us to disperse along the shore of the river.

Like critters and crickets, wild morning glory existed in abundance, even in seemingly dry soil, as long as there was a hint of water underneath. I found a patch of it growing in a crater of rainwater, snapped off a few stems at a time, and stuffed them in a *kroma* slung across my chest like a satchel. The smaller children followed my example, pinching the plants where they broke most easily and naturally. A little girl with wispy reddish hair began stealing bites of the tips whenever the soldier wasn't watching. Her older brother, who didn't seem much bigger, came across a leaf full of tiny snails, plucked it, and furtively pushed the whole thing into the little girl's mouth. Tears stung my eyes as I thought of Radana. I turned away from them and kept working.

Seeing that we didn't much need his guidance, the soldier went to sit under the shade of a tree, pulled his cap down over his eyes, and, in no time at all, dozed off, lulled by the cool breeze from the river and the growing heat of the sun from above.

Around noon the bronze bell rang again, signaling our first meal of the day. We tightened the *kromas* across our chests, now weighed down by morning glory, and, with as much speed as we could muster, propelled ourselves up the incline.

The town center also served as the communal mess, with bamboo tables and chairs in the front and the roughly constructed giant earthen braziers and soot-blackened cauldrons in the back. We dumped our loads into a pile on the ground, quickly lined up in front of the serving table, and were each handed a plate of rice soaked in muddy-looking broth and overcooked greens. Again, it was morning glory soup. But we were too hungry to care. Besides, the alternative was nothing.

I brought my plate to the children's table and, under the soggy mess of the stringy vegetable, found a fish the size of a child's palm! I looked up, my heart palpitating wildly. The other children saw it and licked their lips, but the expression on my face must have told them if they dared touch it, I'd stab their hands with my spoon.

I broke up the rice and spread it out in my plate to make it look full. I put the fish to one side, saving it for last, and began to eat the soaked rice first. When I felt the others still eyeing the fish, I pulled my plate close to my chest and put my arm around it, while I continued to eat the rice in silence, head lowered to avoid their stares. Finally, after realizing they weren't going to get any, the others quickly finished their food and sulked off to wash their plates and spoons. The last person to finish was responsible for cleaning up the table and benches. That was the rule. But I didn't care, as long as I could eat in peace. I finished the last spoonful of rice.

And now the fish! Suddenly I felt a pair of eyes on me. I looked up and saw a woman sitting one table over. She looked like she had a watermelon hidden inside her shirt. She stared at my plate and swallowed, stared and swallowed. I didn't like it.

"Are you going to eat that?" the woman asked, caressing her pregnant stomach.

I made no response.

Noticing me staring at her belly, she said, "I'll be glad when the child is born. He'll get his own share. Right now we're counted as one person, and *he* gets all the food." She smiled, and a tear rolled down her cheek to the corner of her lips. She quickly wiped it away. "Sorry." She tried to laugh it off. "I didn't mean to do that."

Still I said nothing.

"It's all right," she said. "I shouldn't have asked."

My heart felt weak, and my stomach started to whimper. Hers was moaning. I knew the sound. I remembered it. It was Radana the night before she died, wanting my sugared cassava.

"Here I am a grown woman trying to lure food from a child."

I couldn't stand it anymore. I got up and left the fish for her, all the while hating myself for doing it.

As I walked back to the villa to bring Grandmother Queen her ration, I realized what it was that had prevented me from keeping the fish for myself—the thought that if hunger could endure even in death, I never wanted it to reincarnate, to repeat itself in anyone.

Life went on, even as food diminished. Harvest came and I was assigned to be a human scarecrow. "You seem old enough," Mouk said at a meeting one evening, targeting me. "You can tend some fields on your own. How old are you?"

"I-I don't know," I stuttered and, wanting to convince him I wasn't lying, I almost blurted out, *Before the Revolution I was seven,* but thought better of it.

He narrowed his eyes at me. "You're the one with the pretty mother," he said, his scar twitching. "Where is she?"

"You sent her away, her and my father. I-I don't know where they are."

He sharpened his gaze.

"Can I go now?" I asked, my back breaking into a cold sweat.

He waved me away.

The next morning, I got up at dawn and caught a ride in an oxcart to the rice fields on the outskirts of town. The driver dropped me at a tiny hut, said he would be back to pick me up in the evening, and then set off to where groups of people had begun harvesting the rice, their dark silhouettes scattered across the vast expanse.

I lowered myself onto the dirt floor in the middle of the hut, like a guardian spirit looking out at the world, this abundance I'd procured. Before me the rice rippled and rolled like a sea of liquid gold, chanting, *Long grains short grains, fat grains sticky grains, grains that smell like monsoon rains*. In the distance the black figures rose and bent, rose and bent as they harvested the rice, moving farther away. "They look like animals," I mumbled to myself. "Like water buffaloes roaming the fields."

A squawk suddenly rose from the middle of the paddies. I stood up and hollered, more to keep myself from being frightened than to frighten: "I'm a scarecrow! Shoo, shoo, go away, you stupid crow!" I gave a thunderous clap. "I said go away, you stupid bird!"

The crow squawked again, followed by another and another, and soon it became obvious I was outnumbered. "They're everywhere," I gasped. "Now what?" I asked and answered my own question. "Go chase them. You can't just stand here and holler."

I ran along the dikes, throwing sticks and pebbles into the fields, making all sorts of noise. The crows squawked and flapped their wings angrily as if *I* were the intruder. I ran this way and that. One flock flew up and another settled back down into the fields. It was impossible to keep them away. They kept coming, whole platoons of them.

After a while, I gave up. I'd had enough! Who cared if they ate all the rice? It wasn't as if *I* would get it by keeping them away.

Huffing and puffing, I lowered myself onto the dike and tried to catch my breath. In front of me, a crow was pecking at a cluster of grains, not a bit afraid. "Thief!" I hurled a pebble at it. It squawked and flew to another part of the fields. "I'll fry you alive!"

A warm breeze blew, and the rice swayed and danced. It became quiet, peaceful. I closed my eyes and imagined I had the world to myself . . .

When I opened them again, I saw my opportunity. I walked into the middle of one of the paddies, into the soft golden stalks that came up as high as my shoulders. I looked around to make sure there were no Revolutionary soldiers or Secret Guards pacing the dikes anywhere nearby. Far away, black figures continued their work, bending and rising, bending and rising, like insects on the horizon. "Go ahead," I whispered to myself. "No one will see you. Eat some."

Head lowered, I began nibbling the rice right off the stems. I spat out the husks and chewed the tender raw grains. They tasted chalky but sweet, a little like stale sugar. I thought of Mama and Big Uncle. Where were they now?

A squawk from somewhere above me interrupted my wandering. I tilted my head back, expecting to see a crow. Instead, high in the clear white sky, a vulture was circling above a lone palm tree several yards away at the dike junction. I thought of Pok and how he had said that vultures could smell death long before it happened. I thought of Radana and the vultures that circled Pok and Mae's crisscrossed palms. I wondered who this vulture was coming for now. Me?

I didn't care. I was enjoying the rice. I watched the giant bird, following the circular path of its flight. I thought of Papa. His death. What it might have been like. It was the first time I'd permitted myself to think of his absence as such. A death.

Suddenly the vulture swooped down and nestled in the fronds of the palm tree. I could feel it watching me. But I wasn't scared. I stuffed some more grains in my mouth. I looked for young, unripe grains that tasted soft and sun toasted, like green rice flakes, harvest's first *ombok*. I should pocket some for Grandmother Queen.

I kept eating until my stomach started to bloat, until it hurt as if I had eaten a handful of pebbles. If that vulture was coming for me, I thought, I was well fed. I was ready.

twenty-seven

The last of the cool dry wind blew, faint like a sigh, and it was gone. All the rice was harvested and every able body was sent off to build embankments and dig ditches in preparation yet again for the rainy season. The only ones left were people like Grandmother Queen and me, who were broken or damaged in some way. We were the leftovers, Mouk said. The useless odds and ends.

With the rice cut and collected, I was no longer needed as a scarecrow. I returned to my duties around the town. The work of the Revolution was never done. There was always something—vegetables to plant, animals to raise, baskets and straw mats to weave. Even as my body dwindled to skin and bones, I was told I'd become big enough to work alongside the adults. In the mornings, I tended the communal garden, watering the vegetables and pulling out weeds. In the afternoons, I went from house to house and counted the animals, keeping track of every chicken and egg, making sure none was missing. I was a *secret* Secret Guard, Mouk said, and my main duty was to report everything to him. On the rare occasion when there was no spying to be done, I went along the shore of the river cutting bamboo and collecting vines for the weavings. Sometimes I would go with a small group. Other times I was allowed to wander by myself. Alone, I would sneak away to check on Grandmother Queen, making sure she was still moving and breathing, even as I knew the end was near.

At the villa, a young woman—herself gravely ill but assigned to look after my grandmother during my absence—said she could no longer get Grandmother Queen to eat. "She just lies there. Still as a cor—"

Corpse, she was about to say, but caught herself in time.

She turned Grandmother Queen on her side to show me the huge festering welts on her back and buttocks. I held my breath, trying to keep the miasma of rotting flesh from entering my nostrils. She didn't need to show me. I'd known of this decay, lived with it every day, slept beside it every night, grown used to it by now. Grandmother Queen's clothes, the straw mat on which she lay, the pillow and blanket, the entire room reeked of it. Now I knew what it was—the odor of dying. Not of death, but the act of it, of your body giving up even as your mind fights to stay alive.

The young woman stood up and said, coughing, "I'll let you have a bit of time with her. Then we'll have to let her go." She left the room, heaving with her own sickness.

"Grandmother," I said, speaking into her death-embalmed face. She didn't stir. I leaned in and whispered, "Grandmother Queen, it's me." Still no response.

I tried again. "Mechas Mae"—speaking the royal language, testing the weight of it on my tongue—"it's me. Arun . . . your son. I have Ayuravann with me." I placed my hand on my heart. "Yes, he's here with me. He's safe."

She opened her eyes, just a sliver. "I know," she murmured. "I see him."

"He's come to take you back home."

She raised her bony hand and cupped my cheek, her thumb grazing my lips, wet and salty, and it was only then that I realized I'd been crying. My tears soaked her palm, and, as if she'd waited for this moment, for my tears to send her home, she pulled her hand back and, hugging it to her chest, closed her eyes.

I scooted to the foot of the mat and, bending down, touched my head to her feet, the way my father would've done, the way we'd all been taught, bowing to the life that gave us ours, laying bare our gratitude.

Three times—for Papa, for Radana, for the rest of my family. Finally one last time for myself. Then I got up and left.

I went down to the river. I slept on the shore, covering myself with a banana leaf. When I woke again, the morning sky was burning, scathed with streaks of red as angry as the wounds on Grandmother Queen's back. She was gone. She'd died sometime in the night, and by the time I returned to the villa, Mouk had sent his soldiers to cart her body away and dispose of it somewhere in the rice fields. She, like Radana, would fertilize the ground.

All along I'd expected her death, but that she had died this way— without the comfort of her children—made me rage against her demise, against those who'd prolonged her suffering.

The next day I found Big Uncle waiting for me on the front steps of the villa. The sick young woman had sent him word to come and fetch me. I didn't have to tell him what had happened. He knew. He'd seen Grandmother Queen's death long before it arrived.

We hitched a ride on a series of oxcarts we encountered along the way. In the late afternoon we arrived at the work camp, a remote and barren place in the middle of nowhere. Before us stood a naked mountain ridge, holding the sky on its back. Silent black figures weaved their way up and down the long, jagged slope, like ants building a giant anthill in expectation of a great downpour. At the bottom, more silent black figures rose and bent, breaking the earth with hoes and shovels. A funeral, I thought, feeling dizzy. Something must have died. I turned to Big Uncle and asked, "What are they burying?"

"Everything . . ." he said, his voice muffled, faraway. "Everything . . . a whole civilization. Yes, that's what we're looking at. Buried civilization . . ."

There was a ringing sound in my ears, and I wasn't sure if I heard him right. "I thought it was a dragon," I heard myself saying. "A dragon *yiak*."

"Let's hope so," Big Uncle murmured. "Or else we are burying our-selves. A people digging its own grave." He gave me his hand. "Come, we have work to do."

• • •

Thick curtains of dust rose up everywhere. All around us people had their heads and faces covered with *kromas*. I couldn't tell who was who. There was no time to waste. No time to even look for Mama. A soldier handed Big Uncle a hoe and me a *bangki*, one of those bamboo baskets shaped like a half clamshell. While Big Uncle hoed, I pushed loose chunks of earth into the basket with my bare hands and feet. Workers came and traded their emptied baskets for the full ones. Revolutionary soldiers kept a close watch, making sure every hand and foot was moving, occupied in some task. No one looked up. No one talked. The sound of metal banging against the hard dried earth echoed across the sky.

It was a sick sky. A sky burning with welts. Angry and red. The colors of rotting flesh, of dying and death, of one heaving last breath. Of rains that hadn't come, and rains that came a long time ago.

Big Uncle coughed, his face turning dark purple. I thought his tongue would fall out. A soldier looked our way and Big Uncle, suppressing his coughs, resumed his digging, his movements as mechanical as if he'd never known any other way to move, as if his mind was capable of no other thoughts except those of the task before him.

I looked around, searching for Mama, but I couldn't see past the plumes of dust. My eyes felt gritty. When I blinked, I saw sandstorms, I felt fire. When I swallowed, I tasted the desert on my tongue. I felt my inside drying up, fissuring with drought lines, my entire body a cracked coconut shell. Around me the ground was broken and scarred, with holes and ditches that resembled half-dug graves. *We're burying a dragon,* I thought, *but I'm the one dying under the sun. I'm digging my own grave. Or else we are burying ourselves.* Big Uncle's words echoed in my head, mingling with my own thoughts. *Burying ourselves, burying ourselves . . .*

The bell rang, like a series of drawn-out gunshots. People put their tools down and began heading toward an elevated stretch of unbroken land where rows of straw huts stood against a background of trees. I stared and blinked, stared and blinked, my eyes searing with pain. I saw embers and flames, sparks flying everywhere. *Are the huts burning, or am*

I on fire? I couldn't be sure if my eyes were playing tricks on me. Flames leaped and danced, licking my face. *I'm on a funeral pyre. But whose?*

Big Uncle sat down next to me, waiting for the traffic of black figures to subside. Baskets lay scattered all around us, like giant shells, a whole sea of dead clams. *The gravediggers have stopped digging . . .* Hoes and shovels crisscrossed like bones in an open field. Dirt and rocks gathered in small mounds resembling termite hills. *One small mound will be enough to bury Radana . . .* My mind wandered, a long, thin snake slithering across the bare ground. *She was small when she died. Even smaller than when she was born. If she had a grave, it would look like a termite hill. It wouldn't stop the Mekong from flooding the rice fields, but it would keep Mama from drowning in her own tears. Tears that came and tears that haven't come. Like the season's rains. Yes, that's what I'll do. I'll build a grave before I die. Not a grave for the Dragon Yiak. But a termite hill for Mama's sadness.*

I looked up, trying to guess what time of day it was. The sun was right above me, sitting on my head. I was ready to explode. The bell kept ringing. *Ringing ringing ringing . . .*

I was thinking strange thoughts. I was seeing strange things. I saw millions of tiny stars. *Blinking blinking blinking . . .*

A woman walked toward us. Big Uncle said something, but I couldn't understand him. His voice sounded as if it came from the bottom of the Mekong, as far down as where the *naga* serpent lived. *Is Big Uncle a* naga *serpent—a dragon* yiak *called Buried Civilization?* Once he had been a *yiak*. Now he was a gravedigger, digging termite-sized graves. *Why? Why does everything seem so small?* The woman stood before me. She had no face. Only eyes. Black moons in clear white skies. I knew her eyes. She unwound the dust-covered *kroma* from her faceless face. A bandage around her wound. She smiled at me, and when I saw the sadness in that smile, I knew who she was.

The stars stopped blinking. Night met day. A *kroma* covered my body. I was dead before I could build Radana a termite hill next to the Dragon Yiak's grave.

• • •

"You fainted in the sun," Mama said, then added, attempting a smile, "but you're all right now." She felt my forehead and neck with the back of her hand, searching for traces of the sun in my skin.

Night had arrived, it seemed, and the only light was from the torch outside near the doorway of the long communal hut. I swallowed at the sight of its orange-black flame. I tasted its dry heat in my throat. My back was soaked with sweat. Yet I felt cold, shivering with lightness, as if my spirit had lifted and there was only this shell of my body.

Mama pulled the blanket up to my chest. I licked my lips, looking for water in the muted glow of the room, noticing a row of empty straw mats and pillows. Mosquito nets, with their sides thrown over the top, hovered above, like ghosts in flight.

"Here," she said, handing me a bowl of what looked like watery rice soup. "It'll make you feel better."

I sat up and drank the liquid but left the rice. I wasn't hungry, just thirsty. I handed the bowl back to her and, wiping my mouth with the back of my wrist, lay down again on the long communal bamboo bed.

"Are you still cold?" she asked, head tilting, worries fluttering across her face. Or maybe they were shadows of her eyelashes when she blinked. "Do you want to eat something?" She caressed my chin. "I can try to get you something. Fruit, sugar. Just tell me."

I couldn't speak. I could only remember . . . the feeling of her hand on my skin.

"Maybe you just want to sleep now." She let down the mosquito net above me, tucking in the edges under the mat. "I have to get back to work."

I nodded.

She walked to the doorway and then turned to look back at me. In the torch's light, her shadow grew and threw itself on me.

I closed my eyes and pretended to sleep. She left, the light of the torch fading with her footsteps. I turned and faced the wall in front of me. A narrow walking space separated the wall from the bed. I knew she had chosen this place because of the wall. She could climb in and out without having to talk with the other women who shared her hut, and when she slept, she could face the darkness, alone. It was how she had slept since Radana died, hugging the wall, facing nowhere.

I heard noises outside, the hums and drones of night creatures. An owl hooted, and another answered, telling each other an endless tale amidst an endless banging of hoes and shovels, the earth being smashed. When you hear an owl, so they say, death is nearby. But owls were always hooting in Democratic Kampuchea, and when someone died, they were as quiet as people, afraid to speak up, to cry out loud. I had learned not to be afraid of owls or other night creatures. Animals are not like people. If you leave them alone, they won't hurt you. But people will, even if you've done no wrong. They hurt you with their guns, their words, their lies and broken promises, their sorrow.

The crickets made whirring music to accompany the owls' tale. The trees stirred to listen. Once in a while the wind yawned. In the distance metal tools broke the earth in a monotonous rhythm, and nearby, just above my head, whispers echoed tentatively back and forth.

"How is she?"

"I'm losing her . . . Maybe I've lost her already."

"You'd better head back to work. I'll check on her."

At night even the walls had voices.

He walked into the hut. I knew his limping even if I couldn't see his face. He stood at the foot of the bed where she had stood just a moment ago. In the dark Big Uncle was all shadow. "Are you awake?" he asked.

I nodded and sat up in the mosquito net.

"Hungry?"

"No, just thirsty."

"Come outside then."

I followed him, wrapping the blanket around myself. Outside, the moon was a white hole in a black sky. We sat side by side on the giant root of a tree with leaves that resembled turtles' hearts. In front of us a kettle perched on three rocks and, under it, the ash was still warm.

"We borrowed the kettle from the kitchen," Big Uncle said, pouring water into a bamboo cup and handing it to me. "The camp leader allows us to take turns to come and check on you. How are you feeling?"

I kept quiet, my eyes on the Dragon Yiak's grave. It seemed bigger at night. Everything was under its shadow. Bright orange flames dotted the broken landscape, illuminating the endless lines of black figures digging and carrying baskets. Buriers of dragons, I thought. Diggers of graves. Up and down. Up and down. They looked like ghosts. Ghosts burying ghosts.

Big Uncle, noticing my stare, said, "There's no logic to it."

Buried Civilization, he had called it. The Dragon Yiak had a name. It had no logic. But it had a name.

Suddenly, a patch of clouds glided past the moon and, for a moment, I thought I saw the spirit of the Dragon Yiak floating above us.

I put my cup out for more water. Big Uncle refilled it. A warm breeze blew, rustling the leaves above us. Big Uncle looked up and said, "There will remain only so many of us as rest in the shadow of a banyan."

"A prophecy, I know."

The prophecy, Papa had explained that day long ago when Om Bao went missing, said a darkness would settle upon Cambodia. There would be empty houses and empty roads, the country would be governed by those with no morals or teaching, and blood would course so high as to reach the underbelly of an elephant. In the end only the deaf, the dumb, and the mute would survive.

Big Uncle stared at me, startled.

If he meant to comfort me by saying that there was nothing I could've done because Grandmother Queen and the others were among the damned of the prophecy, I wanted to tell him there was no such thing—no such prediction, no such curse. Neither was there a sacred tree under whose shade we'd be safe. There was only this burial ground, and we would all die here, in our communal grave. I couldn't find the words. So instead I said, "Grandmother Queen said it was our karma."

Big Uncle was silent.

twenty-eight

Day and night seemed caught in a rut, sending us round and round in the same monotonous rotation. The only indication that we'd moved forward at all was the growth of the embankment, which appeared to have doubled in size and length since my arrival, its surface scaly with pebbles and rocks and unbroken chunks of hard, dry clay. It was the biggest hand-constructed mound I had ever seen, and the absence of trees and plants, its grave-like nakedness, added to its monstrosity. While steps were dug into the sides to make climbing possible, it was still a dizzying height to overcome. At the top one could see everything in its vicinity. Along one side, beyond the ragged, hollowed-out earth, our huts stood on an elevated tract of land, the women's huts separated from the men's huts by several long, open-air thatch-roofed halls that made up the communal mess, with the kitchen and the soldiers' quarters in the back. Beyond that, past the fields of grass and some woods, loomed the darker, impenetrable silhouette of the much-feared Haunted Forests. On the other side, dry lowland scrub prevailed, stretching endlessly into the horizon. Nowhere though could we see a river, not even a small one, let alone a mighty, raging force that would warrant the construction of this colossal levee.

This morning, as every morning, as soon as the sun rose, I took my place in a large crater with other children, who seemed less like children than little old people with their distended bellies and skeletal limbs.

We, the stronger ones, squatting on our haunches, broke the earth with bamboo spades, while the weaker ones gathered it into the shell-shaped baskets thrown in a pile by a long procession of men and women coming down the embankment. There was a continuous flow, as many lines going up as those coming down. Mama was on her way down and heading toward me, taking the long way around, passing one crater after another where she could have exchanged her emptied baskets for a pair of full ones. If a soldier caught her taking the detour, she would be punished, forced to work longer than everyone or, worse, deprived of a meal. When she got to my crater, she unhooked her empty baskets, lowered them to the ground, slipped me a *krotelong*, a kind of water bug resembling a cockroach, hooked two filled baskets on her stringed bamboo yoke, and was on her way up again. I feigned a coughing fit and, bringing my loaded fist over my mouth as if to silence myself, devoured the water bug in one swallow. Then, both hands again gripping the handle of my bamboo spade, I continued digging around a rock, loosening it bit by bit. There ought to be more water bugs seeking refuge in the cool, moist earth underneath. If not, I thought, there would be other insects. Even scorpions were preferable to nothing.

Several yards away, Big Uncle moved along a deep, narrow ditch, his shoulders rising and falling, as he bent down to dig and pulled up again to throw a shovel of dirt over the edge. At the other end crouched a group of boys, small enough to move along the cramped space. They scraped away the edges to widen the opening, their coughs and gasps falling in rhythm with the sounds of earth breaking around them.

As we worked, the camp leader walked about, bellowing through a bullhorn, "The Organization needs us now more than ever! We're fighting the Vietnamese. They're pushing on our borders, pounding us every which way, trying to steal our country every chance they get."

He was nearly bald and hefty, certainly one of the few meaty bodies among hundreds of skeletal ones. His mouth was always moving, if not speaking then eating. His wife, an equally fleshy being, was the head of the kitchen.

"Yes, they may be Communists like us, but they're Vietnamese first.

So they're our enemies! We must defend ourselves against them! We must strengthen our country from within! And how would we do this? We must build mountains to stop the Mekong from flooding the rice fields."

What Mekong? What rice fields? My mind wandered. I felt hungry, more than ever now that I'd eaten the water bug. I dug harder around the rock.

"All over the country, reservoirs, canals, ditches are being built so that rice can be planted throughout the year! Not just during the rainy season! Democratic Kampuchea is a powerful nation! The rest of the world will depend on our rice! We could have plenty to eat, but who could think of eating when our soldiers need our rice."

My hunger turned to thirst. I wiped the sweat from my nose and licked my palm dry. It tasted salty—gritty with dirt.

"We must continue our struggle! The Revolution is a constant battle! We must search for enemies! Be always on the lookout for them!"

I looked in the direction of our huts, remembering the water canteen I'd left at the foot of the bed in my rush to get to work.

"They're everywhere! Not just outside our borders."

The sounds of digging echoed across the expanse, bouncing from crater to ditch, filling my ears and rattling my bones so that I could not separate myself from every bang and thud, the incessant bark of the camp leader.

"They hide among us, sharing our beds and our meals!"

I closed my eyes and let my body go . . . let the skin fall away . . . let the bones shatter and disintegrate . . . until only hunger and thirst remained.

"And when we find them, we must rout them out!"

Finally, I dislodged the rock and, with all my strength, pushed it over. Nothing. Not even ants. Not one miserable bug to eat. The earth was as dry as it was hot, inhospitable to life.

"We must crush them like termites!"

I dug a hole and buried myself, this seed-like knot I'd become, and waited for rain.

"We must show no mercy!"

Mama came again but had no food to offer, only a faint smile, which I lacked the strength to return.

"Show no pity!"

She put the empty pair of baskets down, hoisted up another pair filled with dirt, and went on her way, following the flow of people in front of her, her steps slower now, her body quaking more with every footfall.

"We must be rid of them, babies and all!"

He bellowed the same message five times over. I wanted to bang a hoe against his head. Reprieve came only when the bell rang.

We were allowed enough time to use the woods or, if we wanted, go down to the creek behind the huts to refresh ourselves with a splash or two of water. Most people stayed put. Except for the call of nature, there was no reason to move, no reason to waste our energy. Big Uncle got out of his ditch and lowered himself next to me in the crater. At some distance away, the camp leader stood talking to Mama, who, every now and then, lowered her head and nodded. He must've caught her taking the detour to visit me and was now reprimanding her. He waved her away, as if allowing her off the hook this time. She seemed grateful and hurried toward us.

"I have to use the woods," she said, offering me her hand. "Come." I didn't understand why she would need me along, but before I could protest, Big Uncle, helping me up, said, "Go with your mama," and to her, "I'll follow in a bit."

He didn't have to say more. I understood. Wherever we were going we couldn't be seen walking off together. Familial closeness was against the teaching of the Revolution, said the camp leader. It eroded the communal structure and lessened productivity. Whatever he meant, it was clear that this was why the men's huts stood separate from the women's huts. Here even husbands and wives were not allowed under the same roof. Breaks and mealtimes were the only occasions a family could be together.

"We'll wait for you by the boulder," Mama said.

Big Uncle nodded, and Mama pulled me along.

We arrived at a secluded part of the woods where the creek curved around a large boulder and spilled into a pool before it dropped off and disappeared under a canopy of bamboo saplings. Mama rolled up her pants and started wading through the ankle-deep water toward the boulder. Bending down, she dipped her arm into the pool and, after some searching, pulled out two stalks of sugarcane, both as long as her forearms. She turned around and waded back toward me. Suddenly there was a loud snap. I spun around and saw a branch falling to the ground. I turned this way and that, my heart beating wildly. There was no one.

"Sit," Mama said, pulling me down so that we were hidden behind a thorny bush. She handed me one of the stalks and right away I bit into the hard covering, peeling it off a strip at a time with my teeth. Gnats swarmed my head, excited by the sweet smell. I broke off a chunk and chewed, grinding it with my teeth, sucking it dry before spitting out the depleted stalk onto the ground. Another branch snapped and this time Big Uncle appeared out of the thicket to our left. He came and sat down beside us. Mama broke the other sugarcane stalk and offered half of it to him. He hesitated, looking down, shamefaced.

"Take it," Mama said, pushing the sugarcane into his hand. "There's no greater humiliation than hunger."

Big Uncle took it, murmuring, "I can't let you risk your life—"

"*What life?*" she snapped, then, as if to put his mind at ease, added, "That pig has as much to lose as we do. If caught, I'll declare in front of the soldiers and guards, in front of everyone, their leader *accepted* our offer." She was talking about the camp leader. "He didn't know what it was—your tie pin. I didn't bother to explain. As long as it's gold, he said, that's all his wife cares about."

Big Uncle said nothing. He bit into the sugarcane, and together we ate in silence, our chewing muffled by the flow of the creek. Afterward, we gathered the chewed remnants and tossed them into the bamboo thicket.

. . .

We barely made it back in time. At the bell's final call, Mama rushed ahead to claim her yoke and baskets, while Big Uncle and I negotiated a narrow bamboo bridge over what would be a reservoir for rainwater. A couple of soldiers brushing past us imitated our walk, one limping right, the other limping left, laughing hysterically, amused by their own theater. I didn't care. Stupid animals.

The sun was bright, brilliantly hard. A sound broke out above our heads, like pebbles thrown against a metal roof. Suddenly millions of silvery darts fell from the sky and melted against our skin. It was raining, just like that. Across the embankment people stopped working and turned their faces up to the sky, and as they did so, the rain stopped, as abruptly as it had come. Not a drop left. Then another shower started and stopped. Again and again the sky played with us; all the while the sun never once blinked.

It went on like this for days, weeks, with small bursts coming and going, disappearing without a trace on the broken earth. *Pliang chmol,* the local folk called them, "male rains." They came when we least expected them, when we couldn't bear the heat anymore, and as soon as they came, they disappeared. Afterward, the sun scorched, the earth heaved, the air became heavy as steel. But the male rains were nothing to fear, we were told. They were only messenger rains. They were sent to warn us of the female rains. "Female rains?" someone asked. "What are they?"

"Rains that weep a whole river," said a woman from a village not far from here, "and flood a plain."

"When will they come?"

"When everything is dead."

"It is time!" the camp leader declared early one morning at a meeting he'd called on the top of the embankment, the bullhorn held to his face like an extension of his oily protruding lips. "It's time to prove our strength! On this auspicious day, April seventeenth, 1977, the Second Anniversary of Liberation, we once again declare our might!" He looked up, as if speaking to the sky, challenging it. "See what we have built? A mountain out of nothing! Have you ever seen anything so amazing? Look! Look at the green rice fields before you!"

I looked and saw on one side our thatched huts, the trees covered with layers of dust, the ground all broken up, and on the other side the parched scrubland, blackened with patches of sun-charred grass. There was no green rice field.

"Imagine them once we have our embankment and reservoir! Yes, this area will be covered with rice. Fields and fields everywhere!"

My temples throbbed, my mind spun.

"All over Democratic Kampuchea our brothers and sisters are building embankments and digging canals! Together we will conquer the sky, the rivers! We will plant rice where we want! Even on rocks! We will have so much that we will be the envy of other nations! The Vietnamese will not bother us anymore."

Why couldn't he disappear like the male rains? I wished there were trees up here, some kind of shade. *Pretend you're riding on the back of the Dragon Yiak,* I told myself.

"If we have rice we have everything! We can do anything! We must unite and demonstrate our Revolutionary might!"

Claps and cheers. I felt my skull cracking, breaking in half. I wanted to run but could not even bring myself to stand up. I stayed where I was, trapped between a grave and a burning sky, between Buried Civilization and disappeared rains, between endless claps and cheers.

The day grew hotter, my stomach emptier. In the late afternoon, it started to rain again. The Revolutionary soldiers and guards let out a victory shout, their guns held high above their heads, as if they had made the rain come, as if they were winning some battle against the sun and heat. They allowed us a brief moment of rest. I stuck my tongue out to taste the warm drops. A cricket jumped in front of me, but I did not have the strength to go after it. My breath felt shallow, filtering through my nostrils rather than rising from my chest. When I tried to breathe more deeply, my rib cage hurt, my head pounded, my vision became blurred. I looked for Mama but could not see her anywhere. Big Uncle leaned against the side of a ditch he was digging, not bothering to come out, taking advantage of this brief moment to close his eyes, letting the fast, heavy drops fall on his lids, soothing the burning underneath.

Then the rain stopped and we started working again. The heat intensified, everything slowed down. I wished the day would end. But the evening wasn't any better. It came with a half bowl of watery rice soup. I drank it down in one gulp and licked the bowl clean. Mama pushed it away and gave me hers. I stared at it, wanting it, not wanting to want it, ashamed of my greed, yet not knowing how to rid myself of the hunger. She nodded for me to go ahead, fingers lifting a clump of hair plastered to my cheek and tucking it behind my ear. I kept my face down as I drank the soup, unable to meet her eyes as she gazed at me. When I finished, she asked, "How do you feel now?"

"Still hungry."

Rain gathered in her eyes and I felt that if she blinked it would drown me.

Night fell, stiflingly hot. Everyone began heading for the top of the embankment, where there was at least some breeze. Mama pulled out a shirt from our bundle and started to mend it. "Come, Comrade Aana," said one of the women in our hut. "It's not often we get the night off. Why waste it mending clothes?" The woman extended her arm out to me, as a way to coax Mama into going with her. I edged off the bed, but Mama, fixing me with her gaze, said, "I need your help threading the needle."

She waited until everyone was gone, then, throwing the shirt aside, grabbed Radana's little pillow and ripped it open with her bare hands. A pair of silvery hoops dropped from the pillow and landed near my knee, the tiny diamond-studded bells jingling with a familiar sound. It took me a few seconds to recall what they were—Radana's anklets. I hadn't seen them since we left Phnom Penh. It was now 1977, the camp leader had said. I didn't know what startled me more—that there was a specific time, a month and a year, to this perpetual darkness, or that a life and a world I once knew had vanished entirely in the span of only two years. I'd completely forgotten the anklets existed. In the torch's light they flickered and gleamed, translucent as a pair of newly hatched snakes. Mama snatched them up from the mat and put them in her pocket.

"Come," she said, pulling me by the arm.

We waited in the woods behind the kitchen. The trees and bushes waited with us. Not a branch stirred, not a leaf waved. Near us heaved a small dark mound of rotting vegetable peels and fish bones. Insects moaned over the mound as if attending a funeral. Suddenly a branch moved and the grass crackled. A soldier, I thought, or maybe a member of the Kitchen Committee. A shadow appeared out of the hazy dark carrying a small clay pot. The shadow kept walking toward us. I wanted to run, but Mama held me still against her.

It was the camp leader's wife. She thrust the clay pot at Mama, and Mama gave her Radana's anklets. The woman examined them, frowning as if they weren't what she'd expected. She tried pushing her chunky wrist into one of the anklets. "They're a bit small, aren't they?"

"Well, they belonged to a child," Mama told her.

The woman looked at me. "Hers?"

"Yes, a long time ago," Mama lied, then added, "but they're yours now."

Satisfied, the woman put them in her pocket and disappeared, becoming one with the dark.

Mama scooted closer and, placing the pot of rice in front of me, said, "They *were* yours."

I pushed one handful of steamed rice after another into my mouth, swallowing the lumpy mush without really tasting it. Mama watched me, resting her chin on her knees, rocking back and forth on her heels.

"The anklets," she continued. "They were yours first. I had them made for you when you were born. I wanted you to wear them as you learned to walk, so that I would always know where you were by the sound of the bells. So that I would never lose you. But you had polio, and I put them away. Then . . ." She paused, unable to bring herself to say Radana's name. "Then your sister was born, and I took what was yours and gave them to her."

I stopped eating and stared at her. I didn't know what to say. My guilt and shame were as overwhelming as hers. We lived, while Radana, who'd done no wrong, died.

"They're the last pieces of our jewelry, what we brought with us. After this . . ." She attempted a smile. "Well, we'll have to figure out some other ways, won't we?"

I swallowed, feeling queasy. The stench of rotting waste was overpowering. I couldn't separate it from the odor of the rice.

"Hurry and finish it," she pushed, looking around, seeming fearful now of being discovered.

I continued stuffing myself, not wanting to disappoint her, even though the rice was rancid—soggy, like it had been sitting in its own sweat all afternoon. Or maybe I'd forgotten the taste of steamed rice. I kept eating, while Mama continued to observe me, lost in her own thoughts.

My stomach churned, not from hunger now but from nausea. Nearby the insects continued to moan and feast on their funeral mound.

When I'd finished, Mama smashed the clay pot against a rock and threw it into a bush. I wiped my hands with the leaves.

Once again she pulled me by the arm and we hurried back to our hut. At the doorway, we paused and looked up at the night sky. Above us, the stars shone as bright as diamonds. Bells of white gold.

The next morning, before the first light, I took my place at the foot of the embankment next to Big Uncle, in a shallow crater with about ten or twelve other people. The taste of spoiled rice coated my mouth and a painful cramp gripped my stomach, but I did not bother to ask a soldier if I could go use the woods. I had emptied my bowels of everything the night before, getting up repeatedly to vomit and relieve myself. The cramps were no worse than the hunger pangs. Besides, it would take too much effort to walk the scarred terrain. There were craters and holes everywhere now, some as big as ponds, some deep as graves. Light from the torches planted in the ground cast long shadows that quivered and trembled like ghosts waking from their slumber. The sound of digging began to fill the air, echoing across the predawn darkness.

In the sky, the stars were still blinking. I tried to find Mama among the figures going up and down the embankment, but it was difficult to tell who was who. At this hour it was impossible to separate people from their shadows, from the baskets and the bamboo poles and their shadows. All had the quality of indefinable sorrow.

I heard Big Uncle's hoe bite into the earth. He pulled out a chunk of dirt and pushed it toward me. I broke it into smaller pieces with a spearlike rock and swept it into a basket. Nearby a soldier sat leaning against the side of the crater, his face hidden under a black cap, trying to steal a few more minutes of sleep.

Finally dawn emerged. But as soon as the sun appeared, it disappeared again. The sky turned moody, its belly hung low like the concave roof of a mosquito net. A big dark cloud drifted overhead, its immense shadow enveloping the entire camp. Far in the distance, the horizon curled like burning paper and rolled toward us, bringing with it more giant dark clouds. A strand of lightning flashed, but it made no sound. A raindrop, fat and heavy, landed on my arm. Another drop fell, and another, and suddenly countless more in rapid succession. Tiny splatters popped up all over the ground, like blisters bursting on damaged, infected skin.

The rain poured, so thick it looked black. Everyone ran down the slope, screaming toward the huts. Suddenly someone bumped into me. I slipped and fell. A hand yanked me up, as quickly as I had been knocked down. "Where's your mama?" Big Uncle screamed through the rain. "I don't know!" I shouted back, trying to hear through the cacophony of sounds. We looked up at the same time. And there she was—a small, dark figure whipping in the wind at the top of the embankment. She was the only one there. Her black clothes looked even blacker wet. Her body swayed, leaning with the rain, like the sail of a boat caught in a sea storm. Suddenly she threw her arms open wide. I turned to Big Uncle and shouted, "The female rains! They're here!"

"What?" he hollered back, leaning closer to me. "I can't hear!"

"The female rains, they're here, and Mama is welcoming them!"

"What?"

It was no use. The storm was deafening. Like thousands of women weeping simultaneously. Lightning crashed and the sky roared with thunder. Water flowed, and soon the whole world was flooded.

The Dragon Yiak's grave was melting. Mud ran down its sides, and the rains kept coming, one storm after another, like waves of flying bullets. We worked day and night to keep up with them. When they slowed down, we sped up. When they rested, we moved forward. We had to take whatever chance there was. It was now the middle of the night. The rains had temporarily subsided. The air was imbued with the premonition of new battles. Thunder resounded, lightning flashed. Above us the moon was full and bright, its luminosity waxed by rains. The camp leader marched back and forth across the embankment, screaming into the bullhorn, "There's no time to waste! We must seize every opportunity to strengthen the Revolution! We must work harder! Faster! The embankment must stand as proof of our strength! We must make it higher! Bigger! We must strive forward! In rain, fire, or storm! We must strive forward!"

I looked up from my hole and saw Mama coming toward me. Even under the white light of the moon, her face appeared red, flushed with fever, her eyes eerily glassy. She put down her empty baskets and picked up two new ones. Knees bent, she lifted the bamboo pole onto her shoulder and pushed herself up, her whole body trembling, vibrating like an overstretched rubber band before it snaps. She turned around and once again began to make her way up.

"OUR REVOLUTIONARY FORCE," the camp leader bellowed as he descended the embankment, coming closer to us now, "IS STRONGER THAN NATURE'S FORCE!"

The moon shivered. Halfway down a man lost his step. He fell backward and tumbled down the steep slope, his baskets rolling ahead of him. No one got up to help. No one even took notice. There was always someone slipping and falling. Accidents were rife. Death was the norm. He might not even be alive.

"WE CAN CONQUER THE SKY!" the camp leader screamed. "WE ARE UNSTOPPABLE!"

Everyone kept working. I didn't know how long I could keep going. My arms felt as if they were splitting off my shoulders. Near me some of the smaller children, the five- and six-year-olds, were busy draining the craters and holes, the rainwater reaching as high as their waists. Some were hidden in ditches so deep and narrow you couldn't see them at all, just water flying from raised clay pots and buckets.

My body was numb with cold. I didn't care if I lived or died. I only wanted the night to end.

The embankment collapsed. It collapsed in the night, while we were working. Four were dead. Three girls and a boy. They had been in one of the narrow ditches when it fell. It happened quickly. We didn't see them, didn't know they were in there. The rain had blurred everything, drowned out the noises—their screams for help, our own voices. They were just the right size for the ditch, we'd all agreed when we put them in there. Not too big, not too small. But when the embankment fell, we forgot them, we remembered only ourselves. Later Big Uncle ran back with the other men, but the ditch was sealed. A covered grave.

If we wash the mud off their bodies, I thought now, *clean their faces and nostrils, maybe then they will open their eyes, maybe then they'll breathe again.*

But they lay so still on the bamboo table, almost hugging one another. They were found that way. Huddled together like baby rabbits in a hole. Big Uncle and the other men had dug them up and brought them to the communal mess. A bucket separated one of the girls from the others. Big Uncle and the men had tried to take it away. They'd tried to pry her fingers open. But her grip was too strong. She was weak strength. Not too big, not too small. Now she was no strength. Nothing at all.

"We have to take them back," Big Uncle said to the crowd gathered around him, his voice small, but calm. "We have to bury them." His eyes were red. Bloodshot. His hands, I noticed, were shaking. He had been like a madman, wouldn't stop digging until he'd found them. Now he untied the *kroma* from his waist and covered the bodies.

Sobs seeped through the silence. A muffled wail. Crying was against the teaching of the Revolution.

We buried them where we'd found them, in the watery grave they had dug themselves. Big Uncle and the men lowered the small bodies, one at a time, into the open ditch. The little girl, the bucket still hanging from her hand, was put in last. *Go back to sleep, baby,* I heard Mama's voice from another night, another fight with death. *It's not morning yet. They're babies,* I told myself. *Yes, babies being put back into their crib.* Why should I weep for them? Why should I be sad? Sad was too small a word. *It's not morning yet . . .*

Next to me, Mama, with her fever-flushed face and hard bright eyes, stared past everything, all the way back to that night when Radana died.

Everyone stepped back. The men began hoeing the earth. The rain had softened to a drizzle. The earth mourned. The sky rumbled with the threat of another downpour.

When the grave was covered, the sun broke through the clouds. It beamed. A bright, glorious smile. The smile of the Revolution.

Later, I went to find Big Uncle. I found him sitting alone in front of the children's grave. I lowered myself next to him. His eyes took in the ravaged landscape. "They rule with the logic of a child in a land where no children remain, Raami." He turned to me. "I buried them myself . . ." His voice was soft as the drizzle that had started to fall again. "Your auntie India squeezed tight between the boys, Sotanavong on the right, Satiyavong on the left. Your Tata on top, facedown, like a mother hen watching over them. I buried them myself, you see. In a single grave I dug with these hands." He held out his trembling hands to me. "They didn't make it, you see."

Yes, I see.

He was a giant who would break at his own words.

Little words.

They didn't make it.

I mustn't let anyone, anything break me.

We found him one afternoon. In Men's Hut Number 5. Big Uncle had hanged himself. With the rope he'd woven with his own hands. He'd lost the will to live, the soldiers said. It wasn't so. His will was broken. He killed himself, they said. But I knew they'd killed him long before.

The female rains came in greater force. They could turn day into night. They came wearing their anger like diamond jewels. They thrashed and whipped and screamed. At night when there were no Revolutionary soldiers, no camp leader, no Kitchen Committee or Burial Committee, when the eyes and ears of the Organization were not watching and listening, I heard them, so close I dreamt they were inside the mosquito net next to me. Some nights they wept and moaned loudly, choking on their own tears. Other nights they cried quietly, correctly, as if they were afraid, as if they knew they were being observed. Once they whispered a child's name, *Rad'na? Where're you running to? Where are you hiding?* I answered, screaming, *She is dead! Don't you understand? She is dead!* And they wept even harder. *Why must you hurt us so?* What could I do then but try to comfort them? *But you have me. I'm your sacred ground. You can dig a hole in my heart and bury all your sadness. I'll be your grave. Please just stop crying. What do you want me to do? Everyone is gone. What are you crying for? Nothing will bring them back. Stop crying or I'll leave as well!* But of course they continued to cry, deaf to my pleas and threats. They would not stop. Not until they'd brought everything back to life. Until the earth was alive again.

I understood the female rains. They were my mother's rains.

twenty-nine

There was no time to mourn. No time to look back. Again planting season came. Mama was sent to another location to dig irrigation ditches, and I was put in a youth brigade that traveled from one area to the next planting rice. There were about twenty of us in the group—all girls—and we worked from dawn until sunset. We slept together in one hut built at the edge of the forest near our work area. Our parents, we were told, couldn't be wasted caring for us. We were not children anymore. This morning at the rice fields, a new Secret Guard was assigned to keep an eye on us. He paced back and forth on the narrow dike, going nowhere, eyes watching. The long gun hanging from his shoulder brushed against the ground as he walked. A black cap shaded his eyes, and the muscles of his jaw flexed in and out on clenched teeth. He tried to look older than he was. If only he knew we were afraid of him *because* he was so young. Around me tiny figures in black rose and bent, up and down, up and down, a step or two back, the rhythm I could count and feel even in my sleep. We moved slowly, pushing rice shoots into the mud, burying the stalks halfway in the water. No one sang, no one spoke, no one looked up. We were just moving figures, up and down, up and down. I could no longer tell the living from the dead. Ours was a world in between.

In the distance was the darker green of the forest, and before it stood a lone sugar palm, so high it appeared to touch the sky. I looked up to where a group of vultures was circling, waiting. They called out softly to one another, to the silence below, and the wind answered, its breath entering my nostrils, the smell of rotten corpses, of bodies abandoned not long ago.

I stole a glance at our brigade leader in the row beside me. She was only a girl, a child like the rest of us, but because she was Mouk's relative, everyone feared her. Through her, the eyes of the Organization were always watching. Her eyes met mine. "You've hardly moved from your spot," she snarled and quickly eyed the others to see how they reacted to her critiquing me. "Don't you think we should punish her?" The others lowered their gazes and made no response.

I did not understand this vague grudge she harbored against me. *Kum,* it was called. Spite. It had no reason, and it seemed too small a thing—a playground sentiment almost—for the consequences it carried. Yet it was not guileless or without purpose. I'd seen it before—in the Fat One's snicker when she eyed Mama's loveliness, in Mouk's scar when it leapt to destroy the district leader, and now in this girl's rage when she saw others pity me. Again and again it appeared in different faces, young and old alike, the vectors of Revolutionary venom, spreading like a disease, expedient and merciless as that from the bite of a death-carrying mosquito. And even if it was petty, it was obvious that when propped up and given the right platform, pettiness became poison.

"Move!" she shouted.

I tried pulling my right leg forward, but it remained stuck in the mud. I struggled, my left leg digging deeper into the sludge. Around me, the girls of my work unit stooped into the rice paddies, pulling farther ahead, pretending not to notice.

"Useless cripple."

I mumbled under my breath.

"What?" she hissed.

"I'm not a cripple."

"Maybe you don't know what you're supposed to do then."

"I know."

"Then do it!"

"Leave me alone." Every day she despised me a bit more. Every day she found something to attack me for. I was tired of it. It couldn't go on. I didn't know where I found the strength, but I challenged, "You're not doing much either—"

"*What?*" She cut me off, teeth clenching.

I didn't answer. The others paused in their work. They knew what I meant. That was enough for me. It gave me strength, even if only to smile to myself.

"I'll report your laziness to the Organization!" she thundered.

I stood up straighter; my breath suddenly halted. I looked up and the Secret Guard was staring down at me. He pushed the tip of his gun deep into my chest. If I moved, it would explode. The others averted their gazes. I opened my mouth but no words came out. My lips started to tremble and I couldn't stop them. I couldn't think straight. Tears welled up in my eyes. I didn't know why. I wasn't afraid. Why was I crying?

"Shoot her!" she said.

I closed my eyes. *When I lie buried beneath this earth, you will fly.*

"What are you waiting for? I said shoot her!"

Her shout forced my eyes open, lids fluttering. The Secret Guard let his gun drop and took a step back. He laughed, and to the girl, said, "Killing her is no loss, but she's not worth a bullet, Comrade."

"That's right—you're a useless cripple!" she declared for all to hear. Leaning into me, she hissed, "You'll die on your own soon enough. Meanwhile, watch what you say, and do as I tell you, do you hear?"

For me, Raami. For your papa, you will soar.

"Do you hear?" She spat on my face.

I blinked. Tears streamed down my face. I tasted the blood on my lower lip where I must have bitten myself. It tasted salty, warm. I let it soothe me. Like the urine trickling down my thigh. No one looked at me now and I looked at no one. I kept my eyes on the muddy bank of the paddy. A tiny crab came out of its hole, with eyes protruding like antennas. I reached for it, but it scurried back into its hole as quickly as it had appeared.

Yes, your papa left you wings.

"Get back to work!"

But it is I who must teach you to fly.

Voices, they came at me now.

They didn't make it . . .

"Why do you stand there?"

And you wonder why she speaks only to ghosts.

Voices of their ghosts, weaving in and out, like filaments of a solitary rope around my neck. *I'm telling you this now . . . so that you will live.*

I took a step back, my feet as light as the crab's. Another step, and another, and further back. Until I reached only silence. Deep within myself, within the dark, grave-like hole, I lay.

They couldn't touch me anymore.

To keep you is no gain, to kill you is no loss. Under the rules of the Organization we were reduced to this dictum. How was I to live by such words? With so many carted away on the tiniest pretense, how could any child believe she would live beyond this day, this moment? How could she hope for tomorrow? In a world of senseless death, I didn't see the purpose, couldn't grasp the meaning. If this was our collective karma, then why was I still alive? If anything, I was as guilty as those who survived and as innocent as those who died. What name then can I give to the force that carried me on? With each life taken away, a part of it passed on to me. I didn't know its name. All I could grasp was the call to remember. *Remember.* I lived by this word.

After that day at the rice fields, I no longer feared guns because I no longer feared death. The brigade leader continued to threaten me. But I never answered her. Instead, silence took root in my blood. I became deaf. I became mute. I thought only of the work in front of me. Standing in the paddy, I planted the rice shoots. When eating, I could only think of eating. In sleep, I thought of nothing else. Hunger made my body frail. Many times I was punished for being too lazy. Without rice, I lived on leaves and small animals found in the mud. The tiniest I would swallow at once. Sometimes I would be punished, though I could never know when. It was futile to worry, to think of tomorrow. The life I'd once known was gone, and with it, the people. There was nothing to say, no one left for me to speak of, so I chose not to speak.

Still, I saw. Still, I heard. In silence, I understood, and I remembered.

Harvest came and for weeks there was talk of plenty. We would eat well again. I knew their lies. All there would be was more to steal. Back in town I was assigned to be a scarecrow again. I had learned to sew large seams into my shirts and pants to hide rice. At dawn I'd catch a ride on an oxcart and return to the same hut where I had come the season before to keep watch on the rice fields and chase away the crows. Alone, with no soldier or guard in sight, I felt the world was all mine again.

Each day I grew more feeble. I felt the disappearing of my body, the deadening of my mind. My skin had become jaundiced, the color of stale turmeric, and I craved the tastes of burnt wood and charcoal. Sometimes, I imagined myself a *beysach,* one of those fabled creatures combing the crematory, yearning for the taste of burnt coffins, for my own ashes. *She's not going to make it,* people would say when I drifted past them. *Poor thing, she's going to die, and her mother is not here to comfort her when she takes her last breath. Poor thing.* Their words would jolt me out of my dark trance, and I'd claw my way back to the light. Once more I fought, seeking every opportunity to stay alive. In the rice fields, hidden behind a termite mound or the trunk of a palm tree, I would light a small fire using a lighter I'd stolen from the communal kitchen and cook the rice in empty snail shells. Often, though, I would eat it raw. I could never be sure who was watching. The eyes and ears of the Organization were everywhere. At night I allowed myself the comfort of dreamless sleep. This, however, was not always possible. Sometimes, I was awoken in pitch blackness by voices of those long dead, and those soon to die. I'd hear their screams, their pleas, the sudden gunshots, and the silence that followed. *Who is it this time?* I'd wonder in the dark, my eyes shut tight. I never knew their names—didn't want to know—those who were taken, or killed on the spot. They had no names, I'd tell myself. I didn't know them. But their screams, their pleas—*Please, comrades, spare my baby*—would echo in the night and lodge themselves inside my head. In such moments I wanted only to get away, from these voices that were not my own, the thoughts I could not speak out loud, the words I could no longer form with my lips.

One night, after the cut rice had been piled in high mounds, I felt a presence inside my mosquito net. I braced myself for death.

"It's me," said a voice that sounded like Mama. I thought I'd imagined it. But then she spoke again, grabbing my arm, "It's me, Raami. They've sent me back to thresh the rice." My eyes adjusted to the dark and I saw her. What had she traded for her escape? Our diamonds and jewels were gone. Papa's notebook? His poetry? Their love? Herself? "We'll never be separated again, I promise," she said, hugging me tight. "Never." I didn't know why, why she promised me anything at all. How could she?

The next day she asked me questions I didn't know how to answer— "Why won't you talk? Why?" She gripped my shoulders, her eyes searching my face.

I said nothing. Deep inside of me, my voice screamed from a hole where I had buried it.

"The wind of the Revolution is blowing too gently! We must take the strongest measures to purify the state! Democratic Kampuchea must be rid of all contaminations! We must weed out the enemies from among the people! We must cut them down! Pull them out! Yank them like weeds from among the rice shoots! No matter how small they are, how harmless they may appear, we must destroy them before it's too late!"

Mouk stood on a stage, a bullhorn in his hand, the sickle-shaped scar on his face twitching even as he paused to survey the crowd before him.

"Remember that servants of the king once lived in the palace, teachers still know how to read and write, and chauffeurs once drove cars. Our enemies are always our enemies! We must seek them out, bring them forward, and destroy them! Destroy what we cannot use! The time has come for another war! A war to purify our state! We must cleanse ourselves! Our Motherland must be pure of foreign elements! We must separate the contaminated Khmer from the pure Khmer! We must eliminate those who *look* and *act* like our enemies! Those with Vietnamese faces, Vietnamese eyes, Vietnamese names! We must separate them from *real* Khmers! Only by taking the strongest, most extreme measures can we speed up the wind of the Revolution!"

The enemy now had a face. Anyone who *looked* Vietnamese, *behaved* like Vietnamese. I didn't know who the Vietnamese were, or what they looked like, but Mouk—who had now become the head of the Kamaphibal—said they were here among us. He ordered his soldiers to drag out an example. It was Mui's father.

"I am Khmer!" Comrade Keng shouted.

"Yes, but your wife is a Vietnamese whore!"

"No, we are all Khmers—"

Mouk shut him up. A bullet through his mouth. I closed my eyes.

When I opened my eyes again Comrade Keng was gone, but his blood seeped down from the stage to the ground and I couldn't help but think how it looked just like any other blood—red, glorious, shining.

Mouk screamed into his speaker, "Vietnamese spy! This is what happens when we find you!"

The next day I woke up as usual before dawn and went to the outhouse behind the villa. In the hazy dark I heard sobs coming through the trees from Mui's house. "Hush!" a voice growled. "Get in the cart!" More sobbing, louder now. I couldn't move. I stayed hiding in the outhouse. A short while later Mama found me on the front steps of the villa, the morning sun shining on my face. "It'll be a scorching day," she said, sitting down next to me, her skin brushing against mine. I made no reply.

She turned and looked at me. "You're shaking," she said, putting her arms around me. "Why are you shaking?"

My teeth chattered, and I hugged her back, glad for her nearness.

We sat in silence, except for the sound of my teeth. After a while she said, "It's still too early. Won't you come back inside?"

I shook my head and pulled myself away. I wanted to be alone. *Go away.* She looked at me, puzzled. Then, nodding, she got up and climbed the stairs back into the villa. I remained where I was, my mind running back and forth, throwing itself in every direction. I wanted to escape—get out of this place. But where? Where would I go?

Finally, my oxcart came. I climbed into it. Again, the driver brought me to the hut where I guarded the rice fields from the crows. Here I could talk without words, without sounds—

"No!" A scream suddenly split the wind from the forest behind me. I heard them. I knew their voices, had recognized them on the first sobs. "No! Please, comrades, no!"—Aunt Bui. "Mother! What's happening?"—Mui. I walked toward the voices. "Please, don't do this! I beg you!"

"Dig!" The same male voice I'd heard earlier at the outhouse. "Do you want me to shoot the girl first? I said dig!"

I stopped. Mui's frightened weeping. I could hear it.

Aunt Bui's giggle—where is it? Vietnamese, the soldiers had called her. Her skin was too light, they said. Her eyes slanty, Vietnamese eyes. *What about her giggle? Is that Vietnamese too? Where is it now? Why won't she laugh? Laugh, damn it. Laugh!*

"Deeper! More!"

The sound of digging echoed and vibrated. I lowered myself to the ground, careful not to make a noise. I waited. I did not know why. Why I waited. Had I not heard enough, seen enough? Had death deepened my appetite for more? Dulled my senses to violence—a friend's murder? Was it shock, paralysis that kept me there? I couldn't explain it, but I remembered all those times when death had brushed by me and I'd close my eyes or turn away. I couldn't do this anymore. I couldn't let those I loved face death alone. From now on, I told myself, I would stay put, be here for them, and when their spirits left their bodies, they would see that I'd been here all along to hear their last words, their last breath, and they would know that I had witnessed not only their deaths but, more importantly, their fight for life, their desire to live.

I pulled my legs up toward my chest and rested my head on my knees, telling myself my fear was nothing compared to that of my friends. I silenced the voices inside my head. I calmed my heart. I braced myself—embraced them.

Then came the thud of a club meeting skull, one, two, and nothing more. Behind me, the crows flew out of the rice fields, wings beating toward the sky.

thirty

Disquiet settled over Ksach. Talk of battle echoed the distant ring of gunfire. We were at war, whispered the townsfolk. Cambodia and Vietnam were fighting. Each day more people were returning from the camps where work had suddenly ceased. They arrived in a constant stream, unaccompanied by guards or soldiers or camp leaders. The town leaders did not question their return. None of them seemed to care. Mouk and many of the soldiers had left for the battlefields some time back. Now the remaining soldiers and Kamaphibal were getting ready to leave as well, not to fight but to retreat into the jungle. Defeat was inevitable, they admitted gravely. They loaded their oxcarts with supplies—food, weapons, and ammunition. The Vietnamese would kill us if we remained, they warned, urging us to go with them. We Cambodians should stick together, they said, as if they had forgotten they were our torturers and killers, as if we would trust them now. Except for their relatives and those close to them, the rest of us chose to stay behind and wait.

Once they were gone, we rushed into the town center and storehouses. There was no squabble, no argument. There were so few of us left and the dead watched us from everywhere. So we each took what we could find, enough to survive one more day, and, if we lived through the night, then we would come back, scavenge for more. Mama, sifting through clothes abandoned by the wives of the Kamaphibal, found a roll of what looked like foreign money. She quickly tucked it inside her shirt. I wondered what she would do with it. She baffled me. I filled my pockets with rice from a pile I uncovered under an overturned basket, stuffed a handful of the grains in my mouth, and drank it down with juice from a nearby pickle vat. A short while later, I threw it all back up. Mama found me a green banana and told me to eat it slowly to calm my stomach. But even this felt like too much food.

Back at the villa everyone talked freely again for the first time in a long time. "I don't understand . . . one Communist regime against another? How can they be fighting each other?" asked a woman, and a man sitting next to her replied, "These Revolutionaries—they feed on chaos." Another murmured, "I'd dreamt of this moment many times. Now it's finally arrived." He was of Chinese background and, like Chae Bui and Mui, his family had been purged for their impurity, their physical resemblance to Vietnamese. The only reason he survived was because he'd been sent away to haul stones in a remote mountain quarry. "Three years and eight months," he continued, "that's how long this nightmare has lasted. Now finally we glimpse dawn, and I am alone."

I watched him, my eyes glued to the Adam's apple gliding in his throat, like a lump of sorrow he could neither swallow nor spit out. I thought of Big Uncle. Mama pulled me away.

An orange glow lined the edge of distant forests. No one slept. We stayed up and waited. The fighting raged on to the morning. The smell of gunpowder filled the air and the sky rumbled as if it would rain. Then at dawn the Vietnamese came. Over the Mekong the sun rose, slowly coming into view, like another world, perfectly round and blazing red. The town was taken over by convoys of army vehicles. A row of camions and tanks parked on the paved road in front of the villa, engines humming with victory, excitement. A Vietnamese soldier, standing atop the roof of one of the trucks, grinning deliriously, called out in broken Khmer, "Anyone? Anyone?" He stared at us, stunned by our appearance and, as if thinking we were ghosts, added, "Anyone still alive? Anyone to leave—come!" He gestured to the vehicles. There was plenty of room, he explained. They were heading in different directions. He and his convoy were heading for Kompong Thom. Several convoys would go to Phnom Penh. We were free, he said. We should go home.

Mama cried and buried her face in my chest. All around us people were crying, the sound like the downpour that came after everything was dead. Like female rains.

"It's over, Raami," she said, wiping away her tears. "Now we can leave." She pulled Papa's small notebook from our bundle of clothes and from between its pages drew a piece of paper folded into a boat the size of her thumb. "Papa left us this." With trembling hands, she unfolded the paper and spread it open, then, in a tentative voice, began to read:

Raami, it is my greatest regret that I'm not able to do more as your father. If your wings should be broken, darling, this paper boat will ferry you out, not across water, but across land. Land between lands. On one side is a border between here and hope. On the other is a border between two hells. To the east is a land where the sun blazes as red as here. To the west is a land of golden temples. Now, you are far from hope. But if there's a sliver of opening, a crack in the wall somewhere, you must take it, walk through to the other side. You must head west, follow the stars until sunrise . . .

Mama paused, clearing her throat, then explained, "A map, he'd called it when he thrust the bundle of his belongings at me that morning. He left us a map, he said, in the folds of his clothes. I read these words a thousand times over, Raami, before I realized they were coded for you and me. I should've known what he meant, should've seen the outline of another place, another life, in the contour of this paper boat. *East . . . where the sun blazes as red as here*—Vietnam. *West . . . a land of golden temples*—Thailand. *You must head west . . . until sunrise*—a new beginning. Listen to me, Raami." She cupped my face, the letter rubbing against my cheek. "I see one red flag coming down and another going up, one regime after another, they're all the same. We can't stay here. This

may be our only chance. Now there's a way out, and we have to take it."
She paused. "I will do what I can. Bargain and compromise in any way
possible to get you out of this place. I thought of going home, Raami,
but there is no one there. Only ghosts await us. I need you to let them go,
the voices in your head. I need you to stay with me, hear me instead, even
if you can't speak." She swallowed hard. "No matter what happens next,
however I may fail, it is life I've chosen for you. Do you understand?"

I nodded. Yes, we were going to leave this land and its ghosts. But if
we failed, if we died along the way, she wanted me to understand that we
would die trying to live. She was fighting for my survival while preparing
me for the possibility of my death. But I understood this already. I'd lived
long with this possibility, and if we survived our next journey, it would be
nothing short of a rebirth.

She looked down at the letter, turned it over, and said, "The rest I
believe is for you." She looked at me. "Would you like me to read it?"

I shook my head.

She held my gaze, and after a moment, said, "I understand." Then
she tucked the open letter back into the pocket notebook and I saw that
it was the same size as the other pages. "I'll go gather our things—I've
collected enough rice to last us a while. Also . . ." She hesitated. "Also, I
went into Chae Bui's house. She'd told me where she'd hidden their gold.
We'd promised each other, Raami, that if one of us should survive, we
would look after the other's child. Mui is not here. But . . . but I believe
Chae Bui would've wanted me to do what I can to save you, even if it
means stealing from them. Their ghosts may follow and haunt us, but
it's something I'm willing to live with." She stopped, as if waiting for me
to respond, but when I didn't, couldn't, she continued, "We'll leave right
away." She placed the notebook in my hand, straightened up, and, as she
turned to go, said, "Once your papa told me there was still hope. He was
right. Always, there's hope."

Hope had wheels like an army truck. It revved and hummed, as lively as
the young Vietnamese soldier beaming at us from the driver's seat of his
vehicle. Mama and I and some of the villa's residents climbed into the

back of the camion and made ourselves as comfortable as we could for the journey. Hope bore us across burnt fields, bombed bridges, broken sparrow-nest hills, and scarred rubber forests. It carried us, even as death pursued us. Corpses littered the roads and rice fields. Those killed by mines were easy to recognize—a limb here and limb there, their flesh scattered on the ground. Those murdered, their bodies whole except for a knife wound in the neck or a bullet hole in the head, we avoided looking at, because their open eyes seemed to follow us, cling to our faces, slow our steps. We rolled into a village populated by ghosts. A rooster sauntered around a family sprawled on the ground in front of their hut, pecking and squawking as if to see who was still alive. One hut after another, it was the same thing. The only difference, the only living presence, was the animals. A duck waddled and quacked, as if calling out for help. A pig snorted, heavy in its despair. A cow ambled back and forth, then lowered itself silently to the ground where its owners lay, keeping watch over the bodies. Word spread that the entire village had been massacred by retreating Khmer Rouge soldiers, probably because the people refused to follow them into the jungle. We looked at one another and considered ourselves fortunate. "At least in Ksach," someone said, "the Kamaphibal and soldiers gave us a choice."

We continued our journey, whenever possible sticking to wide, open roads, driving over tire tracks of vehicles that had gone before us, to avoid land mines.

At nightfall we reached a town. The townsfolk welcomed us, first cautiously, then with obvious relief. Some were blessed enough to recognize faces in our group. Those who recognized one another wept openly. The townsfolk told us only one-third or so of their population was left. A handful had chosen to follow the Khmer Rouge into the forests. "And the rest?" the Vietnamese soldiers wanted to know. "Well, the rest . . . ," said a local man, an elder who, although skin and bones, seemed to have become the strength and pillar of his community, "the rest are here with us. They are invisible, but they are with us nevertheless."

A little girl, who I presumed to be the elderly man's granddaughter from the way she clung to him, came forward and stared at me. I stared back. I hadn't looked in the mirror in a long time, but I recognized my reflection in her emaciated face. We smiled at each other. Neither of us could talk.

Later that night, we camped on the ground beneath their house on stilts, which reminded me of Pok and Mae's hut. Mama offered the elderly man and his granddaughter a can of rice from the supply we'd brought along. They shared drinking water with us and guavas from their tree. The old man told Mama that both of the little girl's parents had disappeared one night. They were still waiting for them to return.

Before dawn the next morning, we boarded our truck in the convoy and left without saying good-bye to our hosts. It was better this way, Mama said, as if I could talk, as if I had a choice. There had been enough good-byes already, she explained.

Several days later we reached Kompong Thom. Our driver said this was as far as his convoy would go. We were told to wait by the road for another truck that would arrive soon. When it appeared, we rushed into it.

Again, hope carried us. It bounced us up and down along Prek Prang Creek, on a small paved road strewn with potholes and craters. We passed choked charcoal kilns, we sped through burning cities and flaming towns. The truck brought us to the face of Masked River, where we took a cattle boat to Citrus Soil then to Blue Bamboo, and to a town called Chhlong that mimicked the sound of a gong, *chhlong . . . chhlong . . . chhlong*, the sound of time. We heard the wind heave. We hoped that time would not end for us. Not here. Not now. We'd come so far.

In Siem Reap, Mama traded charm for a ride on a villager's oxcart. But her beautiful smile and serenading voice could only take us so far. He dropped us at a village called Banteay. Mama took out the roll of foreign money she'd kept tucked in the waist of her sarong and found another villager, a trader in the old days, who was willing to take us all the way to Samrong, where he knew of a caravan preparing to cross the border. He warned us that we might not reach Thailand. It was a dangerous feat we were attempting. He'd heard of many who starved to death in the middle of the jungle, succumbed to malaria, crossed paths with tigers, or simply expired from exhaustion during the arduous trek. Perhaps we should wait, wait a while longer, and maybe our country would go back to normal. Mama shook her head vigorously. The villager took us across the rice fields of Srov Thmey and then through the teak forests of Phnum Chrung. At Samrong he wished us safe passage and passed us on to a man who was readying a caravan of oxcarts to journey through the jungle to the border. Mama paid the leader of the caravan with a necklace from Chae Bui's stash of gold. He found us space in one of the oxcarts up front. There were about six or seven oxcarts and at least sixty of us. It was twilight, the best time to begin, as we would trek through the night.

After weeks of traveling in the caravan, mostly at night with the stars to light and guide our way, we reached an impasse. We abandoned the oxcarts and ascended on foot into one mountain range, then another, always heading west. After a week or two more, we emerged from the dense jungle onto an open plain. We stopped to rest in the shadow of some trees atop a hill. By this time, less than half of our group remained, as some had died along the way, while others were too weak to carry on and thus were abandoned to their fate. It was nighttime, but the moon shone so brightly that we could see the surrounding landscape very clearly. Except for this small rise with its clusters of teaks, it was all grass and flatness. I couldn't tell where one country ended and another began. But the man leading us said that straight ahead was Thailand. He encouraged us to sleep and gather our strength in these brief still hours before dawn. When we resumed our journey at daybreak, we would have to move fast, to slip like shadows across the land. There might be Thai guards and soldiers patrolling the border. If they saw us, we'd run the risk of being shot on the spot or, worse, sent back into the jungle. Some people wondered why we weren't continuing now while it was still dark. Our group leader explained he'd heard that crossing the border by daylight would give us at least half a chance. If we were caught, the soldiers or guards were less likely to shoot for fear that any act of atrocity would be witnessed. If we did make it across, there was hope of finding help.

Perhaps we would encounter some Thai farmers who, moved by our circumstances, would take us in to plant rice alongside them in their villages. We could offer ourselves as tenant farmers to a landowner. We could be servants. Miracles like this were rumored to happen, our group leader said. He himself would be grateful for any labor and food. Anything was better than what we'd endured. Everyone agreed and began to settle down to rest.

Mama spread a pair of *kromas* side by side on the bare ground and made a sleeping place for us under one of the teak trees. She lay down and beckoned me to do the same. But as exhausted as I was, I couldn't sleep, my heart fluttering even as the rest of my body could barely move. I lay on my back, looking at the night sky through the leaves, eyes seeking the moon. Soon, I thought, we would be in another land. I was not ready to leave—to let go. We didn't even know where Papa had been taken, where he might have last been seen. How could I ever return to him—even if only in my mind—when I couldn't imagine the last place my father might have been? Where was his grave? Did he have a grave? I panicked. I held myself rigid beside Mama, afraid that she would read my thoughts. How could we think of freedom when he was trapped here? How could we abandon him? Tears trickled down the corners of my eyes.

Then, as if to comfort me, to calm the tremor of my heart, Mama murmured, her fingers tracing the path of my tears, the contours of my face, "You have his eyes, his cheeks, his nose . . ." She sounded tired but her voice was clear, soothing. "He built a fire, shook himself free of us, and jumped into the flames. But just as he did so, Indra rushed to save him, seizing his spirit, and flew him off to the moon. Henceforth, Indra told him, the world shall know of your kind deed."

I was confused for a second or two. Then I realized what she was talking about.

"You know, for a long time, I could never look at the full moon without seeing it flinch—the pain he must have endured in exchange for our safety. 'I will follow you, and you'll have only to look at the sky to find me, wherever you are.' How could he utter these words to you? How could he have tried to ease you into a life without him by telling you a childish tale? I was overcome with anger toward your papa; I didn't think I could ever forgive him."

I remembered. It was the night before his departure. She'd lain with her back to us, her body hard as a board.

"Had I understood then," she continued, speaking as calmly as Papa would've spoken to me, "that the war, this Revolution, was an old blaze reignited, decades, possibly centuries of injustice manifesting itself like a raging inferno, I could've told whoever were its builders, be they gods or soldiers, they needn't have put him through that test of character. Your papa would've jumped into the fire of a thousand revolutions for us. And . . . and because of this, because of his willing self-sacrifice, he merited a world nobler than the one he'd left behind." She swallowed, hesitating, as if unsure she ought to continue. "We will never know, Raami, how he lived his last moment, what thoughts went through his mind as he took his final breath, nor will we ever know the exact manner in which he perished—" Her voice caught.

Then after a moment, she continued, "I'm certain, though, he remained resolute in his belief that even without him you would live through this nightmare, that life, with all its cruelty and horror, was still worth living. A gift he would've wanted his daughter to embrace. This, I think, was what he was trying to tell you, a story about your continuation."

A story, I had learned, through my own constant knitting and re-knitting of remembered words, can lead us back to ourselves, to our lost innocence, and in the shadow it casts over our present world, we begin to understand what we only intuited in our naïveté—that while all else may vanish, love is our one eternity. It reflects itself in joy and grief, in my father's sudden knowledge that he would not live to protect me, and in his determination to leave behind a part of himself—his spirit, his humanity—to illuminate my path, give light to my darkened world. He carved his silhouette in the memory of the sky for me to return to again and again.

I stayed mute. I could not find the voice to share with Mama what I understood.

She let out a rueful chuckle. "You know, I'd heard the story of the rabbit and the moon from my own father when he was a monk, during one of my visits to the monastery where he lived. Every child, I suppose, is familiar with it. It's a tale you hear often at a temple. But it's only now that I understand it—this creature whose humble form belied its noble spirit, whose action your papa emulated when he shook himself free of us so that he alone would suffer."

I'm the only Sisowath . . . I'd mistaken his words and deeds, his letting go, for detachment, when in fact he was seeking rebirth, his own continuation in the possibility of my survival.

"We will live, Raami," Mama went on, sensing what I couldn't express, speaking the words I couldn't form with my lips. "I'm certain of this now. As for your papa, he lives in you. You are him. I'm certain also that one day you will speak again."

I let out a sob. It was not speech. Nevertheless, it was an expression, a voice of my deepest sorrow. I mourned him aloud, even if only with this single sound.

Mama pulled me to her. I let her hold me until she fell asleep. Then, taking Papa's notebook from our bundle of clothes and slipping it into my shirt pocket, I walked over to a clearing where it was brightest, where I could see in all directions. To my right, in the distance below, a river glimmered like a road, a moving pathway. Light blinked across the inky surface. A cluster of fireflies, I thought. Always somewhere there was light, and, though transient, it flashed all the more brilliantly because of the surrounding dark.

I took the notebook from my shirt pocket, its leather cover Mama had caressed to the softness of Radana's skin. I opened it to the last page, the letter inserted back along its torn edge. In the likeness of the pre-dawn tranquility that inspired my father to write every morning when we'd lived at home, I held it to the moonlight and read the part I hadn't been able to bring myself to read in front of Mama:

Do you remember, Raami, you asked me once what that circle on your shoulder was? A birthmark, I said. But you were not convinced. You told me instead that it is a map. Of what, I never asked you. But now I know. It is the contour of your footsteps' journey. Life, I believe, is a circular path. No matter what misery and awfulness we encounter along the way, I hold out hope that one day we'll arrive at a blessed moment on the circle again. It is my dream that I live beside you always.

It wasn't a dream, of course, that image of him sitting in the doorway of the classroom at the temple ripping out the page of the notebook. In my stupor, I'd believed he was tearing up what he'd written, destroying evidence of himself. Another sob escaped my throat. This time I cried openly, loudly. I allowed myself to wonder what his last moments might have been. Was he murdered right away? Or perhaps, like Big Uncle, taken to some camp for reeducation, beaten and starved? Or perhaps, like Radana, he was claimed by disease, his body afterward left to rot in the forest or thrown in some rice paddy. I gave him the solace of death, myself the consolation that wherever he might be, he was suffering no more.

Following the same creases Papa had made, I folded the paper back into the shape of a small boat. Then, wiping away the tears, my eyes strayed to the inside of the back cover, to what he wrote on the last available space:

> *Bury me and I'll thrive as countless insects*
> *I bend neither to your weapon nor will*
> *Even as you trample upon my bones*
> *I cower not under your soulless tread*
> *Or fear your shadow casting upon my grave.*

A funerary prayer he'd written for the repose of his own soul, I thought. Some kind of chant—a requiem—to give him courage to face his own death. I looked up at the full moon, its blank and luminous surface. There was no face smiling down at me. *Bury me and I'll thrive . . .* I read the entire passage again. Then it hit me what it truly was. An incantation. To bring him back into the world of the living. I reeled from the realization. All these years I'd thought he'd lived in the moon, distant and elusive as light, when in truth he'd hidden in these pages, tangible and tactile, a poem all to himself, with lines and stanzas, a rhythm that was all him.

Dawn was breaking. I looked up, dazed by my discovery, the sight before me—a lotus field at the river's far edge, like a dream reincarnated, each flower a rebirth in this early light.

Even as I could not see his face, hear his voice, I knew I had not lost him.

We descended the hill and resumed our journey, following the curve of the river. Soon after, we slipped across the border, and I wouldn't have been able to tell that we were in Thailand had our group leader not said so. We were not safe yet, however. No sooner had he told us this than we heard a loud, prolonged rumble resound in the air above us. I was certain it was the sound of guns firing at us. Everyone stopped walking and looked up. A black dot appeared on the horizon straight ahead. The dot became a dragonfly, then a helicopter, rushing at full speed toward us, and before we had time to run and hide, it descended to the ground, its heart beating with our hearts. A *barang* stepped out and, amidst the wind and dust stirred by the helicopter's blades, waved and spoke, shouting to be heard. We watched him, stunned, unable to move or respond in any way. Once the noise of the helicopter subsided, he spoke again, in a language that sounded to me now like French. He gestured with his hands, eyes searching for someone who understood him. To my surprise, Mama stepped forward and began to translate, at first haltingly, then more fluently—"He said he and the pilot are with something called the United Nations—an organization." For a brief minute panic broke across the haggard and hungry faces at hearing the word "organization." But she quickly added, "No, no, a different organization. They've been on the lookout for fleeing refugees—us. They've heard of our plight. There is a camp being set up that we could go to. They've radioed for trucks to take us there. But now they'll take the elderly, injured, and children first."

"Yul?" the *barang* asked, his one word of Khmer. "Understand?"

We nodded, and he grinned happily, seeming more grateful than we that he'd found us. He paused now to stare at us, allowing shock and horror to rise to his face. He told Mama that we were not the first group he'd discovered, and that stories of our suffering had filtered across the border, but still his eyes had not grown accustomed to seeing such evidence of inhumanity.

Mama, because she spoke some French and thus was needed as a translator, and I, because of my polio, were among those scurried into the helicopter. It all happened so quickly that we had no time to protest his decision. That we had been spotted and discovered out here, in the middle of nowhere, gave everyone the assurance that the world had not forgotten us.

As we ascended, my gaze leapt ahead to the vast expanse where the river we had been following met up with two others, reminding me of where the Mekong, the Bassac, and the Tonle Sap rivers converged in Phnom Penh. Even as I had no idea how far it was or in what direction it lay, my mind flew there now, toward an image, a stilled memory of my father and me standing on the balcony of Mango Corner, our weekend house, talking about the reversal of currents and fortune. I closed my eyes, letting the past and the present and the future join. *I told you stories to give you wings, Raami, so that you would never be trapped by anything—your name, your title, the limits of your body, this world's suffering . . .* Indeed I was flying. I could leap into words and stories, cut across time and space. Like Papa, I'd become a kind of Kinnara, that half-bird creature, escaping from this world to another. I could transform myself. I could transcend boundaries.

I opened my eyes just as the pilot was pointing back in the direction of Cambodia to a distant border village surrounded by verdant rice fields. Through the heart-pounding din, he shouted, "Cambodge!" Everyone burst into tears. Feeling safe in the cacophony around me, I said his name aloud to myself—"Papa." Mama heard me. She brought her hand over her mouth, as though to hush herself so she could better hear me. But it was all I needed to say to call him forth and take him with me.

Papa! Again and again, I uttered this one-word incantation, the first note to break my silence.

Suddenly, the pilot tilted the helicopter in the opposite direction, and with one quick last glimpse, we left this land, Mama clutching a paper boat and a book of poetry, and I the mountains and rivers, the spirits and voices, the narratives of a country that would in turns shade and shadow me on my journey.

Its prophecy has become my story.

Author's Note

Raami's story is, in essence, my own. I was five years old when on April 17, 1975, the Khmer Rouge stormed into Cambodia's capital city, Phnom Penh, and declared a new government, a new way of life. For centuries before, the country had been ruled by monarchs who styled themselves as *devarajas*, descendants of the gods. The last to hold that mythical stature was King Ang Duong, whose sons King Sisowath and King Norodom gave birth to the two contending lines of Cambodia's modern royalty. My father was a great-grandson of King Sisowath, who reigned in the early part of the twentieth century, when Cambodia was a French protectorate. Like many of his contemporaries who were educated abroad and exposed to the ideas of democracy and self-determination, my father was a member of the intellectual class that became increasingly disillusioned with the corruption and inequity of Cambodian society in the decades after independence. For my father and his peers, this was not only a social critique but also an inward questioning of the foundations of their own privilege. In 1970, when a coup brought monarchal reign to an end and established the Khmer Republic, he and many of his countrymen saw it as the advent of a bright new era in which a democratic system of rule would address the ills of feudalism. Yet this putative democracy failed to bring stability to a country now engulfed by the war spreading from Vietnam. Corruption deepened further still, and in this climate of growing turmoil, a heretofore marginal guerrilla group known as the Khmer Rouge gained strength in the countryside. Its leaders, from the same intellectual class as my father, were equally idealistic but steeled with a radicalism that even the most politically astute could not gauge.

From 1975 to 1979, as the Khmer Rouge leaders attempted to realize their vision of a utopian society—one of the most complete social transformations in modern history—families were separated and put into work camps, systematically starved, and executed. As the regime became more ferocious in its need to rid itself of "enemies," those perceived as politically, ideologically, or racially impure were murdered in vast numbers. Already severely weakened by this internal purge, the regime was finally overthrown by the Vietnamese military in January, 1979, bringing the revolutionary experiment to an end. While the true number can never be known, scholars estimate that between 1 and 2 million people died, perhaps as much as a third of the total population.

Like Raami, I was tormented by my father's disappearance shortly after the Khmer Rouge takeover, his summoning by the regime's leaders for who he was—a prince, a member of the "enemy" class. The losses and the brutality in the ensuing years deepened my desire to understand what happened to him, to my loved ones, and to my country. In writing I have chosen the medium of fiction, of reinventing and imagining where memory alone is inadequate. The broad brushstrokes of this narrative trace my family's journey, set within the context of actual historical events. I have taken literary license to compress time and incidents, collapse places and characters to simplify and give distinction to each, and alter the names and backgrounds of individuals in my family as well as those we came to know during our journey. The one name I have retained is that of my father. While he was a pilot by training, it was the "poetry of flight," I remember him telling me often when I was a child, that took him to the sky. Thus, Raami's father not only bears the various names and titles my own father held—among which was the affectionate moniker Mechas Klah, or the "Tiger Prince"—but also embodies my father's hopes and ideals, his fervent wish for my survival. He is imbued with the memories of the man I loved and love still to this day.

It was this love that led me in search of him again and again. While the present Cambodia is far from the paradise of my childhood home, or the sacred land my father once believed it to be, it is the burial home of those sacred to me. In 2009, I was invited to the palace and granted my first audience with His Majesty King Norodom Sihamoni, to be formally reintroduced into the royal family. I was presented as Neak Ang Mechas Ksatrey Sisowath Ratner Ayuravann Vaddey. Sitting in Khemarin Hall, with my hands pressed together in front of my chest and speaking the royal language, I told the king I came as the daughter of the Tiger Prince, son of His Royal Highness Prince Sisowath Yamaroth, son of His Royal Highness Prince Sisowath Essaravong, son of His Majesty King Sisowath. I'd brought a gift of three tons of rice as donations for the poor, in my father's name. His Highness Prince Sisowath Ayuravann— I stopped. I could not say more. The silence I'd known as a child took hold of me again, and I fought back the tears that threatened to rush forth as the full realization of this visit hit me, what it meant that I was now taking my father's place, sharing his name.

I remembered once my father tried to explain to me what that was— what it meant to be royalty. I was perhaps four. At a marketplace in the city, we encountered a beggar on a street corner sitting cross-legged on a torn burlap bag that looked to be his entire home and only possession. The beggar was blind, so that as he looked up, the cloudiness of his eyes seemed to reflect the white of the sky, and as he lifted his hands beseeching passersby, he seemed to implore the gods. This gesture—his whole being—moved me deeply. If the gods couldn't grant him sight, I thought, I wanted to give him *something*. So we bought rice wrapped in lotus leaf, and just as I was about to take it to the beggar, my father stopped me and told me not to forget to take off my sandals. I didn't understand. Removing one's shoes is only done when giving alms to Buddhist monks, to show respect for their spiritual path. We are all beggars, my father said. It doesn't matter what we wear—rags, a saffron robe, or silk. We each ask the same of life. I may have been born a princess. But that beggar, that blind man, who was probably born poor and no doubt had suffered greatly, discerned enough beauty to want to continue living. He deserved our highest respect. His life had as much nobility as ours, as anyone's, and we ought to accord it dignity. I cannot recall my father's every word exactly, but as young as I was, it was clear what he wanted me to understand. His gesture and words resonate with me to this day. For all the loss and tragedy I have known, my life has taught me that the human spirit, like the lifted hands of the blind, will rise above chaos and destruction, as wings in flight.

I wanted to tell the king this, to intimate who my father was, but it wasn't a time for stories. Instead I spoke what I felt most immediately— that however my father died, however his last moment might have been, I wish he could've known that one day I would sit in this same hall where he sat countless times in his short life, that his name would be invoked again and again, that he would not be forgotten.

As my father's only surviving child, it is my endeavor to honor his spirit. This story is born of my desire to give voice to his memory, and the memories of all those silenced.

V.R.

Acknowledgments

My profound thanks and gratitude:

To my editor, Trish Todd, for her astute critique and calm guidance. The quality of her questioning allowed me to bring to the surface what was hidden. To Jonathan Karp and the team at Simon & Schuster, for all the support they've given to this book.

To my agent, Emma Sweeney, for the sharp eye and honed instincts she brought to her comments on the manuscript, and for her diligence in finding it a home. And to Suzanne Rindell, for rescuing me from the slush pile!

To Gillian Gaeta, for her timely advice.

To Jane McDonnell, my dearest friend and mentor, for seeing the storyteller in me even when I had neither language nor voice. To Penny Edwards, for her enthusiastic reading. To my best buddy, Neil Hamilton, for his belief in me, and for many moments of revelation. To my darling friend Maria Herminia Graterol, who always saw me as a writer.

To my family, for their gifts of love: my sisters, Leakhena and Lynda, who mean the world to me; E. K. Kong, a father to the three of us; Ann-Mari and Mitchell and Juliana, who have always supplied me with great books; Ann-Mari Gemmill, Sr., and Henry Gemmill (Mormor and Morfar) and Melvin and Ida Ratner, in memory of their generosity; and Joann and Patrick, who have followed me around the world, arriving at moments when I needed them most.

To my husband, Blake, for his immeasurable support, for taking on the burden of work and caring for our family to give me the stability and comfort of a writing life. *Your love transcends all boundaries and I feel I have traveled with you many lifetimes.*

To my smallest but most magnanimous supporter, our daughter Annelise, for her wisdom and patience, for mothering me when I exhausted myself with writing. *You are the reincarnation of so many hopes and dreams.*

To my mother, who gave me life, again and again. *To you, I owe everything.*

About the Author

Vaddey Ratner was five years old when the Khmer Rouge came to power in 1975. After four years, having endured forced labor, starvation, and near execution, she and her mother escaped while many of her family members perished. In 1981, she arrived in rural Missouri as a refugee not knowing English, and later, living in the low-income Torre de San Miguel housing project in Saint Paul, Minnesota, graduated as her 1990 high school class valedictorian. She is a summa cum laude graduate of Cornell University, where she specialized in Southeast Asian history and literature.

Vaddey is a descendant of King Sisowath, who ruled Cambodia in the early part of the twentieth century. In 1970 her father's first cousin, Prince Sisowath Sirik Matak, led the coup that ended monarchal reign and established a short-lived republic, soon engulfed in the chaos of the broader Vietnam War. Once the Khmer Rouge took power, forcing the entire urban population into agrarian work camps, the royal name that once meant protection and comfort now marked them for death.

Vaddey spent nine years in Southeast Asia while researching and writing *In the Shadow of the Banyan*, her first novel, which is being translated into seventeen languages. She now lives outside of Washington, DC.

Simon & Schuster Paperbacks
Reading Group Guide

In the Shadow of the Banyan

Introduction

"To keep you is no gain, to destroy you is no loss." For seven-year-old Raami,
the collapse of her childhood world begins with the footsteps of her father
returning home in the early dawn hours, bringing details of the upheaval
that has overwhelmed the streets of Cambodia's capital city, Phnom Penh.
It is April 1975, and the civil war between the U.S.-backed government
and the Khmer Rouge insurgency has reached its climax. As Raami plays
in the magical world of her family's estate, she is intrigued by the adults'
hushed exchanges that pit hopes for the long-awaited peace against fears
that this might be the end of the life they know, a life protected and
cushioned by their royal lineage. On the morning of the lunar New Year,
a young soldier dressed in the black of the Revolution invades that world
of carefully guarded privilege. Within hours, Raami and her family join
a mass exodus as the new Khmer Rouge regime evacuates Cambodia's
cities.

Over the next four years, as she endures the tragic deaths and violent executions of friends and family members, Raami clings to the only
remaining vestige of her childhood—the magical tales and poems she

learned from her father. Whenever Raami comes close to giving up hope, she looks up at the moon and recalls the intricate tales that her father created for her, stories of fortitude and love that instilled the values that will keep her alive.

Topics & Questions for Discussion

1. According to the prophecy that Grandmother Queen tells Raami at the beginning of the novel, "There will remain only so many of us as rest in the shadow of a banyan tree." What does the prophecy mean to Raami when she first hears it? How does her belief in the prophecy change by the end of the novel? After reading, what does the title of this novel mean to you?

2. Tata tells Raami, "The problem with being seven—I remember myself at that age—is that you're aware of so much, and yet you understand so little. So you imagine the worst." Discuss Raami's impressions as a seven-year-old. How much is she aware of, and how much (or little) does she understand?

3. Review the scene in which Raami tells the Kamaphibal her father's real name. How does this serve as a turning point in the novel—what changes forever after this revelation? How does it affect Raami, as well as her relationship with both Papa and Mama?

4. Papa tells Raami, "I told you stories to give you wings, Raami, so that you would never be trapped by anything—your name, your title, the limits of your body, this world's suffering." How does the power of storytelling liberate Raami at different points in the novel?

5. Compare Mama's and Papa's styles of storytelling. When does each parent tell Raami stories, and what role do these stories serve? Which of Papa's stories did you find most memorable? Which of Mama's?

6. Consider Raami and her family's Buddhist faith. How do their beliefs help them endure life under the Khmer Rouge?

7. Discuss Raami's feelings of guilt over losing Papa and Radana. Why does she feel responsible for Papa's decision to leave the family? For Radana's death? How does she deal with her own guilt and grief?

8. What does Big Uncle have in common with Papa, and how do the two brothers differ? How does Big Uncle handle the responsibility of keeping his family together? What ultimately breaks his spirit?

9. Raami narrates, "my polio . . . time and again, had proven a blessing in disguise." Discuss Raami's disability, and its advantages and disadvantages during her experiences.

10. Although Raami endures so much hardship in the novel, in some ways she is a typical inquisitive child. What aspects of her character were you able to relate to?

11. Discuss how the Organization is portrayed in the novel. How does Raami picture the Organization to look, sound, and act? How do the Organization's policies and strategies evolve over the course of the novel?

12. Names have a strong significance in the novel. Papa tells Raami he named her Vattaaraami, "Because you are my temple and my garden, my sacred ground, and in you I see all of my dreams." What does Papa's own name, Sisowath Ayuravann, mean? What traditions and stories are passed down through these names?

13. Consider Raami's stay with Pok and Mae. Discuss what and how both Raami and Mama learn from them, albeit differently. Do you think their stay with Pok and Mae gave them hope?

14. "Remember who you are," Mama tells Raami when they settle in Stung Khae. How does Raami struggle to maintain her identity as a daughter, a member of the royal family, and a Buddhist? Why does Mama later change her advice and encourage Raami to forget her identity?

15. Mama tells Raami after Radana's death, "I live because of you—for you. I've chosen you over Radana." Discuss Mama's complicated

feelings for her two daughters. Why did Raami assume that Radana was her mother's favorite, and how does Mama's story change Raami's mind?

16. At the end of the novel, Raami realizes something new about her father's decision to give himself up to the Kamaphibal: "I'd mistaken his words and deeds, his letting go, for detachment, when in fact he was seeking rebirth, his own continuation in the possibility of my survival." Discuss Papa's "words and deeds" before he leaves the family. Why did Raami mistake his intentions, and how does she come to realize the truth about him?

17. How much did you know about the Khmer Rouge before reading *In the Shadow of the Banyan*? What did you learn?

Enhance Your Book Club

1. Greet your book club members with traditional Cambodian food. A cooking school in Phnom Penh provides some classic recipes here: http://www.cambodia-cooking-class.com/recipes.htm

2. Imagine you're planning a trip to Cambodia with your book club. What historical, religious, and natural sites would you want to visit? Start planning your virtual trip by visiting the Cambodia Ministry of Tourism website: http://www.tourismcambodia.org/

3. Study a map of Cambodia and chart some of the places depicted in the novel, including Phnom Penh, Kratie Province, and the border with Thailand. If you don't own an atlas, you can view a map here: http://www.worldatlas.com/webimage/countrys/asia/lgcolor/khcolor.htm

A Conversation With Vaddey Ratner

In the Shadow of the Banyan is a novel, but it is based closely on your family's experience in Cambodia during the genocide perpetrated by the Khmer Rouge regime between 1975 and 1979. Why did you decide to write it as a novel rather than a memoir?

I was a small child when the Khmer Rouge took over the country. Revisiting that period of our life, I found that I couldn't trust myself completely to recall the exact details of the events and places and the chronology of our forced exodus from the city to the countryside, the journey from one place to the next during the span of those four years. I did initially try to write it as a memoir. But sorting through my own memories and what my mother was able to share with me, as well as the historical record, I kept asking myself again and again, *What is the story I want to tell? What is my purpose for telling it?* It isn't so much the story of the Khmer Rouge experience, of genocide, or even of loss and tragedy. What I wanted to articulate is something more universal, more indicative, I believe, of the human experience—our struggle to hang onto life, our desire to live, even in the most awful circumstances. In telling this story, it isn't my own life I wished others to take note of. I have survived, and the gift of survival, I feel, is honor enough already. My purpose is to honor the lives lost, and I wanted to do so by endeavoring to transform suffering into art.

That's not to say that a memoir doesn't demand artistry and skill. I've read many beautifully crafted literary memoirs—*Angela's Ashes, Autobiography of a Face, Running in the Family, I Know Why the Caged Bird Sings, The Woman Warrior* . . . In my case, because I was so young when the Khmer Rouge took control of Cambodia, and with hardly any surviving family records or pictures as source material, I had only my own mostly traumatic recollections and the understandably reluctant remembrances of my mother to rely on. What's more, those whom I wished to write about, whose sufferings I felt deserved to be heard and remembered above my own story, are gone. I didn't want them to be forgotten, and while, as Elie Wiesel has said, one cannot truly speak for the dead, I wished still to reinvoke the words and thoughts they'd shared with me. I felt compelled to speak of their lives, their hopes and dreams when they were still alive. And to do this well, I realized, required me not only to cull from memory and history but also to employ imagination, the art of empathy.

Speaking of art, what was your inspiration for writing?

In writing, one often speaks of voice as if it belongs exclusively to each of us as a writer, as if it emerges from a source that's all our own. More than twenty years ago, when I was a high school student, I came across *Night* by Elie Wiesel. I didn't know what it was, whether a memoir or a novel. I don't think it even said on the book. It was a slim volume, just over a hundred pages, and I read it in one sitting. And then again and again. It was the first piece of Holocaust literature I read, even though I didn't know what the word *holocaust* meant at the time. It was this writing that set me on a search to find the voice for my own story at a time when I could only communicate the mundane in a language new to me. Elie Wiesel's journey through death and inhumanity so moved me that I aspired to one day write a book that would give voice to my own family's struggle for survival, for life, in the face of a different atrocity in Cambodia.

You were five years old when the Khmer Rouge took over Cambodia, and your protagonist, Raami, is seven. Why did you decide to make her two years older?

In my own experience, I have the sense I began to perceive and understand much of what was happening about halfway through the Khmer Rouge regime, which was around when I turned seven, even though I wasn't sure how old I was at any given time. Still, I was aware that I was growing up, maturing. I was forced to be an adult by what I endured and witnessed. Yet, there was this part of me that wanted desperately to remain a child—to be protected, to escape from all the violence and suffering. I sought beauty wherever I could find it and I clung to it. So in choosing an age for Raami, I wanted her to have that balance between insight and innocence. In the beginning of the book she is a precocious and inquisitive child, but as the story progresses, she becomes quieter and more reflective, and her curiosity turns to seeking—a search to understand.

Is Raami's experience very similar to yours? How does it differ?

Raami's experience parallels mine. There's not an ordeal she faces that I myself didn't confront in one way or another. The loss of family members, starvation, forced labor, repeated uprooting and separation, the overwhelming sense that she's basically alone but also the tenacious belief that there's a spirit watching over her—all this I experienced and felt. Raami had polio as a baby. I had polio also when I was still an infant. Raami's long name, Vattaaraami, means in Sanskrit a "small garden temple." My own name, in the vernacular language, alludes to something similar. Vaddey, or "Watdey" as you pronounce it in Khmer, sounds like the "ground of a temple." This was why my father chose the name for me.

Where Raami's experience and mine diverge is in the minor details—the size of our family, the number of towns and villages we were sent to, the names of those places, the dates of various incidents. There are countless other small variations like these. As we discussed, she's two years older, but she's also a lot wiser than I was. She certainly regards the world with greater equanimity than I probably could at the time, than most of us can, even as mature adults. Even so, as a child, I always had faith in people. In spite of the atrocities around me, I never failed to find kindness, to encounter protection and tenderness when I most needed it. I had a strong intuition about people. In writing *In the Shadow of the Banyan,* I needed to draw on that intuitive understanding, that ability to see and perceive people's humanity in a way that enlarged my own. Raami shares my faith in people. Perhaps the big difference is that she can articulate it, and in so doing magnify it even more. Her intuition becomes prescience.

Are the characters in your novel based on real family members?

Yes, but my actual family—the group of uncles, aunts, and cousins who left the city with us—was much larger. The novel is a contained universe, so each character is there for a reason. If I were to include everyone in my family, it would be a mammoth book! In some instances, I had to combine family members to create one character, or make other changes. My father was actually the youngest of five children, for example. But in the story, I made Raami's father the older brother in order to capture the solemnity of my own father, his role as the pillar of the family. Every one of us looked to my father for reassurance.

So many scenes in your novel bring to life the unspeakable horror of this era of Cambodian history. Which scenes did you find the most difficult to write?

Every page was a struggle. I labored and labored, from a single word to a sentence to a paragraph. Each ordeal that had broken my heart when I was a child broke my heart again as an adult writing it. There were moments when I spiraled downward, to a depth I didn't think I could come back from. It was a painful story to write, to relive.

You write of your father in the Author's Note, "This story is born of my desire to give voice to his memory, and the memory of all those si-

lenced." Did you find it difficult to capture your father's voice all these years later, or did his way of speaking come naturally to you?

I've lived with my father's voice for so long. He's always with me and I've had countless long conversations with him. The challenge was not so much reaching back in time to capture his voice but reaching across languages. Essentially, I had to make my father speak English, and I had to do it in a way that wouldn't change the way he sounded in Khmer. In our language, one rarely addresses people by their names: it's either too formal or too disrespectful to use someone's name. For example, my father would almost always call me *koan*—"child"—which in Khmer is extraordinarily tender and intimate, but if Raami's father were to call her "child" or "my child," it would sound rather formal and distant, archaic even. So he calls her by her name and simply "darling" or other terms of endearment that my own father used with me.

The voice has to fit the character. I remember my father as solemn but never morose. He not merely saw beauty in the world, he reflected upon it as well, often aloud to me. He was always hopeful, and rather idealistic—as my mother often points out—but because there was a touch of sadness about him, I've always thought there was a poetic quality to his person. He spoke like a poet. While he was not a poet, he was an avid reader of poetry, especially those Khmer epics in verse like the *Reamker* and *Mak Thoeung*. He loved words, and was himself a ceaseless weaver of stories. I wanted to capture my father's essential qualities and instill them in Raami's father. In a way, having Raami's father speak English helped me to write, to progress with the story. There were moments in the writing when, remembering my father's exact words as he'd spoken them to me in our language, the tenor and tenderness of his voice, I would break down completely, and it would take many days, weeks, to come back to the writing.

Your family, like Raami's, lost everything. Were you able to salvage any personal belongings or memorabilia?

Coming out of the experience, I thought we'd lost everything. Then, in 1993 in America, on my wedding day, my mother gave me a diamond brooch that she had received from my *sdechya*, my grandmother on whom Grandmother Queen is based. The brooch had been a wedding gift to my mother from my grandmother. More recently, as a gift to congratulate me on *In the Shadow of the Banyan*, my mother gave me a pair of diamond earrings. The settings are new, she said, but the diamonds are hers from before the war.

I also have this tiny wallet-sized picture of my father from when he was young. My mother pried it apart from an ID paper after my father was taken away. She feared the ID paper would link us to him, so she threw away the paper but kept the photo. Years later in the United States, I noticed that his name, A. Sisowath, was embossed on the right-hand side. It was a poignant discovery because in those early years in America it was the only tangible link I had to him—aside from my mother. No one else I knew then was aware of his existence. Looking at the picture now, I imagine unease in his pose—the asymmetrical slant of his shoulders, the questioning arch of his left brow, the tentative smile—as if he were uncomfortable with this attempt at permanency. I imagine him walking into the room, addressing the camera skeptically, and walking out again, his spirit always in constant movement, in flight.

Did you and your mother flee to a refugee camp in Thailand just as Raami and her mother did? How did you end up in the United States?

Our escape from Cambodia was even more obstructed and circuitous. At one point along an abandoned road, we were recaptured by Khmer Rouge soldiers on the run from the invading Vietnamese troops. The Khmer Rouge took us from one village to the next, then into the forest, and deeper still into the jungle. We thought this was the end—here they would kill us. What I saw, what I witnessed, on that journey alone is enough for another novel.

In 1981, you arrived in the United States as a refugee speaking no English, but went on to graduate as your high school class valedictorian in 1990, and *summa cum laude* from Cornell in 1995. How, after witnessing all of the terrible atrocities in Cambodia, were you able to not only move forward, but to thrive and succeed?

When we left Cambodia, the images that stuck with me, that overwhelmed my mind, were of corpses—corpses and flies. Then, landing at the airport in California, I was struck by all the shiny glass and stainless steel, not a single fly anywhere! Everyone and everything was humming with energy. Even the luggage carousels rolled with magical vitality. I was so far from death. Right then and there, I realized that we had so much to catch up with. The world hadn't forgotten about us, but neither had it waited for us. It had moved on, prospered. I felt so fortunate to be part of it. In Cambodia, staring at a muddy rain puddle, I could conjure up a whole underwater kingdom. Imagine what went through my mind when I walked into a supermarket in America! I remember the Safeway supermarket our sponsor took us to after we'd resettled in Jefferson City, Missouri. *Safeway.* Even the name sounded like a haven! I had such a yearning . . . a hunger to learn, and that hunger overtook all else. I absorbed everything this country had to offer me. Whatever ordeals we faced in America were nothing compared to those in Cambodia. We were given so much. How could I not thrive and succeed? I believed this, and still do.

You only began to learn English at age 11, on arriving in the United States. How did you learn to write? What was it like reinvoking the story in a language entirely different from the language of that experience?

It began with reading. I was a copious reader in my own language, and I was a copious reader as soon as I learned to read in English. I'd devour anything I could get my hands on. I read things I didn't quite understand. *Jane Eyre,* I remember, was my first grown-up novel. I thought it was so illicit—the man keeps his wife locked up in another part of his mansion while he develops romantic feelings for his young employee, this impoverished governess. Sounds like a Cambodian love story! But it wasn't just literature I read. I'd linger over descriptions on shampoo bottles, lost in the shower, deaf to my mother's call, soothed by adjectives—*foamy, invigorating, silky* . . . I'd move on to the list of ingredients—all those scientific names had a ring and rhythm to them, almost like poetry. In chemistry class, learning to decode the letters and numbers in formulas, I came across *tetra*, its familiarity heavy on my tongue. Then suddenly there was this flash in my memory. *Tetracycline*. I remembered that it was medicine—yellow and valuable as gold—that we'd had in our possession during our time in the countryside when medicine was almost nonexistent. Reading introduced me to an endless range of expression, from the thematic language of "family secrets" and "complicated love" articulated in a novel like *Jane Eyre* to small, incidental words that jogged my memory, revealing buried recollections.

Then, when it came to actually learning how to write, I basically did it on my own, at my own slow pace. Except for a summer writing camp I went to through a community arts program in Minnesota called COMPAS when I was in high school, and a short-story writing course I took at Cornell University, I've had no formal training in writing. But I believe there are no better teachers than great pieces of writing: classics that tackle universal and timeless questions, and contemporary writings, from many cultural and linguistic backgrounds, that not only delve into these existential queries but also enlarge my world by transplanting me to a whole new geography of thoughts, feelings, and beliefs.

I wanted to do something similar with this story. I didn't want just to *translate* my family's experience, a Cambodian experience, to a foreign audience; I wanted to take the readers and *replant* them in the fertile ground I'd sprung from, to let them take root and sprout, and to see my world as their own. I wanted them to see Cambodia before it became synonymous with genocide, before it became the "killing fields." It was once a place of exquisite beauty, and I try to show that, not only by locating the readers in the loveliness of the natural world but also by immersing them in the rhythm of a people's thoughts and sentiments, in its literature and art. Only when we know what existed can we truly mourn what is lost.

So, I feel, writing *In the Shadow of the Banyan* was not just a retelling. It was an act of creation, a long journey toward its realization.

In the Author's Note you tell the story of visiting the royal court of Cambodia in 2009. Can you describe that experience? What was it like to return after all of those years?

Even before my visit to the royal palace, I had visited Cambodia countless times, always in search of my father. Each time, I see him in all that's lost and in all that's found. My first trip back was in 1992. I went to my family's estate in Phnom Penh. Our house was not there. Everything was gone, except, I believe, for one charred column from the bath pavilion. But even though our home was gone, I revisited other places I remembered my father and I had frequented—the promenade along the river, the lotus fountains near the Independence Monument, temples around the city . . . During a trip several years later, I visited the royal palace, just the grounds that were open to tourists, and I came across a golden statue that took my breath away. It was of a man on a horse, with a sword in his raised hand. Very gallant! I remembered that statue! For a long time I had thought it was on our estate and that it depicted my father. But it turned out the statue was of one of the kings! When I told my mother about being shocked by that encounter and the confusion in my own remembering, she had a very simple explanation: I had often accompanied my father to the royal palace, and the statue, with its lovely surrounding gardens, was where my father and I would escape from the formality of a ceremony or a function inside the courtly halls. There, beside the statue, he would tell me stories and tales, using the ornate setting to launch into mythical adventures. In my memory, I suppose, my father and the statue became fused—a single entity.

From 2005 to 2009, when I returned with my husband and daughter to live in Phnom Penh, a lot of things became clear in my mind. In particular, I got to witness the power of the monsoon, how in a single day the rains could flood the land; the different ways rice is grown and harvested through the seasons; the monumental struggles of the tiny creatures against the elements. I would spend hours with my little daughter watching a dung beetle fighting its way out of a cow pie! It was an epiphany. Living there—while at times difficult because of its proximity to the past—helped tremendously with the writing of *In the Shadow of the Banyan*.

In late 2009, just before returning to live in the States again, I was invited to have an audience with His Majesty King Norodom Sihamoni, to be formally reintroduced into the royal family. I didn't want to go, actually. I panicked. What would I bring as a gift for the king? One ought to bring a gift, right? But what could His Majesty possibly desire? Chocolate? I didn't think so. I called my mother, and she said that I ought to consider a gift that would honor my father's name, his spirit. So I brought three tons of rice for the poor, as a contribution to His Majesty's humanitarian effort. At the royal palace, facing His Majesty, I could barely speak. All I could think about was my father, the sacrifice he'd made so that a moment such as this, my taking his place, would be possible. And yet, I couldn't help thinking, he couldn't have known with absolute certainty that I would survive. He'd only hoped, and I felt that hope in my throat. When I swallowed it, tears rushed to my eyes. The next year, when I had another audience with the king, I was much more prepared and composed.

As *In the Shadow of the Banyan* makes clear, one of the Khmer Rouge's primary strategies was splitting up families. How do you maintain your

connection to your family members today—including those who only live on in your memory?

I have an uncle in Cambodia now, one of my father's two elder brothers, the middle son. I despair every time I see him. I mourn his lost self. Once when he rode in a car with us to go to lunch, he became suddenly agitated. He explained that he was not used to being in a car and was completely disoriented. He was once a lover of cars. Now, no longer a prince, he lives a humble life, has kept the name he took on when we'd relinquished our royal identity, and feels most balanced when he shuffles along the uneven streets of Phnom Penh barefoot or in flip-flops. Whenever I look into his eyes, I think there are small deaths like these, some parts of ourselves that were buried with the others. My uncle cries every time he sees me, as I do when I see him or read the letters he sends me.

When I returned to live in Cambodia with my husband and daughter, one of the first things I did was to surround our new home with flowers I remembered from my childhood home. I filled our small garden with orchid, jasmine, bird of paradise, lobster claw, and also frangipani of different colors, even though, I learned, Cambodians believe that the flower attracts ghosts. If so, I thought, it was a fitting offering. I filled our vases each day with fresh stems of lotus. A couple of years later, we bought a piece of land in Siem Reap and built a house there, which for me was very therapeutic, a willful act to counter the destruction I had witnessed helplessly as a child.

How does your family, specifically your mother, feel about your decision to write In the Shadow of the Banyan?

My family is extremely supportive. They've watched me persevere for so long with this. They've seen me not only tormented by my recollection, by my reckoning with the past, but also by the labor of writing itself. They are very happy that this is a story I can now share with the world.

As for my mother, she's very proud. I couldn't have written this book without her blessing, and, of course, her sharing of painful memories. Some of the stories about family members she told me have made their way into the narrative. We've been through everything together. This book is hers, too.

An important theme of your novel is the power of stories. What do you hope readers will take away from your own storytelling?

I've always loved stories, the written word. Even at a very young age, I sensed their intrinsic power. Like Raami, I saw and understood the world through stories. In Cambodia, under the Khmer Rouge, when I was lost in a forest or abandoned by my work unit among the vast rice fields because I moved too slowly, I would recall the legends my father or nanny had told me or those tales I'd been able to read myself. I'd invoke them like incantations, chanting aloud descriptions and dialogues I'd memorized, to chase away my fear of being alone in the middle of nowhere, in the silence around me. Stories were magic spells, I felt, and storytelling, the ability to tell and recall something, was a kind of sorcery, a power you could use to transform and transport yourself. I still feel this way, and I think it shows in crafting *In the Shadow of the Banyan* as I did. But I hope the story is layered enough so that every reader finds the inspiration or message they seek.